New York Times
bestselling author and
WINNER of the Romance
Writers of America
Lifetime Achievement Award

ELIZABETH LOWELL

IS
"GREAT!"
Johanna Lindsey

"INCOMPARABLE!"
Romantic Times

"A LAW UNTO HERSELF IN THE
WORLD OF ROMANCE!"
Jayne Ann Krentz

Books by Elizabeth Lowell

Contemporary

FORGET ME NOT • LOVER IN THE ROUGH
A WOMAN WITHOUT LIES • DESERT RAIN
WHERE THE HEART IS • TO THE ENDS OF THE EARTH
REMEMBER SUMMER • BEAUTIFUL DREAMER
MOVING TARGET • AMBER BEACH
JADE ISLAND • PEARL COVE • EDEN BURNING
RUNNING SCARED

Historical

ONLY HIS • ONLY MINE • ONLY YOU
ONLY LOVE • AUTUMN LOVER • WINTER FIRE
ENCHANTED • FORBIDDEN
UNTAMED • MIDNIGHT IN RUBY BAYOU

And in Hardcover

THIS TIME LOVE

ELIZABETH LOWELL

To The ENDS of The EARTH

(Previously published as *The Danvers Touch*)

AVON BOOKS
An Imprint of HarperCollins*Publishers*

To the Ends of the Earth was previously published in an altered form entitled *The Danvers Touch* by Silhouette Books in 1983.

AVON BOOKS
A division of
The Hearst Corporation
1350 Avenue of the Americas
New York, New York 10019

Copyright © 1983 by Ann Maxwell; 1998 by Two of a Kind, Inc.
Excerpt from *Jade Island* copyright © 1998 by Two of a Kind, Inc.
Cover art by Nick Gaetano
Published by arrangement with the author
Visit our website at **http://www.AvonBooks.com**
Library of Congress Catalog Card Number: 97-94417
ISBN: 0-380-76758-9

First Avon Books Printing: May 1998

AVON TRADEMARK REG. U.S. PAT. OFF. AND IN OTHER COUNTRIES, MARCA REGISTRADA, HECHO EN U.S.A.

Printed in the U.S.A.

OPM 20 19 18 17 16 15 14 13 12 11

For Evan
man to my woman

PROLOGUE

SHE WAS perfect. Sleek, sensuous, responding to the lightest touch.

And therefore dangerous to the man who tried to control her. He would have to be catlike in his reflexes. A moment's inattention would—

The phone rang, destroying his concentration.

Travis Danvers looked up from his computer screen and blinked like a man surfacing after a long dive into uncharted waters. His blue-green eyes were unfocused. He rubbed his short, tawny beard, shook his head briskly, and tried to concentrate on the here and now rather than on the ever-changing interplay of wind, hull, water, and sail.

Through an open window near the desk, the scent and sound of ocean waves poured into the room, calling to Travis at a level deeper than words. The Santa Ana wind had blown Southern California's usual smog all the way to Catalina Island. The land lay revealed in all its bronzed, late summer splendor. The ocean was a shimmering, restless blue.

He should be out there on the water, feeling the *Wind Warrior* heel over as her sails filled and she stepped into the wind.

The phone kept on ringing.

Travis glared at the dainty instrument. He hated all phones in general and this one with a special passion.

1

Pink.

Bloody hell. What was my cousin thinking of when she redecorated the house—Easter eggs and nurseries?

The phone rang for the eighth time. Travis blew out a breath and flirted with the seductive idea of ignoring the phone and slipping back into the computer-driven virtual world where he tried out new ideas for catching every last whisper of wind in a ship's sails.

The phone rang. Number nine.

With a muttered curse he saved his most recent design changes, grabbed the silly pink receiver in his big hand, and snarled his usual telephone greeting.

"What!"

"Swear to God, Danvers, you gotta work on your manners."

Most of Travis's irritation vanished the instant he recognized the voice. Rodney Harrington was one of his favorite people.

"Why should I work on my phone etiquette?" Travis asked, stretching his long, rangy body and yawning at the same time. "You're the only one who has my cousin's telephone number."

Harrington made a pleased sound. "Then you're actually in Laguna Beach? My call hasn't been forwarded to Tierra del Fuego or some other benighted place?"

"I'm here, pink phone and all."

"Excuse me?"

"My cousin redid the house since my last visit. Pink. Pink. More pink. Repeat. PINK."

"You're surrounded by pink?"

"Mostly, yeah. Lavender, too."

"Um. I'd like to see that. The thought of a man your size lolling around in a pink villa is . . . piquant."

"So visit me," Travis retorted. "I'll put you in the special guest room, the one with the candy-striped canopy bed."

Harrington snickered. "Does this mean you'll be having the *Wind Warrior*'s hull repainted in fuchsia?"

"Was that the reason you called, to find out if I'm repainting my ship?"

"Actually, yes."

"Good-bye."

Harrington laughed and then spoke quickly. "I just wanted to be sure the *Wind Warrior* is all slicked up for her debut."

Travis looked at the pink receiver as though it had licked him. "Harrington, are you all right?"

"In the pink, actually."

"Awful pun. You're fine."

Travis flexed the muscles in his back and shoulders, trying to work out kinks that came from spending hours bent over a computer. His tall, rawboned body had been designed for physical work. If it weren't for his lengthy morning swims, he wouldn't have been able to sit still long enough to use his fancy computer.

"What's this about my ship's debut?" he asked. "She's hardly a virgin, you know."

"Remember my idea for a splashy coffee-table book featuring you, your ship, and your designs?"

Travis remembered. "Suddenly the pain in my neck just moved lower. A lot lower."

"Stand up and walk around," Harrington said cheerfully. "God made bodies like yours for action, not computers. I've hit upon the perfect photographer."

Travis had no problem following the non sequitur. His brain was as quick as his body was rangy. "If this is another of your—"

Harrington kept talking in the manner of a man who knew he was going to have a hard sell for a pet project. "Cochran! I don't know why I didn't think of her sooner. She—"

"You did," Travis interrupted ruthlessly. "I vetoed it."

"Did you? Why?"

"One word. Female."

"Rather narrow-minded of you, boy-o."

"Thank you."

There was silence, then a long-suffering sigh. "Swear to God, Danvers, you can be a real pain in the butt."

Travis grimaced and looked out the window to the rock-lined beach and the endless sweep of Pacific Ocean. He knew he was being unreasonable. Using one lame excuse or another, he had also turned down all the male photographers Harrington mentioned. Travis didn't want to be bothered with having an outsider underfoot on the *Wind Warrior*, or someone looking over his shoulder while he tinkered with sail and hull designs on his computer.

But he owed Harrington a lot, and Harrington had wanted to do this book for several years.

"You're in Laguna," Harrington said neutrally. "Cochran lives in Laguna."

"Rod—" Travis began.

The other man ignored him. "You're going to be there for at least a few weeks. Your ship is at Dana Point. Cochran has a car. She's familiar with ships, both power and sail."

Silently Travis groaned. He had always known he was going to give in to his friend about the damned book.

He just hadn't thought it would be today.

Maybe he could hold out a little longer, until the new sail design was stitched, rigged, and ready to try out at sea.

"Rod, have you thought of—"

"Stop interrupting," Harrington said crisply. "It's rude. The publisher is on board, so to speak. He's willing to pay a nice advance to the photographer."

"What about me?" Travis asked dryly.

"What about you? You're as rich as I am. Richer, probably, if you followed my advice about the stock market."

"Now that you mention it, I was going to ask you about—"

"Nice try, but no," Harrington interrupted. "The subject of this conversation is a book about you and your exquisite, ruthlessly efficient designs. You won't be paid because all you will have to do is ignore the photographer and do what you would be doing anyway."

"Does that mean you've given up on the idea of me writing the damned book?"

"I'm not entirely stubborn. Some poor grunt will do the captions for five free copies and a pat on his balding head."

"I never thought of you as a 'poor grunt.' "

"Swear to God, you never think of me at all or you wouldn't be such a wart on the pickle of my progress!"

Travis started laughing and knew he had lost. "All right, all right. Set up a meeting with this photographer for— What day is this?"

"Sunday."

"Toward the end of the week, then. We'll see. No promises."

"Next Thursday. I'll leave the details on your answering machine."

"I don't have one."

"Buy one. Or use E-mail. You're a hard man to get hold of."

"I like it that way."

"In-the-Wind Danvers. You and Cochran should get along fine."

An uneasy prickle went over Travis. "What does that mean?" he asked suspiciously.

"Such a nasty bark. All I meant was that Cochran, like you, gets too wrapped up in her work to care about mundane things like sleep or answering telephones."

Travis wasn't buying it. "My bite is worse than my bark. Keep it in mind."

"Truer words were never muttered. Don't use your teeth

on Cochran. She's a particular friend of mine.''

"As in mistress?''

"Cochran?'' Harrington laughed sadly. "Not in the past, not now, not ever. She doesn't like the opposite sex. Another thing you two have in common.''

"I'm quite fond of the opposite sex.''

"You like sex. It's not the same.''

"And you don't?'' Travis retorted.

"I like women,'' Harrington said simply. "Sex is part of it, but not all of it. Women genuinely see the world from a different point of view than we do. It's fascinating. Each time I think I've figured women out, they surprise me.''

"Rather like designing and sailing a ship.''

"If you really believe that, you're getting far too intimate with your ship,'' Harrington retorted.

"Ships don't screw you. What you put into them is what you get back.''

"Tina was a long time ago.''

Travis's hand tightened around the phone, but only for an instant. Tina had been a savage lesson in the difference between women and men. He had had years to get used to the depth of her betrayal. He couldn't change his past, but he could make damn sure it never happened again in his future.

And he had.

He had simplified his relationships with women to mutually beneficial business transactions. No hard feelings and no regrets between consenting adults.

"Tina was a very bad mistake,'' Travis said matter-of-factly. "Unfortunately, the highest price was paid by the most innocent. Considering that price, I would be a cruel, stupid son of a bitch not to learn my lesson, wouldn't you say?''

"Hell,'' Harrington said gruffly. "Sorry. I didn't mean to bring her up.''

"No apology needed. I don't talk about my former wife if I can help it."

In fact, Travis could count on one hand the number of times he had discussed his disastrous ex. Four of those times had been with his lawyer. The fifth time had been with Harrington, over a bottle of very, very old Scotch. While the *Wind Warrior*'s hull rode on the dark blue breast of the sea, they had toasted the past's bitter lessons under the endless daylight of the Antarctic summer sun.

"How much time will this book project take?" Travis asked.

Nothing in his voice even hinted at the rage that still coiled in his gut at Tina's memory. He wasn't even aware of his feelings. They were so deeply burned into him that he would have been aware of them only if they were absent.

"Depends on how much time you give the photographer," Harrington said. "It shouldn't be tough duty."

"Why? Is she easy on the eyes?"

"Cochran is a pro. She could teach you about hard work."

"So she isn't good-looking."

"She's a photographer, not a future mistress. What do you care what she looks like?"

Travis laughed. "Just curious. Bet that she asked you about me."

"Nope."

"Not even whether I was married or ugly or lecherous or gay or—"

"Nope," Harrington interrupted. "Cochran's only questions were when, how long, and what was the advance. She's no more eager to dillydally than you are. She's supporting three other people."

"Children from a bad marriage?"

"Bad luck. Her mother's, not hers. Cochran is putting her twin siblings through medical school and keeping the wolf from her dear, ditsy mother's door until January."

"What happens in January?"

"Her mother marries one of my friends."

"Rich?"

"But of course."

Travis's voice turned sardonic. "Found a dumb one to support her, huh?"

"He's quite bright for a tax lawyer. Worships the ground she walks on, et cetera. She returns the favor and sets up elegant charity dinners for his law firm. Quite a good match, if I do say so myself."

"You introduced them?"

"Little old *moi*," Harrington agreed smugly. "One of my better efforts."

The prickle of unease went over Travis's body again. Harrington took too much pleasure in nudging people—or shoving them, if it came to that—in a new direction.

"About this photographer," Travis said evenly. "I won't sign up for anything at all until I've seen her work."

"I should hope not."

"I don't want a series of full-color postcards."

"Absolutely not."

"Or sappy—"

"Wouldn't think of it," Harrington interrupted, satisfaction oozing from his voice.

"Damn it, you're purring. I hate it when you purr!"

Harrington was still laughing when he broke the connection.

Travis glared at the receiver, smiled ruefully, and hung up. Then he turned back to the computer screen and looked at his latest sail design.

It was good, but not nearly good enough. Maybe if he flared a corner here and took two long, curving tucks there . . .

He crouched over the computer again. As the hours went by, the changing design on the screen was reflected in his tourmaline green eyes. He was lost in curving lines of force, wind, and the infinite possibilities of the sea.

For the next three days Travis didn't think about his ex-wife, the photographer, or the book he didn't want to do. Except for his strenuous dawn swims, he was consumed by the endless, changing, fluid beauty of ocean and wind, hull and sail, design and freedom.

Freedom most of all.

Freedom from a past he couldn't change and couldn't stop regretting.

ONE

CATHERINE COCHRAN was too caught up in the sensuous beauty of ocean and sunset to realize that the tide was creeping up on her. Earlier, when the light had begun to slant and deepen into late afternoon, she had picked her way out on the rocky point below her house, set up her camera, and settled in to wait for the moment when the sun would set fire to the serene face of the sea.

She hadn't noticed that the tide was coming up as the sun was going down. The inward sweep of each deceptively smooth wave brought her an inch closer to real trouble. But each wave also brought her closer to the picture she had spent weeks trying to get.

Everything was perfect today. The tide was low, the sky was clear, the sun was setting, and the surface of the sea was a liquid gemstone shimmering with light. If she was patient, the moment she had been waiting for would finally come.

Behind Cat a ragged line of rocks thrust out of the water, gathering height and power until they finally became a headland braced against the seductive rush of waves. In front of her the ragged tongue of land dissolved into random rocks covered by thick beards of mussels and slick green water plants.

That was what held Cat's attention now. The textures of shells and seaweed, smooth waves and slanting light, were what had lured her out beyond the tide pools and slippery intertidal rocks to this spot midway between land and sea. She had been daring but not foolish in her quest for just the right photo; at low tide, the top of the rock she crouched on was dry and beyond the reach of all but the biggest waves.

The rocks behind and in front of Cat were below water most of the time. Their rough, powerful faces emerged only during an unusually low tide. As soon as the balance of sea and moon shifted, the rugged rocks would sink again into the ocean's liquid embrace. Then the image she had worked so hard to capture on film would be beyond reach until the next time that tide, sun, and weather worked together again.

As the evening sea swept toward the outer rocks, Cat counted out the seconds between the rhythmic waves. When she sensed that the light and time and wave finally would be right, she braced herself more securely and let out her breath. At the exact instant the fluid curve of water met the rocks, she triggered the motor drive on her camera.

Well beyond the six-hundred-millimeter lens, wave met rock. Water exploded into creamy cataracts. Fountains of iridescent bubbles licked over black stone.

That was the moment she wanted to capture, the fragile caress of foam and the rock that had broken a billion waves . . . the rock that was itself being melted by rainbow bubbles until finally it would be one with the sea it had so long withstood.

Not defeat, but equality, for wave and rock defined each other. Without the wave, the rock would never know the power of surrender. Without the rock, the wave would spend itself quietly on the shore, never finding a way to transform its smooth perfection into a fierce explosion of beauty.

Cat lost count of the waves, of the times she triggered the camera, of the rolls of film she loaded into the Nikon's compact body. Her legs cramped, protesting their unnatural position. She ignored discomfort. Until the light was gone, she wouldn't allow anything to break her concentration on the changing images pouring through the long lens into her camera.

Beneath her practiced, calm motions, excitement threaded through Cat. Her trademark was the kind of photos that made the viewer stop, stare, and reassess reality. She knew the shots she was taking now would be some of her best work, combining stark light and shadow, elemental textures, and the changed perspective that was possible only with the use of a very long lens.

With no warning, water leaped up over Cat's perch. A cold diamond spray stung her legs. The cramps had been more painful, but hadn't threatened her camera equipment. Seawater did.

She raised her head, blinked, and focused for the first time on the world outside her camera lens. When she looked back toward shore, she knew that she had stayed too long on her rocky perch.

The thirty feet back to the beach might as well have been thirty miles.

The path to the shore was gone. What had been a tricky journey out beyond the tide line was now a witch's brew of surf, foam, and slick black rocks. To keep from being swept off her feet by the powerful waves, she would have to cling to the rocks with teeth and fingernails. Yet she needed her hands to hold her expensive photographic gear beyond the reach of the sea.

Water foamed up toward Cat, then hissed down the hard rock. In the reflected glow of the dying sun, the wet stone looked like a primitive sculpture of hammered gold.

For once she didn't enjoy the rich light. She looked at the water with clear gray eyes and the cut-your-losses attitude of someone who had made a mistake and knew it.

"Damn!"

Even if her hands had been free, she would be lucky to keep her feet underneath her on the trip back to the beach. But her hands wouldn't be free. She had thousands of dollars worth of equipment to carry, equipment she needed to earn her living.

Equipment she couldn't afford to replace.

Cat wasted no more time on curses or regrets. She measured the height of the water against the rocks she had used to scramble out to her present perch. Even in the troughs between waves, the water was well above her knees. Add more than three feet of wave onto that, and she was in trouble.

But she had no choice except to get ashore as quickly as possible. Waiting would only make the trip harder, the water deeper. She would have to hold her equipment above her head, abandon the treacherous rocks entirely, and wade a diagonal course to the sandy beach that curved back from the headland.

And pray very hard that she wasn't knocked off her feet by the deceptively frothy waves.

Cat didn't look around for anyone to help her. She had been on her own so long that the thought of someone else coming to her aid never even occurred to her.

She checked the fastenings on her carrying case to be sure that nothing would come open, spilling her cameras into the salt water. The bag itself was meant for protection against rain, not for a swim in the ocean.

The most valuable piece of equipment she had with her was an autofocus zoom lens as long as her arm and a lot heavier. The lens was mounted rifle style on a stock that fit against her shoulder. The whole piece of gear was too big to squeeze into the uncertain protection of her camera case.

Reluctantly Cat decided she would have to make two trips. She set down the case that held camera bodies and smaller lenses. Holding the big zoom lens above her head, she cautiously began to climb down from her rock.

Never once did she notice the rangy man who had been trying to catch her attention from midway up the beach.

Hands on his hips, Travis Danvers shook his head in disgust and gave up trying to shout his way into her attention. The lady with the great legs and fiery, French-braided hair must be deaf as well as crazy. There wasn't a chance in hell that she would get to the sand before she was trashed by the surf.

Travis started toward her at a run. And as he ran, he wondered if the rest of her matched her legs. Doubtful, but a man could always hope.

Cat stayed upright through the first wave without too much problem. Because she was still clinging to the rock, the water reached only to her waist. The wave felt cold to her sun-warmed skin and much too powerful. It forced her against the rock in a breathless hug. The cutoff jeans and cotton halter top she wore weren't much protection against the sharp edges of rock, barnacles, and mussels.

"Get on with it," she told herself through her clenched teeth. "You swim in a lot less than you're wearing now."

Watching the sea rather than the shore, alert for the occasional larger wave, Cat eased all the way down the rough shoulder of the rock. She had to cross a narrow trench, then a smaller ridge of rocks, before she reached the sandy shelf leading to the beach. The waves were coming so quickly that she wouldn't be able to take more than a few steps in the lull between breakers.

The next wave was a big one. It caught Cat and slammed her back against the rock she had just abandoned. She scrambled desperately for balance on the slippery, uneven surface. The boiling surf wrenched off one of her canvas deck shoes. She felt a searing pain along the side of her right foot as unprotected flesh scraped over sharp barnacles. Her arms waved wildly, trying to balance her straining body.

It was impossible.

When she felt herself falling, she cried out against the destruction of her trademark lens.

Just before Cat went beneath the wave, something yanked her upright. At the same instant the weight of the zoom lens lifted from her fingers. Reflexively she fought losing her grip on the costly, vital lens.

"Hold still, wildcat. I'm not going to steal anything."

The deep drawl startled Cat, but not as much as the lazy amusement reflected in the stranger's sea-colored eyes. He was standing easily in the powerful surge of surf, his lips curving in a smile that was as seductive to her senses as sunlight tangled in a breaking wave.

"Well, you have some sense, at least," Travis said when she stopped struggling. "Turn around."

"What?"

With an impatient sound, he spun her around so that she faced the rock again.

"Up," he said curtly.

"But—"

Cat felt his big hand on her butt, and gasped. She fairly flew out of the water as he gave her a hard boost.

"Hand me the camera case," he said.

She stared at the man who was holding her zoom lens beyond the reach of the sea—and her. He was tall enough to rise well above the foam. He wore cutoff jeans and a blue-green rugby shirt that matched his eyes.

Because he was already wet to his shoulders, the shirt was plastered to his body, outlining the strength that had so casually lifted her beyond the reach of the waves. His tawny hair was short, well cut, thick, and sun-streaked. His short beard and mustache were clipped to conform to the male planes of his face.

Despite the grooming, he somehow looked uncivilized. He certainly wasn't conventionally handsome. His face was too hard, too individual, for easy labels. If he hadn't been smiling up at Cat, she might have been very wary of him.

Common sense told her that she should be wary anyway.

It was the tawny beard that persuaded her to trust the tall stranger. She had an irrational weakness for the way his beard transformed sunlight into burning curves of gold.

"That's my life you're carrying," Cat told him in a calm voice as she handed down the camera case.

Travis—who had been sizing up the rest of her and deciding that it lived up to the legs—looked at her face in startled reassessment. She might be reckless enough to put herself at risk for a few pictures, but she wasn't stupid. There was fierce intelligence in her luminous gray eyes. It was matched by the determination in the line of her mouth.

"I'll be careful," he said, turning toward the shore. "Stay up there until I get back to help you. The waves are stronger than they look."

"So am I."

Cat's words were lost beneath the hissing thunder of surf as another wave broke around the rock. She watched her unexpected savior wade toward shore carrying her equipment above his head.

The artist in her approved of him. His balance was remarkable, indescribable, a combination of strength and animal grace that made her hands itch to hold a camera again. In his own way, the man was as elemental and compelling to her as waves sweeping over rocks.

Suddenly she realized that not only was she staring at him as though she had never seen a man before, she was waiting like an obedient child for him to return and pluck her off the rock. The idea of being so entranced by a stranger's male grace both irritated and amused her.

Irritation won. She wasn't going to wait like a good girl for him to rescue her. It had been seven years since a man had told her to do anything. She hadn't obeyed then, either.

But her ex-husband's demand had been degrading. The stranger's was merely reasonable.

Impatiently Cat pushed away the past and its unwelcome memories. Reasonable or not, she wasn't going to sit around like some limp-wristed princess waiting for a brawny knight to rescue her. Life had taught her that if she needed rescuing, she had better get on with the job herself.

In a pause between waves, she started easing down the slippery rock once more. A wave rushed up, tugging at her with immense, blue-green power, tumbling around her, shaking her until she felt like a leaf being torn from its branch by a storm.

He's right, she thought. *The water is much rougher than it looks.*

Cautiously Cat lowered herself farther into the sea. It wasn't a tropic lagoon. Instead of a comfortable eighty or eighty-five degrees, the water temperature was in the seventies. But it was bracing rather than chilling. The first shock of wetness passed quickly.

She was used to Southern California's rich, cool ocean. She swam in the calmer waters around Dana Point as often as she could. It was as close to freedom as her life got.

January, she thought automatically. *Then I'll be able to take a deep breath and relax a little.*

But she would never get to January unless she got to shore first.

Cat crept away from the rock, moving by careful inches rather than long strides that would leave her off balance in the surging, playful surf. She shuffled along in the water, never really lifting her feet, always keeping her side turned toward the incoming waves so that the water had less of her to push against.

Once she was beyond the point where breakers could pick her up and slam her onto the rocks, she relaxed. The surf still could tumble her around a bit, but the thought of a dunking didn't worry her. Keeping an eye on the waves, she edged toward the small sandy beach. Her right foot

burned and ached with each step, reminding her that she
had lost a shoe and some skin as well.

"You really don't have the sense that God gave a
goose."

The voice came from behind Cat, startling her again—
but not as much as the arms that lifted her off her feet and
held her above the reach of waves. She stiffened suddenly,
aware of the stranger's sheer animal warmth, the intriguing
texture of his skin against her bare legs, the muscular length
of his arms supporting her body. She had never sensed a
man in such an elemental way. She wasn't sure she liked
the feeling.

Yet the photographer in her couldn't help but notice the
play of light over his slanting cheekbones, the contrasting
textures of slightly curling beard and sculpted lips, the
depth and changing color of his eyes.

Cat had an uncanny feeling that she knew this man. At
the same time she was certain that she had never met him
before. He wasn't the kind of man a woman would forget.

Yet she trusted him. The same instinct that had prompted
her to hand over her cameras to him urged her to relax and
accept being helped by the hard-looking man who was simultaneously familiar and a stranger.

"I'm a good swimmer," she said.

It wasn't an objection to being carried. It was the simple
truth.

But as she spoke, unhappy memories surfaced in her
mind: a desperate two-mile swim through a midnight ocean,
her only beacon a glittering yacht, her only strength the
rage that had made her dive over the railing of her husband's boat wearing nothing but moonlight.

Yes, she was a very good swimmer.

Cat realized that the man was watching her, his eyes
intelligent, speculative.

"I'll bet you've got a temper to match your fiery hair,"
he drawled.

She smiled a bit. Her rich auburn hair was as close as she came to beauty. The rest of herself she dismissed as average. She had the normal number of fingers, toes, and everything else in between, and it was all in working order.

Well, almost all.

And that was another thing she wouldn't think about.

"Don't you have any happy thoughts?" he asked softly.

The question went through Cat like a shock wave. Her eyes widened, revealing the shadows in their gray depths. Then her dark lashes came down, shutting him out. He was far too perceptive for her comfort.

"I have thoughts that aren't unhappy," she said in a clipped voice.

"Not quite the same, is it?"

"Close enough," she said, trying to keep the bitterness out of her voice. She almost succeeded.

With a feeling of relief she saw that the beach was only a few feet away. Soon she would be out of reach of the unnerving man she had just met and felt like she had known forever.

"Do you always settle for second best?" he asked.

"It's called growing up."

"It's called giving up."

Anger shot through Cat. With a quick, supple twist of her body, she slipped free of the stranger's arms. Landing on her feet, she splashed out of the shallow water to get the camera equipment he had left well above the high-tide mark.

With every other step she took, her right foot felt as though she was walking on bees. Sand mixed with blood stuck to her foot, scrubbing against the raw flesh. Ignoring the pain, she slung the camera bag over her shoulder, settled the sling for the zoom lens over her arm, and turned around to head for her house.

Travis moved with deceptive laziness. Deceptive because he was much quicker than he looked. In two strides he was standing calmly in front of her, cutting off her retreat.

It wasn't something he had stopped to think about. He simply did it. He had no intention of losing such an intriguing, if touchy, female. The combination of great legs and clear-eyed pragmatism made him wonder what it would be like to be her lover.

Not that he was likely to find out. His social skills were beyond rusty. They were a solid lump of corrosion. After his divorce he had discovered that a diamond tennis bracelet brought more smiles and sexy cooing from his women than social lies about beauty and such.

Too bad she isn't Harrington's photographer, Travis thought ruefully. *Then I wouldn't have to worry about how to stay close to her.*

But Harrington had said Cochran wasn't much to look at. This woman was. Not to everyone's taste, certainly. She was no Barbie doll or slickly oiled Playmate. Yet Travis was drawn by her sleek lines and poise, and by the in-your-face independence that would have warned off a less confident male.

"You've had a lot of practice landing on your feet, haven't you, little cat?" Travis asked.

Cat stared up at him, startled again. *How does he know my name?*

Then she realized that he was referring to the way she had twisted out of his arms and landed on her feet. She smiled in wry acknowledgment of the compliment and moved to step around him.

"Thanks for keeping my cameras dry," she said.

"My name is Travis."

"Thanks for keeping my cameras dry, Travis."

When she would have walked on past him, he moved with a speed that was surprising in such a rangy, soft-spoken man.

Cat stopped abruptly. It was that or run right into him.

She shifted the camera bag again, wincing as a jagged piece of shell bit into her right foot.

"Don't you at least owe me a name?" he asked.

"Several," she agreed coolly, "but my mother taught me not to swear."

Travis smiled. "The cat has claws. Not even a purr for me? Such gratitude."

"On the contrary," Cat said, stepping around him. "I'm so grateful I'm not even going to tell you to go to hell."

His laughter was as unexpected as the strength that swept her up off the sand again.

"Put me down," Cat said. There was no coy pleading in her voice. It was as icy as her eyes.

"Your foot is bleeding."

"It's a long way from my heart."

Travis looked down at her face. His eyes lingered over the tempting curve of her lower lip.

"Buy a postcard next time," he said huskily. "It's safer."

"Postcards lack staying power."

His eyes widened. He stared as though seeing her for the first time.

"I'm beginning to believe you aren't just another pretty face," he said.

"And I'm beginning to wonder how you keep your feet out of your mouth long enough to brush your teeth."

"Come and watch me. I'll even let you squeeze the toothpaste."

His slow smile was a parody of a sexy leer, and he knew it. It was his way of inviting her to share a joke that was on him.

"You're impossible," Cat said, smiling despite her irritation.

"Actually, I'm very easy."

She groaned at the ancient joke.

Cat would have warned off any other man with a single

cold glance, but Travis was too outrageous to take seriously. Obviously he didn't expect anything more from her than a shared moment of amusement. She gave him that, succumbing easily to the lure of laughter, realizing as she did that it had been too long since she had really laughed.

His expression changed when he saw the tense lines of her face changed by laughter. Her gray eyes were radiant, as warm in their own way as her hair with its hidden fire.

"Tell me your name," Travis said softly.

The sudden huskiness of his voice was a caress.

Cat's eyes widened suddenly. She saw the male intensity in him and wondered how she had made the mistake of taking him lightly. An odd feeling raced through her, making her shiver. She blamed it on her wet clothes.

"My name is Cat," she said. Then she added quickly, "Catherine."

"Do your friends call you Catherine?"

"No."

"Cathy?"

"Yes."

"And your men," Travis said smoothly, "do they call you Cat?"

There was no mistaking the cynical calculation in his sea-colored eyes. She couldn't have missed it if she had wanted to. The regret she felt surprised her. A corner of her mouth curled in a bitter smile.

This joke was on her, definitely.

"Fun's over, Travis. Put me down."

"What do your men call you . . . *Cat*?"

She lifted one dark auburn eyebrow and watched him with cool, unblinking eyes, waiting to be released.

After a long moment he loosened his grip on her legs, letting go of her in such a way that she slid intimately over the length of his body before her feet touched the ground.

And even when she was standing, his arm stayed around her back, holding her against his body.

Cat knew that struggling against Travis would be a waste of energy. Even worse, it would increase her awareness of his disturbing male strength. Her skin burned with the tactile memory of his body rubbing over hers.

Finally, slowly, Travis removed his arm.

Unconsciously she readjusted the weight of the camera bag and shifted the awkward sling to a more comfortable angle. While she did, she studied Travis as though he was an interesting rock formation she was thinking about photographing.

He would have been a good subject. Sunset light transformed his hair and beard into fine, radiant wires. His eyes had changed color again, green tourmaline now, so deep they were like a sea without a shore. His wet clothes clung to every line of tendon and sinew, outlining muscular shoulders and thighs.

Distantly Cat realized that Travis was much bigger than he seemed at first glance. Like a perfectly proportioned tree, she had to stand close to him to appreciate his true size.

And his confidence. He was watching her, waiting for her to move. Nothing in the blunt lines and angles of his face suggested softness.

Not a handsome man, she thought. *Yet there's something about him . . .*

She could look at Travis for a long, long time and still find new aspects of him to appeal to her. He was a complex man.

And she was used to boys.

"I'm the only one who calls me Cat. I don't have any men. And," she added neutrally, "I'm not looking for any." She turned away. "But thanks twice, Travis."

"Twice?" he asked quickly

There was surprise in his deep voice. Surprise and something else, something uneasy. He rarely was wrong in his estimate of people, yet she kept taking him off guard.

Cat looked back over her shoulder, caught by the odd

inflection in Travis's voice, as though he was echoing her own regret.

"Once for the cameras," she explained, "and once for the laugh."

"I was right, wasn't I? You don't have many happy thoughts."

She pretended she hadn't heard. Without another word she turned and walked away from the surprising, compelling stranger.

Travis watched her proud long-legged stride, the faint hesitation caused by her bloody foot, and the ease with which she shouldered the weight of her camera equipment.

It didn't take a crystal ball to know that she wasn't going to look back.

TWO

STRUGGLING NOT to limp, Cat crossed the narrow strip of sand that stood between the ocean and the ragged cliff ahead of her. Houses spilled down the steep face of the land, trailing stairways like tentacles down to the beach. The bluff was so heavily eaten by weather and sea that deep ravines separated homes whose outer walls were no more than twenty feet apart.

To visit neighbors, Cat had to climb up to street level and cross over on the city sidewalk or climb down to the beach and take a private stairway up to the neighbor's house. The arrangement wasn't unusual in Southern California cities like Laguna Beach, where waterfront land was so valuable it was sold by the inch.

A rock concealed beneath the sand made a joke of Cat's attempts not to limp. She bit her lip against the pain.

"Cat."

She froze. She hadn't heard Travis come up behind her, yet he was so close to her now that she could feel his warmth radiating against the bare skin of her back.

"Will you let me help you?" he asked.

The words were soft, spoken against the braided mass of her hair. His breath was as caressing as sunlight on naked skin.

When she didn't answer, he slowly picked her up again, giving her every opportunity to object.

Cat could have told herself that it was all right not to protest, that her foot hurt too much to walk on, but she had given up that kind of comfortable self-delusion when she dove into a midnight sea seven years ago. She was letting Travis carry her because it felt right, as though he was an old friend helping her rather than a stranger who intrigued and annoyed her by turns.

"Thank you," Travis said softly.

She shook her head in a gesture of disbelief that was directed at herself. Then she sighed and relaxed against his strength. It *did* feel good not to be walking on her bloody foot.

"I'm the one who should be saying thanks," Cat said.

"Maybe. But you don't allow many people to help you."

Surprise and wariness flickered through her. She didn't like being so transparent.

"How did you know that?" she asked coolly.

"I watched you on the rock. The rest of the world just doesn't exist for you."

"Nothing mysterious in that. Concentration is simply part of being a photographer."

Travis smiled down at her, but his eyes were intelligent rather than amused.

"When that wave sprayed your legs," he said, "you knew you were in trouble. You didn't look around for help."

"Why would I? I was alone."

"You acted like you were on Mars. You didn't even notice me when I yelled."

"The surf was too noisy," she said.

He shook his head. "It took you about three seconds to get to the bottom line. No whining, no hand-wringing. You saw your best chance and you took it."

"Your point?"

"That kind of independence is unusual for a man, much less for a woman. It comes from living alone."

"Like you?" Cat challenged.

"Yeah," he drawled. "Like me."

"Well, don't cut your foot. You're too big for me to carry."

He laughed and his arms tightened in what could have been a hug.

"Kitten, I—" Travis stopped abruptly, aware of the sudden stiffness of her body. "Don't like being called kitten?"

"Right the first time, Travie-boy."

"What happened to the last man who called you kitten?"

"The last *boy* who called me kitten decided it was a case of mistaken identity."

Cat smiled, but her eyes were narrowed against the painful flood of memories. For a time, Billy had called her kitten. Billy, the pretty, petulant, too rich boy she had married before she was old enough to know better.

"Another unhappy thought," Travis said.

"You seem to have the touch."

He winced. "Sorry."

"Why? You can't be blamed for my memories."

"You made them, and you'll live with them," he said. It was a summation, not a question.

Cat cocked her head and looked at Travis again. She was becoming used to his uncomfortable insights.

"Have you been reading my mail, or are you a practicing warlock?" she asked.

One corner of his mouth lifted slightly. "It would take a warlock to pet a red-haired cougar, wouldn't it?"

"I'm told that warlocks have green eyes. Yours are, sometimes."

"Not often enough to count on the warlock scale. Actually, I'm a pirate."

"A pirate . . ." Cat said slowly, testing the thought.

She looked at his profile, his beard luminous with the fading light, his teeth a slash of white beneath an arrogant nose. An uncompromising face, utterly male, fully suited for a pirate.

"I'll buy that," she agreed. "A southern pirate."

"Southern?" Travis asked as he began climbing the stairs at the far right of the beach. "How did you guess?"

"The name. And the sexy drawl. East Texas?"

"Guilty."

Belatedly Cat realized that she was being carried up the wrong stairs. "I'm the next one over on the left."

"I'm not."

"You live here?" she asked, surprised.

"For a while."

"House-sitting?"

"After a fashion."

Then Cat remembered the man she had seen for the last eight dawns when he dove into the waves and swam out beyond the cove, his body as sleek and powerful as a dolphin's.

"I didn't recognize you with your clothes on," she said, thinking of the brief black trunks that were all Travis wore at dawn.

He stopped at a midpoint on the stairs and stared down at her blankly.

"Your dawn raids," she explained, smiling.

Her smile revealed the white shine of teeth against the tip of her pink tongue. Reluctantly Travis glanced from her mouth to the multilevel redwood-and-glass house that was one stairway over. Understanding hit.

"And I didn't recognize you with your clothes *off*," he said wryly.

He looked back at her, taking in the thick auburn braid sliding over her shoulder, the wet halter top outlining two very tempting breasts, and the cutoff jeans that only emphasized the feminine curve of her legs draped over his arm. Slowly his glance returned to the halter and her nipples drawn tautly against cloth.

"The lack of clothes is a definite improvement," Travis added.

Cat looked down at herself, wondering if her halter had been ripped on the rocks. The cloth was intact, but for an instant she saw what he had seen—a woman whose breasts were perfectly revealed through the halter's thin cloth, every curve, every swell, nipples puckered by cold. Everything.

She had never seen herself through a man's eyes. The experience was both shocking and . . . intriguing.

"Do I embarrass you?" Travis asked.

His voice was gentle rather than teasing. She reacted to the drawl as though she had been caressed.

"I don't know," she admitted.

"Honest little cat, aren't you?"

"Always," she said flatly, not bothering to be polite. She looked at his face again, fascinated by an elusive *something* about this man that appealed to her. "I keep feeling we've met before."

His sun-bleached eyebrows shot up in surprise or disbelief.

Hearing her own words, Cat groaned. "You've reduced me to clichés."

"I know the feeling."

Slowly Travis bent his head down to her. She didn't protest when his lips brushed across her forehead. His short, sleek beard smelled of sun and salt and man. She closed her eyes, accepting his caress as easily as he had given it.

"For the last three days I've seen you at dawn," he said against Cat's hair, "stealing down your stairs like a shadow. You're all but hidden by equipment. Are the baggy jeans and sweatshirt a disguise to keep off predatory males?"

"It's cold at dawn."

"Not if you're in the right bed."

The thick crimson light of sunset concealed his expression, but Cat could feel Travis waiting for an answer to the question he hadn't asked. Not quite.

"I'm always in the right bed," she said. "Mine."

She wondered whether that had been the answer he wanted to hear. His expression told her nothing.

Travis continued walking up the stairs, breathing evenly, carrying her with every appearance of ease. Cat appreciated his strength on more than a simple feminine level. Her own career—and pride—demanded that she keep the flexibility and stamina she had enjoyed as a teenager. At twenty-nine, that wasn't easy.

Cat guessed that Travis was at least five years older than she was. She respected anyone who had the discipline to stay fit on the other side of thirty. She knew several men who got breathless just climbing up her steps from the beach. She had worn out more than one eager male simply by walking down to the water, swimming for an hour, and walking back up to her home.

It was piquant to realize that it would take more than a bit of exercise to wear out the man called Travis.

"Now, that looks like a good memory. Or at least," he amended, taking the last step and walking onto a cantilevered wooden deck, "not a bad one."

"It's a new one. Fully worth cutting my foot for. In fact—"

Cat's words stopped abruptly as Travis turned, giving her a view of the sun balanced on the edge of a shimmering magenta sea. The whole world had turned burning gold and shade on shade of purple. There were no clouds, no smog, nothing to interrupt the razor clarity of the horizon.

And then Cat saw a sailing ship sweeping before the wind like a great black bird. Soon it would fly across the incandescent eye of the sun.

"Put me down," she said urgently, struggling without realizing it, intent on the image that was forming in her mind.

Cat didn't see Travis's surprised look or the instant of anger that quickly became puzzlement. Once she felt the deck beneath her feet, she forgot her wet clothes, her cut foot, even the disturbingly sensual presence of the man who stood watching her.

Her hands flew over the camera case. She found an empty camera body with one hand and high-speed color film with the other. She loaded the camera, secured it to the autofocus zoom lens, and zeroed in on the sailboat.

Less than a minute after Travis put her down, Cat was taking the first picture. She worked rapidly, with a precision that reflected the years she had spent looking through a lens. The long lens was sensitive, well balanced in its rifle-style holder, and easy to use.

Yet the lens felt very heavy after a solid day of photography. Even as Cat braced her arm, part of her mind cursed her relentless schedule of work in the past twelve months. Her reserves of strength were gone. She was weak when she desperately wanted to be as strong as the beautiful ship skimming over the incandescent sea.

But most of Cat's mind ignored regrets and emotions. Pouring herself into the camera, she focused entirely in the moment, forcing her weary body to obey her commands.

The ship cut the burning wake of the sun. In silhouette the purity of the ship's lines became breathtaking, more work of art than simple transportation. Curve on curve singing of speed and distance, flight and patience, power and silence, endlessly poised on the edge of creation.

The last frame of film whirred through the camera. The motor drive fell silent.

Quickly Cat looked at the sun and the ship. There was neither time to reload nor enough light left for photography. With an expression of yearning, she lowered the camera and watched the elegant ship sail into the condensing night.

Not until the ship vanished completely did Cat notice that her foot throbbed, her arms were shaking with fatigue, and Travis was bracing her with one hand and holding the heavy zoom lens with the other. She sagged against him but still said nothing. Her eyes searched the darkness beyond the setting sun, looking for a ship. She found nothing but colors draining into night.

"It's gone," she said.

Travis stared at Cat. Her eyes were luminous, intense. Her voice was barely more than a sigh, as melancholy as the descending night.

"Oh, God," she whispered, "it must be incredible to sail that ship over the curve of the world and into the soul of beauty."

Travis clenched his jaw against the anger uncoiling in his gut. *She's just like the others after all, out for everything she can get from me.*

A seagull cried, breaking the spell the ship had cast over Cat. She looked up at Travis. His expression was distant, his eyes unreadable.

"Didn't you see it?" she asked. "It was the most beautiful ship ever created. Someday I'll take a photo as perfect as that ship. Then I'll smash my cameras and never take another picture again."

Travis didn't say anything. His disappointment in finding that Cat was just like the other women he had known was so intense that it was almost pain.

It infuriated him.

Fooled again, he told himself bitterly. *Just when I was congratulating myself on finding a woman who was interested in me before she ever knew about my bank account.*

I should have known better.

"Travis?"

He didn't answer.

She looked at him again, wondering why he looked so remote, so grim. Then she replayed her own words in her mind. For the first time in years, a flush climbed up her cheeks. She laughed self-consciously.

"Sorry," she muttered. "Not everyone feels the way I do about light and shadow and the shape of freedom."

Travis didn't trust himself to speak. Anger and disappointment were too strong, shockingly strong.

I barely know her. Why the hell do I care that she's another gold-digging, lying female?

Cat smiled slightly, trying to understand the expression on his face.

"I'm not really crazy," she assured him. "Not all the time. I've just never seen anything quite that beautiful before."

She waited for Travis to speak. He didn't. His eyes were a reflection of deep twilight—mystery and darkness and something else, something bleak that she couldn't name.

"Travis?" she whispered.

His fingers tightened on her arm to a point just short of pain.

"What kind of game do you think you're playing?" he asked roughly.

Cat stared at him, not understanding the question. All she knew was that the expression on his face was as cold as the wind lifting off the darkened sea. The lazy, approving masculine warmth was gone as though it had never existed.

Abruptly she felt so tired she could hardly stand up. The weakness sweeping over her was frightening.

No, she thought instantly. *I can't be this tired. Not yet. Not for four more months.*

But she was. Exhaustion was stealing through her like twilight, taking all warmth and color. She couldn't allow it to happen. Her reserves of strength had to last until January.

In January she would be able to crawl into bed and pull the covers over her eyes and sleep for a year.

Until then she must do what she had been doing. Work, followed by more work, followed by much more work. There was no other choice that she could live with. She had already failed life's bitter little tests once. She would work herself into the grave before she failed again.

This time she was counting only on herself.

"I'm not playing any game," Cat said flatly. "I'm way too tired for games. I saw something incredible, and for once there was someone worth sharing it with. That's all."

Travis didn't say a word.

She looked at his expression and finally recognized it. Contempt.

"My mistake," she said, trying to step away from him.

The big hand that was clamped on her arm held her where she was. Close to him.

"What's my last name?" Travis demanded.

"I don't know."

"Guess," he said sarcastically.

"I said I was too tired for games."

Cat tried to move away, but Travis's fingers were like iron, caging her. She turned on him with narrowed eyes and a mouth that no longer smiled.

"Smith," she suggested acidly. "No? How about Johnson? Or Jones."

Then she jerked her arm sharply. This time she didn't take Travis by surprise. This time there would be no easy escape for her.

"Smith, Johnson, and Jones are the three most common names in the English language," she snarled. "After them, the odds of guessing right go straight to hell."

Travis saw and recognized Cat's anger. It was like his own—the instinctive rage of a thirsty animal that had finally found water, only to discover it was tainted.

Cat shivered again. Warmth had drained out of the evening as surely as color. She moved, but remained imprisoned by his grip.

"I suppose you don't know the name of the ship, either," he said coldly.

"The lens is powerful, but it can't read print a half mile

away against the sun.'' Her tone was as cold as his.

Travis stared at her for the space of several breaths, hungry to believe her, afraid to be wrong again. The cost was simply too high. Not in money. He could afford that.

But he couldn't afford the personal wreckage that came from misjudging a woman's motives.

Cat waited, watching Travis with remote gray eyes. Gradually his expression and his grip on her arm gentled. His fingertips moved over her skin as lightly as a butterfly sipping nectar. She shivered beneath his sensitive touch, feeling as though she had never been caressed by a man before.

''If the ship was yours,'' he said softly, ''what would you call her?''

''Freedom.''

''Is your world a jail, Cat?''

She looked up at Travis's face. His expression was intense yet oddly gentle. Instinctively she gave him the honesty his waiting silence required.

''Not always,'' she said. ''But the next few months are going to be really tight.''

He dragged a key from the wet pocket of his shorts and unlocked the door to the gleaming white house. ''Tell me about it while I take care of your foot.''

Before she could accept or refuse, Travis picked up her camera equipment and gestured her inside with a sweep of the hand holding her big zoom lens.

Cat hesitated for only a heartbeat. His shifts in mood were unsettling, but they were no worse than her reckless concentration on taking photos or her babbling about freedom and the soul of beauty.

She stepped into the house. The unglazed terra-cotta tile of the entryway felt cool beneath her sore foot. Her remaining canvas shoe squeaked with each shift of her weight.

Sand grated as she and Travis walked side by side into

the center of the luxurious foyer. She looked at their gritty feet and the pale pink carpet that waited beyond the white marble tiles.

"We're going to ruin your carpet," Cat said.

"I can only hope," he muttered. Then he said, "Linda assured me that I can't do anything to the house that her parties haven't done already. Twice."

Cat glanced at the expanse of pink and wondered. It looked spotless to her. "Are you sure?"

"Positive. Have you been to my cousin's parties?"

"No. I've only lived next door for six months, but your, um, cousin's parties are legend in Laguna."

"Figures. My cousin has been in London for the last six months. It must have been real quiet around here."

He caught Cat's quietly cynical smile at the word *cousin.* But he didn't say anything.

Neither did she. She simply looked around the glass-walled, lushly carpeted living room. There were modern crystal sculptures and mirrors and beveled glass, suede couches in startling pink, and minimalist art like sliver exclamation points scattered around the room.

After a time Cat realized that Travis was watching her, waiting for her attention to return to him.

"Having second thoughts about the carpet?" she asked.

"Screw the carpet. Linda really is my cousin. My mother's sister's daughter."

Cat studied Travis for a moment, then nodded slowly. "Cousin it is. You have no more reason to lie to me than I have to lie to you."

"You act as though men never lie to women, and vice versa."

"*Men* don't."

Travis smiled crookedly. "I take it that your definition of 'man' has little to do with age."

"It has nothing to do with age." She looked down at her foot. "Why don't you bring the disinfectant or whatever out here? My blood is the wrong shade of pink for the rug.''

''No problem.''

He set aside Cat's camera gear, picked her up, and carried her through the room. Other than making a soft, startled sound, she didn't object.

Glass doors slid open to reveal an interior garden. A hot tub steamed invitingly in the midst of greenery and concealed lights. Somewhat cynically, Cat waited for Travis to suggest that she would be more comfortable if she took off her cold, wet, sandy clothes.

''Do you have a special definition of woman, too?'' he asked, setting her on the broad lip of the tub.

The question was not what Cat had expected. It slipped past her defenses without warning. A memory went through her like black lightning, darkening everything it touched.

Billy had been very cruel on the subject of her womanhood. But then, he had been very disappointed. He had wanted to found a dynasty.

''No,'' Cat said, trying not to let her memories color her voice. ''No special definition. Honesty. Warmth. Intelligence. Endurance. The usual things.''

''Usual?'' Tawny eyebrows lifted. ''The usual things are bust, waist, and hip measurements.''

''Which, added together, invariably exceed the IQ of the boy doing the measuring.''

Travis smiled. ''Wise little cat, aren't you?''

''Eventually. It's called survival.''

He pulled off his wet shirt and tossed it aside. The hair on his chest gleamed wetly. Cat half expected him to take off his jeans, but he didn't. He simply slipped into the tub and pulled her in with him. At no time did he so much as hint that either one of them would be more comfortable without clothes.

Cat couldn't help relaxing as the heat of the water went through her like a benediction. She sighed with pleasure.

"I didn't know how cold I was," she admitted after a time.

"You mean that interesting shade of blue isn't lipstick?"

Smiling slightly, she flipped her braid outside the tub and sank farther down on the bench that circled the interior. With a groan, she rested her head on the lip of the tub. Eyes closed, she let heat seep into muscles that were tied in knots from the tension and fatigue that had ruled her life since the twins hadn't been able to find enough grants, loans, and scholarships to get through medical school.

Cat had made up the difference, even though her mother was a sweet, incessant drain on her daughter's bank account. She had worked herself into the ground and she knew it.

I can hang on until January. I've done it for four years. I can do fourteen weeks and four days standing on my head.

She repeated the words to herself, and the promises. In January she would cut her workload in half and take proper care of herself again. Until then, life was going to be a jail of sorts, with each bar carefully chosen and set in place by her own hands.

"Tell me about your jail, Cat."

THREE

"YOU *ARE* a warlock," Cat muttered into the foaming water.

"I am?" Travis asked, startled.

"Mind reading. Definite warlock trait."

He smiled. "It wasn't tough. We had already brought up the subject of jail. Then you leaned back into the tub looking like someone who has just been paroled."

Cat also looked like a woman who thoroughly enjoyed heat, liquid, and her own senses. He couldn't wait to find out how she reacted to having a man's mouth all over her. But he didn't say anything for the same reason that he hadn't urged her to take off her clothes.

Cat was well named. If he crowded her, she would rake him from heels to head.

"Jail," she repeated, making the word a sigh. "No wonder you seemed so familiar."

"Fellow inmates?"

She looked at his off-center smile and felt more heat than the water could account for.

"We think along the same lines," Cat said, closing her eyes again. "That makes you seem familiar."

Travis was tempted to get a whole lot more familiar, but he knew he would get clawed if he tried. Besides, watching the taut lines of her face relax was a kind of pleasure. He had a hunch that bordered on certainty that his wary Cat didn't let many people close to her.

What he didn't know was why.

"Tell me about your jail," he said quietly.

"Nothing special," she said, smothering a yawn with dripping fingers. "I work for myself. That means when I have time, I don't have money, and when I have money, I don't have time."

Travis's eyes narrowed at the mention of money. He watched her with sudden, predatory intensity.

Cat didn't notice. She had given herself over to the glorious luxury of heat.

"Is money so important to you?" he drawled, but his lazy tone was belied by the cold intelligence of his eyes.

For a time she didn't answer. She didn't want to spoil the sense of well-being that was stealing through her. Yet talking held a real lure. She had no one other than the next-door neighbor to talk with, and Sharon was buried under infant twins and a precocious seven-year-old.

"Cat?"

She sighed. "My twin brother and sister are just finishing their medical schooling. Neither of them is able to work enough to earn more than pocket money."

"You're putting them through school?" Travis asked, surprised.

"Yeah. Until January."

"What about grants and loans?"

"Oh, we've got them, too," she said, yawning. "Do you have any idea how much it costs to put your kid through an advanced degree these days?"

The thought of a child took the last light from Travis's eyes, leaving only bitterness. "No," he said softly. "I don't."

"Thousands and thousands and thousands of dollars. Lord, I wouldn't have believed it." Lazily Cat swirled water with her fingertips. "Then there's my dear, gently crazy mother. She had never written a check in her life until Dad died. Then she wrote too many checks, for all the wrong reasons, until all the money was gone.''

Travis looked carefully at Cat's expression, but saw only a weary affection for and acceptance of whatever her mother was and was not.

''Twins and a mother, huh?'' he asked quietly, wondering why it sounded familiar. But then, hard luck stories all tended to sound the same.

''Yeah. Not to mention my home. I can't really afford the monthly toll on the lease-option until I make the last payment on the twins' education in January.''

''In over your head?''

If Cat noticed the edge to Travis's voice, she didn't react.

''Nope. I'm a good swimmer,'' she said, settling even deeper into the luxurious heat of the tub. ''I fell in love with my home six years ago. It came on the market six months ago. If I'd waited until January, the house would have sold and I'd be back to yearning over it from afar.''

''So you took out a loan?''

''Are you kidding? I'm in business for myself. Banks hate me.''

''How did you get the money? Rob one of the banks that hated you?''

She smiled and yawned. ''Nope. I just increased my workday from twelve to sixteen hours.''

Travis laughed, thinking Cat was joking.

''If seven days a week doesn't get it done, try working nights, is that it?'' he asked.

''Oh, I do that, too.''

''Work nights?''

''Of course.''

''Money is very important to you, isn't it?''

This time there was no ignoring the edge in Travis's voice. Cat opened her eyes and saw the mingling of anger and disappointment on his face. At that instant his face was a study in hard angular shadows. His lips were flat, almost invisible beneath his thick mustache. His teeth were a thin line of white. Savage gold lights glinted through his beard.

"Put a knife in those teeth and you'd be Bluebeard incarnate," she said.

"You haven't answered my question."

"About what?"

"Money," he said flatly.

Cat looked at Travis as though he was as impractical as her mother. "Of course money is important."

"Not to everyone."

"The only people money isn't important to already have it."

"Maybe. And maybe some people are quite happy without money."

"They don't have to pay my bills."

"And you would be so grateful if some good ol' boy paid your bills," he drawled.

The understanding and subtle disdain in Travis's voice sent a shock of adrenaline through Cat, giving her false energy.

"Don't worry, Travie-boy. I'm not going to hit you for a loan."

With a fast twist of her body, she pulled herself out of the tub. The movement was savage, unexpected, like the disappointment slicing into her. She ran through the house, swept up her camera equipment, and opened the door to the beach stairs.

Two big hands shot over her shoulder, slamming the door shut before she could even start to go through it. She looked at the tanned, dripping, powerful forearms holding the door shut.

Travis was so close to her that his breath stirred the fine hairs at the nape of her neck.

"Open it," Cat said through her teeth.

"You're shivering. Come back to the tub."

"It's warmer outside."

"Cat, it's not—"

"Let me out," she interrupted harshly.

Travis both sensed and saw the outrage vibrating through her. Whatever the state of her bank account, at that moment she wouldn't have taken a bent coin from him.

"I didn't mean it as an insult," he said calmly. "It's just a fact of life."

"Not my life. *I earn my keep.*"

The savagery of Cat's voice told Travis that he had opened a very painful subject. He hesitated, then let out a long breath, wanting to believe her when she said she hadn't been looking to him for money.

Needing to believe her.

He hadn't known until this moment how much of a jail his money had become, and how anonymous he felt within its bars.

"I'm not used to women like you," Travis said finally.

"I'll bet you aren't used to *women* at all. With your manners, you must have to rent female company by the quarter hour. The door, Travis. Open it."

Cat expected anything but the wry male laughter that sent an entirely different variety of shiver through her body, not cold at all, but a delicate kind of heat.

"Do you always draw blood with your claws?" he asked, not blaming her, simply curious.

She shifted her weight, wincing as her foot complained. The hot tub had taken away most of the sand, but it had done little else except make her realize how exhausted she was underneath her determination to do what must be done.

"Game's over, Travis, whatever game you were playing."

"I wasn't—"

"Sure you were," she interrupted in a clipped voice. "You found the cat, you found the cage, and then you started shoving sharp things through the bars just so you could watch the cat scratch and howl. That makes you feel powerful, and the cat . . ." She shrugged. "Hell, who cares how the cat feels? It's just an animal and you're a *man*."

A charged silence settled over the foyer.

Cat watched Travis's hands change from flat against the door into fists, solid and heavy. Muscles coiled and slid beneath tanned skin, telling more clearly than words of the emotions seething in the man behind her.

Stiff-spined, she waited for him to let her go.

"Don't be afraid," he said. "I won't hurt you."

"I know."

"How?" he asked starkly, looking at his own fists.

"The same way I knew my cameras would be safe with you. In some ways we know each other frighteningly well. It makes the misjudgments all the more . . . painful."

"Cat in a cage," he whispered. "I would like to know who left such scars on you."

"Believe me, you wouldn't like knowing him at all. He isn't a likable boy."

Gradually Travis's hands relaxed. He let out a long, weary curse.

For the first time Cat noticed the fine scars crisscrossing his fingers. Some of the scars were new, some were so old they had all but faded beneath the sunbrowned skin. She wondered what kind of work he did that left such spidery marks on him.

And then she wondered what kind of female had left invisible, much deeper scars on him.

"Was he really that bad?" Travis asked finally.

"My ex?"

"Is he the boy who put you in a cage and tormented you?"

Cat shrugged. "He probably wasn't any worse than the female who soured you on half the world's population."

"Are you so sure it was a woman?"

"A female," Cat corrected evenly. "And yes, I'm sure.

Most people have to be taught that kind of soul-deep wariness of the opposite sex.''

"Were you?''

"Of course.''

"When?''

Cat didn't answer, but the stiffness slowly left her spine. Her shoulders sagged. She didn't have the strength to fight Travis and her memories, too.

With a bitter word she stopped trying to pull open the door and simply leaned her forehead against it, letting her camera bag rest on the floor. For the first time she noticed that she was standing in a spreading pool of pink-tinged water.

Travis saw it, too. He didn't ask if he could pick her up again. He simply did.

The strap of the camera bag slipped from Cat's fingers. Automatically she made a grab for it, but it was already beyond her reach.

"My camera gear,'' she said.

"It will keep.''

"But—''

"Relax,'' he interrupted, talking over her. "All I'm going to do is bandage your foot. If you want to leave afterward, I won't get in your way.''

Cat told herself that she was probably a fool, but she believed Travis at a level of her mind too deep to deny. Despite their mutual wariness, something in him called to her. She had never felt that with a man before. Any man. Even her ex.

Especially her ex.

It made Cat wonder if there was more to the man-woman dynamic than she had managed to discover in twenty-nine years.

This time Travis set her down in a bathroom done in shades of lavender, lemon, and pale fuchsia. His brown, powerful back looked so out of place amid the pastel splendors that she couldn't help smiling.

But when he touched her foot, the smile became a gasp.

"Hurt?" he asked mildly.

Cat gritted her teeth against an unladylike answer.

"It will get worse," he assured her. "The sand has to be scrubbed out." He looked up at her. "Do you want me to do it or would you be more comfortable doing it yourself?"

At first Cat didn't answer. She simply pulled her right foot into her lap to inspect it. There was more than one cut. None was deep enough to require stitches. All the cuts began on her sole and then wrapped around to the outside of her foot, a place that was almost impossible for her to reach.

And Travis was right. There was sand in every cut. Even if she soaked the foot thoroughly, some sand would remain. It was the nature of sand and barnacle cuts to stick together.

Making a disgusted sound, Cat thrust her foot back into his hands.

"Thank you," he said.

"Haven't we had this conversation before, the one where I should be thanking you instead of vice versa?"

"That's okay. We'll just keep on doing it until we get it right." He looked up and smiled slowly at her. "I guarantee it."

Cat knew better than to touch that line. He was no more talking about repeating conversations than she was thinking about it.

Still smiling, Travis put warm water and disinfectant in a basin, set her foot in it, and left the bathroom. He returned almost immediately, carrying a thick, dark blue bathrobe in his hands. Without a word he wrapped it around her. Then he settled cross-legged on the floor and picked up her cut foot.

She wasn't surprised that he was both gentle and quick

as he worked over her foot. Any man who moved with his innate coordination was bound to be good with his hands.

With a minimum of pain and no wasted time, Travis cleaned Cat's cuts, put on salve, and wrapped her foot with gauze. When he was done, he held her bandaged foot in one hand and kneaded her calf almost absently with the other. His eyes were focused on something only he could see.

She was focused on him. His hands were warm on her cool skin, his fingers strong and sure as he soothed away the cramps that had come as she tensed her muscles against pain. As she looked at him, she forgot her stinging foot. His tawny hair was alive with every possible shade of brown and gold. Light moved through his short beard and highlighted the subtle difference in the texture of his skin against hers. His fingers curved tenderly around the arch of her foot.

Cat longed to photograph him, the fluid lines and blunt strength, the sleek light and masculine shadow. He was as compelling to her as the great black ship had been.

"What are you thinking?" Travis asked quietly

"I want to photograph you."

His eyes widened, revealing brilliant tourmaline depths. He laughed softly, shaking his head. "Will you always surprise me?"

"Depends on what your preconceptions are, doesn't it?"

His smile faded. "I hereby abandon all my preconceptions about the opposite sex. And you, Cat, will you abandon yours?"

"I don't have any where men are concerned. Only boys. I've never known a man."

Except you, she thought. *Are you what you seem, Travis? A man, not a boy?*

Travis was as baffling as he was compelling to her. She had just met him, she had always known him, she didn't know what to do with him, and she didn't want him to go away.

Cat waited while he studied her in turn, visibly weighing her words against his previous experiences, deciding whether to take her the same way the sailing ship had taken the night—openly, with nothing held back.

"May I call you Cat?"

"Haven't you always?" she asked lightly.

He rubbed his beard along her bare calf. She was smooth, resilient, smelling of salt and a faint perfume that was essentially woman. He would have brushed his lips over her, tasted her, but he had seen the flashes of wariness and confusion in her eyes. He understood them.

They were very like his own feelings.

"Yes, I think I've always called you Cat," Travis said, gently releasing her foot. "That will make our dinner plans a lot easier."

"What plans?"

"I'm taking you out to dinner."

"Thanks," she said, bending over to look at the neat bandage, "but I don't think my foot is up to a night on the town."

"Then I'll bring some dinner in. What do you want?"

"How does salad, rolls, and swordfish sound?"

Travis made a growling sound of enthusiasm, but it was the bare nape of Cat's neck that he was looking at.

"Which Laguna restaurant does take-out fish?" he asked.

"Chez Cat," Cat said dryly, straightening up. "But I insist that customers eat with the chef."

He smiled and wished he could nibble on her nape a little. Sort of an appetizer.

"How about if I cook?" he asked.

"You haven't been here long enough to know your way around your cousin's kitchen."

Travis couldn't argue that. Linda had enough bells and

whistles in her kitchen for a fire station. After one look at the stainless steel, matte black, and fuchsia appliances, he had started exploring the local restaurants.

"You sure you want to cook?" he asked, standing up and setting Cat on her feet. "I know some really good places to eat."

"I won't poison you," she said, heading for the front door, "if that's what you're worried about."

She stopped long enough to pick up her camera gear. He was behind her. Right behind her. If she turned around, she would be in his arms. She forced herself not to turn around. Instead, she reached for the door handle.

A large, male hand beat her to it. Unlike some big men, there was nothing slow about Travis. She hadn't turned around, but she was still halfway to being in his arms.

"Who has the best local swordfish?" he asked.

"The seafood market at Dana Point marina. Kind of pricey, but—"

Cat's breath broke. For an instant it had felt as though her bare nape was being caressed by a silky brush.

Travis's mustache. She was certain of it.

"Good is always pricey," he said. "Always worth it, too. Want to come and help me pick it out and watch me while I cook?"

When Cat looked over her shoulder, she found herself staring into a pair of sultry blue-green eyes. She didn't have to be a mind reader to know what Travis was thinking about.

She was thinking about it, too.

I must be nuts, she told herself wildly.

Herself shot back, *If this is nuts, I'll take it.*

"I like to cook," Cat said.

She turned back to look at the door. She didn't trust herself to look at Travis any longer without doing something really stupid, like finding out if he tasted as appealing as he looked.

The thought of being the sexual aggressor startled Cat. Her ex had made it brutally clear that men wanted that role. Aggressive women left men cold.

"Sure?" Travis asked.

She wondered if he was talking about her thoughts or about leaving or about cooking dinner, but she knew better than to ask. She cleared her throat of the huskiness that had gathered after the silky caress of his mustache against her neck.

"Very sure," Cat said briskly. "I've got some things to do before dinner. Why don't you and the swordfish show up at my door in about two hours?"

"One hour."

The certainty that Travis was as reluctant to see her leave as she was to go made Cat feel almost light-headed with a combination of pleasure and relief. Whatever was happening, she wasn't alone.

"Ninety minutes," she said.

"You drive a hard bargain. Eighty minutes it is."

"But I said—" Cat began.

The door handle clicked beneath Travis's left hand. The front door nudged against her breasts. The fingertips of his right hand traced the line of her throat and collarbone. With a reluctance that had Cat holding her breath, he stopped short of touching the curves that showed so clearly beneath her wet halter.

"Run while you can, Cat. With every breath you take, this pirate is becoming less willing to let you go."

FOUR

EVEN AFTER Cat shut her own door behind her, she still felt as though Travis was watching her with elemental hunger in his eyes, a hunger she couldn't help sharing.

Too soon, she told herself. *Way too soon. I've never done a quickie with a stranger. I'm too old to start now.*

Besides, I have more brains than that.

Don't I?

Hurriedly Cat showered, chose some casual slacks and a hunter green blouse, rebraided her hair, and went down to her office on the lowest floor. There were messages waiting on the answering machine. She hit the play button and started jotting down notes for tomorrow's work.

The first voice brought a smile to her face. She was always glad to hear from Rodney Harrington.

"Hi, Fire-and-Ice. Hope you and the poet octopus are doing better."

Cat grimaced. At the moment Blake Ashcroft was one of her least favorite people. The guy gave the idea of lecher new dimensions. But he sold well and he wanted photographs to go with his lush words. A lot of photographs.

She wasn't in a position to be picky about the number of hands her clients had.

"Remember the Danvers book I talked to you about last year? I have a publisher's name on the dotted line as of today. I'll finalize a few things with Danvers and then get back to you. *Ciao.*''

Cat blinked, trying to remember what Harrington was talking about. She and her "green angel" discussed so many projects, and she was lousy at remembering names. Frowning, she ransacked what passed for her memory. All she came up with was a vague mention of someone Harrington had nicknamed In-the-Wind Danvers or Hell-On-Women Danvers, depending on the occasion. He built ships, or something like that.

For a few moments Cat wondered how she would make a shipbuilding facility look fascinating on film. Then she shrugged. If Harrington got the job for her, she would figure out something.

After Rodney Harrington, the rest of the calls were routine: slides ready to be picked up, a camera body that had been repaired, someone selling aluminum siding, a gallery wanting to know when she would be bringing some more work by, someone selling windows, and the bank telling her that there hadn't been any mistake, her balance was dismal.

She deleted the messages and went through the mail, sorting everything into three piles: To Be Paid; To Be Billed; Trash. The To Be Billed pile was depressingly small. If Energistics, Inc., didn't come through with her check in the next few weeks, money would get really tight.

Cat thought about calling Harrington to see if he had any paying jobs other than the Danvers book in her future, but decided not to. She was too tired to think about taking on new work, even though she really needed the money.

Energistics will pay me soon. It's been six months, for God's sake. They agreed that I had done my work well and their payment is due.

Overdue, actually. They should pay me interest.

When Cat finished the mail, she eyed the pile of small film boxes that were heaped in a basket. Each box held thirty-six color slides that needed to be edited, indexed, duplicated, and then sent to the photo banks that represented her.

Usually she was eager to edit the results of her photo shoots. If she wasn't eager, all she had to do was think about a simple fact: she couldn't make any money on slides that were hidden in boxes.

Even so, tonight the thought of editing lacked any appeal. All she really wanted to look at was Travis.

I wonder what his last name is. And why was he so sure I knew it?

The slides boxes had no answers for her.

Cat glanced at her watch. Time was moving like a square wheel. Twenty-two minutes to go.

"I should have taken his first offer—one hour," she muttered as she headed for the kitchen. "Then I'd only have two more minutes to go."

Before she got to the kitchen, there was a knocking on her back door. She laughed aloud, pleased that Travis was as impatient as she was and not afraid to show it. Quickly she crossed the kitchen.

"Fish delivery?" she asked, smiling as she opened the door.

Cat's smile slipped when she looked up at Travis. No man had ever attracted her more than he did at this moment. He was freshly showered, wearing a navy T-shirt and white cotton beach slacks. His tawny hair gleamed like skeins of rough silk.

She wanted to stand and simply enjoy the way his eyes transformed light into jeweled tones of blue and green. She wanted to run her fingertips over his beard and the subtle swells of muscle beneath his shirt.

But most of all she wanted to grab her camera and capture him forever, an image of sensuality to warm the cold center of her nights.

"Are you sure you want to cook?" Travis asked, looking at Cat's odd, intent expression.

"What? Oh, yes. I told you. I really like to cook."

"I knew we were a great match."

She blinked.

"I really like to eat," he explained, handing over two swordfish steaks wrapped in white paper.

Smiling, Cat took the package from his hand. As she did, she noticed again his long, tanned fingers and their hair-fine scars. She wondered if it would be rude to ask how he had acquired them.

Then she thought about her own, hidden scars, and kept her mouth shut. There was rude and then there was painful. She didn't want to add to whatever past pain had made Travis so wary of women.

"Have a seat somewhere," Cat said. "I'll just be a minute."

There was a big bay window at the end of the kitchen overlooking the water. The deep shelf of the window was filled with a pile of local shells. Travis ran his fingers through them, but his eyes followed Cat as she worked over the charcoal brazier outside and then came back to the open kitchen.

Her hair shimmered and blazed beneath the overhead lights, making all other colors look lifeless. Her dark green shirt was tucked into a pair of sand-colored slacks. Though loose, the slacks couldn't conceal the curves and subtle, essentially female swing of her hips. The white bandage on her foot made her skin look like honey.

Despite the sore foot, she moved with a grace and economy that was pleasing to watch. She pulled various fresh vegetables out of the refrigerator, washed them, and began slicing them with a big chef's knife.

"Sure I can't help?" Travis asked in the drawl that sounded so lazy and concealed so much intensity.

"You've carried me enough for one day."

"But I like carrying you."

Cat glanced up, saw the crooked grin that was as familiar to her as her own hands, and felt both warmed and chilled. Right now she didn't need any more complications in her life.

Yet it felt so good to laugh, to glance up and see his blue-green eyes approving of her every movement, to watch his hands and remember their gentleness on her skin.

She knew she shouldn't pursue the fire she sensed within Travis.

And she knew she was going to.

Even in the short time she had spent with him, he had filled spaces in her that she hadn't even known were empty. It was as though he knew her better than she knew herself.

Cat smiled and shook her head. "Travis, you're . . ."

"Impossible?" he suggested hopefully.

"Incredible," she said, her voice revealing too much. "Really incredible," she added briskly.

With casual skill she went back to work. White slices of mushroom piled neatly to one side of the large, honed knife. With a deft motion she gathered slices onto the blade and dropped them in a bowl. The mushrooms fell on top of thinly sliced scallions, nearly transparent rounds of radishes, and circles of carrot as thin as gold coins.

Without pausing, Cat squeezed a lemon over the vegetables, added a generous tablespoon of her homemade garlic-basil olive oil, and set the bowl in the refrigerator to marinate.

"You look like you've done that once or twice," Travis said.

"I cooked my way from the Virgin Islands to Dana Point."

Though Cat's voice was neutral, something in her manner made Travis look at her sharply.

"Do you do it often?" he asked.

"Cook?"

"Go from the Virgin Islands to Southern California."

"Just once."

"You sound like you didn't enjoy it. Seasick?"

"No."

Cat pulled the core out of the leafy lettuce, turned on the tap, and held the lettuce underneath.

Travis waited, knowing there was more to the story.

She turned off the water and shook the lettuce so that excess water could drain off. Methodically she began taking leaves and patting them dry on clean cotton towels.

Part of Cat wanted to tell Travis why she hadn't enjoyed the trip. The rest of her wanted to forget the past.

"I loved the ocean," she said finally. "It just wasn't the best time of my life."

Travis waited until he was certain she wasn't going to volunteer any more.

"I'm glad you don't get seasick," he said. "I'm going to take you sailing."

"Does a boat come with your cousin's house?" Cat asked, wrapping up the lettuce in a damp dish towel and putting it in the refrigerator.

"No. I come with the boat."

She stood on tiptoe and peered out the kitchen window to check the progress of the coals in the small grill on the deck. They would be ready by the time she got the biscuits made.

Silently Cat began cutting butter and flour together in a bowl, making biscuit dough. Travis watched her while she kneaded the dough, rolled it out, cut it into circles, and tucked the biscuits into the oven.

"Aren't you going to ask me what kind of boat I own?" he asked.

"Sure. What kind of boat do you own?"

"A sailboat."

"That's nice. The coals are ready. I'll just dab some herb butter on the swordfish and we'll be eating in no time."

Travis shook his head at Cat's lack of interest in the possibilities of sailing with him.

"Are you sure you like sailing?" he asked.

"I love the ocean," Cat said as she spread a sheen of butter over the swordfish. "I don't know beans about rag sailing. So if you're one of those avid sailors who expects me to care about sloops and catamarans and jibs and the six thousand boring shapes of canvas you can hang from masts, you're going to be one disappointed puppy."

Travis smiled ruefully. "I learned a long time ago that my love of wind, sail, and water isn't something most people give a damn about."

"Like me and photography. I could go on for hours about light and texture, shape and weight and shadow and— Get the door for me, would you?"

He opened the door and followed Cat out to the back deck. Her hands were full of fresh swordfish. His eyes approved her unconscious grace as she bent over the grill.

"But I'm more than willing to listen to you talk about wind and all," she said without looking up. "I'll even make soothing noises, as long as there isn't a pop quiz at the end."

He laughed out loud. "Some other night, maybe. I won't ask that much of a sacrifice on our first date."

Cat went back inside and began setting the small table. Travis took the silverware and plates from her.

"I can do this," he said.

"Thanks. The napkins are on that roll by the sink."

He looked at the paper towels and grinned. "I thought I was the only one who did that."

"My mother did her best to civilize me," Cat said with a shrug. "It worked until I figured out that life isn't civilized."

While she tore up lettuce for the salad, Travis wandered over to the bay window and picked up a handful of shells from the pile by the sill. Slowly he let the shells pour from his hand. They made a whispering, strangely musical sound as they fell. He repeated the motion slowly, thinking about the curves of shells and sails and Cat's sleek body.

He looked back at her. As though hypnotized, she was watching his hand and the liquid fall of shells. Her gray eyes were soft, luminous. Wisps of hair burned around her face in the lamplight.

When the last shell had fallen, Cat glanced up to Travis's face, to his eyes, and felt as though she had stepped off her solid world. She was floating on a tourmaline sea the color of his eyes.

It was an effort to look away. The silence shimmered with possibilities, a sensuality as deep as his eyes.

"Jason likes those shells too," Cat said.

"Jason?" Travis's drawl vanished, leaving his voice as smooth and cool as a wave-polished shell. "Who's he?"

"My neighbor on the other side. Most of those shells are his. Or were. He refuses to take them back."

Travis looked at the pile of unimpressive shells. Privately he didn't blame Jason for unloading the whole lot. What he didn't understand was why Cat had kept them.

"What made him think you wanted them?" Travis asked.

"He found me photographing a shell one day. The next thing I knew he had given me his whole collection."

"Generous of him."

She laughed softly. "It's just an excuse to visit me. He's a smart one, all gorgeous blue eyes and earnest conversation. It would go to my head, but I know I'm just a stand-in for his mother."

The clear, deep affection in Cat's voice sent a wave of unease through Travis. Somehow he hadn't thought there was a boyfriend in the wings, especially not one who could make her mouth soften and her eyes radiate happy memories.

"I thought you didn't like boys," he said.

"I make exceptions for the seven-year-old variety," she said dryly. "Especially when he finds himself the not-so-proud older brother of newborn twins who take up every second of his mother's time. We have a breakfast date whenever he can sneak out."

"Seven, huh?" Travis dug into the shells with renewed pleasure.

"A very grown-up seven."

From the corner of his eyes Travis watched Cat combine all the ingredients of the salad, toss it, and put it on the small table. She turned the fish on the grill, took out the biscuits, and put them on the table next to the salad.

"Time for the fish?" he asked hopefully.

"Hungry?"

"Like I said, eating is one of the things I do well."

Travis proved it when Cat brought in the fish. He ate as she did, without hurrying, but a lot of food disappeared in a very short time. When they were both finished, he sighed, picked up a final crumb of biscuit, popped it into his mouth, and smiled at her.

"You were right," he said. "You can cook. It's a wonder you don't weigh as much as I do."

"Eating alone isn't much fun."

"What about the kid next door?"

"Jason is only allowed to show up for breakfast. Not my rules. His mother's. Sharon threatened to put a collar and leash on him if he doesn't stop 'bothering' me. But he's just lonely."

Cat pushed back her chair and began carrying dishes to the sink. Travis took them from her hands, gestured for her to sit down again, and cleared the table. It didn't take long. He spotted the dishwasher, opened it, and looked dismayed.

"No room," he said.

"Sure there is."

She slipped past him and took over, finding places for

everything but the salad bowl in the already full dishwasher.

"So you don't mind having the neighbor kid underfoot?" Travis asked, wiping off the table with a sponge he had found. "I thought you were busy."

"I am. Jason is an excuse for me to relax."

"You need an excuse for that?"

The sharp question made Cat glance up. She shut the dishwasher and reached for a towel to dry her hands.

"I must have pushed the button marked preconceptions," she said. "What are you really asking?"

"Are you so busy chasing money that you need an excuse to be human?"

Saying nothing, she wiped her hands on a kitchen towel and leaned against the dishwasher. The tiredness that came from too little sleep and too much work rushed back at her like a great gray wave.

Four months to go.

January.

Wearily Cat reminded herself that she could do anything for a hundred-plus days without breaking down. All she had to do was take them as they came. One at a time.

She drew a deep breath. "I suppose you could say I'm too busy chasing money. There's enough truth in it for most purposes."

Cat didn't have to look at Travis to sense his disappointment. He washed the salad bowl with abrupt motions of his hands. She took it and began drying the wood with unnecessary care. She was glad to have something to do that concealed the fine tremor in her hands, a tremor caused by fatigue and emotion.

"Why does that bother you?" she asked neutrally.

"Money is such a shallow thing to spend your time on."

"No exceptions?" she asked, setting the dry bowl on the counter.

"Not one." The words were implacable, the tone utterly certain.

Absurdly, Cat felt her throat tighten around tears. She hadn't cried in seven years. That, more than the burning ache in her back and arms and legs, told her how very tired she was.

Anger came finally, giving her the temporary strength of adrenaline. With deceptive calm she tucked the dish towel over the corner of a cupboard to dry.

Then she turned and faced Travis.

"Are you finished?" she asked.

"With the dishes?"

"No. With passing judgment on me."

"Cat—"

"It's my turn," she interrupted tightly. "I don't know what paragon of womanhood you're measuring me against. I do know that I'm damn tired of coming up short. Two choices, Travis. Take me as I am or take a hike."

He propped his hip against the counter, crossed his arms over his chest, and looked at her. "What if I told you I was rich? Would you still want me to leave?"

"Why is it that boys seem to feel money excuses all manner of shortcomings?"

"Because girls tell them so as soon as they're old enough to know the difference between nickels and dimes," Travis retorted.

"Your choices have just narrowed. Take a hike."

"But what if I'm very rich?"

Yet there was no real question in Travis's voice. He already knew the answer. Rich made everything right. Rich also made a man feel as interchangeable and anonymous as a hundred-dollar bill. One was pretty much like another, as long as the zeros added up.

"If you're very rich," Cat said, "that would explain everything except my stupidity. I thought I was a fast learner, but I guess some things just have to be gone through twice.''

"You lost me."

"That's the way it goes," she said, turning away from Travis. "Win some, lose some, some never had a chance. If you're rich, we fall into the third category."

"You're not making sense."

There was impatience and something more in Travis's voice. Something urgent. Something uncertain. She couldn't be turning away from him.

But she was.

"What's so hard to understand about good-bye?" Cat asked.

"You don't believe I'm rich," he said flatly. Women didn't turn their backs on a really wealthy man. He had found that out the hard way.

"Travie-boy, you could spit diamonds and still not impress me."

"I doubt it. Women like you don't—"

"You don't know anything about a woman like me," Cat interrupted bitterly.

"I doubt it."

"I don't."

Cat wanted to stop there, to say no more, but anger and an irrational sense of betrayal forced words past her stiff lips.

"I once swam two miles at midnight through the open sea just to get away from more money than you'll ever count. *Rich*," she snarled. "Sweet God above, preserve me from rich boys!"

For a moment there was only silence and the echo of Cat's rage quivering in the room. Travis looked at the rigid line of her back and knew he had made a mistake. She was telling the exact truth about herself and rich men.

She despised them.

Thinking hard, Travis crossed the kitchen to the window

where the pile of shells lay gleaming in the overhead light. Slowly he began running his fingers through the shells.

"Who is he?" Travis asked finally.

Cat stared out the kitchen window where coals still burned hotly inside a cast-iron trough.

"Cat?"

She looked back toward him. Her eyes were the color of winter. She said nothing.

Travis left the shells and walked over to Cat with the coordination of a man accustomed to balancing on the uncertain deck of a ship.

As she watched him approach, she wondered if that was why he seemed so familiar to her, because he walked like a man who had been to sea, like her dead father, like the man she had thought her husband was.

Billy, the worst mistake she had ever made in her life.

"Who is he?" Travis asked again, his voice gentle, coaxing. "Did he seduce you and abandon you? Is that why you hate rich men?"

Cat looked through Travis to seven years ago. Memories poured over her despite her desire to forget it all, especially that last night when she and Billy had been anchored in the Virgin Islands with a group of his friends. As usual, Billy was sullen. As usual, he was mostly drunk.

The smell of rum and pineapple turned her stomach. He was yelling at her and waving a lab report that said his sperm count was low, but adequate for conception.

It's your fault I don't have sons. You're not good for a fucking thing, and that includes fucking most of all.

It's all your fault. Your fault! You're no good as a wife, no good in bed, and you're sterile. What the hell good are you, kitten? Huh? How are you going to earn your keep? You can't run home to Mummy because she's broke now, and you never went to school.

All you were good for was having babies, and it turns out you can't even do that. You're sterile, you useless bitch!

*You can't earn your keep. It'd serve you right if I kicked
you overboard to drown.*

"Cat?" Travis said softly, calling her attention back to
him.

When she didn't answer, his hands kneaded her shoulders and rigid neck. He looked at her gray eyes, filled with
memories and pain.

Slowly Cat focused on Travis. For a moment she gave
in to the silent promise of his touch, letting his warmth
seep into her. Then she realized what she was doing and
pulled away.

"Cat? What is it?"

She couldn't find the words to tell Travis of the need
welling up in her, consuming her.

And Travis was that need.

Wearily she wondered if she would be this vulnerable to
him in January, when she would no longer feel like a
woman being pulled to pieces by too many demands, all of
them utterly necessary. In January she wouldn't be impossibly drawn to Travis. Travis, who looked so strong, so
competent, so capable of love.

But that was always how the masculine trap was baited.

Billy had looked strong and competent too. Capable of
love? No, not even before he knew she couldn't be the
source of his dynasty. Boys loved only themselves.

Cat closed her eyes. *How many times will I have to be
hurt before I learn that simple lesson?*

*And why am I so weak that I want to believe Travis is
different?*

A man, not a boy.

"Cat, say something."

"Why are you still here?" she asked with false calm.

But she couldn't mask the tremor that began beneath the
warmth of his hands on her shoulders and radiated through
her body.

Slowly Travis lowered his head. She felt the heat of his

breath on her cheek, the rough silk of his mustache on her mouth, then his lips moved over hers.

The kiss was gentle, sweet, safe. He demanded nothing, gave everything, warmth and the taste of him slowly filling her senses until she sighed his name. She had never been kissed like that, had never even dreamed such gentleness and caring was possible from a man.

When Travis lifted his head, tears stood like crystal at the ends of Cat's eyelashes. He caught each drop on the tip of his tongue, then bent and kissed her again, sharing the taste of tears.

"Why are you doing this to me?" she whispered, trembling between his hands. "I'm not strong enough to lose again. Not now."

"You won't lose. The last thing I want to do is hurt you." Travis framed Cat's face with his hands. He closed his eyes against the confusion and fear he saw in hers. "Don't look at me like a cat with her paw in a trap. Trust me."

"But you don't trust me."

His eyes snapped open. A trick of light made them nearly black.

"I was twenty when I married Tina," he said in an empty voice. "She was eighteen, pregnant, and very much in love with me, she said. I thought I was in love with her. I knew I wanted the child she carried. Two weeks after our marriage she had an abortion."

Cat stiffened, but Travis didn't notice. This time he was the one gripped by the freezing violence of the past.

"She told me it was a miscarriage. I believed her. Later, I found out the truth. Thank God the second baby she got rid of wasn't mine."

Travis's hands flexed, pulling Cat's hair almost painfully. He didn't notice. Nor did she. Both were caught in the past. His past.

"I paid her off. One million dollars. Being shed of that

creature was one of the few things money could buy that was worth having.'' His eyes focused on Cat again. His voice was harsh. ''What about him? Do you still love him?''

She couldn't speak. She was stunned by the brutality of his wife's betrayal.

Cat had accused Travis of not trusting her, and he had told her something she was certain he told very few people. Now he was asking the same honesty of her.

She didn't want to talk about Billy. But then, Travis hadn't wanted to talk about his past failure.

For a long moment Cat studied Travis's face, weighing her instinct to trust him against the lessons of a past that had almost destroyed her. If she was wrong about Travis, if he was more boy than man, trusting him would be the worst mistake she could make. She would lose more than she could regain by a midnight swim, more than she could regain at all.

She would lose herself.

Closing her eyes, Cat tried to shut out the familiar stranger who stood so close to her. Maybe if she couldn't see him, she wouldn't soar or drown in his compelling eyes, eyes that offered her the sensual release and the freedom of a great black ship skimming the edge of creation.

''I married Billy when I was nineteen,'' Cat said. The words were rough, forced past her unwillingness to remember, memories choking her. ''My father had just died. My mother had all she could do to take care of my younger brother and sister. I needed love. I thought Billy loved me.''

Remembering, Cat shuddered and tried to speak. No words came. She couldn't speak about exactly what had happened. Not yet. Maybe not ever.

''I was very, very wrong,'' she whispered. ''Money had spoiled Billy. He didn't know the difference between a woman and a whore.''

Cat closed her eyes, knowing she owed Travis more but

unable even to form the thoughts that would lead to words. She had spent seven years trying to forget her husband's degrading demands the night he learned she was sterile.

I'm going to teach you, bitch. Whore's tricks. Not the kind of thing a man wants the mother of his sons to know, but you're never going to be a mommy, so what the hell does it matter?

"No, I don't love him," Cat said thinly. "Most of the time I don't even hate him."

Travis kissed her eyelids, then rocked her against his chest, comforting both of them. Slowly her arms went around his waist. They stood together in a closeness that demanded nothing, gave everything. A man and a woman holding each other, creating warmth where before there had been only chill, a simple moment of peace where there had been only pain.

Finally Travis tilted Cat's face up to his and looked at her, just looked at her. Then he brushed his fingertips over her cheek, released her, and walked out of her kitchen into the night.

Cat was too shaken to protest his leaving. Like him, she needed to find out again where self ended and other began, because for a single, shattering instant there had been no difference.

It was an instant neither one of them had been prepared for.

FIVE

THE NEXT morning, dawn came to the sea like a magenta dream. Cat stood by the kitchen's bay window, a cup of tea steaming in her hand. She was staring at the water beyond the rocks that lined the little cove. When she saw a dark, powerful shape cut across the shimmering swells, she put down her tea, grabbed her camera gear, and ran out on the deck.

Through the zoom lens she could see Travis almost as clearly as if he were across the room. But even with autofocus, keeping him in sight wasn't a sure thing. The big lens saw only a narrow slice of reality and had a very shallow depth of field. She had to hold utterly still in order not to jiggle the lens and lose her subject completely.

Normally, standing still wasn't a problem for Cat. But this morning her heart was beating so quickly that she finally had to fasten the camera onto a tripod. Then she stared through the lens with the pleasure of a miser counting gold.

Travis's arms and legs moved rhythmically, tirelessly, propelling him through a dawn world where shades of magenta gathered and ran and glimmered with each shift of his body on the sea.

Watching him, Cat could believe that yesterday had been real, that this man had kissed her, held her, then gently let her go. Caught in the shimmering, ecstatic light of dawn, she could believe anything, even that she had met Travis yesterday and known him forever.

The phone rang from somewhere in the house. She ignored the sound. The answering machine would get it.

Intently Cat followed Travis with the lens, tracking him as she triggered the motor drive. It beat as quickly as her heart, attempting to capture the man and the moment. Even knowing that such a photo was probably impossible, she still had to try. She wanted an image of Travis as he appeared to her: half shadow, half dawn, a power and mystery and fascination to equal the radiant sea.

And like the sea, he could change between heartbeats—gentle, savage, serene, turbulent—shaking the certainties of anyone who dared his depths.

The phone rang for the seventh time. Apparently the answering machine was on strike.

Reluctantly Cat put away her dreams and ran inside. Rodney Harrington, her green angel from New York, was the only person who would call her at this hour and keep ringing until he got through. It had been on Harrington's yacht that she had cooked her way to California from the Virgin Islands. He was also her agent, the man who had nagged and flattered her into a career as a photographer at a time when she had no self-confidence and less self-respect.

"Hello," she said breathlessly.

"Morning, Cochran. Catch you sleeping for once?"

"Not this year, angel. Maybe in January. I was taking pictures out on the back deck."

Harrington sighed. "Swear to God, you work too hard."

"Tell me something I don't know."

"You're sexy."

Cat laughed out loud. Harrington was the only man she had ever met who could say such things, mean them, and never crowd the No Trespassing signs she had set out against the male world after her disastrous marriage.

"Well," Harrington said smugly, "you told me to tell you something you didn't know. How are you coming with Ashcroft?"

Cat was glad her green angel couldn't see her expression. She reminded herself that the trendy poet's book would be an oversize, beautifully made, very expensive, top-quality color production. In short, a photographer's dream. She was grateful to Harrington for getting her the assignment.

But she wished that Ashcroft wasn't so single-minded about getting into her jeans.

"Did he call you?" she asked.

"Was he supposed to?"

"The last time I told Ashcroft to put his hands in his pockets instead of mine, he told me if I didn't play, he'd get another photographer."

"Oh, that." Harrington sighed. "Yes, he mentioned that."

"And?"

Cat's hand tightened on the phone while she waited for the answer. She needed the work, needed the money for her mother's living expenses and the twins' tuition, but she definitely didn't need the hassle.

"I told him you had herpes," Harrington said casually.

There was a stunned silence. Then Cat choked on laughter.

"Don't know that it will do you much good," he admitted when she stopped laughing. "Ashcroft said that was okay, he had it too."

She groaned. "Thanks a lot, angel."

"Yeah. Ready for the good news?"

"Should I sit down?" she asked dryly.

"T. H. Danvers." Harrington spoke as though the words meant something fabulous.

"Huh?"

"You do remember that book we talked about? T. H. Danvers, the ship designer? The man whose hull designs win every race they're entered in? It's gotten so bad that the handicappers are talking about making entirely new categories for Danvers hulls.''

''Is that good?''

''No. It's flat incredible. He's revolutionized hull dynamics. Swear to God, he's a genius, and the most private man since Howard Hughes. Danvers is also a friend of mine. I've been after him to do a book for years, but he never stayed in one place for more than a few weeks at a time. He's on your coast now, and has found something interesting enough to make him change his plans. He's going to stick around for a few more weeks. Then he'll probably—''

''Wait. Back up. A few *weeks*? You expect me to do the art for a whole book in a few weeks?''

''You can do it. You're good, Cochran. Very, very good.''

''Angel, you're sounding as otherworldly as my mother. I'm up to my lips in work. The next few months are going to be brutal.''

''I know you're busy,'' he said soothingly. ''Hell, I got most of the assignments for you, but this Danvers thing is too good to pass up. You simply have to do it.''

''What, precisely, am I supposed to do?''

''Shoot images for a book called *The Danvers Touch*.''

''Keep talking.''

''Danvers thinks the book is going to be about designing hulls and sails, particularly the Danvers racing hull. Well, that's part of it. But it's also going to be about the man. I want people to see him as the complex artist he is. I want them to read the book, look at your images, and *know* what it's like to design and sail a Danvers hull.''

''Swear to God,'' Cat said sardonically, using Harrington's favorite phrase, ''that shouldn't take more than a day or two.''

He laughed. ''The money's not bad. Fifteen thousand up

front, all expenses paid, fifteen thousand when your images pass muster, and an extra fifteen grand if the work is really good.''

She closed her eyes. That much money would make the difference between sinking and treading water if Ashcroft dumped her overboard on some pretext or another.

The money would allow her to pay enough on the twins' school loans to keep the creditors quiet for another six months.

She would be able to pay the rent and still buy an occasional bottle of wine.

She couldn't buy the forty-thousand-dollar digital camera setup she needed, but she might be able to make a down payment on enough computer equipment to enter the twenty-first century the only way a photographer could expect to survive—electronically.

''You're awfully quiet,'' Harrington said.

''I'm thinking.''

''Think out loud.''

''I'm about finished with Ashcroft's art. He hasn't seen any of it yet, but it's good. That show you set up in L.A. for late November is crowding me a bit. I haven't picked out more than three of the thirty images they want, much less done anything about the printing, matting, and framing.''

She winced at the thought of the money involved in taking images from slides, blowing them up, and framing them suitably for an upscale gallery. She should have put off the show until March, but galleries like Swift and Sons only asked an artist to participate once. If the artist couldn't be bothered, neither could the gallery.

''Do all the framing stuff when it's too dark to take pictures,'' Harrington advised. ''If it gets tight, I'll find someone to do it for you. If it gets down to the short strokes, I'll do it myself.''

''Ummm.''

"Yeah, I know. If you can't do it yourself, you damn well won't let anyone else do it. Independent as a hog on ice."

"Your midwestern roots are showing."

"Soybean money is as good as other kinds and better than most. Take Energistics, for instance."

"I'd love to. Have they sent my check yet?"

Harrington sighed. "Sorry, Cochran. I've camped on their accounting department for the last nine business days, and all they give me is some lame variation of 'Your check is in the mail.' "

Cat swore under her breath. She had spent six weeks on the Energistics assignment, gone all over hell and back shooting art for a massive, full-color report on energy systems of the twenty-first century. They had loved her work, praised her endlessly to Harrington, and had yet to pay a single cent of the fifty thousand dollars they owed her.

They hadn't even gotten around to reimbursing her for the three thousand dollars of her own money that had gone toward renting a helicopter, not to mention several thousand dollars worth of film and development.

Yet no matter how Harrington threatened or pleaded, the Big Check from Energistics eluded Cat.

"Why is it that I'm expected to pay my bills on time and the rest of the world isn't?" she asked.

"Just lucky, I guess," Harrington said sardonically.

"Yeah. How soon would I get money from the Danvers book?"

"As soon as you sign the contract."

"Translation: as soon as you can pry money out of the publisher after I've signed the contract. Anywhere from three to six months, usually."

Harrington laughed. "Not this time, Cochran. The publisher is a friend of mine."

"I'd feel better if your friend was the accountant."

"Accountants don't have friends. Three weeks after you sign, you'll get the money. Swear to God."

Cat closed her eyes. If she didn't have a sinking feeling about Energistics, she would have tried to delay the Danvers assignment. But she did have a sinking feeling. A bad one.

If Energistics didn't pay her, the Danvers assignment would be all that stood between her and bankruptcy.

"I'll take it," she said grimly.

"I'll set up a meeting with Danvers tomorrow and call you."

"I suppose he's another drooling octopus."

"Not to worry. He likes ships better than skirts. If he wants a woman, he buys her for a while."

"Female."

"What?"

"You buy females, not women."

Harrington laughed. "Is that how it works? Well, whatever you call them, they're standing in line for In-the-Wind, Hell-on-Women Danvers."

Cat shook her head in disgust. "No accounting for tastes."

"I'll talk to you soon, Fire-and-Ice. Keep your answering machine on, okay?"

Smiling, Cat hung up, made sure the answering machine was turned on this time, and raced back to the deck.

Travis was no longer in sight. She was tempted to wait on the deck until he reappeared on the return leg of his morning swim, but she didn't have time.

If she was going to do the Danvers book, she didn't even have time to sleep.

She set a watch alarm to remind her of her doctor's appointment in two hours, stuffed the watch in her camera case, and set off for the beach.

*   *   *

Even with the alarm, Cat was late for her appointment. As she rushed into the doctor's office, she realized that she was nervous. She was afraid of what the tests she had taken two weeks ago might have uncovered, afraid that her sterility and unpredictable periods were caused by something unthinkable.

"Dr. Stone will see you in her office," the nurse said.

Cat knew the way without help. She walked quickly down the narrow hall, through the open door, and into the doctor's office. She had never met anyone more unlike her name. Dr. Stone was a warm woman in her fifties rather than the cold male gynecologist Cat had expected on her first visit eight months ago.

"Sit down, Catherine," Dr. Stone said, smiling up from a pile of papers. "All your tests came back negative, which is good news for you and bad news for me."

"Bad? Why?"

"There's no obvious organic reason for your menstrual cycle to be as erratic as it has been in the past year, especially in the past few months."

Cat let out a long sigh. "Thank God. But I'd like to know why my period is so late."

"You still haven't gotten it?" Dr. Stone asked, looking at her patient sharply.

"Oh, it came two days after I had the tests." She smiled wryly. "Scared me into it, I guess."

Dr. Stone scanned Cat's file with professional speed. "Your cycle is highly unpredictable. Six weeks, three weeks, seven weeks, sixteen days . . . all over the map. Spotting?"

"Sometimes. No pattern."

"Of course not. That would be too easy. Cramps?"

"Sometimes. Nothing severe enough to keep me from working."

"And according to the tests, everything is in the right

place, nothing missing and no extras. How do you feel?''

"Tired.''

"Taking the vitamins and iron I prescribed?''

"Religiously. There are days I think that's all that keeps me going.''

Dr. Stone set aside the file and leaned back in her chair. "Tell me about your days, Catherine.''

"I get up, I work, I go to bed.''

The doctor's lips curved in something that wasn't quite a smile. "Take me through an average day.''

"Up an hour before dawn. Exercise if there's time, shower, breakfast, and out the door. The poet I'm working for has a thing about 'rosy-fingered dawn.' ''

"So did Homer.''

"Homer did it better. Blake Ashcroft is a bit soft for my taste.'' Cat shrugged. "Anyway, I shoot the Ashcroft assignment for a few hours, then I do a few hours on various business stuff—bookkeeping, query letters, billing, and the like. Then I edit, duplicate, and file slides until the light starts slanting again. Or I go out and argue with the processor who loused up the color on my prints, or with the framer who can't cut a right angle on the mat, or with accountants who can't seem to write out checks paying me for work I've already done.''

"I thought your agent did that.''

"Only on the assignments he gets for me. The smaller stuff I handle myself. Where was I?''

"Arguing.''

"Right. After three o'clock I go out shooting again. That lasts until dark. Sometimes I have a night shoot, but not often. When it's dark I spend more time on office work. Filing, filling orders for particular slides, whatever. Then I go to bed.''

"How much sleep do you get?''

She smothered a yawn. "Five hours. Sometimes less.''

Dr. Stone's silver eyebrows lifted. "Are you one of those

people who only needs a few hours a night?''

"No. I'm one of those people who only has a few hours a night to spare.''

The doctor looked at the file. "What about your weekends?''

Cat looked puzzled. "What about them?''

"Do you get time off?''

"No," she said, yawning outright. "Unless I'm traveling. Then I sometimes get the afternoon off if a flight is delayed or the art director doesn't show up. That sort of thing.''

Dr. Stone shook her head slowly. "Seven days a week, no time off for good behavior?''

"That's the trouble with working for yourself. The hours suck.''

The doctor's capable hands flipped through Cat's folder again. "Nothing has changed since the first visit? There's still no possibility of pregnancy?''

Cat felt her expression change, saw the doctor's suddenly intent look, and wished the question had never been asked.

"No. No possibility of pregnancy," she said stiffly.

"Cathy, I'm hardly going to be shocked if you tell me you've been sleeping with a man and were either careless or unlucky and ended up pregnant.''

Cat didn't say a word.

"It helps if you cooperate," Dr. Stone pointed out. "Without that, I can't do much except doodle in your file.''

Closing her eyes, Cat said dully, "I can't get pregnant.''

"What?''

"I'm sterile.''

The chair creaked as Dr. Stone suddenly leaned forward. "From the beginning, please.''

After a moment Cat opened her eyes. They were as haunted by memories as her voice. "I was married for three years. I never tried *not* to get pregnant. My husband was certified fertile. That means I'm sterile.''

"Were your periods irregular then?"

"No."

Dr. Stone frowned and reviewed Cat's file. "I don't see any reason why you couldn't become pregnant. None of the ordinary causes of infertility appear to be present. Are you sure that your husband was fertile?"

Cat closed her eyes. She could still see Billy's face as he waved the lab report at her: *Adequate for conception.*

"Yes, I'm sure," she said.

"What did your tests show?"

"I didn't have any tests. Why bother?"

"Infertility is often curable."

"A bad marriage isn't." Then, seeing that Dr. Stone wasn't satisfied, Cat added, "Even if I was as fertile as a frog, pregnancy isn't at the root of my irregular periods. To get pregnant there would have to be a man. There isn't."

The words were no sooner out of Cat's mouth than she remembered Travis and wondered what it would be like if he was her man.

"Would you agree to some tests to pin down the cause of infertility?" the doctor asked. "Sometimes it's as simple as bad timing or as subtle as incompatible body chemistries."

"Not unless you think it's causing my cycle to be so damned unpredictable."

Dr. Stone snapped shut the file, folded her hands, and stared at her stubborn patient.

"What's throwing off your cycle is the same thing that's causing those dark bruises beneath your eyes. Overwork. You're a prime candidate for whatever virus might come along. And one will. Ease off, Cathy. Take your weekends and sleep. Play a little. Eat well. Build up your reserves."

"In January I'll be glad to do that. Just get me through until then."

"What happens in January?"

"Easy Street," Cat said promptly. Then she sighed. "Well, at least Easier Street. The twins' last payment for medical school will be done and Mother will be safely married. I just have to get there from here."

"Sounds like quite a jump."

"I'll make it. Besides, I love my work."

"Try loving a man. It's less strenuous."

Again an image of Travis haunted Cat. She hadn't even known him a day and she couldn't stop thinking about him. She cursed her photographer's awareness of texture and line, light and shadow, clear tourmaline eyes reflecting her in their depths.

"Here." Dr. Stone's brisk voice brought Cat's attention back to the office. "I'm changing your prescription. This one is guaranteed to put color in your cheeks. The nurse will give you a B complex shot and take a blood sample. Make an appointment for a week from today. If your blood count isn't up by then, I'm giving you iron shots." She smiled slyly. "My patients tell me they're quite painful."

"I hate shots," she muttered, getting up to leave.

"Cathy?"

Cat turned and looked back.

"It's just as well you can't get pregnant now," Dr. Stone said. "You're in no shape for it."

"My silver lining for the day," she said flippantly.

The doctor shook her head. "Get more sleep. Eat regularly and eat well. I'll see you in a week."

SIX

LATE THAT afternoon Cat met Blake Ashcroft at the foot of the cliff that was near her house, but much farther down the beach toward town. Behind her, surf foamed and creamed in the rich, slanting light. But instead of shooting it, she felt more like shooting the sulky poet.

"Ashcroft," she said distinctly, "I've photographed this spot on this cliff at sunset every day for the last three weeks. What makes you think you'll like the results any better this time?"

He stepped closer to her, smiling slowly. "Cathy-baby, any time you'd rather shoot the interior of my jockstrap, just say the word. Until then you'll shoot cliffs at dawn or sunset or any other time that suits me."

Cat looked at the fair-haired, blue-eyed male standing between herself and the water. She wished very sincerely that she could rearrange Ashcroft's perfectly formed face. He didn't need this shot of the cliff any more than he had needed any of the others she had done for him in the past three weeks. It was simply his way of screwing her because she wouldn't screw him.

Deliberately Cat turned her back on the cable TV poet and measured the cliff face once again. There were many fine images buried in those eroding rocks. Ashcroft wanted none of them. Yet the images were there—powerful, compelling, calling out silently to be seen and known.

Cat shrugged off the broad straps of both camera bags and sighed in unconscious relief. It seemed like the bags weighed more every time she picked them up. While she studied the cliff, she absently rubbed her aching shoulders.

It had been a long day, beginning at dawn, pausing for Dr. Stone, then full throttle until now. Lunch hadn't happened. She had been on the phone trying to straighten out a problem of double billing with the photo lab. From there things had gone from bad to worse to Ashcroft.

Cat wished the fair-haired toad would just take one of his many groupies, crawl off under a rock, and screw himself senseless. There was no reason for him to badger the only unwilling woman west of the Mississippi. She should be home now, fixing dinner.

If she had been at home, she might have seen more of Travis than a glimpse through a long lens.

Impatiently she brought her mind back to the cliff. By slow degrees she moved to the right, shifting her perspective. From that angle heavy gold light turned the rock to black velvet. Random plants clinging to the cliff became golden sculptures radiant with life and mystery. The air itself seemed to quiver with magic, reflecting light as though shot through with diamond dust.

Without looking away from the cliff, Cat stepped back and reached for a camera bag. Her hand bumped into Ashcroft's hip. Before she could recover, he grabbed her wrist and held her hand against his crotch.

She made a sound of disgust and tried to pull free, only to find that she couldn't. Ashcroft's poetry might have been soft, but he wasn't. He was both taller and stronger than she was.

And he was ready for sex.

"Cathy-baby," he said, smiling narrowly, "I've put up with your teasing little sex games long enough. I'm going to fuck you whether you like it or not. I know that *I'll* like it."

A look at Ashcroft's face told Cat that he wasn't kidding. He was perfectly capable of raping her and blaming it on her for being a tease.

She looked around quickly. There was no one in sight. She and Ashcroft were standing in a deep trough between water-smoothed rocks, shielded from casual observation. Nearby a stairway twisted up the cliff, but she could see only the middle of the stairs. They were empty. She was utterly alone with Ashcroft.

Fear shot through Cat, followed by a surge of raw, hot rage. Whatever happened, she would guarantee that Ashcroft would *not* like it. She bent and grabbed a fistful of sand.

Before she could fling it in the poet's smiling face, Travis appeared between the boulders that hid the bottom of the stairway. Long, powerful fingers wrapped around Ashcroft's wrist, found the nerves between the wristbones, and squeezed. Hard.

The pain was so quick, so paralyzing, that Ashcroft's only response was a gasp as his hand went limp.

Cat jerked free and looked at her attacker with bleak gray eyes. It was all she could do to keep from slapping the stunned expression off his face.

"Is he someone I should know?" Travis drawled.

"No," she said harshly. "If I had a choice, I wouldn't know him either."

"That can be arranged."

For the first time Cat looked at Travis's face. She took a half step backward before she realized that she had no reason to fear him.

But Ashcroft did.

Violence seethed in Travis's narrowed eyes. Violence waited in the unyielding planes of his cheeks. Violence begged to be free in the purposeful coiling of muscle and sinew.

"Well, Cat?" Travis asked softly.

"Don't tempt me." Then she sighed wearily. "Let him go. He'll behave now that he has had his nose rubbed in the fact that I wasn't playing games. I said no and I meant it."

Travis released Ashcroft's wrist and waited.

The poet wasn't entirely stupid. He didn't move.

"Who is he?" Travis asked Cat bluntly.

"Blake Ashcroft, wunderkind of American poetry," she said. "He's also a spoiled little boy. I'm doing the art for his latest book."

"You *were* doing the art, you teasing bitch," Ashcroft snarled. Then he flinched at the expression that came to Travis's face.

"I *am* doing the art," Cat shot back. "If you don't believe me, ask Harrington. You try to dump me over this and I'll sue you for everything from breach of contract to attempted rape."

Travis looked at Cat with a startled expression. Then he smiled and wondered why Harrington had let him think that his photographer wasn't much to look at. He certainly hadn't mentioned that Cochran had elegant legs, tempting breasts, and hair as red as an autumn fire.

And a temper to match.

"No one would believe you," Ashcroft said to Cat, rubbing his burning wrist. "Women fall all over themselves to unzip my fly."

Cat glanced quickly at Travis. He was watching her with a curious smile.

"I have a witness," she pointed out.

Ashcroft looked at the big, barefoot man wearing cutoff jeans and a faded blue T-shirt.

"An overgrown beach bum," Ashcroft said with contempt. "Who will believe his word against mine? You're through, Cathy-baby. *Finis*. Kaput. The End."

Travis leaned over and spoke so softly to Ashcroft that Cat couldn't hear him.

The poet went as pale as his hair, stared in disbelief at Travis, and tried to speak. Nothing came out.

Travis waited with the patience of a cougar stalking dinner. His cold, measuring eyes never left the other man's face.

"For God's sake," Ashcroft said in a hoarse voice, glaring at Cat. "You can do the damned book. But the pictures had better be great or I'll—" He looked sideways at Travis and shut up. Then he asked her angrily, "Instead of teasing me, why the hell didn't you tell me you had a famous, jealous maniac for a lover? I wouldn't have touched you!"

Cat's eyes widened. Surprised laughter tugged at her lips as she turned to Travis. "Are you a famous, jealous maniac, Travis, er, *lover*?"

His lazy smile changed the lines of his face from bleak to inviting. When he turned to face her, sunlight transformed his eyes into brilliant blue-green jewels.

She stared at Travis, forgetting everything but his compelling male presence. She wanted him.

The shock of wanting went through her in a wash of heat.

Travis's eyes narrowed as though he was reading her thoughts before she was even aware of them. The same fingertips that had brought pain to Ashcroft caressed the slanting lines of her cheekbones and the curves of her mouth.

"I'm jealous as hell of everything that touches you," Travis said, "even the sunlight. Especially the sunlight licking all over your smooth skin."

Cat's lips parted in surprise. Slowly his fingertip slid over the small serrations of her teeth.

She shivered at the intimacy of the gesture. Without thinking, she closed her teeth delicately around his finger, silently demanding that he prolong the tantalizing, unexpected caress.

Travis's expression changed again. He focused on the

moment with a consuming sensuality that was as exciting to Cat as the feel of him between her lips.

"Shit," Ashcroft said. "I can see that she doesn't have her mind on photography. Tomorrow, Cathy-baby. Same time, same place. I don't care who your lover is, you'll get that cliff the way I want it or the deal is off."

"She'll be there," Travis said without looking away from Cat's smoky gray eyes. "And so will I."

Ashcroft wanted to object but thought better of it. He stalked off without another word.

After a few moments Cat blinked as though emerging from a deep sleep. Slowly she released Travis's finger. When he didn't withdraw, she moved her tongue over his skin with catlike deliberation, tasting him thoroughly.

Then she realized what she was doing and flushed to the roots of her russet hair. Quickly she turned her face, ending the contact.

"Cat?"

She shook her head, too ashamed to look at Travis. Billy had taught her what men thought of women who were interested in sex. They were whores, sluts, and worse.

They were what Billy had tried to make Cat into the night she dove over into the sea.

"I'm sorry," she whispered. "I wasn't thinking."

The sensual touch of Cat's tongue hadn't startled Travis, but her obvious shame did.

"What are you talking about? That sorry bastard Ashcroft?"

She shook her head without looking at Travis.

"Then what?"

"What I—I did. To your finger."

Travis caught Cat's face between his hands. Her cheeks were hot against his palms. Although his grip was gentle, it was impossible to escape.

After a few seconds, Cat didn't even try. She turned back to Travis, but didn't lift her eyes.

"Look at me, Cat," he said softly.

Reluctantly she did as he asked. Her breath went ragged at the desire burning in the depths of his eyes. She would have said his name, but it was all she could do to breathe.

Travis bent down and spoke against Cat's lips. "There's nothing to be sorry for. You can 'not think' like that with me any time you want. Now, for instance. Right now."

The kiss began as gently as dawn, a simple flow of warmth. Then the tip of his tongue teased the outer line of Cat's lips and burrowed into a corner of her smile. Before she could do more than take a startled breath, his tongue slid between her teeth to taste and caress the tender heat of her mouth.

Though Travis held Cat much more gently than Ashcroft had, she couldn't move. She was too stunned by the sensuality of the man whose taste was spreading across her tongue like wine. She was nearly thirty, divorced . . . and learning for the first time what it was like to be well and truly kissed.

When Travis finally lifted his mouth, Cat was trembling. Slowly she realized that he, too, had tremors running through his big body.

"Travis . . . ?" The word was a sigh and a breath and a question.

He kissed the pulse beating at the base of Cat's throat and felt her heartbeat quicken. He caressed her pulse with the tip of his tongue, then with his teeth.

This time there was no question in her voice when she whispered his name. She was his, melting and running like warm honey in his hands.

It was an effort to let her go.

Finally Travis lifted his head and looked down into Cat's dazed, misty gray eyes. The temptation to simply take her down on the sand and sink into her was so great that for a moment he couldn't think.

"I feel like throwing you over my shoulder and sailing

off into the sunset," Travis said huskily. "But I'm too old to make love with a woman who doesn't know my full name."

For a long breath Cat looked at him. She realized that beneath his humor, Travis was as hungry to taste her all over again as she was to be tasted. He was hungry, period, every bit as ready for sex as Ashcroft had been.

Yet unlike the poet, Travis was a man. He would make certain that his woman was not only willing, but eager.

The thought sent heat scattering through Cat.

"You don't know my full name, either," she pointed out in a low voice.

"You mentioned a man called Harrington."

She nodded.

"Is that," Travis asked, "Rodney Swear-to-God Harrington, promoter extraordinaire, the best friend and most devious man ever born?"

Despite Cat's surprise, she smiled at the description of Harrington.

"That's him." She cocked her head and looked up at Travis. "But he never mentioned you."

"He never mentions anyone by the first name. Only the last. Or by title, as in Ashcroft, the Crown Prince of Treacle."

She snickered. "You must know Harrington very, very well. He's careful who he shares his nicknames with."

"Like Fire-and-Ice Cochran?" Travis asked.

Cat drew her breath in sharply. It was Harrington's pet name for her, one he had coined in the Virgin Islands the night she climbed up his yacht's sea ladder and walked naked into his lounge, dripping rage and salt water.

"Who *are* you?" she demanded.

"Has he ever mentioned anyone with the nickname In-the-Wind?"

"You?"

Travis brushed his lips over her. "T. H. Danvers," he said in a husky drawl, "at your service."

For an instant Cat told herself that she hadn't heard correctly. Then she knew that she had. She stiffened and stepped back from Travis.

"You're *Danvers*?"

"Is that a problem?" Travis asked, suddenly wary.

Cat's fingers were still clenched around a handful of sand. From the look on her face, she was prepared to use it.

"How long have you known my full name?" she demanded.

"For certain? About three minutes. When you threw Harrington at the poet, I guessed you must be Cochran. There can't be too many women photographers in Laguna Beach who have Rodney Harrington for an agent."

Cat studied Travis with level gray eyes, obviously deciding whether to believe that he had just found out who she was. After a long moment, she sighed and let sand sift away between her fingers.

"I don't like coincidences," she muttered, looking at her feet, "but I know they happen all the time. That's why we have a name for them."

"I'm not very fond of coincidences myself."

Her head snapped up. Travis's mouth looked hard beneath the tawny mustache. His sea-colored eyes were suddenly distant, measuring her as though he had never seen her before.

"Did Harrington tell you that I wouldn't guarantee you the job until I saw your work?" Travis asked bluntly.

Cat's eyes narrowed. "You think I knew who you were all along, don't you?"

He shrugged.

"Well, Mr. T. H. Danvers, you can relax. I'm not one of the females standing in line waiting for a paid vacation with you. If you don't believe me, ask Harrington. He'll tell you the simple truth. I never mix men and business.''

"He already told me. It was the only reason I agreed to try out a woman photographer. No chance of involvement other than professional.''

"Exactly.''

Travis smiled slowly. "Yeah. Right. Then I saw this woman balanced like a cat on the rocks above the waves. She was taking pictures as though there was no tomorrow— and no tide. How was I to know that the beautiful red-headed idiot I rescued would be Harrington's Cochran?'' His voice lightly stressed the possessive: *Harrington's*.

"Three out of five wrong,'' Cat said in a clipped voice.

"What?''

"I have red hair and my name is Cochran.'' She held up two fingers. "But I'm not beautiful, I'm not an idiot, and I most certainly am not Harrington's.''

"He's very fond of you.'' Travis's tone was cool and subtly probing.

"And I'm fond of him. I owe him more than I can re-pay.''

"What's wrong with the usual method?''

"Sex?'' Cat asked.

"Like I said. The usual method.''

Her mouth thinned to a line of distaste. "A simple business transaction, so many minutes at so much per groan? No thanks, Travie-boy. Not now. Not ever.''

Travis simply looked at her, unconvinced.

Cat bent over, picked up her camera bags, and shrugged the straps into place on her shoulders.

He waited, watching her.

"I'll call Harrington tomorrow,'' she said, "and tell him to find you another photographer.''

Surprise flickered over Travis's hard face. "No. Not yet.''

"Not yet? What are you waiting for? A definite 'go to hell' from me? Fine, I'll make it definite. Go—''

With a swift motion Travis put his mouth over Cat's, smothering her words.

His quickness gave her no chance to object. Nor did she really want to. The feel of him on her lips, his breath sweet around her, his warmth stealing into her bones . . . she enjoyed it all with an intensity that should have frightened her.

Instead, it tempted her unbearably. Each time Travis touched her, he made her understand all over again how much she had been missing without him. Whether or not he realized it, he had taken her habit of honesty and used it as a weapon to get through her defenses. Cat couldn't tell herself that she was responding to Travis only because of long abstinence or temporary hunger, that she would react the same to any man. She responded because he was Travis, unique; and she was Cat, vulnerable to his uniqueness.

And she was very much afraid he knew it.

"Stop," she whispered.

"Such a prickly little cat," Travis whispered against her lips. "Are you angry because I won't guarantee you the job?"

"No."

"Then what?"

Very carefully, Cat eased out of Travis's arms. He let her go, but so slowly that the act of releasing her became another kind of caress.

"I'm angry because I don't mix men and business," she said. "And suddenly I find out I've done just that."

The corner of his mouth turned up in a sardonic smile. "And I have a rule against mixing women and anything *but* business."

The look on Cat's face almost made Travis laugh out loud. "What an expression. You can't be that innocent."

"I'm not innocent at all."

"Good. Then you know that men want sex and women want money. There's no reason both can't have what they want. A simple business transaction."

"You're talking about boys and females, not men and women."

"You're dreaming, Cat. Wake up. This is the real world."

Travis bent his head again and traced the sensitive outline of her lips with the tip of his tongue. Her breath broke in surprise as a rush of pure heat flushed her skin.

"But the real world has real compensations, doesn't it?" he asked softly.

Cat couldn't conceal her response, but she could refuse to give in to it. And she did.

She jerked her head away. "I'm not a prostitute."

"Who said anything about prostitutes?"

"You did."

Travis sighed and straightened. For a time he simply looked at Cat with brooding eyes. When he spoke, his voice was gentle and oddly sad.

"I'm not naive or selfish," he said. "I don't expect a woman to be my lover and get nothing in return."

"She's getting the same thing you're getting."

He shrugged. "That's not enough for a woman. More important, if it's a business transaction, both parties know exactly what to expect. No accusations and no nasty surprises."

Cat's mouth thinned as though she had just tasted something bitter, but she didn't say a word.

"Despite what your expression says," Travis continued mildly, "it's not prostitution. The women I've enjoyed weren't prostitutes. Mistresses for a time, yes, but never whores."

Cat looked at him for a long, silent moment. "Your wife really burned you to the bone, didn't she?"

His eyes narrowed until almost no color showed through

his eyelashes. "She completed my education."

"And just what did you learn, that women are whores?"

"No. I learned that I'll never be able to trust, much less marry, a woman who has less money than I do. And I'm very rich, Cat. Very, very rich. If I find a woman who appeals to me, I put it on a business basis. Frankly, it doesn't happen very often. I'm too old to be ruled by my dick."

Cat barely heard above the echoing of her own past words in her head. *Win some. Lose some. Some never had a chance. If you're rich, Travis, we fall into the third category.*

She was appalled at the sadness she felt, and the pain, a razor of regret turning inside her. It told her how terribly easy it would be for her to fall in love with Travis Danvers.

And how terribly stupid.

She closed her eyes, unable to look at the face of the man she could have loved. "I'm sorry."

"You've done nothing to be sorry for," Travis said, surprised by the sadness that thickened her voice.

She laughed a little wildly because it was better than crying.

"Cat? What's wrong?"

"You're rich."

Travis said nothing. He didn't understand why *rich* was a curse on her lips. He tried to gather Cat against his body and comfort her, but she stepped out of his reach. With a tired sigh she readjusted the weight of her camera gear and faced him.

"Do you want to call Harrington or should I?" she asked.

"Why should either of us call Harrington?"

"To tell him to get another photographer."

Surprise and something like anger swept through Travis. He kept on misjudging Cat, yet in the next instant he was certain he knew her as well as he knew himself.

Wrong again.

"You're quitting just like that?" he asked in a clipped voice. "Just because I won't guarantee you the job until I've seen some photos of my ship taken by you?"

"Of course not. You have every right to decide whether my images fit your needs."

"Then why are you quitting?"

Cat's false calm went up in a flash of anger. "It's simple, rich man. You have no right to turn my world inside out, breaking my rules, making me feel—" She stopped abruptly. "I don't mix men and business, period."

"I'm not 'men,' I'm just Travis," he drawled in a reasonable voice that made her want to scream. "And I'll try to make working with me more pleasure than business."

She gave him an icy gray look.

"Cat, I'm not Blake Ashcroft. I won't make life hell for you if you don't sleep with me. Besides," Travis added neutrally, "can you afford to turn down work?"

Her lips thinned. She needed money and he knew it. She had told him herself.

Fool.

"If I agree to do the book," Cat said in a clipped voice, "it's publisher rather than you who pays me. A simple business transaction, Mr. T. H. Danvers, something you should be able to appreciate. Nothing personal at all. Certainly nothing intimate."

"And no possibility of . . . intimacy?"

"We both have our rules. You don't have a woman unless you buy her, and I'm not for sale. What could be clearer than that?"

"The fact that you want me as much as I want you," Travis said ruthlessly.

Cat looked up and saw herself focused in his brilliant blue-green eyes. She saw him look at her hair, her lips, the shape of her breasts against her cotton pullover, the curve of her legs below her cutoff jeans.

His desire was almost tangible. Her response was all too tangible. Her nipples tightened against the cloth as though it was wet.

"No," she said. "It wouldn't work."

Yet her husky, yearning voice denied the words even as she spoke them.

"Bullshit," Travis said politely.

His hands snaked out, lifting the camera equipment off her shoulders.

"Travis, I'm not—"

"We'll argue about it over dinner," he interrupted. "My treat this time. Think of it as a business meeting."

He started walking toward Cat's house, carrying the heavy camera bags with an ease she envied. Then she realized that nothing had been settled. She ran until she was ahead of him, stopped, and turned to confront him.

"That's exactly what it will be," she said. "Business."

"Business, huh?"

Travis's slow smile sent heat shimmering through her body. She swallowed. "Yes."

"Whatever you say, sweet Cat. Business it is."

Too late Cat remembered what kind of business Travis conducted with his women.

SEVEN

THE RESTAURANT was Italian, but not a spaghetti parlor. It had exquisite leaded-glass windows whose frames were painted a glossy forest green. The heavy carpet was woven in patterns of deep red, cream, and a dark green that matched the window frames. There were red linen table-cloths, fresh flowers, gleaming china, spotless silver, crystal glasses dividing light into rich primary colors. And over all was the hushed ambience of wealth.

Cat didn't have to look at the menu to know the place was expensive. Really expensive.

"No," she said, turning on Travis.

"You don't like Italian?"

"I don't like the cost."

He blinked, surprised. "Sorry, but it's too late to change now. I can hear your stomach growling. When did you eat lunch?"

"I didn't."

"Cat, be sensible. You have to eat."

She took in a deep breath.

It was a mistake. The scent of food made her dizzy. Breakfast had been a long time ago. Too long.

Get more sleep, Cathy. Eat regularly and eat well. I'll see you in a week.

Cat sighed as she remembered Dr. Stone's words. There

wasn't much she could do about the sleep, but eating well was all around her.

"I let you cook last night when I didn't want to," Travis pointed out neutrally.

"Look at me. I'm wearing slacks, a blouse, and sandals. They won't even seat me in a place like this."

"Want to bet?"

The hostess approached with a professional smile. Though she was wearing a floor-length black dress, high heels, and pearls, she obviously had no problem with seating more casually dressed patrons.

"Two?" she asked.

Travis looked at Cat.

It was the incredible aromas that undermined her will. She couldn't remember the last time she had eaten a good meal prepared by someone else.

"All right," she said, sighing. "Just this once. Right now I'm too tired and too hungry to argue about how much the meal costs."

Travis smiled slightly. He had seen Cat breathe in the food-scented air, rich with garlic and oregano, roasted chicken and lamb. His own mouth was watering and he had eaten a big, late lunch.

Taking her arm, he followed the hostess to the private booth he had requested. Instead of sitting across the table from Cat, he slid in beside her.

"So tell me," Cat said as she settled into the lushly upholstered booth. "What does a ship designer do?"

"Design ships."

She gave him a sideways look.

Travis opened a menu. "If you like scallops, I'm told there aren't any better in Southern California."

"I love scallops."

"Good. Anything you can't or don't eat?"

"Vegemite."

"What?"

"Australia's answer to peanut butter. Nasty stuff."

Travis grimaced. "Now I remember. One of my crew comes from Australia. Said he left just to get away from Vegemite."

"How many men do you have on your ship?"

"Enough to get the job done."

Cat looked at the ceiling and took a deep breath. "You're not helping me."

"What do you mean?" he asked without looking up from the menu.

"How can I plan my shots if you won't tell me what you need?"

"Right now I need food. You can shoot me later."

"Don't tempt me. This is a business meal, remember?"

"I don't conduct business on an empty stomach. You shouldn't either. Leads to bad decisions."

After the server took their orders, Cat tried to bring the conversation back to business. Travis promptly took it away again.

"You're determined to turn this into a date, aren't you?" she asked tightly.

"I'm determined not to talk about anything that matters until you've eaten."

The silence that followed was uneasy at first, but Cat was too tired to sustain anything, even frustration. When the meal came she gave the food the attention it deserved.

By the time Cat ate her fill, she knew that Travis was right; she had been too hungry to be particularly reasonable about anything, especially food. She took a final bite of buttery scallop, sighed, and sipped her wine.

The Chardonnay tasted like sunlight. Eyes closed, she savored the intense, complex flavor. It had been years since she had tasted a wine that suited her so exactly. Long ago she had discovered that wines praised by other people often were bitter, sour, or acid to her. At first she thought it was her untrained palate. Later she realized that her body chemistry was simply different.

"Still mad?" Travis asked quietly.

Cat glanced at him. His eyes were very dark, reflecting only the graceful dance of candlelight. With a faint smile she shook her head.

He smiled in return and watched candlelight run like melted rubies through her auburn hair.

"Good," he said. "I didn't choose this restaurant because I thought it was a way to buy you. I didn't even think about it. If I had . . ." He shrugged. "I'd have taken you somewhere else. The last thing I wanted tonight was a fight with you."

Cat remembered the intense pleasure and hunger in their shared kiss and wondered if Travis was remembering it too. She suspected he was.

"I know," she said. "And you were right, the food here is wonderful." She smothered a yawn and looked longingly at the scallops she was too full to eat. "I just wish I could finish it all."

"That good?" he asked, smiling lazily.

"Don't take my word for it. Try one."

With a skill left over from years of feeding the younger twins, she slid her fork under a plump scallop and popped it into Travis's mouth.

Too late Cat realized the unthinking intimacy of her gesture. Frowning, she looked back at her plate and wished that Travis didn't seem so very familiar to her. She had to keep reminding herself that she had known him only one day, and that everything she had learned about him was a clear warning not to become involved.

Rich men just didn't know how to love.

If she knew that and was fooled by him anyway, then she was indeed a fool. As her father had always told her: Fool me once, damn you; fool me twice, damn *me*.

Travis's tongue licked up a stray bit of sauce from his lower lip. "Mmm. Incredible. Again."

He opened his mouth slightly, waiting. She hesitated, then deftly fed him another scallop.

"You're very good at that," he said. "Do you have children?"

Cat's fork made a ringing sound against the china plate. Instead of answering the question, she took a sip of wine.

"Cat?"

"No." Her voice was low, almost savage. "No children." She looked up at him with pale eyes. "More scallops?"

Travis hesitated, curious and cautious at once. He knew his question had hurt her, but he didn't know why.

"Yes, please," he said finally.

He waited for Cat to feed him another scallop; the intimacy of the gesture was like a caress. And like a caress, it aroused him. Yet instead of offering to feed him from her fork, she switched plates with him. A single look at her eyes told him that he would have to feed himself.

Cat watched in silence while Travis finished her dinner. If she had hoped to cool the sensual heat by not feeding him, it wasn't working. Seeing him eat from her plate, sip from her glass because his own wine was too assertive to drink with scallops, use her fork, lick the silver tines clean . . . all of it gave her a feeling of intimacy with him that was as hot as the flame dancing at the tip of the scented candle.

Travis poured more wine in Cat's glass before he returned it to her. He watched her mouth as she drank, wanting to know if she tasted him as well as the wine. But she hid her eyes, so he was left with only his own memory of her taste.

"Dessert?" Travis asked when she set aside the wine.

Cat shook her head.

The server appeared as though conjured out of candle-light.

"Cognac," Travis said. "And something chocolate."

The server returned with a crystal brandy snifter and an elegant dark chocolate mousse. Travis tasted the cognac, nodded, and turned to the dessert. A single bite told him that the mousse was light, creamy, and just sweet enough to offset the rich natural bitterness of the chocolate.

"Very good," he said.

The server smiled and vanished.

Travis heaped the silver spoon with mousse and held it out to Cat. "Open up."

After a brief hesitation, she opened her mouth.

They were sitting side by side, well within reach, but he had no experience with the gentle art of spoon feeding. Part of the mousse ended up just below her lip.

"Damn," Travis muttered.

He leaned over and neatly licked up the evidence of his bad aim. He was so quick, so casual, that Cat had no time to object. He turned her chin with his fingertip to make sure that he hadn't missed any mousse. He hadn't.

But he leaned down and flicked the tip of his tongue over her lower lip anyway.

"You can tell I'm not experienced at this feeding thing," Travis said.

"That must be why you asked for a private table," she said dryly.

He smiled, took a bite of mousse, then held out another spoonful of dessert to her.

Cat knew she should refuse it. And she knew she wasn't going to. The expectation in his blue-green eyes was as sweet to her as the dessert itself.

"How did you know that chocolate is one of my weaknesses?" she murmured.

He tucked the mousse into her mouth. "Because it's one of mine."

Cat savored the dessert with the same intensity she had savored the wine. Travis watched her pleasure and wanted nothing more than to share the taste of chocolate and the memory of wine with her. He swore softly.

"What's wrong?" she asked. "You did it perfectly this time. Not a speck of mousse out of place."

"I know." He looked regretfully at her clean lower lip. No excuse to tease her with the tip of his tongue. "Maybe next time."

He held out another bite to her.

"You really are a buccaneer, aren't you?" Cat muttered just before her lips closed around the silver spoon.

The smile Travis gave her was as lazy as his drawl. "Because I like licking chocolate off you?"

She swallowed and shook her head. "Because you do what you damn well please when it damn well pleases you."

"Are you saying this doesn't please you?"

"The mousse?"

"Among other things."

Travis took Cat's hand and kissed her palm. With melting tenderness his teeth closed over the pad of flesh at the base of her thumb in a primitive caress. Her breath caught, then resumed, but not before he heard the ragged sound. Smiling, he rubbed her palm against his beard. He had met few women as responsive as Cat, and none who appealed to his senses the way she did.

For a moment Cat allowed herself to enjoy the warmth and silky roughness of Travis's beard. Then she withdrew her hand. Though the motion wasn't quick, it was final. To her relief, he didn't make an issue out of it.

"Last bite," Travis said, holding out a spoon heaped with mousse.

"I've had more than my share already."

His expression changed, as though he understood that she was refusing more than a bite of chocolate.

Cat wished Travis was less perceptive or she was less vulnerable to him. But she was too honest—or foolish—to wish that she hadn't met him. Even knowing that she would burn herself if she came too close to his fire, it felt wonderful to be warm again, tingling with life.

Silently Travis cradled the snifter of cognac between his big hands. When the liquid was properly warmed, he held the glass out to Cat.

She shook her head. "I'm half asleep as it is."

"Go all the way to sleep. I'll get you home." He caught and held her eyes. "It's all right to let down your guard with me. I'm not Ashcroft."

Cat told herself that was exactly why she should be on guard against Travis. Yet it was impossible, like being on guard against her own heartbeat. There was no point in fighting the silky intimacy that wove more securely between them with every breath.

The heady scent of expensive liquor curled up to Cat's nostrils from the snifter Travis held out to her. She inhaled deeply and sighed. Then she dipped her head to take amber liquid from crystal that was warm with his body heat.

Travis watched her sip with an intensity that would have dismayed Cat if she hadn't been watching him in exactly the same way. A primal curiosity was consuming them, a mutual fascination that was both sensual and mental, a silent recognition of the other's unique *rightness*.

It wasn't until Travis tucked Cat into the front seat of his gunmetal Mercedes that she realized how sleepy she really was. Headlights on the opposite side of the freeway moved by in a dazzling, hypnotic silver river. Ahead, a ribbon of taillights glittered with ruby fire. The car's throaty growl was oddly soothing, for it spoke eloquently of restraint as well as power.

The fine food, the wine, and the cognac uncurling in her body all combined to unravel Cat. She sagged against the seat and slept, silently announcing her trust in the utterly familiar stranger called Travis.

He looked over at her and smiled, understanding more than she did about her declaration of trust. A woman as fiercely independent as Cat was didn't accept anything easily from anyone, especially a man.

Travis drove quickly, skillfully, not disturbing her sleep. The car's powerful engine consumed the night, devouring miles of darkness and the twisting Laguna Canyon road. As he drove, he glanced often at the woman sleeping next to him.

Streetlights and moonlight made a fluid, changing mystery of her face. Now young, now old, now laughing, now sad; and always hauntingly *right*. In the shared darkness of the car he felt as though he was sinking into her, and she into him.

Or am I just recognizing what always has been? Travis asked himself. *Cat and me and the night, peace within and possibilities all around.*

Yet beneath the peace was uneasiness and a prowling hunger that had nothing to do with food. The sexual tension of his body Travis both understood and knew how to cure within the sweet violence of Cat's body.

The uneasiness he also understood, but he didn't know how to cure it. He wanted Cat as he had never wanted another woman, yet she would reject the no-strings, I'll-pick-up-the-tab kind of affair that was the only relationship he had permitted himself since Tina.

Tina, the woman who had wanted his money, not his baby.

Tina, who had killed the possibility of their child before it even had a chance to live.

If Travis ever married again, he knew the kind of woman his wife would have to be. Rich. Very, very rich. The kind of woman who didn't need his money but wanted very much to have his child.

No matter how much Travis wanted Cat, no matter how *right* it felt being with her, she needed money too much for him to trust her. An innocent life had been snuffed out because he had trusted the wrong woman. He simply couldn't risk a loss like that again.

Even to have Cat.

Broodingly Travis downshifted and looked again at the sleeping woman who called to him in so many ways.

She won't mix men and money. I won't have women any other way. One of us will have to break our rules, Cat.

It won't be me.

It can't be.

Travis started to turn in to his own driveway, then decided against it. He knew Cat would resent waking up in his bed, as though he had purchased her along with the dinner that seemed so expensive to her and meant no more than a peanut butter sandwich to him.

He parked in Cat's driveway, used a key from her purse to open the front door, turned on the lights, and went looking for her bedroom. The first door he opened was next to the kitchen. It had a view of the midnight ocean, a slightly oversized single bed, an antique oak rocking chair, and a matching dresser with a beveled mirror. The sunrise colors of the bed quilt were repeated in a thick wool throw rug.

The combination of polished wood and glowing colors pleased Travis. It was a room that a man as well as a woman could be at home in. Assuming that this was a guest bedroom, he shut the door again and resumed his tour of the house.

Only after he had opened every door on every level without finding another bed did Travis realize that the room with the single bed in it was Cat's.

He went back to the room. For a long time he stood there, looking at the bed. Hesitant to disturb her privacy in even such a small way, yet unable to stop himself, he turned down the crisp sheets. The sunrise colors of the quilt were matched in the sheets. The delicate scent of Cat's perfume rose from them, pervading his senses, making his head spin like fine cognac. Gently he stroked the pillow, wishing she was there, looking up at him, smiling with a woman's timeless invitation to her lover.

Then Travis thought of Cat sleeping in his car. He wondered how long it would take her to accept what she couldn't change.

She wanted him.

Wary, independent Cat. I should grab her before she wakes up and sail with her over the edge of the world.

He smiled, eyes narrowed, temptation plain in the piratical lines of his face.

"Someday, Cat," he promised. "Someday soon. But not tonight. You're not ready."

Neither was he. They had the details of their affair to work out. He was accustomed to such delicate negotiations. He was very much afraid that she wasn't.

Cat was still asleep when Travis returned to the car. As he lifted her out and shut the door, she shifted in his arms and murmured sleepily.

"It's all right," he said softly. "Go back to sleep. I've brought you to your own home."

She half opened her eyes, saw his familiar smile, and smiled dreamily in return. With a murmured word she let herself slide fully back into the sleep her exhausted body craved.

Smiling, Travis carried Cat into her bedroom, laid her on the narrow bed, and began undressing her. After he removed her black sandals, he stacked them to one side and gently rubbed away the small marks the straps had left on her arch. Then he took out the silver clasp that held her hair in a disciplined coil on top of her head.

Strands as soft and warm as dawn spilled into his hands. He buried his face in the untamed silk of her hair, inhaling deeply. He knew he should stop there, pull the blanket over her and leave.

He knew, but he didn't leave.

Slowly Travis began unbuttoning the teal blue blouse that followed Cat's curves so tantalizingly. Silky folds of cloth fell away beneath his hands. He paused for a moment, looking at her creamy body, glad that she wasn't awake to see the fine trembling of his hands.

"Do you know what you do to me?" Travis whispered. "I'm shaking like you're my first woman."

There was no answer.

He hadn't expected one.

He slipped off Cat's slacks, careful not to hurt the foot she had scraped on the rocks yesterday. Only when he reached for her lacy bra and panties did he hesitate.

"You wouldn't like that, would you?" he asked very softly. "Prickly, independent Cat. I know I should leave you to sleep alone. But I . . . can't."

With the ingrained neatness of a man who had spent a long time at sea, Travis folded Cat's clothes and his own and set them on the antique rocking chair. Though he had stopped short of fully undressing her, he had no concerns about his own clothes. He was quite naked when he lay down beside her in the small bed, gathered her into his arms, and eased the covers over both of them.

She moved slightly, neither awake nor fully asleep, sensing his presence.

"Travis . . . ?" she murmured, her voice slurred with sleep.

"Shhh," he said, stroking her hair soothingly. "Go back to sleep, Cat. Everything is all right. You're home."

She sighed and relaxed into his warmth.

A shudder of need and something more, something Travis couldn't name, swept through him. He rested his lips on her hair, baffled by the emotions that were warring inside him.

The single bed told him that she was accustomed to sleeping alone. Yet she fell asleep in his arms with a smile, as though they had always been lovers.

Everything he had seen and sensed in her told him that they would be very good together, that she was the right woman for him in all ways but one.

And that one way was the only one that mattered.

Damn it, Cat, why didn't I meet you before Tina taught me about women and money?

Cat burrowed into Travis's warmth like a sleepy child. Her fingers curled into the warm mat of hair on his chest. Her long sigh was sweet and warm against his throat.

Need knotted in Travis, a need both sexual and simply human. He wanted the peace that was stealing through Cat as much as he wanted her body.

Her trust was a sweet, cruel razor slicing into the scars left by old certainties.

What am I going to do with you, Cat? You make me want to believe in . . . too much. And the cost of being wrong is too high.

It's one of the few things on earth I can't afford.

For a long time Travis lay in the darkness holding her and thinking. No matter how he approached the problem, nothing changed.

He was rich.

She was not.

That meant they would have to sort out the terms of their affair very quickly. If Cat refused to quantify their relationship, Travis would do what he had done before when the restraints of land and human nature imprisoned him; he would step aboard his ship and sail to the ends of the earth.

The clean, limitless beauty of the sea would renew him as it had so many times in the past.

Yet even as he assured himself of that, he breathed in her scent and knew that nothing on earth or ocean could replace it.

EIGHT

DAWN SHIMMERED over the ocean in tints of rose and gold, lavender and cream. It was a radiant fantasy that filled Cat's bedroom with a soundless rush of light. Her inner alarm clock prodded her, telling her it was time to be up.

She stirred in silent protest—and realized that she was moving against something warm and very solid. Beneath her cheek a heart beat in the slow, steady rhythm of sleep.

Eyes still closed, barely awake, Cat realized that she was lying half on top of a man, breathing as he breathed, her arm thrown across his warm torso, her leg wedged between his.

Travis.

She didn't have to open her eyes to know who shared her intimate sprawl. It wasn't so much the vague memories of being carried inside and tucked in bed by Travis that told her who was lying so close by. It was the simple fact that only Travis could have slipped through her defenses to the point where she not only fell asleep on him, but didn't wake up even when he got in bed beside her.

Deliberately Cat kept her eyes closed. She didn't want to wake up and face the working day. It was deliciously warm lying next to Travis, and dawn was usually so cold. She rubbed her cheek sleepily against his chest and snuggled even closer.

An instant later there was a change in his heartbeat, in

his big body, in the tension of the arm wrapped around her waist.

Travis was awake.

That was when Cat realized that he was naked and she wasn't. Not quite. Her whole body stiffened.

"Don't be angry," Travis said softly.

A large hand slowly stroked her hair. The touch was gentle and undemanding.

"If you had finished undressing me," she said after a moment, "I would be furious."

"I know."

Her breath broke. "How?"

Smiling, he let his fingertips drift over her eyebrows. "I just do."

"How can I—" Cat began, then stopped abruptly.

It wasn't the sort of question a smart woman asked aloud: *How can I defend myself against a man who knows me so well?*

The answer was both simple and frightening. She couldn't.

"Mmmm?" Travis asked.

"How can you be so smart?" she muttered.

"Just about you. Sometimes. And sometimes you surprise the hell out of me."

Cat hesitated, then sighed and relaxed into his body again. For a few slow breaths she allowed herself to enjoy the feel of his hand moving over her hair.

"If you weren't bigger than me," she said finally, yawning, "I'd throw you over the deck into the surf for your morning swim."

Silent laughter rippled through Travis. "But I *am* bigger, so what are you going to do with me?"

"I'm thinking about it."

He slid a hand beneath Cat's hair and rubbed sensually down to the small of her back.

"May I offer a suggestion?" he asked.

As he spoke, his nails scraped very lightly over the base of her spine.

Cat shivered and arched against him with an instinctive motion. Travis's breath caught as his heartbeat and his body leaped almost painfully. There had been no calculation in her movement. She simply had responded to his caress with a bone-deep sensuality that made his whole body tighten in anticipation.

He had been right. They were going to be good together. Very, very good.

"A suggestion, huh?" Cat said sleepily.

"A small one."

She lifted her head and looked down at Travis. Dawn had transformed the arrogant lines of his face into velvet shadows and luminous planes. His eyes were such a deep green they were almost black, yet light turned in their depths, light and intelligence and laughter. Beneath his thick mustache his lips shaped a pirate's smile.

"Don't tell me," she said dryly. "Let me guess."

"Okay. Here's your second hint."

His hand slid up into her hair. Slowly his fingers rubbed over her scalp until she sighed and lay against him again. When he spoke, his voice was even deeper than usual.

"Have you guessed my suggestion?" he asked, but there was no real question in his voice.

"Yeah. That I get to work."

"On me."

"You don't need work." Cat propped herself up on her elbow. "You look all together to me."

Travis's big hands framed her face. "I'm just half together, looking for the other half." He pulled her gently down to his lips, tasted her. "We'll fit together very well, two halves that are finally whole."

"But—"

His mouth moved over Cat's before she could finish the rest of what he was afraid would be a refusal.

"Don't say anything yet," Travis said against her lips. "Just kiss me. That's all I ask, a single kiss. Just one. You know you can trust me. Say you trust me, sweet Cat, show that you trust me. A kiss. Just one kiss for the well-behaved pirate who wanted to steal you and sail off over the edge of the world, but brought you back to your own room instead."

Cat felt herself giving in to the gentle power of his words, pulled like a bright leaf into the whirlpool of his desire. No man had ever wanted her like this. His need was as irresistible to her as dawn. Slowly she bent her head until her lips touched his in a breathlessly gentle kiss.

His fingers tightened very slightly around her face, simultaneously reminding her of his strength and his restraint.

Just a kiss.

Just one.

Trusting Travis's control, Cat moved her lips lightly on his. She felt the sensual tension that rippled through him in response. It told her how desirable she was to him as no words could have. Shivers of heightened awareness went through her. With them came a feeling of feminine power that was as new and heady to her as the cognac she had sipped from warm crystal last night.

Her ex-husband had required that she lie still and be quiet until he was finished, because women who enjoyed sex weren't fit to be the mothers of children. Wives were passive. Whores cooperated. Sluts enjoyed.

Following Billy's rules hadn't been a problem for Cat; he wasn't an enjoyable lover. The only pleasure she had ever found from sex had been some hasty, furtive, and finally rather embarrassing petting in high school.

While Travis was in no way as boring as Billy or as embarrassing as a high school boy, Cat didn't expect anything from Travis once the brief preliminaries were over.

Sex was one of Mother Nature's jokes on women. Men were fast and hard and women weren't.

But on the plus side, it had been very nice for Cat to wake up feeling Travis's heartbeat under her cheek and his warmth all along her body. She had slept better than she had in years. If the price of that kind of peace and companionship was a few hurried, uncomfortable minutes underneath him . . . well, she had learned after her father died that nothing in life was truly free.

Even while Cat brushed her lips lightly against Travis's mouth, she expected the soft kiss to end immediately in an assertion of male sexual prerogative. Yet he showed no signs of impatience, much less of a headlong rush toward sex.

Curious in a way she hadn't been since high school, Cat increased the pressure of her kiss. She didn't stop until she could savor the firmness of his lips, sense the smooth hardness of his teeth, and feel the warmth of his breath blending with hers.

Long fingers flexed in her hair, encouraging her without imprisoning her, coaxing rather than demanding that the kiss continue. With a ragged sigh she opened her lips and recklessly traced the line of Travis's mouth as he had once traced hers.

The instant Cat realized what she had done, she froze. Three years of marriage to Billy had taught her that men disliked anything but straight-line, quick sex. Kissing just got in the way.

She tried to raise her head, to end the kiss, but found she couldn't. She was held tenderly, immovably, in Travis's hands. Their lips were still touching.

"Travis?" she whispered.

"Yes," he said simply.

"What?"

"Whatever you're asking, the answer is yes. As long as it doesn't mean that the kiss ends before I taste you. I have to taste you, Cat. Is that so very much to ask of a kiss?''

Her eyes opened in shock.

Travis was watching her. His eyes were a blue-green blaze that filled her world.

"You don't mind?" Cat said against his lips.

"Mind what?"

"This."

She closed her eyes and probed the corners of his mouth with the tip of her tongue. As she did, she wondered if Travis was as sensitive there as she had been when his tongue teased her.

"Mind?" he asked huskily. "Hell, no. I like that."

"What about this?"

She licked his lips with catlike neatness. The sultry little caresses made him want to open her thighs and seek out flesh that was even hotter, wetter.

But it was much too soon. She was as skittish as a girl with her first man.

"I like that," Travis said. "A lot."

His fingers kneaded down Cat's back. She didn't notice the fine trembling of his hands against her skin. She was too busy memorizing the shape of his smile with her tongue to let anything else distract her. She had never guessed how sensitive her tongue could be. Each caress she gave returned to her in warmth and quickened breathing.

"And this?" Cat whispered. "What about this?"

Her tongue pressed inside his lower lip, then delicately touched the serrations of his teeth just as he had once touched hers. The temptation to sink into him and pull him around her kept warring with her experience of men and sex.

Cat hesitated against the inviting warmth of Travis's mouth, not touching him with her tongue. She didn't want the slow, sensual exploration to end in a jarring rush of sex.

"Do it," Travis whispered. "Taste me the way I want to taste you."

The heat of his voice was like a tongue stroking sensitive nerves. She shivered with pleasure and sought him in the warm darkness of his mouth. Instinctively she moved her lips and tongue over his, finding the points of greatest mingling, most intense pleasure.

Travis met and matched the kiss, teased and retreated, encouraged and enjoyed; and always he lured Cat deeper and deeper into his embrace.

After a time she forget to tense against the instant when she would find herself flat on her back with Travis sweating over her. She forgot Billy's harsh teaching, forgot that she hadn't known Travis long, forgot everything but the heat and restrained power of the man who was confident enough to let her test herself on him.

The kiss became a timeless sensual awakening for Cat, a hot sunrise that ended her long night of ignorance and misunderstanding of what sexual play could be with the right man. With a ragged sound she stopped thinking of anything at all. She gave herself completely to the hot, wild kiss.

In time not even the deepest kiss was enough for Cat. She had to be closer to Travis, then closer still. But no matter how she tried, she couldn't get close enough to him, couldn't hold him tightly enough, couldn't take enough of his mouth. Her legs tangled with his as she pressed herself against his chest, trying to melt into him as completely as he was melting into her.

His hands shifted and his arms flexed. Without breaking the deep kiss, he lifted her over himself like a hot satin blanket.

But that still wasn't close enough for Cat. With a low sound she pulled herself against Travis, caressing him with sinuous movements of her body that at first eased and then savagely increased her need for him.

"Closer," Cat whispered without knowing what she was saying. *"Closer."*

Travis spread his legs and let Cat sink between them. Then he slid his legs around and over hers, pulled her ankles apart with his heels, and opened her soft, flushed core. Her response was another of the reckless, sliding movements of her hips over his that made sweat stand out on his skin.

The temptation to slide beneath her lacy briefs and push deep inside her was so great that he shook. But he wouldn't do what he wanted so badly. He would not take her.

He hadn't had sex without a condom since Tina had aborted his baby. He wasn't going to start now, no matter how wild Cat made him.

And from Cat's odd combination of hesitation and headlong sensuality, Travis was very much afraid that she didn't practice the kind of offhanded sexuality that meant a box of condoms in the bedside table, just in case she ended up astride a date.

Travis groaned deep in his chest and pushed his erection between her legs in a blunt, sensual questing. She made a broken sound against his mouth, shivered, and melted over him. Her instant, sultry response made him wonder if he was wrong about the contents of her bedside drawer.

Cat barely noticed Travis's hands moving over her body. Dark scraps of lace slid away, leaving her as naked as he was. She didn't object. She welcomed it. She wanted to be still closer to him, skin to skin, hunger to hunger, burning away a lifetime of chill in his unique fire.

It was Travis who finally ended the passionate kiss. He lifted Cat's face until he could see her eyes, smoky with hunger, and her lips, reddened with all that she had given and taken.

"Are you sure?" Travis asked simply.

Dazed, breathing hard, Cat trembled full-length against him. She didn't understand his question or why he had stopped.

"I've never wanted—like this," she said raggedly. "Is that—what you mean?"

Desire ripped through Travis. His elemental response to her words made his whole body rigid. He slipped the leash on his control for just an instant, long enough to tell her without words what her admission meant to him. He pulled her down and kissed her hungrily, achingly, penetrating her mouth with his tongue in a single, swift stab, filling her in the only way he would permit himself for now.

Then he held Cat away from him once more and fought to control himself.

"That's more than I asked," he said thickly. "I'm not contagious, but I have to know if you're protected against pregnancy."

At first Cat didn't understand. When she did, she stiffened against Travis. She was well, painfully well, *protected* against getting pregnant.

With a small cry she rolled away from him. She didn't want to see his eyes change when he knew that she wasn't a whole woman. She couldn't bear to know the exact moment when he would no longer desire her.

Swiftly Travis turned onto his side. His long arm slid over Cat's waist and gathered her close to him again. His rigid arousal lay against her, hot and heavy, urgent. Yet his voice was calm rather than harsh.

"Ah, Cat, don't be angry with your blunt pirate. I have a right to know."

She let her breath out slowly and relaxed a little, but still refused to look at Travis. "I'm not angry."

His lips brushed gently over her shoulder. Though he said nothing, she knew that he was waiting for an answer to his question.

The words simply wouldn't take shape on her tongue.

"Cat?" he asked.

She closed her eyes. "I won't get pregnant."

The words sounded flat to her, harsh, but there was nothing she could do to soften them. She had told the truth.

She wouldn't get pregnant.

Bothered by the change in Cat's voice and her refusal to meet his eyes, Travis turned her face toward him. When he spoke, his own voice was as hard as hers had been.

"Look at me," he demanded. "Are you certain you won't get pregnant?"

Anger raced through Cat. Travis had the right to ask the question once, but no more.

"I'm very certain," she said distinctly. "But it doesn't matter."

He raised a tawny eyebrow. "Like hell it doesn't. I was caught in the baby trap once. Once was more than enough."

Cat's smile made him flinch.

"Not to worry, Mr. T. H. Danvers," she said in a brittle voice. "I'm fresh out of baby traps."

"What does that mean?"

"I'm sterile!"

As Cat spoke the last words she twisted aside, trying to get out from under his weight, out of bed, out of his reach, out of the room . . . *out.*

Her quickness wasn't enough. Travis had sensed her tension, guessed what she was going to do. He flattened her on the bed beneath him.

"Not so fast, Cat. Not before you tell me why."

Her body twisted violently as she tested his hold. She quickly realized that Travis not only had position on her, he also had even more sheer power than she had guessed.

His strength didn't frighten Cat the way she had been frightened when she realized Ashcroft's power. The difference between the two men was both simple and devastating—Cat trusted Travis not to rape her and chalk up her struggles to coyness.

But trusting Travis didn't mean that she was pleased to be his captive.

"Why what?" she asked in a stranger's voice. "Why am I sterile? Or don't you believe that I am? Would you like a note from my gynecologist certifying my defect?"

His breath came in sharply. "Don't, Cat. Please don't." Travis bent to kiss her gently, realizing too late how much the subject hurt her. "I believe you."

She jerked her head aside, avoiding his kiss. "Then if your curiosity is satisfied, get the hell out of my bed."

"Try to understand," Travis said against her cheek. Between words his tongue delicately traced the contours of her ear. "After my divorce, I swore I'd never be caught in the baby trap again. I'd be a regular Boy Scout, always prepared."

He laughed without humor. "And I have been. If I'd taken you to my own bed, this never would have happened. But when I saw your single bed, I knew that Harrington was right, fire and ice, and I couldn't leave you. I had to stay and warm myself with your fire."

"Stop it!" Cat said, shaking with anger and the desire Travis could call out of her with a look, a touch, a word.

"Why?" he whispered. His breath stirred her hair as his hips slid hungrily over hers.

Her body went rigid. *"No."*

Gently Travis turned her face toward his, forcing her to look at him. "Why?"

"I don't feel like celebrating my defect right now," Cat said bitterly.

"It isn't a defect," he said, his voice certain.

"That depends on your point of view, doesn't it? Billy wanted a dynasty. You want a roll in the hay."

Travis touched her hair with fingers that trembled very slightly. "And you, Cat. What do you want?"

She said nothing at all.

He looked at her and was afraid that he had lost everything before either of them even had a chance to win. Her face was framed in a cloud of auburn hair that shimmered and smoldered with each rapid breath she took. Her eyes were pale as ice, staring through him. She was proud and distant, quivering like a racing sloop under full sail, heeled over dangerously far, pursued by a storm.

"I can't change the past," Travis said, watching Cat with eyes that shared her hurt. "But I can give you a chance to run before the storm, to feel ecstasy in every motion, every touch. And when the storm finally breaks, I'll be there. Let me love you, Cat."

Like a warm, soft wind his lips brushed over her cheek, her shoulder, her breast, stealing away her anger while the gentle warmth of his hands gave her back the gift of passion.

Slowly Cat's stiff body relaxed, softening beneath Travis. Her breath trembled out in a sound that might have been his name. He answered it with a kiss whispered against her ear. His weight no longer imprisoned her. There was no need. She was held more securely by the pleasure he was giving her than she had been by his strength.

His tongue teased her breast for long moments before he drew her nipple into the heat and pressure of his mouth. She shivered at the unexpected sensations consuming her. His hand surrounded her with warmth. His fingers slowly, deliciously kneaded her breast.

Cat made a startled sound as streamers of heat shot through her. When his teeth caressed her hardened nipple, she arched wildly. Her fingernails sank into his shoulders, clinging to him urgently. He was the only solid thing in a sea of swirling pleasure.

Slowly Travis released her nipple and lifted his head, wanting to see the tight crown he had drawn from her flesh.

"No," Cat said on a broken breath. Her hands slid into his hair, bringing his head back down to her breast while she moved beneath his mouth. "Don't stop. Please. It feels so good."

Travis laughed softly and gave her a sweet, biting caress that made her gasp.

"It's too soon to worry about stopping," he said huskily. "We've barely started."

He bent his head and feasted on her breasts until she was shivering and crying, twisting beneath him, moving her hips against him with a hunger that she didn't even try to hide.

With any other woman Travis would have ended the preliminaries then and there. But she wasn't any other woman. She was Cat, wary and welcoming by turns, mysterious and yet sometimes as familiar to him as his own breath.

"Travis, I—" Cat's voice broke as he caressed her breasts with fingers and tongue. The pleasure shooting through her was good, wonderful, incredible.

And it wasn't enough.

"I know," Travis said in answer to her incoherent words. "We'll get there. Let the storm build for a while. Let me find out."

"What?"

"How good we're going to be."

"I'm not—I mean—I—"

Cat gave up trying to make sense. Travis was moving over her with the smooth power of a breaking wave. She was pinned again beneath his big body and she loved every inch of it. She stretched and twisted against him, her skin on fire with pleasure everywhere she touched him.

"You're trying to push me over the edge, aren't you?" Travis asked, hungry and laughing at the same time.

The dazed look Cat gave him said better than words could have that she wasn't aware of what she was doing. She was simply responding to him and to the wild, unexpected storm he had called from her core. The knowledge almost stripped away his control.

Abruptly Travis took Cat's mouth with his own, needing to sink into her in some way. His tongue probed her lips with increasing pressure, demanding that she share the kiss. When her mouth opened, he asked for more, took it, his tongue sliding between her teeth until he was in complete possession of every soft, hot bit of her mouth.

She responded with a need that equaled his, invading his mouth with her tongue, trying to consume him even as he consumed her. Her hands moved recklessly down his back, glorying in the rippling strength of his body, digging into the tensed muscles of his buttocks, seeking his hardened flesh, finding it, holding it.

His breath broke, then came out in a hoarse groan that was a warning of how close to the edge he was.

Too late Cat remembered all that her ex-husband had taught her about a woman's role in bed. Instantly she snatched back her hands.

"I'm sorry," she said raggedly.

"For what?" Travis asked. His voice was rough with pleasure and his hands were seeking her as intimately as hers had sought him.

"I know that men—don't like—aggressive women. I forgot. I'm sorry." Cat's words jerked out, sharp with the humiliating memories.

"Are you talking about that sorry bastard you married?"

Numbly Cat nodded.

"Billy was a fool," Travis said. "You're passionate, not aggressive. That might frighten a boy, but it's exciting as hell to a man."

As he spoke, he pulled Cat's hands back down his body, then shuddered openly when her fingers brushed against him. He was so hard that his flesh jerked with every racing heartbeat. Her touch was heaven and hell at once, but above all it was a storm swirling around both of them, a storm building toward the moment of breaking.

"I'm not afraid of you," Travis said, moving between Cat's hands, letting her see and feel his pleasure. "I want my woman to touch me all over, everywhere, any and every way she wants to.''

Cat stared at him, wanting to ask what he meant, unable to think of the words. He felt so exciting between her hands, hard and smooth, hot and quivering with life.

Travis smiled down at her in lazy contradiction to the smoldering blue-green fire of his eyes.

''That's it,'' he said almost roughly. ''Touch me all over. Anything. Everything. It's the way I'm going to touch you. All over, everywhere, any and every way I want.''

She shivered at the sensual promise that radiated from him, the certainty of ecstasy burning in his eyes, the intense pleasure that rippled through him when she curled her fingers around him. The feel of him was unbearably arousing. She buried her face in his neck, caressing his skin with her tongue, biting the hard tendons, then licking away the marks her teeth left.

Travis made a raw sound of pleasure and hunger. He could sense her liquid heat close to him, so close, it would be sweet hell to slide into her. The scent of her arousal infused the air like lightning. Her hands teased and praised him, measuring and caressing him in the same sexy movements.

''That's it,'' he said, laughing softly, triumphantly. ''Test me, Cat. See how hard I am.'' As he spoke, one of his hands moved between her thighs, opening them. A long finger slid into her. ''And how soft you are.''

Cat gasped with surprise at the sensations surging through her body. She tried to say Travis's name, to ask what he was doing to her. All that came out was a ragged sound of need.

Deliberately Travis circled the soft, sleek folds of skin until he found the point of greatest pleasure for her. Then he stroked and teased and rubbed until she cried out and melted in his hand.

''Travis?'' Cat asked almost desperately. ''What—''

Her voice broke as another gust of pleasure shook her, a storm wave cresting endlessly within her, sweeping her toward an unknown shore.

Body arched, she closed her eyes and gave herself over to the storm and to Travis. She lived only where he touched her, and he touched her everywhere, the storm building until she couldn't bear it anymore. She cried out with a pleasure so intense it was almost pain.

His hips flexed and he sank into her. The powerful movement joined their bodies deeply, completely. Lightning scored her with searing pleasure. She clung to him, frantically matching his rhythmic movements, sharing his strength as they raced before the storm they had created, wanting both to outrun and be consumed by it.

Then they could run no further and the storm broke around them, consuming them.

Cat would have been frightened, but Travis was there, surrounding her, sheltering her while ecstasy shattered her world, then holding her while her world slowly re-formed. It was a different world now, for he was part of her.

NINE

CAT AWOKE to sunlight pouring in silent golden cataracts across her bed. She stretched with a slow, feline thoroughness and smiled at the memories unfolding inside her, memories more beautiful than light.

When she opened her eyes Travis was there beside her. He looked good to her, as golden as the sunshine, as warm as her memories, strong and wonderful and very, very male.

Travis smiled at the approval in her eyes. He ran a lazy, possessive fingertip from her nose to her knees and back again. Then he traced the dark smudges beneath her eyes.

"You don't get enough sleep, do you?" he asked.

She patted back a yawn. "Whose fault is that?" she asked, then caught his wandering fingertip between her teeth.

"I'll take the credit—um, blame—for this morning. But what's to blame for all the other mornings that left marks under your eyes?"

"Work."

"Not men?" Travis teased, sure of the answer. The utter lack of calculation in Cat's response in bed had already told him that she wasn't part of Laguna's indiscriminate sexual games.

"You're the only man I've found who will put up with my bed," she said, yawning again.

"I've been meaning to bring that up."

"My lack of other men?"

"Your bed." Travis's eyes caressed Cat as she lay softly tangled in sheets. "I was delighted to find that you slept single, but . . ." He dangled his feet over the end of the bed and at the same time bumped his head against the wall. "Do you think we could give my bed a try?"

"For sleeping?"

"Eventually."

He moved his body slightly, all but crowding Cat off the mattress. Only the fact that his arms were around her kept her from falling off the bed.

"You're at my mercy," he pointed out. "I'm not only bigger than you are, I'm bigger than you and this bed put together."

Cat wrapped her arms around Travis, measuring his length with her own supple body. If she was worried about the fact that he had a good seven inches on her, she didn't show it.

"You're right," she said huskily. "I'm at your mercy."

"I can hardly wait. Do that again."

"What?"

"Rub up against me like a hungry cat."

Smiling with pleasure that Travis approved of the sensuality he had lured out of her, Cat moved slowly against him again. The sensation of being naked and alive with him was so delicious that she licked her lips as though savoring a fine wine.

Travis laughed and moved over Cat. Slowly he lowered part of his weight onto her, pinning her beneath him.

"I was going to offer you lunch," he said as he nuzzled her breasts, "but I think I'll just eat you instead."

"Lunch?" Cat asked, startled. "What time is it?"

Travis looked at the angle of the sun with a sailor's measuring eye. "Nearly noon. Why?"

"It can't be!"

"All right. It can't be." He nibbled around the top of

one breast, loving the way her nipple instantly pouted to be in his mouth. "Maybe dinner is the best idea of all."

"Travis?"

"Mmmm," he said, smiling down at her breasts.

"Is it really almost noon?"

"It really is."

Cat swore softly, then her breath caught as Travis sucked on the tip of one breast.

"Travis, I was supposed to be somewhere at nine."

Reluctantly he released the tight, eager nipple. "It's okay. Jason's mother called at eight to tell you that he has a slight fever. I told her that you'd be glad to reschedule whatever you had going with him."

Cat stared at Travis. She hadn't even heard the phone.

"You aren't glad to reschedule?" he asked.

She frowned and thought aloud about her schedule. "I reserved Thursday morning for meeting T. H. Danvers." She smiled distractedly at him. "Except for dawn and sunset, of course. They belong to Ashcroft."

"Like hell they do," Travis said. "Dawn is definitely *mine*."

"But I have to shoot Jason for the Laguna Realtors."

Travis watched Cat with an expression of patient curiosity that didn't quite suit his pirate's face. "That sounds rather extreme, shooting a child."

She smiled. "Film, not bullets. It's for the 'Laguna, a Fine Place to Raise Children' campaign," she added, as though that explained everything.

"Of course," Travis said gravely, but laughter turned in the blue-green depths of his eyes.

"The light is best in the early morning and late afternoon," she explained, "unless there's a nice lively storm with lots of broken clouds and wind."

She frowned and looked out the window.

"Not a chance," Travis said. "Fair weather and smooth

sailing, world without end, amen. Or until the weekend, whichever comes sooner.''

"Then I'm afraid it's Jason at dawn and Ashcroft in the evening.''

"And T. H. Danvers?'' Travis asked, his voice light, his eyes very intent.

"I'll fit him in every chance I get.''

"Fit me in, huh? I love it when you go all wild and demanding on me.''

One of his hands slid up between Cat's thighs.

"But this isn't the time,'' she said quickly. "Travis, I—oh!''

Her breath came in on a gasp as his fingertips ruffled the hair between her legs. He prowled around the soft, hot core of her.

"You'll at least promise to see my ship, won't you?'' he asked.

"I can't—think when you—''

She shuddered as his finger slid slowly, deeply into her. Her nails sank into the strong muscles of his shoulders. She could feel a liquid warmth seep out to meet him, bathing both of them in her helpless response to his touch.

Smiling, he repeated the long, gliding caress several times before he said softly, "Don't think, Cat. Just say, 'Yes, I'll go with you to see your ship.' ''

"Yes, I'll—*oh*—do whatever you—''

She made a low sound and forgot what she was supposed to say. Travis was circling the violently sensitive knot of flesh he had discovered hidden in her soft folds. His wet fingertips plucked her sweetly. She gave up trying to think or speak.

"I think I like your version better,'' Travis said, smiling at her unguarded, hot response to his touch.

His breath sucked in as one of Cat's hands slid between his legs and cupped him lovingly. Then her fingernails scraped over him with excruciating care. He couldn't breathe for the shocking pleasure of her hand returning all the sensual tricks he had taught her last night.

"Cat," Travis said in a strained voice, "if you're planning on getting out of bed today, one of us has to be sensible about this."

"Let me know when it's my turn. Anyway, it's all your fault."

"What is?"

He closed his eyes and savored the feel of her hands cherishing him. He was hard and heavy, as though it had been months rather than hours since he had last had a woman.

"This."

Cat's nails ran lightly from Travis's neck to his hips. Her fingertips ruffled the tawny hair on his chest, traced the subtle ridges of muscle down his abdomen, tangled again in darker hair, then teased his aroused flesh without quite touching him.

"If you hadn't told me that you like being touched," she said, "I'd be lying on the bed like an inflatable doll and you'd be—"

"Bored as Lucifer in church," Travis finished, laughing.

He caught Cat's wandering hand, bit her palm with restrained power, then smoothed her hand back down the length of his body. Her fingers curled around the base of his erection and then slowly moved down between his legs until she could cup him in her palm.

"I love feeling how tight you get," she said in a low voice. "And I love holding you in my palm when you come."

Travis's body leaped in response to Cat's words and his own memories. They had proved to be even better matched as lovers than he had hoped. She was neither shy nor coy. She was simply, stunningly, sensual.

"How anyone as sexy as you is still running around

loose is more than I can understand,'' he admitted, shaking his head. ''But I'm damned grateful.''

''I could say the same of you,'' Cat pointed out, caressing him gently. ''While I won't claim great experience, I can guarantee that the other men I've met didn't make me want to touch them. You, though . . .'' She closed her eyes, tracing the strength and changing textures of his body. ''You make me *want*.''

''What do you want?'' Travis asked softly.

When she didn't answer, he looked up to her face. His breath caught as he saw her intense pleasure in simply touching him. Her eyes were closed, her face taut as she concentrated only on him.

''I want to pull you around me like a warm velvet blanket,'' Cat whispered, seeing Travis only with her sensitive fingertips. ''To feel you change as I touch you. To cover you like sunlight covers the sea. To sink into you until neither one of us knows who is being touched and who is touching. To . . .'' She laughed raggedly and shook her head. ''I can't explain.''

''You don't have to.'' Travis lifted Cat onto his body with a single powerful motion. ''You make me *want* in the same way. And that's as new to me as it is to you.''

Her eyes snapped open, revealing silver depths of surprise and desire. Before she could speak he rolled over slowly, lazily, taking her with him as he turned.

Then he was over her, surrounding her, sinking into her while she made small sounds of welcome, sounds he echoed. They spoke to each other as they had last night, without words, their bodies swept up in a gathering wave of mutual need as they taught each other pleasures that neither alone had believed possible.

And when they could climb no higher, they held each other while the wild wave broke around them. Then they forgot which was self and which was other, for both were one.

*   *   *

Turned halfway in the car seat, Cat watched Travis drive the Mercedes toward Dana Harbor. By the time they had dragged themselves out of the house, it was after two o'clock. The day was cloudless, sunny. He had declared it a perfect time to introduce her to his ship.

The ship she would be photographing, assuming he liked her work.

Cat hadn't forgotten that no deal would be made until Travis saw samples of her photography. She didn't resent his caution. Last night and this morning she had learned just how passionate a man he was. Passionate people cared deeply about their work. If the roles had been reversed, she would have insisted on the same kind of proof of ability before she allowed him to touch her work.

"You're awfully quiet," Travis said, glancing up from the road. "Are you falling asleep on me?"

"Not yet." Cat swallowed a yawn. "Just thinking."

"About what?"

"This and that. Mostly that."

Travis smiled. "Sounds important."

Cat gave up and yawned openly. "Nope. You've unraveled my brain."

He changed lanes to pass a huge motor home that belonged on the multilane interstate highway, not on Laguna's crowded streets.

She enjoyed watching him control the car with ease and precision. When he downshifted, sunlight ran like gold water over the tawny hair on his arm. As he transferred his grip from gearshift to steering wheel, the tendons on the back of his hand moved beneath tanned skin. His fingers closed firmly over the leather-sheathed wheel.

Cat remembered the intense pleasure Travis could give to her with a simple caress. Sudden, stark need coursed through her, leaving her shaken. She wanted to touch him, taste him, take him so deeply into her body that she could feel every wild pulse of his release.

"If you keep looking at me like that," Travis said, "I'm going to pull over to the side of the road and do things to you that will get us arrested."

His husky drawl did nothing to cool Cat's blood. She looked away from his knowing hands to his lips smiling beneath his tawny mustache. She remembered the feel of his beard sliding down her skin, the exciting silky roughness against her neck, her breasts, her stomach. She wondered what it would be like to feel him . . . everywhere.

With a small groan Cat closed her eyes. "What am I going to do with you?"

"I'll pull over so we can find out."

"Not a good idea."

"Chicken."

"Cluck cluck. I can't afford bail."

"I can."

"They'll put us in separate cells."

"Damn. I didn't think of that. Then you better stop looking at me like a cat with cream on her mind. I don't want to spend the night alone."

As Travis slowed to turn off the Pacific Coast Highway, the Mercedes made a well-bred, throaty sound. The sound deepened when the car accelerated along the winding road into Dana Point Harbor. To the right of the street, a deeply eroded bluff wore the skeleton of a failed hotel like a gap-toothed smile. To the left, yacht basins held row after row of pleasure craft, countless boats tied side by side, creating a forest of white masts with seagulls turning and crying overhead.

"Close your eyes," Travis said.

Startled, Cat looked at him.

"I promise not to get us arrested," he added, smiling slowly.

"Oh," she said, disappointed.

He slowed the car, caressed her mouth with the ball of

his thumb, then gently closed her eyes. "Keep them closed until I tell you otherwise."

"Yes, Captain," she said, saluting badly. "Whatever you say, Captain."

"Don't tempt me."

Cat licked her lips, tasted him, and kept her eyes shut.

The car growled through a few more turns, then slowed. Travis pulled into a parking lot next to the bluff, which had been named after Richard Henry Dana.

"Stay put," Travis said. "And keep your eyes closed."

She made a sound like a grumpy cat but didn't open her eyes.

Smiling in anticipation, he got out of the car, came around to her side, and opened the door.

"I can lead you or carry you, little Cat," he said against her ear. "Your choice."

The feel of his lips brushing her earlobe made Cat's breath catch.

"Lead on," she said. "But I should make you carry me and eat your words. At five feet seven inches, I'm hardly little."

Without warning, Travis lifted Cat out of the car and settled her across his chest, carrying her as he had when she'd hurt her foot.

"I was just kidding," she said, laughing. "Let me go."

"Not yet. Never threaten a pirate, sweetheart. It will get you . . . this."

He kissed her slowly, completely, then let her slide down his body until she was standing. He could feel her heartbeat. It was as fast and hungry as his own.

"Remember," Travis said. "Eyes closed."

"It's hard to walk that way."

"I'll help." He took a firm grip on her upper arm, supporting and reassuring her at the same time. "First we walk across the parking lot, then the pier. Ready?"

"A pier? Aren't you tied up with the other boats?"

"No questions."

"But I just—"

Travis silenced Cat by tracing the line of her lips with his thumb. She sighed, kissed his thumb, and allowed herself to be led through the parking lot while he kept up a running commentary on whatever might get in the way.

"Big car to your left, and one backing out on your—wait—okay. Left about three steps, then right. Good. There's a curb, then a ramp going to the pier, a kid riding a skateboard and carrying a surfboard, and—ah, the hell with it."

Ignoring Cat's muffled laughter, Travis picked her up and strode past the obstacles. There was no one out on the end of the pier. He set her on her feet, wrapped her hands over the railing to orient her, and put his hands on her shoulders.

"All right, you can look now. Her name is *Wind Warrior*."

Cat opened her eyes, looked out over the yacht basin, and forgot to breathe. There, beyond the other boats, riding alone at anchor, was the great black bird she had seen flying across the face of the dying sun.

Even with its dark maroon sails furled, the ship was superb. The bold masts and rigging made elegant patterns against the empty sky. The ship's graceful ebony hull rippled with the reflected dance of light on water. Although wholly at rest, the ship was alive, potent, a tangible consummation of wind and wave and one man's extraordinary vision.

Cat turned and looked at Travis as though she had never seen him before. And in one vital way, it was true. She had never before seen T. H. Danvers, designer and builder of the most beautiful ship ever to fly the seas of Earth.

"I'm dreaming," she said. "First you, then that ship." Her words ended in an odd sound that wasn't quite a laugh. "Don't wake me up, Travis, not yet."

She looked over the water again at the ship lying sleek and quiet at anchor. Very quickly she glanced back at Travis, then at the harbor, as though expecting both the ship and the man to vanish before her eyes, leaving her as empty as the sky.

Wind Warrior.

"No wonder you wanted to wait and see my work before you agreed to let me do your book," Cat said.

"I didn't mean—"

She touched his mouth with her fingers, cutting off his words.

"It's all right," she said. "The ability to shape beauty out of nothing is one of the few things I truly respect. I won't belittle your creation with cute, safe pictures. And," she added softly, honestly, "it is a rare, rare pleasure to meet an artist like you, T. H. Danvers."

For a long moment Travis stared down at Cat, drinking in her appreciation and wonder until she thought she would drown in the depths of his sea-colored eyes. Then he gathered her in his arms, holding her as though she was sunrise after a lifetime of night.

"Thank you," he said.

"For not insisting you hire me?"

"No. For seeing the *Wind Warrior* as I do." He smiled wryly. "The first time people see my ship, most of them say, 'Oh, what an unusual boat,' and then they turn away, not really liking what they see."

"You make them see too much," Cat said simply. "You make them see that beauty is fierce, not soft, that it has the power to turn your soul inside out, forcing you to think again about the world and your place in it. Your *Wind Warrior* makes people afraid."

"But not you," Travis said. "You're like me, a wild creature caught in a civilized world." His hands framed her face. "Come away with me," he said, low-voiced, intense. "Avalon. Ensenada. Or farther. Hawaii. Papeete. The Seychelles or Tasmania or the China Sea. Anywhere in the world the wind blows, and it blows everywhere, Cat. *Come with me.*''

Wanderlust was a strike of lightning that shook her to her soul, bringing memories like thunder in its wake. The scent and feel and sound of the sea, the long reaches where only a ship moved beneath the silent dance of stars. No one to worry about, no obligations to meet. Free.

Free to photograph the fierce images that haunted her without being concerned about their commercial appeal.

Free from worries about the Big Check and all the little ones.

Free to be a woman with her man.

Free as a great black bird skimming a sunset sea.

Free.

Yet nothing was free, not really. Cat had known that since she dove over the railing of her husband's ship. She couldn't run out on the twins, who depended on her for their education. Nor could she abandon her mother, a woman never made for the hardships of independence.

''I can't,'' Cat said, her voice raw with longing and regret.

Anger drew Travis's mouth into a harsh line. His hands tightened around her face. Abruptly he released her and turned away.

''Travis?'' she said, putting her hand on his arm.

He spun back toward her. For an instant Cat saw again the leashed violence that had made Ashcroft turn as white as his hair.

Travis saw her expression and stopped as though she had struck him.

''I'm sorry,'' he said, holding out his hand to her. ''I didn't realize how much I wanted to sail away with you until you said no.'' He tried to smile. ''Don't say no to me, Cat.'' Then, quickly, ''If you can't say yes, don't say anything. Not yet.''

She took the hand he held out to her.

"January," she said huskily. "By January I'll have paid all my debts that matter. Then I'll sail to the ends of the earth with you. "

His expression changed again. Cat couldn't read his emotions, but she could sense . . . something.

And then she knew.

"You'll be gone by then, won't you?" she whispered.

"Cat," Travis said softly.

He moved to hold her, but she let go of his hand and stepped away from his arms with a sad, understanding smile that was worse than tears or anger would have been.

Then Cat looked away to the ship he had built. She couldn't bear to look at Travis. Not yet. Not until she stopped feeling as though the earth had been cut away beneath her feet.

"I'd like to go aboard the *Wind Warrior*," she said carefully. "It's hard to judge camera angles from here. Would it be possible to row around the ship?"

There was a long silence behind Cat. She felt the pressure of Travis's will reaching out to her, demanding that she turn back to his arms. He was a wealthy, ruthless brigand who wasn't used to hearing the word *no*.

And she was an independent cat accustomed to going her own way.

"Is that really how you want it?" Travis asked finally.

Cat turned to face him with a determination that equaled his.

"It's the way it has to be." Her voice had no emotions, certainly not sadness or regret. "I can't leave until January and you'll be long gone by then. Wanting doesn't have a damned thing to do with it."

"But—"

"I don't expect you to understand," she interrupted.

"Why?"

"You're rich," Cat said simply. "You've done whatever

you wanted whenever you wanted to. You've forgotten that for most people, wanting and getting are rarely the same thing.''

''You judge me very easily,'' Travis said. His voice was remote, his eyes narrowed.

''I know what it's like to be rich.''

Surprise widened his eyes, revealing their unique color.

Cat smiled thinly. ''I was born rich, and I married richer. Along the way I learned that there really are some things money can't buy.''

''Such as?''

''Self-respect. That shouldn't surprise you. If money automatically bought self-respect, you never would have designed your ship.''

He looked beyond Cat to the *Wind Warrior* riding at anchor in the tranquil water. A man was walking along the deck toward the bow to check the anchor cable.

Without warning Travis covered Cat's ears with his palms and whistled through his teeth. The shrill, ascending sound carried like a siren over the water.

The man on the *Wind Warrior*'s stern straightened and shielded his eyes against the glare of the sun. When he saw two people standing on the pier, he returned the questing whistle.

Travis waved, covered Cat's ears again, and whistled, two short and one long. The man whistled once, waved, and vanished behind a mast.

Cat looked at Travis, her clear gray eyes silently asking what was going on.

''In a few minutes Diego will bring the Zodiac around to the pier,'' Travis explained after he took his hands off her ears.

Then, as though there had been no interruption, he picked up the conversation where he had left it.

''You're right about me and ship designing and self-respect," he said. "I was born rich, like you, and like you, I turned my back on it."

"You did?"

He smiled ruefully at the surprise in her voice. "When I was sixteen I left home to work on international freighters. It was very different from what I'd known before. The men, the women, the fights."

"Fights?" Cat asked, startled.

"Yeah. I grew up fast. One of the things I learned was how much I missed true sailing, wind and sails and the sea. I didn't have to be without sailing—I knew I could go back to the life my father had made for me, the kind of life that had sailboats as toys."

"Are you the oldest son?"

"The only child, boy or girl. Dad was waiting for me to grow up, to accept the responsibilities of my family name. Once I'd done that, I could afford a sailing ship again. Hell, I could afford a hundred of them. A thousand."

Travis looked beyond Cat for a moment, his blue-green eyes absorbing the beauty of the *Wind Warrior*.

"But the thought of sitting on the boards of sixteen corporations and being listed on thirty select committees left me cold," he said. "I didn't want to juggle money and people. The only power I hungered for was the pull of a clean sailing ship in a good wind."

Cat followed Travis's glance out to the *Wind Warrior*. She recognized the hunger in him for the untouchable, the unknowable, a world without boundaries. It was the same hunger, the same need, that she answered with her photography.

"Since I couldn't afford to buy a sailing ship," Travis said, "and was damned if I'd give up my freedom to own one, I decided to build a ship of my own."

"Just like that? Build a ship?"

"Not quite. I apprenticed myself to an English shipbuilder. He was a big, hard old man who knew more about ships and the sea than he did about anything else. Especially people. His granddaughter became my wife, but that was later.''

Cat looked at Travis's distant, hooded eyes and didn't say a word. She was afraid that any interruption would stop him from speaking at all. It was clear that he hated talking about his ex-wife as much as she hated talking about Billy.

''The day I finished my first ship, my father died,'' Travis said neutrally. ''I couldn't believe how much it hurt. I'd had some childish dream about sailing my ship alone across the Atlantic, tying up at his dock, and saying, 'See, you aren't the only one in the world who can do something special. There's more to me than my family name and money.' But Dad was dead and couldn't hear me, and in any case I was no longer a child.''

Cat's eyelids flickered. She reached toward Travis, but he didn't see the small gesture.

''I sold my ship and flew home because I'd grown up enough to know that I couldn't turn my back on my family when they needed me,'' Travis said. ''Tina—the old man's granddaughter—followed me. Later I figured out that it was my money she wanted. Just after I left England, she found out that I was the son and heir of *the* Thomas Danvers. She was determined to marry me.'' He shrugged. ''She did, for a time.''

Cat bit her lip against the need to comfort Travis. She knew he wouldn't want it. All he wanted was to get the bitter story told.

''I was determined to fill my father's boots,'' Travis said. ''In time, I did. The family fortune doubled under my management, then doubled again. Yet I dreamed of the sea and a great black ship. If all my money couldn't buy me that, what the hell good was it? So I found men and women I trusted, and trained them to run the companies. Then I built my ship and stepped into the wind.''

Cat looked from Travis to the great ship with its wings

folded calmly, floating on quiet blue water. Before she could speak, he did.

"What happened between you and money, Cat? Why do you look so frightened every time you realize I'm rich?"

She closed her eyes. Travis was a warm presence from her shoulders to her heels. Her memories were ice chilling her all the way to her soul.

She didn't want to put the brutal past into words, yet she knew she should. She owed it to herself.

And to Travis.

TEN

"You want to know what happened with me and money?" Cat smiled with bleak humor. "I can give it to you in one word. Billy."

Travis waited. Beneath her self-control he sensed the savage tides of old rage and bitterness.

"When I left Billy he was one of the hundred richest men in the world. *Rich*." Cat's upper lip curled. "So rich he kept score with people instead of balance sheets."

"What did he do to you?" Though Travis's voice was soft, there was the hardness of demand just beneath his drawl.

"It wasn't the love match of the century," Cat said, not answering his question immediately. "I wanted the security of a husband, and Billy wanted enough sons to make him feel like a man."

"Are there that many sons in the world?" Travis asked sardonically.

"No. But I didn't know it then. Anyway, as long as I was Billy's wife, the question was academic. When he found out I was the reason we weren't having kids, he . . ." Cat took a broken breath. "He was furious. Since I couldn't have babies, he demanded to know how I would *earn my keep*. I wasn't educated, my mother had spent all the money, and I was sterile. What damn good was I to a man?"

141

Travis's eyelids flinched. He knew now why Cat was so touchy about being independent. And about being sterile.

"He kept flicking that lab report across my face," she said, her eyes unfocused. *"Sterile. Can't earn your keep. Sterile. No damn good."*

Strong arms came around Cat, wrapping her in warmth, pulling her close. Slowly her stiff body softened, accepting the comfort Travis silently gave.

"The worst of it was that I believed him. When he . . ." Cat's voice thinned until it broke.

"You don't have to tell me any more," Travis said.

His voice was as tight as hers, as tight as the arms holding her, wanting to protect her from everything, especially her own memories.

"I want to tell you," she whispered. "I have to. I've never told anyone what really happened, not even Harrington, but I have to tell you. I want you to understand why I can't just put my hand in yours and step into the wind with you for a week or a month."

Cat took a breath as though preparing to dive into cold water, but she didn't move away from Travis. His warmth made it possible for her to face the past without flinching.

"Like I said, it wasn't much of a marriage to begin with. It's not that I minded Billy's other women." Cat's lips twisted down. "Sex with him wasn't so special that I wanted to keep it all to myself."

"You're lucky he didn't bring home something lethal."

"He used condoms when he was screwing around. Not for my protection, of course, or even for his own, but for the son I was going to conceive. He didn't want to infect his dynasty with anything that antibiotics couldn't cure."

Travis said nothing. He knew a few people like Billy, slow learners who hadn't figured out that promiscuity wasn't worth the price no matter how many condoms you wore. Sooner or later, everyone paid the piper.

"The night he found out I was sterile . . ." Cat swallowed and fought to keep her voice level. "That night Billy brought his latest bar girl on board. I was asleep. When I woke up, he was shoving her into bed with me."

Travis's breath came in sharply.

"When I tried to get out of bed, Billy tore off my night-gown and told me that since I was a dead loss as a wife, I could *earn my keep* as a whore."

"Cat, don't," he said in a low voice. "I understand now. I'm sorry."

But she kept talking, driven by the need for Travis to understand all of it, the rage and the shame.

"When I tried to get away, Billy started slapping me, shouting at me that tonight he was going to teach me how to fuck. When I was good enough, he would take me to meet some drinking buddies on the boat anchored next to ours. He couldn't wait to watch them take me back to front."

The muscles in Travis's arms were like steel, but Cat didn't notice his fierce tension. She was held in the poisonous coil of memories that still sickened her.

"I don't remember exactly what happened after that," she said hoarsely. "I think I went crazy. Somehow I grabbed the glass shield from a hurricane lamp. It was cold and smooth. I hit him as hard as I could in the face."

"I hope you killed the son of a bitch."

Cat laughed a little wildly. "No such luck. There was glass and blood everywhere and that drunken slut was screaming with laughter and Billy was cursing and kicking me."

Travis stroked Cat's hair, trying to call her out of the past, but she couldn't leave it behind yet. She still had to make him understand why she couldn't run off with him on a moment's notice, even though she wanted to so much that the thought made her weak with yearning.

"Somehow I got away from him," Cat said. "There were boats anchored nearby, but they were full of Billy's friends. Out in the dark I saw a light from a small boat anchored farther off out to sea, away from the noisy parties. There wasn't time to lower the dinghy, so I just dove over the rail and started swimming toward that boat.''

"Was Billy too drunk to lower the dinghy and follow you?''

"No, but he was looking for me in the wrong place. He thought I'd swim toward shore. I didn't. I swam straight out to midnight. It was the only place I would be out of Billy's reach.''

Travis whispered Cat's name and gathered her even closer. She shuddered and put her forehead against his chest for a few moments. Then she straightened and kept talking.

"It turned out that the boat I was heading for wasn't small after all,'' she said. "It was a huge power cruiser strung with lights. And it was a long way off. A long, long way. I thought I was going to drown before I reached it. But I didn't. I'm a good swimmer.''

Distantly Cat realized she was trembling all over. She drew a strained breath and laughed oddly. "I'll never forget the look on Rodney's face when he first saw me.''

"Harrington?'' Travis asked, surprised.

"It was his cruiser I swam to. Poor guy. He was entertaining a lady when I came up the sea ladder wearing nothing but salt water and some bruises.''

Travis wished he could laugh as Cat was laughing, but he couldn't. A cold rage was choking him.

I thought I was going to drown.

He held Cat as he had the first night, rocking slowly, comforting her without words.

After a time she continued her story. Her voice was steady now, almost calm. The worst of the memories were behind her, bitter words spoken aloud, poison draining away into the past where it belonged.

And Travis was warming her with his own life, holding her as though he would never let her go.

"I've always wondered how Rodney explained me to his lady," Cat said.

"He probably didn't have to explain. Women of all kinds follow Rod like puppies."

"It's his eyes. He looks for all the world like a lonely teddy bear some child forgot to put away."

"Don't be taken in by those sad brown eyes," Travis retorted. "Rodney Harrington is about as shrewd as they come."

"He's also very kind. He was so calm, as though strange naked women crawled up his sea ladder five times a night. He wrapped me in a blanket and fed me hot soup. As soon as he figured out what had happened to me, he ordered his crew to weigh anchor for California."

"I'm surprised he didn't find Billy and beat the hell out of him," Travis muttered.

"I begged him not to. All I wanted to do was get as far away from Billy as I could." Cat let out a long, long breath and continued in an even tone. "Harrington's lady was about my size and very sympathetic. I shared her clothes. She even taught me how to cook at sea. When we docked in Acapulco I sold my wedding rings to buy a Mexican divorce. Then I went back on board the yacht and worked my way to California as a cook."

"A good one, if the dinner you fixed me was any measure," Travis said, kissing her hair gently.

"I wasn't good at first," Cat said, smiling even though her lips still trembled with the fading echoes of the past. "I learned a lot that trip. Some of the other passengers asked me to take a picture of them with their Polaroid. They showed me what to do, I did it, and when I saw the image condensing out of nothing on that little piece of cardboard, the hair on my neck lifted. I knew I had found something miraculous."

"Photography?"

"Yes" She looked up at Travis intently, wanting him to

understand. "Putting a camera in my hands was like putting a fish in water. I *earned my keep* cooking, saved until I could buy my own camera, and then worked my tail off until Harrington insisted that I let him represent me."

"So that's how he became your agent," Travis said. "I always wondered."

"I'm good at what I do," Cat said, her voice smooth and certain. "I'm a dead loss in the baby department, but no man can say I don't *earn my keep* as a photographer."

A sound came over the water before Travis could speak, a noise like a chain saw. A Zodiac skimmed the surface of the marina toward them. When the inflatable boat reached the pier, the engine cut off suddenly. The black boat coasted smoothly to the stairs beneath the pier.

In the sudden silence, Travis's words sounded harsh, almost brutal. "You didn't keep Billy's last name."

It was a statement, not a question, but Cat answered anyway.

"No, I didn't keep anything of his. Not his name, not his rings, not one dime of his damned money. Nothing but my freedom and a few bruises."

"What is Billy's last name?"

Her head snapped up to look at Travis. His voice belonged to a stranger. His expression was distant, savage.

Yet his arms were very gentle around her.

"Nelson. Why?"

"I sail everywhere," Travis said, bending down to take Cat's lips. "Someday I'll meet him. I promise you."

She was too surprised to say anything. Nor would she have known what to say if she could speak. Travis's combination of leashed violence and tender protectiveness was new to her. It left her feeling confused, off-balance, and . . . safe.

"Come on," Travis said as though nothing had happened. "Diego is waiting for us."

He led her down the stairs to the water and handed her into the Zodiac.

"This is Diego," Travis said, gesturing toward the compact, dark-haired man at the stern of the little boat. "Diego, meet Catherine Cochran. If you behave yourself, she just might let you call her Cathy."

Cat smiled and held out her hand. Instead of shaking it as she had expected, Diego kissed her fingers with Old World grace.

"I always behave," Diego said in a clear tenor voice, "and most especially I behave for beautiful women." He smiled, transforming his looks. He had a Mediterranean beauty in his face that only smiling revealed. "And you are very beautiful, señorita. *Muy, muy hermosa,* like a rose in winter."

"*Gracias,* Diego," Cat said, wishing her Spanish was up to returning the compliment. The corner of her mouth curled in a slight smile. "Why is it that I look at you and see a string of broken hearts circling the world?"

Diego's dark eyes lit with laughter. He looked over to Travis and nodded approval.

Travis put his hand on the small of Cat's back in an unconsciously possessive gesture that Diego noted and instantly understood.

"You see broken hearts," Travis drawled, leaning down to put his lips on Cat's auburn hair, "because Diego is a heartbreaker. If you listen carefully, you can hear women crying, too."

Cat cocked her head, pretending to listen but actually enjoying the play of light in Travis's hair. When she spoke it was without thinking, for most of her mind was framing a photo.

"They don't cry for you, do they?" she asked Travis in a low voice. "Tears come from hope, and when you go you leave nothing behind, not even the hope that you'll return. No hope, no tears."

The expression on Travis's face changed, anger and regret and an emotion that could have been pain. Then there was nothing at all but distance and restraint.

Cat realized what she had said and tried to make a joke of it. "Ah, my secret is out. Your great-grandfather might have been a pirate, Travis, but I come from a long line of Scots witches. Second sight and third as well." She winked at Diego. "So be on your best behavior, *hombres,* or I'll turn you into toads and gingerbread cookies."

Diego smiled brilliantly, ignoring the grim lines of his captain's face. "I am warned, señorita. Only the best for you." He turned his attention to the engine.

"Wait," Travis said.

Diego froze, his hand on the starter.

Cat looked at Travis and wondered if he had changed his mind about taking her aboard his ship. She wouldn't particularly blame him. What she had said about him was thoughtless, nearly cruel.

The fact that it was also true made it worse, not better.

"Your cameras," Travis said.

"What?" she asked, off-balance.

"Your cameras are locked in the trunk of my car."

"I know. They'll be safe there, won't they?"

"Cat," he said patiently, "don't you want to take pictures of my ship? That's why we're here, isn't it?"

"If it makes you feel better, I'll get my cameras. But I'll just throw away whatever I take today."

"Why?" Travis asked, startled.

She looked beyond him to the elegant, powerful ship floating at rest on the water. "Something like the *Wind Warrior* can't be taken by storm. I'll need time to absorb her presence, her lines, her silence." Cat's mouth turned down in a self-mocking line. "I know it sounds crazy, but . . ." She shrugged. "That's the way I work."

"Seduction rather than force?" Travis suggested softly, his expression no longer grim.

"I never thought of it that way, but yes."

His finger followed the line of her eyebrows. "Whatever you say, my Scots witch. Diego, take us to the ship."

Smiling to himself, Diego started up the engine.

Cat settled into place and concentrated on the ebony shape that loomed larger with each second. The ship was even more beautiful up close. The feeling of power and endurance and grace was almost overwhelming.

How will I ever capture that on film? Cat asked herself silently.

She followed Travis aboard, barely hearing as he described the *Wind Warrior*'s dimensions and attributes. She was lost in the feel of the ship, the glow of polished brass and new paint, dark rigging and black masts, the muscular bulge of sails furled along the booms. Traditionally ships were referred to as "her," but there was a masculine potency to *Wind Warrior* that reminded Cat of the man who walked beside her.

". . . fathoms," Travis concluded.

"Mmm," Cat said.

It was her all-purpose answer when she didn't want to be distracted. At the moment she was fascinated by the subtle, clean sweep of the railing and wondering which lens would best capture its line.

Travis stopped, took Cat's chin in his hand, and forced her to look at him instead of the ship.

"You haven't heard a single thing I've said, have you?" he accused.

Cat blinked, called out of her private thoughts about how to capture on film the appearance and reality of the ship called *Wind Warrior*.

"Sure I have," she said. "Two masts, schooner-rigged, thirty meters long at the waterline."

He smiled and shook his head in mock despair.

"Forty meters?" she hedged.

"Closer, but no prize. I'm glad you aren't trying to bring my ship alongside a dock."

Cat gave him a guilty smile. "You're right. I was thinking of . . . images. But I'm not going to photograph the *Wind Warrior*'s exact dimensions or her bilge or her precise speed in a forty-knot wind with following seas and full sail, so what's the point of remembering all that?"

"What are you going to photograph?"

A man's soul.

But Cat knew she shouldn't say that aloud. She had already said more than her share of foolish things to Travis. So she simply shook her head and said, "You'll see."

Travis led her below, saying very little about the ship's construction and inner dimensions.

It was just as well. Cat wasn't listening again. She was running her fingers over hardwoods from every part of the world, rare woods inlaid and polished to make a table or frame a door, the lives and histories of individual trees laid out grain by grain in swirling patterns.

T. H. Danvers designed and built state-of-the-art racing hulls that were poured and formed and polished to exact computer specifications . . . but his cabin was filled with the traditional, exquisite textures of wood and brass. The sheets on his oversized bunk were made of smooth linen. An antique beveled mirror was set like a diamond in the hull, and the overhead light shone through a carved crystal globe.

Cat looked around the room again, seeing with a photographer's eye, missing nothing. At some wordless level she realized that there was no contradiction between the metal masts and the textured richness of the cabin. Both were the culmination of long traditions, both were essentially sensual, both were powerful rather than meek in their beauty. And besides, where was it written that an engineer couldn't be a pirate too?

Smiling to herself, Cat watched the play of light through carved crystal.

"Talk about the cat that licked up all the cream . . ." Travis said in a low voice. He put his hand behind her head, burying his fingers in the auburn hair that fell loosely down her back. "Share some with me."

Cat's lips parted even as she felt long, strong fingers kneading her scalp. Warmth uncurled along her nerves, the heat that always came when Travis looked at her with blue-green fire in his eyes.

Hunger leaped inside Travis when she sighed and gave herself to his kiss. His hands moved over her almost roughly, molding her to the hard lines of his body as though he wanted to take her into his very bones.

It was a long time before Travis lifted his mouth from Cat's. He started to say something, but the temptation of her flushed lips was too great. He groaned deep in his throat and kissed her again, not stopping until her hips moved against him and her eyes were nearly black with passion.

Pushing her away was like tearing off his own skin, but he had to do it. There wasn't enough privacy for what he wanted so much his hands were shaking.

"Go back up on deck," he said huskily.

"Why?" Cat asked, her voice as dazed as her eyes.

"If you don't, I'll take off your clothes and taste every bit of you until you're hot and wet and crying for me with every breath you take."

Hunger shook Cat, a need to equal his.

Travis saw it. The certainty of her welcome was a fire in his veins.

"The hell with it," he muttered, reaching blindly behind him for the open door. "I'll just have to keep my head enough to muffle your screams."

But before he could find the door, Diego was calling to him.

"Captain? Are you still belowdeck?"

The sound of footsteps descending the ladder was very distinct. Travis swore softly and spun around with his back to Cat. His body blocked the doorway, concealing her flushed face and misty, hungry eyes from Diego.

"What is it?" Travis asked curtly.

Diego stopped just outside the open cabin door and looked at Travis a bit warily. "Some official wants to know how much longer we'll be anchored here."

"Does it matter?"

Diego grinned. "Not to me. I think the man just wants a guided tour of the *Wind Warrior*."

"So give it to him."

"When?"

"For the love of God," Travis snarled. "Now, Diego! Give it to him right now!"

"*Sí*, Captain."

Diego turned smartly and headed for the stairs, but not before Travis saw his first mate's knowing smile. Travis swore and looked ruefully at Cat.

"The things you do to me, Ms. Cochran, sweet Cat, Scots witch, woman. That most of all. Woman." Then, softly, "Go topside, woman. I'll be along as soon as my pants fit again."

Cat looked and wanted nothing more than to feel Travis naked between her hands, her legs, inside her. With a ragged sound she slipped by him to the door, watching him with eyes that were very dark. She was careful not to touch him.

She didn't trust herself to stop with just one touch.

ELEVEN

CAT STEPPED out of Travis's car and turned to look back at him. "Are you sure you won't come in?"

"Very sure. I don't trust myself," he said with a wry smile. "Diego almost got a real eyeful back on the ship."

"Diego isn't here."

"The big circles under your eyes are."

"Comes with the territory called self-employment."

Travis grunted. "It's at least three hours before we have to meet Ashcroft. Sleep for two hours and—"

"Alone?" she interrupted.

"If I come in with you, it won't be to watch you sleep."

She smiled slowly. "Promise?"

He laughed despite the hunger pulsing through him each time he thought of pushing into her velvet heat. And he thought of it often, like a teenager who had just discovered sex.

"Take a nap, Cat. I've got plans for keeping you awake later tonight. And that's a promise. I'll pick you up in two hours for dinner. Until then, I've got some work to do on the ship."

Cat stood in her driveway until the growl of the car's engine dissolved into the rhythmic, powerful sound of the surf breaking below her house. Then she sighed and turned toward the house.

As soon as Travis was out of sight, she realized that he

was right. She was tired to the soles of her feet. Ignoring
the fatigue that had become as much a part of her as her
gray eyes, she went into her house and walked right past
her bedroom.

If she hurried, she could squeeze in an hour or two of
sorting slides and still catch a little nap before dinner.

I've got plans for keeping you awake later tonight.

Heat snaked through Cat as she remembered the look in
Travis's eyes. She couldn't wait to find out precisely how
he planned on keeping her awake. And she had a few ideas
of her own for keeping him awake, things she had heard
about but never wanted to try. Until Travis.

Smiling, she hurried down the stairs to her office on the
lower floor of the house, hit the replay button on the answering machine, and began laying out slides on the light
table while she listened. There was only one message that
mattered. Ashcroft had called off the sunset shoot tonight.

"Good," Cat muttered, bending over the light table.
"Travis and I can have a peaceful dinner and not have to
rush out to meet the platinum blond toad."

Less than ten minutes went by before she heard a knock
on the outside door, one of two in the house that opened
onto the beach stairway. The other was in the kitchen upstairs, next to her bedroom.

"Cathy?" called a young voice. "You home?"

"Sure am. The door's open."

An instant later a boy's head appeared. He gave her a
brilliant smile. "Hello."

"Hi," she said, smiling back. "Does your mother know
you're here?"

Jason hesitated. "Uh . . ."

Electric blue eyes peered out at her from beneath a fringe
of heavy black lashes. Black hair fell in soft, unruly curls
over his forehead. His skin was tanned, making his lips
appear quite pink in contrast. He was saved from mere pret-

tiness by the unusual maturity of his expression and the intelligence that gave depth to his eyes.

Looking at the boy, Cat knew she wasn't going to get any work done for a while. She didn't really mind. She loved Jason as much as she would have loved her own child. Having her love returned with Jason's own brand of headlong enthusiasm had softened the bleak edges of knowing that she was sterile.

Pushing away from the light table, Cat held out her arms to Jason.

Grinning, the boy ran to her, gave her a big hug, and looked up earnestly at her. "The twins were hollering and Mommy was trying to change both of them at once and Daddy's coming home late and I spilled my juice and—"

"You sneaked out the back way," Cat finished.

He nodded a bit sheepishly.

"That's okay, tiger. We all have days like that."

She ruffled his hair and went to her desk. As she reached for the phone, she hesitated. Travis had said something this morning about Jason being sick.

"Are you feeling okay?" Cat asked, looking intently at him.

"Sure."

"No fever?"

"Nah," Jason said with a grand gesture. "Only babies get fevers."

"Baloney."

"Sliced and diced?" he asked eagerly.

Cat laughed and shook her head. Sliced and diced baloney was Jason's favorite "madword."

"Come here," she said.

He trotted over to her. She bent down and put her cheek against his forehead. Jason didn't feel hot, nor did he look ill.

"Okay," she said. "We'll see what your mother says."

She dialed Jason's mother and waited for the six rings it

usually took Sharon to get to the phone. A breathless voice finally answered.

"Sharon? Cathy."

"Oh Lord. Jason?"

"Right. Bedtime?"

"You're sure?" Sharon asked anxiously.

"I'm sure."

Smiling, Cat hung up. She and Sharon had exchanged so many calls on the subject of Jason that they had it down to a code.

The small boy whooped and all but danced in place. "Can we go shell-hunting, Cathy, huh? Can we, huh?"

"I'll think about it."

Moving quickly, she stacked and put away the slides she had been sorting. The white plastic surface she was working on glowed softly, illuminating the slides from below. Not only did the light table make sorting slides easier, it was much better for the delicate color emulsion than running the slides through a hot projector.

Someday Cat wouldn't need to worry about such things. She would take her pictures electronically and store them the same way. But there was a lot of money standing between her and that kind of high-tech freedom.

"What do you think? We gonna get shells?" Jason asked, watching Cat with big blue eyes.

"First we'll do some pictures like we agreed on, okay?" Cat smiled down at him. "It was nice of your mom to dress you in a red T-shirt, clean jeans, and red sneakers."

He smiled proudly. "Not Mommy. Me. I remembered you said red was good for pictures."

"It's the best," Cat said, hugging Jason. "Like you. You're very smart to remember."

Jason wound his arms around her and snuggled in tight. "Where are we going this time?"

"Bluebird Park. Then Main Beach for a while. Then back here for shells."

"Oh, boy! Shells!"

Cat smiled. At least she wouldn't be spending another futile sunset with Ashcroft.

Which reminded her. She should leave a message for Travis.

"But first I have to make a fast call," she told Jason.

She dialed the number Travis had told her was his cousin's. Nothing answered, not even a machine.

"We'll just have to do it the old-fashioned way," Cat said.

Jason was too busy prowling around a small forest of camera tripods and lighting equipment to answer. Prowling, but not touching. He knew better. His grown-up friend was very firm about that. If he wanted to be in her office, he couldn't touch anything that she didn't hand to him.

Cat wrote Travis a quick note, stuffed it in an envelope, and put his name in block letters on the outside. As she closed the front door behind herself and Jason, she wedged in the envelope. When Travis came to pick her up for dinner he couldn't miss it.

Jason watched impatiently. "Who's that for?"

"Travis."

"Who's he?"

"A friend of mine. He might meet us later. You'll like him."

The little boy's face settled into tight, stubborn lines. "Won't."

There was a world of loneliness and jealousy in that single word. Remembering her own feelings when her newborn twin siblings had taken two hundred percent of her mother's attention, Cat knelt in front of Jason.

"Yeah," she agreed. "You probably won't like Travis. Most people don't like pirates."

"He's a pirate?" Jason asked, interested despite himself. "A really for sure pirate?"

"Yup."

"How do you know?"

"He sails a black ship," Cat said, standing again.

"A really for sure pirate!" Jason crowed, spinning in happy circles. "And I get to meet him! Boy, that's something baby twins can't do!"

"Sure is. Only big kids can play with pirates."

"Yippee!" Suddenly Jason stopped spinning and looked at Cat with hope in his eyes. "Does your pirate steal kids? I mean really *little* kids, like babies?"

"Um," she said, swallowing her laughter. "I don't think so, but we can ask him. Come on, tiger. We're wasting sunlight."

Hand in hand, Jason and Cat headed for her car. He didn't let go of her hand even when she bent to raise the heavy garage door. He simply ducked beneath the door as it went up.

"Do I have to wear a seat belt?" he asked plaintively.

"Only if you want to go with me."

He sighed and allowed himself to be strapped in. She fastened her own belt and backed her Toyota up the steep driveway to the street.

As Cat wove through summer traffic, she planned her first shot for the "A Good Place to Raise Kids" campaign while Jason chattered about a beautiful playground, Disneyland and Magic Mountain and Sea World rolled into one, a place where good kids got to go, a place where no one under seven was allowed. . . .

By the time Cat got Jason back to the beach in front of her house, the sun was low in the sky. Santa Ana winds had blown through the day, bringing the dry warmth of the Mojave Desert to Laguna Beach, which had been flirting with tropical storms all summer. This summer El Niño, with its sultry heat, violent storms, and huge waves, had come with a vengeance.

With the "real" photography over, Jason was stripped

down to jeans and nothing else. He prowled the tide pools like a small black panther, pawing the sun-warmed water and then emerging triumphantly with a bit of wildlife wriggling on his palm.

For her own pleasure, Cat caught it all with her camera—Jason's intensity and intelligence, his curiosity and laughter, his endless delight in the scent and sound and feel of the world around him. She forgot how tired she was, forgot her unspoken promise to Travis that she would take a nap before dinner, forgot everything. The camera was her only reality, a mystical window that allowed her to see the universe condensed into a child's smile.

Jason brought her shell after shell, piling them at her feet, pale offerings against the radiance of his smile. She took photos until the rich light was gone. When it was no longer possible to catch all the nuances of his expression, she put away her cameras, lifted the sandy, delighted boy in her arms, and hugged him.

"What a good trooper," Cat said. "You've earned yourself a hamburger, fries, *and* a milkshake."

"A milkshake, too?" Jason asked, throwing sandy arms around her neck. "Chocolate?"

"Is there another kind?"

She shifted the boy's weight in her arms, trying to find a more comfortable position. No matter what she did, her back and shoulders stilled burned fiercely. Wishing she wasn't so close to the ragged end of her physical reserves, she set Jason back on his feet in the sand.

"If you gain another ounce, I'll need a crane to lift you," she said, groaning dramatically.

"That's because I'm seven, " Jason said, proud to be so big. Then he sighed. "Mom says I'm a little man now."

Kneeling, Cat smoothed back the boy's black curls, revealing the wistful depths of his blue eyes. Though he liked the idea of being grown-up, he wasn't quite ready to let go of being his mother's baby. But the arrival of the twins didn't leave any choice.

Cat understood the paradox of Jason's eagerness to grow up and his hurt at no longer being a baby. She had felt the same way at his age, and for the same reason. Eventually she had come to love her own twin siblings, but not right away. Not for several years.

"Tell you what," she said, dropping a kiss on Jason's short nose, "you can be a little man for your mother and a little boy for me. Deal?"

"Deal." His smile faded into a serious look. He asked hesitantly, "Does your pirate like chocolate milkshakes?"

Cat blinked. She was used to the unexpected turns of Jason's conversations, but this one was more off-the-wall than most. "My pirate?"

"He looks like a pirate." Jason stared over Cat's shoulder. "Do you have a black ship?"

"That boy knows a pirate when he sees one," drawled a deep voice behind Cat's back.

She turned her head so quickly she almost hit Jason with her flying French braid. "Travis!"

The delight in her voice was obvious. She didn't care. It seemed like a very long time since she had seen him, days instead of hours.

"Do you like chocolate milkshakes?" she asked him.

Travis sank to his knees next to Cat. Even kneeling, he towered over Jason.

"I love them," Travis said. He held his hand out to Jason. "I'm Travis. Are you the boy who gave Cat all those nifty shells?"

"Yeah." Jason shook hands in a manner his mother would have approved, little man to big. "Cathy's too busy taking pictures to find shells, so I do it for her."

"It's a shame that someone can't sleep for her." Travis gave Cat a sideways look. "I thought you were going to take a nap."

"Ashcroft canceled, Jason appeared, the light was good." She smiled and shrugged. "No nap, but lots of fine shots."

Travis seemed on the point of saying something, then looked at Jason's eager face and changed his mind.

"Did I hear dinner mentioned?" Travis asked.

She smiled apologetically, hoping Travis wouldn't mind including a lonely boy in their dinner plans.

"Jason takes his modeling fees in food," she explained.

"Um," Travis said, "that means there will be a third for dinner?"

Cat touched his arm in silent appeal that he not spoil Jason's pleasure. "There's always room for one more."

The hard lines of Travis's face softened into a gentle smile. "As long as that one is Jason, there's room. I'll call the restaurant and change the reservations."

"Just cancel them," she said quickly, thinking of last night's expensive dinner. "Jason's favorite scarf-and-barf is only a few blocks away."

Travis grimaced, looked at the boy's eager expression, and gave in. "I hope the food isn't as bad as the description."

"It isn't," Cat assured Travis with a smile. "It's worse."

Naked, relaxed, warm to her core, Cat lounged chin-deep in the gently steaming water and tried to stay awake. She clenched her jaws against a yawn but didn't fool Travis. No matter how careful she tried to be, his eyes measured her tiredness with unflinching precision.

"Sharon was very grateful to you for getting Jason out of her hair for an evening," Travis said.

"She has her hands full and then some. Twin babies are bad enough, but her husband is on the fast track at his accounting firm, so he's doing eighty-hour weeks. A promotion—and a move, naturally—are in the air. Sharon is going nuts. Not to mention Jason. He was the properly spoiled only child of older parents, and then wham! He's got two screaming competitors."

"Do you take Jason under your wing a lot?"

"Sure. He's a wonderful kid, bright and full of energy and mischief. I would have liked . . ." Cat's voice died before she could put the painful truth into words. She would have liked to have a child like Jason. "Anyway, he and I do just fine together."

"I could see that. He didn't want to share you."

"He got over it when you bought him an extra order of fries. Not many boys have a real for sure pirate at their beck and call."

Travis laughed. "He's a crafty one. When we went to the rest room, he asked me if I kidnapped babies."

Cat yawned. "He's got two in mind. His competition."

"I picked up on that," Travis said dryly. "It was as obvious as the fact that you're falling asleep."

"I'm just relaxed."

"Is that what you call it?"

Travis turned Cat so that she faced away from him. Strong fingers rubbed her shoulders and back, easing muscles knotted by balancing camera equipment and crouching in odd positions for hour after hour. She relaxed against his strength, letting herself drift. Inevitably, she yawned again.

"Bedtime for you," he said.

"It's not even nine."

"So? You're yawning."

"I yawn every night."

"Try sleeping."

"I do. Midnight to five. Or four. Depends."

His hands stopped. "That's all?"

Cat's only answer was swallowed by a yawn.

"If you weren't here with me," Travis said neutrally, "what would you be doing?"

"Sorting slides. Duplicating slides. Mailing slides to photo agents. Writing pay-me-or-die letters. Choosing mats and frames for the L.A. showing.'' Abruptly Cat sat up straight. "I've got to choose the rest of the images for Swift and Sons. They were supposed to go in yesterday."

Travis couldn't believe what he was hearing. "Tonight, after a day that began at dawn?"

"Uh-huh," she said absently, thinking about her schedule. "But I don't have to start this minute. Later."

He was glad that her back was turned to him. He had a feeling that his expression would have sent her running. He had never met anyone so obsessed with work.

With money.

Yet not once had she even hinted to Travis that his money would be a welcome relief.

Grimly Travis realized that every moment, every breath, he expected Cat to ask him for money. The fact that she hadn't made him wary . . . and hopeful.

Don't be a moron, he told himself savagely. *She'll get around to asking for money. They always do.*

And if she's too coy, I'll bring it up. This nonsense about just liking to be together has got to stop.

Travis didn't mind helping Cat out with some cash gifts. She certainly needed a break more than any woman he had ever met. But he did mind pretending that their relationship was anything other than what it was—a simple, adult business transaction.

He had learned the hard way that not nailing down all the details was a good way to find yourself fucked without being kissed.

For a time there was only silence and the small groans of pleasure Cat made as Travis soothed the aching muscles of her back.

"When are your days off?" he asked finally.

"No such animals," she said, fighting a yawn and losing.

"No weekends?"

"No. Price of being self-employed."

"Do you always work this hard?"

She shook her head. "You just had the bad luck to meet me during a cash crunch."

Travis's hands went still.

Too late Cat remembered his contempt the first time she had mentioned her money difficulties.

"But that's my problem," she said quickly.

She leaned forward and reached for a towel. His hand closed over her arm.

"It's mine, too, if it keeps you away from me," Travis said.

"So lean on Energistics," Cat retorted, looking at him over her shoulder. "They owe me fifty thousand."

He didn't bother to hide his surprise. "That's a fair chunk of change."

"Yes," she agreed coolly. "I do rather well for myself, all things considered. *I earn my keep.*"

Travis heard the echo of Billy's cruelty and was reminded of what drove Cat. Yet he still wasn't satisfied that the past was motive enough for the price she was paying in the present—no time for anything but work.

"Self-respect is very cold comfort," he said. "It took me years to learn that. Let's see if you're smarter than I was."

As Travis spoke, he turned Cat in his arms. Before she could say anything, his mouth closed over hers in a demand that she knew she should resist. But she couldn't deny him, not when his tongue began to probe her lips and his breath was sweet in her mouth. She sighed and let herself melt into him, enjoying the sensations that came when her breasts rubbed across the wet mat of hair on his chest.

A shudder went through Travis as he felt her nipples harden against him. "Cat, witch, woman, sail with me, just two days, Catalina Island and back. You can spare two days for me, for yourself, for us."

His husky whisper shimmered over Cat's nerves, making her breath stop and then come back in a ragged surge of desire. She wanted the time with Travis as much as he did.

No, she wanted it even more.

She knew that someday very soon he would step aboard his ship and sail over the edge of the world. In-the-Wind Danvers, never ashore more than a few weeks at a time.

"When?" Cat asked simply.

"Tomorrow."

She closed her eyes. Her nails dug into the palms of her hands. "I can't," she whispered. "I . . . can't."

Travis hadn't really expected Cat to pick up and go off with him before a price had been agreed on, but it angered him that she kept pretending she didn't have money in mind at all.

"Can't?" he asked. "You mean you *won't*. All you care about is measuring your self-respect by the amount of money you make." He stood and grabbed a towel. "Well, I sure as hell won't get in your way."

Cat watched Travis with eyes that were too bright. She blinked back exhaustion and frustration and tears.

"That isn't true," she whispered, because a whisper was all she could force past the tightness of her throat.

Saying nothing, Travis climbed out of the tub and began drying himself. He didn't look at her, yet she couldn't look away from him, each muscle and tendon outlined in honey-colored light, water drops sparkling and sliding down his strong body. He was the most beautiful, most powerful thing she had ever known . . . and she would surely lose him.

"Why?" she asked. "Why couldn't I have met you in January, when we might have had a chance to love?"

Then Cat heard her own words and realized what she had said, what she had revealed. Anger finally came to her, driving out exhaustion, giving her strength.

She reached blindly for a towel, stood, and fumbled with the thick cloth, unable to control her fingers long enough to tie a simple knot. She didn't look at Travis again, couldn't, because if she did, she knew she would cry.

She hadn't cried for seven years. She had no intention of starting now. Certainly not over another rich bastard.

Travis watched Cat make a muddle of tying the towel and knew that whatever monetary agreement they would eventually reach, she wasn't ready to be realistic tonight.

And neither was he. Not if it meant watching her walk out on him.

"Cat," he said quietly, "you're so tired that you're coming apart, but you won't even let me hold you together."

She put her hands over her ears, not wanting to hear Travis's words melting her anger, his concern making her want to run to him, trust his strength, love him.

"No, oh God, *no,*" she said in a strained voice. "Not that. Not now!"

"Not what? Cat, what's wrong?"

She looked at Travis wildly, then put her face in her hands and looked at nothing at all. Her body shook with the force of her effort to control her emotions.

"Damn it," he said tightly. "You're working yourself into the ground! Can't you see that?"

Travis wrapped Cat in his arms. Her tension vibrated in every line of her body. Silently he cursed himself for pushing her too hard, too soon. She simply wasn't as experienced in the mistress game as the women he was used to.

And he was much more impatient than he had ever been in the past.

"It's all right," Travis said gently. "Tell me what's bothering you, sweetheart." His voice coaxed her and his body warmed her cool skin. "If you want to talk about money in any way, *any* way at all, I won't get angry." He kissed her eyelids lightly, warmly. "Tell me, little Cat. Let me help you."

"No," she said in a rough voice, turning her face away from him.

Fiercely Cat held on to Travis, wanting him and at the

same time afraid if he made love to her again, she wouldn't be able to keep from loving him. She couldn't afford that.

Rich man.

A man who didn't know how to love.

"I don't want to love you," she said bleakly.

There was such desperation in Cat's words that it took a moment for Travis to understand what she had said. When he did, he stopped thinking about money and women and business.

Knowing he would regret not setting out the rules of their relationship, yet unable to stop himself from bending his own unbendable rule, he lifted Cat's face and kissed her until she was hot and supple against his body. His hands slid from her shoulders to the towel wrapped around her breasts. When she stiffened, he stopped.

"Cat . . . ?"

She shivered, cold and hot at once, caught in a trap she didn't know how to escape. Or maybe it was simply that she didn't want to escape.

And then she knew it didn't matter. She couldn't lose more of herself to Travis than she already had.

"Yes," she whispered, "yes."

Without another word Travis picked her up and took her into his bedroom. He unwrapped the damp towel from around her and replaced it with a silk comforter. She shivered continuously as he got in bed and covered both of them with the quilt. He held her until he felt warmth return to her skin.

Finally Cat gave a shaky sigh and relaxed against Travis. Once again he became aware of the dark hollows beneath her eyes, the paleness beneath her tan, the bones pressing against her skin. He wanted her until he couldn't think, but she was so tired. She needed rest more than he needed sex.

"Sleep, Cat." Travis brushed a gentle kiss over her cheek. "You're exhausted."

Her arms slid around his waist. She kissed the hard muscles of his chest. Her tongue lingered to tease his flat nipples into tiny hard buttons. Though he was rigid and ready against her thigh, he made no move to caress her in return.

"Travis?"

"You're too tired," he said simply. "You wouldn't be able to enjoy making love."

"Try me."

Cat's cool fingers kneaded against his chest until her hands became like him, very warm. She teased his nipples again, then his navel.

Travis shuddered and caught his breath. "On one condition."

"Name it."

"Stay with me tonight. No more working for you."

He saw her frown and knew that he had guessed right. Cat had been planning to go right to work after she got home tonight.

"Deal?" he asked.

When she didn't answer immediately, he caught the peak of one breast between his fingers and squeezed gently. Her back arched in helpless response.

"No fair," she said breathlessly.

"Sue me."

He bent over her, rubbing his bearded cheek between her breasts. Her hands slid down to his hips. He caught her wrists in his fingers just before she would have captured him.

"If you put those hot little hands all over me, I'll take it as an unqualified yes," Travis said.

"Yes," Cat sighed, closing her eyes.

"Good. I'll make this as easy on you as possible."

"What?"

"This."

His mouth caressed her breasts until she moaned and moved blindly. He smiled and traced the flush spreading across her body. Even exhausted, she responded to him.

"Now, the second condition," Travis said.

Cat groaned. "Unfair. You said just one."

He laughed and shifted his weight in a fluid movement. His mouth slid down her like warm water until his hands held her hips in a hard embrace. Gently he sank his teeth into the smooth curve of her thigh.

"Travis . . . ?" Cat whispered.

He raised his head just enough to meet her eyes. Her breath wedged in her throat. The look in his eyes was a sensual threat and an exciting promise.

"It may shock you, my red-haired Scots witch," Travis drawled, "but I've wanted to do this since I carried you off that rock, and I'm damned if I'm going to wait any longer."

Breath held, Cat watched as he kissed her thighs and belly and nibbled along the edges of the dark mahogany triangle that shielded her soft core. Deliberately he nuzzled through the warm thatch. Then his mouth opened and heat shot through her.

Whatever shock she might have felt at the love play didn't survive the first wave of pleasure that swept over her. When the second wave hit she made a choked sound and gave in to the subtle pressure of Travis's hands separating her thighs. With a rippling breath of surprise and pleasure she opened herself to his intimate kiss.

Travis rewarded her with a hot, hungry caress that made her cry aloud. The changing pressure and texture of his lips, his tongue, his teeth, moved over her slowly, completely.

Cat tried to say his name, to tell him the exquisite pleasure he was giving her, but she had no words, only her body twisting and melting, her voice crying with need of him.

When she thought she could bear it no longer he came to her in a rush of power, filling her, answering her with his own elemental need until neither of them knew who gave and who took, for giving and taking couldn't be sep-

arated from the ecstasy that consumed their interlocked
bodies.

When Cat woke up, she was still in Travis's bed. The
light of another beautiful day was flooding the room.

And she was alone.

"Travis?"

No answer came.

With a feeling of unease, Cat sat up, looking for a clock.
She found one, but couldn't read the time. As though Travis
had known that her first thought would be of time, he had
taped a note across the face of the clock.

Gone sailing.
I wanted to take you with me.

TWELVE

THE *WIND Warrior* flew before the southern storm like the great ocean bird she was. Normally the crew would have enjoyed the chance to try their ship under a clean, strong wind, but not much about the past five days had been normal.

Nothing pleased the captain. Not the new sail designs, not the wind, not the clever rigging he had designed to go with the sails, nothing. Travis stalked the decks like a caged cat, snarling at anyone careless enough to get within reach.

"We will outrun the rest of the tropical storm before we get to Laguna," Diego said.

Travis grunted.

"The new sails have performed well," Diego said. "Only a ship as strong and well made as this could carry so much wind."

Travis grunted.

"The crew has learned quickly how to manipulate the new rigging," Diego added. "Don't you think?"

Travis grunted.

"Your conversation, my captain, leaves much to be desired."

Travis caught himself before he grunted again. Overhead, the sails quivered with wind, filled to the point of groaning. The ocean parted with a long, continuous hiss around the bow of the ship. The slant of the deck and the creak of rigging told of a ship doing what it had been designed to do, skimming powerfully over the timeless face of the sea.

The captain had absolutely nothing to complain about.

With a muttered curse, Travis raked a handful of fingers through his windblown hair and faced the dark eyes of his first mate.

"The men have done very well," Travis said evenly.

"They would like to hear it from you."

"What am I, a cheerleader?"

Diego winced.

"Hell," Travis muttered. "I'll tell them at mess tonight."

"Thank you."

Travis had the grace to look uncomfortable. "No thanks needed. The men have done a fine job."

"They would not have dared to do less," Diego said dryly. "Their captain is, as they say, on a rip."

Travis's lips twitched in a smile. "That bad?"

"*Sí.* That good, too. We have done two weeks of work in less than five days and we are on our way back to harbor where beautiful women wait. No one is complaining about that!"

Travis smiled rather grimly. "Only five days, huh?"

"Less."

"Seemed more like five weeks."

"Next time bring your red-haired woman along. Then time will run at its usual pace."

Travis gave his first mate a look.

Diego held up his hands in surrender. "Jurgen wins the pool, I see."

"What pool?"

"The one trying to guess what put you out of temper and what it will take to bring you back to your normal, smiling self."

"Normal? Smiling? In their dreams," Travis retorted.

"I am shocked, Captain. Simply shocked. You are a man

of most even disposition." But Diego's wry smile said just the opposite. "The men are proud to work under a captain who demands their best. The only time they grumble is when their best is not appreciated."

"I know how they feel," Travis said, thinking of Cat, who had turned down a few days at sea with him as though the days they had shared ashore were . . . nothing.

Anger shot through him again, the same anger that came every time he thought of how much he had enjoyed Cat and how little she must have enjoyed him.

Cat, witch, woman, sail with me, just two days, Catalina Island and back. You can spare two days for me, for yourself, for us.

Travis had never expected to be reduced to begging for a woman's company. But to be on his knees and still end up sailing alone baffled him as much as it infuriated him.

Next time he wouldn't be put off by Cat's protests about too much work, too many responsibilities, and all the rest of the excuses. Next time he would do what he should have done five days ago. He would put their relationship on the only kind of footing that was reliable, predictable, and comfortable. Money, pure and simple.

Part of Travis wondered what Cat's price would be. Most of him didn't care. Money had to be good for something.

Dr. Stone studied the results of Cat's most recent blood tests and sighed. Over the rim of her reading glasses, she glared at her patient.

"Your red cell count is too low," the doctor said flatly. "You're strong, but you haven't learned the working woman's truth: You can do *anything,* but you can't do *everything.*"

Cat grimaced. "I'm not crazy. I know I can't do everything."

The doctor's smile took years off her age. "But do you practice what you know?"

Cat looked at her hands and said nothing. In the five days Travis had been gone, she had worked herself mercilessly. She spent the long hours of darkness choosing images for her Swift and Sons show, sorting and resorting slides until her eyes refused to focus on the dancing colors.

Only then did she go to bed. If sleep wouldn't come or didn't continue until dawn, she got up in darkness and began the endless round of bookkeeping that went with running her own business.

When dawn finally came she looked out over the ocean and remembered . . . and tried not to ask herself why she had thought Travis was different, why even now her body longed for him, why the sound of his laughter haunted her sleepless hours, why she could not forget the first time he had held her and taught her that peace as well as pleasure could flow between a man and a woman.

And with each dawn came the worst question of all. *Did he leave because I didn't please him as much as he pleased me?*

The one bright spot in Cat's life was that Blake Ashcroft had stopped trying to crowd her into his bed. She still shot sunsets for him, but she shot them alone. Tonight he was coming over to sort through the slides she had taken for his book.

Cat wasn't looking forward to having Ashcroft in her house, though she doubted that he would revert to caveman tactics. The poet was also a pragmatist, and the pragmatist had a healthy fear of a certain hull designer.

If that wasn't enough, Cat wouldn't be taken by surprise again. It wouldn't have happened the first time if she hadn't been focused on her photography instead of on the spoiled poet who couldn't believe that she didn't want him.

Lacing her fingers together, Cat wished heartily that Ashcroft hadn't insisted on having her around while he reviewed the slides. Not that he didn't have every right to expect her presence. It was his book, after all, his poetry, and his choice of images. He could hardly be expected to explain what he liked and disliked over the phone.

But it would have been very nice just the same.

"Cathy?" Dr. Stone said.

Cat glanced up from her interlaced fingers. "What?"

"I asked if you were taking the new vitamins."

"Yes."

"They aren't meant as a food substitute," the doctor said dryly, looking at Cat's drawn face.

"I know."

"How many meals a day are you eating?"

Cat tried to focus her thoughts on something besides Travis or photography or the growing mountain of bills waiting to be paid. The Big Check from Energistics hadn't come.

"I don't really have time to cook," she said.

"There are many good restaurants in Laguna."

"Too expensive."

"No time to cook and no money to eat out. What does that translate to in actual meals for you?"

"When Jason comes over at dawn, he makes breakfast."

Dr. Stone waited expectantly, but her patient wasn't feeling chatty. "What does Jason make for you?"

"Cocoa and peanut butter toast."

The doctor laughed and shook her head. "Well, at least your body can put the carbohydrates and fat to good use. But you might teach your Jason how to make scrambled eggs."

"I tried. Took me two days to get rid of the smell." Cat smiled slightly. "Besides, I've acquired a taste for peanut butter."

"What about lunch and dinner?"

"Soup. Eggs. Cheese and crackers. Whatever."

"Fruits? Vegetables?"

"They're the whatever," Cat said. "Whatever looks good when I get to the store."

"I want you to keep track of what you eat between now and next week's appointment."

Cat sighed and kept quiet. She knew she should eat better meals, but had neither the time nor the desire to cook real meals for herself. As a result, the more tired she became, the less she ate. And the less she ate, the more tired she became.

Dr. Stone called the nurse in and left instructions for B complex and iron shots. A few minutes later Cat left the office rubbing her hip. The doctor had been right—iron shots were a literal pain in the rear.

On the way home Cat stopped at the camera store and picked up her latest batch of processed film. The majority of the slides were duplicates of slides in her files, duplicates she hadn't had time to make herself because she was too busy with the Swift and Sons show.

Cat had long since given up mailing her original slides across country to various photo agents. They didn't like getting duplicates, but the quality of the slides was such that they put up with it, knowing that the alternative was no slides at all from the photographer known only to them as Cochran.

She was careful not to send identical slides to different agents. Each agent had slides no one else had. It was more expensive that way, but it paid off in the long run because agents could assure clients that the precise slide or slides they were buying weren't available anywhere else, at any price.

Even so, Cat flinched at the cost of duplicating so many slides, especially when she didn't do it herself. Including her professional discount but not including the cost of the film itself, the bill came to just under one thousand dollars.

And this was only the first of several batches of slides she had sent off to be processed.

Even though the long nights of work were bearing fruit in terms of more images indexed and sent to her agents, she would rather have caught up on her backlog of slide editing in some other way than driven by loneliness and anger.

Cat carried the cardboard carton full of slide boxes to her car and thought gloomily of all the sorting, indexing, filing, and mailing to various agents that lay ahead of her. It was a part of the business of photography that least appealed to her. It also was vital at this point in her career.

As Cat pulled into the garage, she heard the phone ringing. Simultaneously she remembered that she hadn't turned on the answering machine when she left. She ran down the stairs to her tiny front yard, vaulted the little white gate, and unlocked the front door.

Then she remembered that she had left the portable phone on the lowest floor of her three-level house. She raced down the stairs connecting the levels and snatched the receiver out of its cradle, promising herself that as soon as the Big Check came, she would buy a phone for every level of the house.

"Hello," she said breathlessly.

"Forgot your machine again, Cochran."

Disappointment went over Cat like winter surf, cold and powerful, numbing. It wasn't until that instant that she admitted to herself how much she had wanted the voice on the other end to belong to Travis.

She swallowed, took a steadying breath, and hoped she responded in her normal teasing tones.

"Hi, Harrington. Going to be my green angel again?" she asked, referring to his gift for getting highly paid assignments for her.

"I'm trying," he said with a sigh. "It'd be a hell of a lot easier if I could talk to you from time to time. Swear to God, I'm getting you a pager for Christmas. Maybe I won't wait that long. Hold it for a minute."

There was a pause while Harrington turned away from the phone. Cat heard one of his six assistants speak hurriedly to him. His answer was muffled and abrupt.

"Swear to God," he sighed into the phone, "the bigger the boobs, the dumber the booby."

The assistant's response was muffled, creative, and explicit. So was Harrington's.

"They're going to get you for sexual harassment," Cat said, amusement curling in her voice.

"Jim? Nah. He's been lifting weights. I get out of line, he'll just hammer me into a thin paste, right, Jim?"

"The 'booby' with the boobs is a man?" she asked, startled.

"On a man, they're called pecs. Besides, there isn't a woman here who could give a C cup a run for its money."

There was a chorus of outraged and outrageous responses questioning Harrington's eyesight and more personal functions. Unruffled, he continued speaking loudly into the phone, drowning out the comments.

"They've got no sense of humor," he complained. "I hope you do."

"Uh . . ."

"Good. You're gonna need it. Energistics has stopped returning my calls. Word is they're in a cash-flow crunch."

Cat closed her eyes and swallowed hard against the turmoil in her stomach. She had been counting on that check to survive.

"They can't do that," she managed.

"I said about the same thing to them in a registered letter," Harrington said. "I mentioned accountants, contracts, lawyers, courts, and other obscenities."

Cat swallowed again, harder. She couldn't afford the time or expense that a lawsuit would involve.

"That bad?" she asked finally.

"Let me put it this way, Cochran. I'm tired of being jerked around by Energistics. I'm so tired of it I'm going to sue their tight asses off unless they pay."

Cat let out a long breath. She trusted Rodney Harrington

too much to start questioning his business judgment now. If he said a suit was necessary, then somehow she would find money to pay the lawyers.

"How much do you need and when?" she asked, her voice only slightly hoarse.

"How much what?"

"Money, what else?" she asked wearily. "All those obscenities you mentioned cost a lot."

"Nothing right now. If it gets serious, three to five grand should take care of it."

"Three to five." Cat hoped the dismay she felt didn't show in her voice.

"Think of it as an investment, because sure as God made little green apples, we'll get every cent of it back out of their corporate hide and more for the insult. But it probably won't come to that. Usually these business types come across when you wave a lawyer at them, especially when you have them by the balls. And that's where we have Energistics."

"Then squeeze," Cat said bluntly. "I need that money. The twins' next-to-last school payments aren't very far away. And my mother . . ."

She hesitated, not wanting to criticize the very dear, very helpless woman who was her mother. Mrs. Cochran still believed that checks were a magic form of money unrelated to dollars and common sense.

"Well, you know my mother," Cat said finally.

"Lovely lady," murmured Harrington. "A real old-fashioned woman. Wouldn't know a balance sheet if it walked up and introduced itself."

"January," Cat said, code word for freedom.

"I'll drink to that."

Cat almost smiled. Of all the people in the world, it was Harrington who best understood the pressures she was under. He had been the one who introduced Cat's mother to her future husband. Privately Harrington had been heard to say that it was the best piece of work he'd ever done for Cochran.

"I have some good news, too," Harrington said. "Well, it could be good, anyway."

"I'm listening."

"Remember that new account of mine, the guy who started a face-goo company?"

"Er, no. Does it matter?"

"He'll pay fifteen thousand dollars per shot for every shot he uses in an ad campaign. He's looking for five good ones."

"What does he want—beach, flowers, hills, skin?"

"Just pretty, Cochran. Whatever you have that would go well on a slushy greeting card or a postcard. You know, the kind of shot that makes people say, 'Ohhh, isn't that pret-ty,' and then they walk away and never think of the image again. Not your usual style, but you must have some little cuties hiding away in that wall of filing drawers."

"Boxes and boxes," agreed Cat. "There's a lot of demand for pret-ties. Photo banks love them. Most common denominator and all that. Like Ashcroft's poetry."

Harrington laughed. "How has the octopus been behaving? Did the herpes gambit work?"

"No. He tried to get physical." Cat flinched and held the phone away from her ear for a moment. "It's okay, Rodney. Travis happened to be nearby. He cut off most of Ashcroft's arms and tied the rest in knots."

"Travis? As in T. H. Danvers?"

"The same. He has chivalrous instincts and the strength to enforce them. Ashcroft has been very well behaved since he met Travis."

"Chivalrous?" Harrington said in a rising tone. "Cochran, are we talking about T. H. Danvers, the ship designer? About six foot two, odd-colored eyes, hard-faced, and meaner than a junkyard dog?"

"Hard-faced?" Cat asked, unaware that her voice had

softened as she remembered Travis's face close to hers, Travis smiling with pleasure as he lifted her into a kiss. "Mean?" Memories of laughter and gentleness, his sensitive fingertips bringing warmth to her, his body sharing with her the gift of passion and shimmering release. She laughed softly. "Must be talking about two different men."

"Cathy."

Harrington's quiet use of her first name shocked Cat. He had called her Cathy only once before, when she had comforted him after his brother died in a yachting accident.

"Are you listening?" he asked gently.

"Yes," she whispered, wishing she wasn't, knowing she wasn't going to like what she heard.

"I'd give my life for Travis and consider it well spent," Harrington said, his voice calm and absolutely sure. "He would do the same for me. He's unique, brilliant. A man couldn't ask for a better friend to share a bottle or a fight or a dark night of the soul." He paused. "But, Cathy . . ."

"I'm listening."

"That man is hell on women."

"What do you mean?" Cat asked, her voice flat, afraid that she knew the answer before she heard it.

"Nothing physical. He would never hurt a woman in that way. It's just that they fall for him and he gets in the wind. Something to do with his ex-wife, I think."

"Yes. He told me."

"He did?" Harrington asked, startled. "Then you're the only person other than the two of them who knows what burned him. He never told me a damn thing except that he was divorced."

Cat didn't know what to say.

There was a long, not entirely comfortable silence.

"Oh, hell," Harrington said. "You're a woman grown and all that. But be careful. For women, Danvers is like one of the big storm waves at Oahu—glorious and fascinating as hell until you get caught in it. Then it's out of control and damned terrifying. I care about you too much to want to pick up the pieces after the wave goes out again.''

''I know,'' Cat said softly. ''I'm a good swimmer, angel,'' she added, keeping her voice light. ''Remember? But thanks. I care a lot about you, too.''

''Send the pret-ties,'' he said gruffly. ''Turn on your machine. And, Cochran . . .''

''Yes?''

''Take care of yourself.''

Harrington hung up before Cat could answer. She stood and stared at the phone for a long time.

They fall for him and then he gets in the wind.

Maybe that was the answer to the worst of her dawn questions. It certainly fit. There was no doubt that she had fallen for Travis like a breaking wave, curling over and tumbling until she was little more than spindrift glittering on a sandy shore.

But she thought Travis had been with her, riding the crest of the wave.

Cat closed her eyes, angry that she missed Travis the way she had never expected to miss anything. It was futile to care about him. Rich men didn't know how to care about anyone but themselves. Surely she should have learned that by now.

Yet Travis's great black ship flew across her mind, as unforgettable and compelling as the memory of his touch. She couldn't believe that a man who created such wild, fierce beauty was as shallow as her ex-husband.

With a dispirited curse, Cat went to her cluttered desk, drew out boxes labeled ''To be paid,'' ''Overdue,'' ''Owed to me,'' and began adding columns with the aid of a small calculator. She worked for several hours, writing checks, delaying some bills and paying part of others, trying to make the outgo balance with the income. She worked until her jaw ached from the tension of her clenched teeth.

No matter how many times Cat juggled the figures, they came up dripping red.

She rubbed her eyes and the back of her neck and thought about deadly serious corporate portraits, handshakes between smiling politicians, advertising brochures, and all the other small jobs that might add up to enough money to survive.

It took several minutes before Cat geared herself up to sound cheerful and energetic. She hated what she was about to do, but there was no choice. She had to keep going until the Energistics check or the Danvers assignment came through.

At the moment, neither seemed a good bet.

Grimly Cat reached for the telephone and punched in a number she hated to call. "Hi, Dave. It's Catherine Cochran. You still buried in weddings, gala openings, corporate portraits, and the like?"

THIRTEEN

PUSHING AWAY from the desk, Cat stood, stretched, and kneaded the small of her back. The bills were in different pigeonholes now. That, some small jobs from Dave's Lifetime Memories, and a hip that ached from iron shots were all she had to show for the morning.

She was tired, bone-tired, but she ignored exhaustion without even realizing what she was doing. She had learned that hard work was the price of freedom.

Besides, the checks always came. Eventually.

With a sigh Cat sat down at the typewriter, pulled over the box marked "Owed to Me," and began writing the biweekly round of dunning letters. As soon as she finished with them, she should call the custom color printers and find out if the first batch of prints for the L.A. show was ready.

If the prints were in, she would have to pick them up, assuming they passed her inspection. If they didn't pass, she would spend time arguing about cropping and color register. If the prints were good, she would pay for them with her credit card, if it wasn't maxed out.

Then she should take the prints immediately to the framers and spend more time—and credit—trying out various combinations of mats and frames.

Part of Cat hoped that the prints weren't ready. Part of

her knew they had better be. She simply must get everything in shape for the Swift and Sons gallery showing.

But even if the prints weren't ready, it didn't let her off the hook in terms of office work. There were all those slides to sort, query letters to write, slides to index and file, slides to duplicate. Slides, slides, and more slides.

Cat muffled a yawn and thought longingly of a nap. It would take only a moment to shift the boxes of slides off the low couch and make room for herself. She could lie beneath the open windows and listen to the surf thunder and dissolve on the beach.

Today the sound was unusually deep, almost hypnotic. A southern storm was churning off of Baja California, sending tropical clouds and ten-foot breakers up to Laguna Beach.

For a few minutes Cat closed her eyes and let the powerful, unhurried thunder of the surf lull her. But she resisted the temptation to stretch out on the couch. She was having enough trouble sleeping at night without taking a nap during the day.

Besides, when she was working she wasn't thinking about Travis "Hell-on-Women" Danvers.

After a last look at the couch, Cat reached for another piece of paper, rolled it into the typewriter, and began writing to yet another Dear Sir who hadn't found the time to pay her.

It was five o'clock before Cat remembered lunch. Only the thought of having to write down "peanut butter and crackers" for Dr. Stone drove her to the kitchen upstairs. She looked in the refrigerator, hesitated, then decided on a cheese-and-whatever omelet. Tonight whatever turned out to be limp scallions and two dubious mushrooms. She assembled the ingredients, then cooked and ate the omelet without enthusiasm.

Fuel, not food. Food was something you prepared with pleasure and shared with someone.

Like Travis.

Abruptly Cat pushed away from the table. Her stomach was gnawing on the omelet as though uncertain what to do with it. The muscles along her shoulders and spine felt like braided, red-hot wire.

Ignoring the tension and tiredness that warred for control of her body, Cat wrote out a grocery list on the pad hanging next to the refrigerator, cleaned up the kitchen, and tried not to listen for the phone to ring.

In the pauses between the muscular thunder of surf, there was no sound but that of her own footsteps. The rhythmic surf should have soothed and relaxed her. It didn't. Between listening for the phone and dreading the sulky poet's visit, she was wound tighter than a roll of film.

"What I need is a long, hot bath," Cat told herself briskly, trying to break the silence that never had bothered her before Travis. "The bath will be therapy, not a waste of time. It's either lazy bath or a glass of wine. Maybe both. Yes. Both. Definitely."

Cat had to be more in control than she was now if she hoped to cope successfully with the Crown Prince of Treacle. At the very least she had to stop listening for the phone, stop straining to see the *Wind Warrior* flying across the evening sea, stop remembering . . . too much.

"And while I'm at it, I'll stop breathing, too," she said bitterly.

The continuous rush and thunder of water into the tub drowned out the surf. Cat sank into the welcome heat with a groan of pleasure. By the time she finally dragged herself out of the tub, her skin was flushed pink and steam hung in every corner of the bathroom.

She took a long time drying her hair, enjoying the thick, silky weight of it as it tumbled in auburn waves below her shoulder blades. Subdued fire licked through her hair, gold and bronze, flame and orange, hot colors burning beneath the darker auburn.

Travis had enjoyed her hair, enjoyed burying his face in it, enjoyed having it fall cool and sleek across his naked skin.

He had enjoyed it, but not enough to stay.

Blindly Cat set aside the hairbrush. Working from habit alone, she lifted her hair and sprayed a subtle perfume on the back of her neck. When she glanced in the mirror, her face was pale. She flinched at the taut, wan face that even a steaming bath hadn't been able to warm.

"I look like something the cat dragged in and decided not to eat after all."

Automatically Cat reached for some makeup. Then she changed her mind. The bath had been for herself. The makeup wouldn't be. She didn't care if she looked—or smelled—like dead fish for Blake Ashcroft.

With quick motions she twisted her hair into a coil on top of her head and pinned the slippery mass in place with an ebony comb. Black underwear, black jeans, and a high-necked, long-sleeved black cotton sweater completed her outfit.

Cat measured the image in the mirror and nodded with bleak satisfaction. No one could mistake her somber clothes for a come-on, not even a man as self-absorbed as Ashcroft.

What she didn't see was the effect of her hair quietly burning above an unsmiling face. Sleepless nights had made her eyes larger, more silvery, reflecting the emotions seething beneath her pale surface. Just below her high cheekbones were velvet shadows, gentle hollows to tempt a man's lips. Though her sweater and jeans weren't tight, they revealed the woman beneath in the same way that her hair revealed fire—with each breath, each movement, aloof and alluring at the same time, a red-haired sorceress with eyes of ice.

In one way Cat was correct in her view of herself. She was a woman to tempt a warrior, not a poet. At least not a poet like Ashcroft.

The doorbell summoned with three impatient bursts of sound. Ashcroft had arrived. Cat yanked on black ballet shoes and went to the front door.

"Somebody die?" Ashcroft asked the instant the door swung open.

"Don't tell me, let me guess. You like your women in pink ruffles."

Ashcroft bit back whatever he was going to say and followed Cat down the twisting stairs to the next level. Without a word, she flipped switches until the only illumination in the room came from the light table.

"Where's lover boy?" Ashcroft asked, looking around.

"In the freezer with the other things I don't have time to eat."

The poet blinked. "I never can tell when you're kidding and when you mean it."

"No problem. As long as you keep your hands off me, you don't have to worry about ending up with the ground meat."

Ashcroft shrugged. "Your loss, babe."

"I'll survive it. Here."

Cat handed him a photographer's magnifying glass. It was about four inches high, a topless cone that was wider at the base than at the eyepiece where the magnifying lens was. It was a tool that had been specifically designed for use with slides that were laid out on a light table.

"What's this?" Ashcroft asked.

"A way to look at slides."

"What about a screen and a projector?"

"Too much heat from the projector light will fade the colors on the slide's emulsions, which means that whatever print you make from the slide will be washed out."

Doubtfully Ashcroft looked at the magnifying glass. "Which end is up?"

"Watch."

Cat opened one of the boxes she had stationed around

the light table, pulled out a slide, and put in on the glowing white surface. She took the magnifying tool and put the wide end down on the plastic that framed the delicate slide.

"Here," she said. "Close one eye and look through this with the other eye. If you like what you see, put the slide in the tray to the right. If not, put it in the one to the left."

Ashcroft looked at the magnifying glass and the boxes of slides stacked around the luminous table. "I still think a projector would be easier and quicker."

"It's your book. Your choice. I'll set up the projector and cook some slides."

"Okay, okay. I'll try it your way for a while." He bent down to the first slide, then realized that Cat was walking away. "Where are you going?"

"To brew a cup of tea."

"Sounds lovely. Make one for me."

"You'll have to drink it somewhere else. I don't allow food or drink at the light table."

"Then forget it," Ashcroft said curtly.

He bent over the first slide.

With a sense of relief, Cat closed the door behind her and hurried up to the kitchen. After she made a cup of tea, she went out on the deck by her back door. The deck was cantilevered, jutting out from the steep slope of the bluff. Twenty-five feet below, surf prowled and growled over rocks concealed by darkness.

At one end of the patio a cement stairway zigzagged down to the beach. During the rare storms that whirled up from the south, the cement stairs took the full force of breakers two or three times as tall as Cat was. The stairs had been built with just such storms in mind. A cold iron railing as thick as her arm lined both sides of the concrete stairway.

And for the last ten feet leading down to the beach, the rails were twisted and bent, a silent reminder that the ocean could be as violent as it was beautiful.

Tonight the sea was quiet, a dark playground where

moonlight danced to secret music. Cat looked longingly at the stairs that led down to the beach. She could tell by the low sounds of the surf that the tide was retreating, drawing back into the restless body of the ocean. The beach would be wide and empty, perfect for someone who wanted to feel the gentle kiss of foam on her feet while she watched the moon's tilted smile.

Cat scuffed off her ballet shoes and rolled her pants to her knees. With her teacup in one hand and tension whipping through her body, she walked down the stairs to the sea. The sand was dense, dark, infused with spent waves. As her feet squeezed water out of the sand, her footprints gleamed, only to return to darkness within seconds as the sand drank back the moisture.

The first touch of the ocean was chill, almost cold. Cat didn't retreat. She stood where the water had found her, letting waves curl around her calves and sift sand over her motionless feet.

Staring with unfocused eyes into the night, Cat remembered what it was like to sail a silver moon trail and to see sapphire light glinting in the crests of black satin waves. She wondered if Travis was out there somewhere, moonlight like a benediction on his hard features, strong hands holding the helm of a huge black ship.

Is he looking at the fluid curl of waves and thinking of me?

There was no answer but the emptiness of the night and the sigh of the sea spending itself on the shore. A cool breeze lifted from the water. Cat barely noticed. She wanted Travis so badly that the wind could have been acid and she would have felt nothing at all. The tearing ache of loss was so great that she couldn't feel anything else.

When Cat finally lifted the teacup to her lips, she was startled to find that the tea was colder than the ocean. She had been outside for a long time, long enough for the waves to retreat beyond her feet. Lost in the moonlight and night, thinking of many things, of black waves flexing, of sea gleam and moon smile, but most of all she had thought of Travis.

And now she was cold.

Cat shivered without looking away from the sea. She knew she should go back inside, yet what she really wanted to do was to walk a few feet farther down the beach and let the waves wash over her calves again, setting her mind adrift . . . spindrift gleaming on a hot, distant shore.

And then Cat knew why she was drawn to the dark body of the sea. It made her feel closer to Travis. The same ocean that touched her also touched the *Wind Warrior*.

Touched him.

Cat spun around and ran up the stairs, spilling cold tea at each step.

"Where the hell have you been?" Ashcroft snapped as soon as she reached the deck. "I've been looking for you."

"Here I am."

She set down the nearly empty teacup, washed her feet at an outside faucet, and turned to face the surly poet. A single look at his face told her that he hadn't liked the slides. Yet she had been counting on the money she would get when he approved her work.

"Finished?" she asked curtly.

"I've seen enough, if that's what you mean." Ashcroft's full upper lip lifted slightly. "I don't like them."

Cat walked past him into the house.

He hesitated, eyed her almost warily, and then followed her into the house.

She didn't look back to find out if Ashcroft was coming to the workroom with her. She simply wanted to see the extent of the problem.

As soon as Cat opened the workroom door, she knew there wasn't a problem. There was a disaster.

The tray she had told Ashcroft to put the slides he liked in held precisely two slides. Two out of the two hundred

she was contracted to supply. The reject tray was a disor-
derly pile of slides. Most of the boxes of slides stacked
around the light table hadn't even been opened.

Apparently Ashcroft had indeed seen enough and then
decided not to waste his time looking at any more.

Automatically Cat sorted out the mound of rejected
slides, putting them correctly into the tray. She was neither
hurt nor particularly surprised that Ashcroft didn't like her
images. After all, she didn't like his poetry.

Unfortunately she needed his money. And she was a professional. If he could tell her what he wanted, she could
deliver it.

Cat picked a handful of slides at random from the reject
tray and put them in a vertical line on the light table. On
the opposite side of the table, she put the two slides Ashcroft had selected. Only then did she turn and face him.

"Look," he said quickly. "I want you to know that this
has nothing to do with what happened a few days ago. I
mean, nothing personal. Hell, even if you were sleeping
with me, I still wouldn't like those pictures."

She watched him with unblinking gray eyes, measuring
the emotions in his voice—uneasiness, frustration that had
nothing to do with sex, irritation. He was telling the truth.
He didn't like the work she had done, period. Nothing personal about it. Just a simple, fundamental difference in
taste.

"Babe, I'm telling you the truth. It has nothing to do
with sex!"

"I believe you."

Cat turned away, bent over the light table, and picked up
the magnifying glass. She began with the two slides Ashcroft had selected as suitable to accompany his poetry.

The first slide was a breaking wave, a side view that
showed many shades of blue-green fading into creamy
foam. The lighting was correct if not particularly compelling. The image showed everything in the first glance.

Technically there was nothing wrong with the slide. It was simply rather shallow. Pret-ty. Cat had included it more for contrast than content.

The second slide showed Jason working over a ragged sand castle. He was smiling, his cheeks and lips rosy, his blue eyes like cut glass, his black hair curling every which way. He looked cuddly and adorable, the image of a perfect child.

Cat bit back a curse. Again, there was nothing technically wrong with the image Ashcroft had picked. Light, focus, composition, everything was in place. But after one glance there was nothing more to see. The picture lacked complexity.

She had another picture of Jason that she liked much better. He was standing at the edge of the ocean, holding his cupped hands in front of him, watching water drain back into the sea. He was unsmiling, intent. The sidelight picked out his round cheeks and tiny teeth, shadow of the baby he had been. The same light also illuminated the intelligence behind his deep blue eyes and the intensity of his taut body, foreshadow of the man to come.

It was a riveting image, one that repaid study. But it wasn't pret-ty.

Cat turned to the five slides she had picked at random from Ashcroft's reject pile. The first slide was a close-up of a single shell lying on wave-smoothed sand, sidelit by the setting sun. A thin line of spindrift glittered in an irregular, curving diagonal across the damp sand above the shell, a line that was echoed by the transparent gleam of a retreating wave below the shell. The shell itself was old, imperfect, its spiral worn by the ceaseless roll of waves, its exterior milky rather than opalescent, matte-finished rather than gleaming.

The purity of line and colors had appealed to her, the sensuality in the contrasting textures, the feeling of time and completion and peace. But again, not pret-ty. This shell would never end up in a tourist shop along with bright plastic fish and beach thongs.

The third slide was of a rock at the instant a wave broke against it. It was a late afternoon shot, and she had deliberately underexposed to silhouette the rock against the molten sky. The wave and spray were liquid gold, the rock a black dragon rising out of the sea, orange blood running from its jagged mouth. Mystery and power, fire and night, myth and violence, darkness and light defining and refining one another.

No, not pret-ty at all.

Yet to Cat, it was an image well worth nearly losing her cameras for. And lose them she would have, if a tall stranger hadn't grabbed her off the dragon's back and carried her to shore.

Travis, she thought bitterly. *Always Travis, everywhere I look, every breath I take. Everything.*

With a hand that wanted to tremble, she set aside the magnifying glass and turned toward Ashcroft. He looked very bland after the midnight and fire of the last slide, about as appealing as skim milk.

"I think I know why you don't like the slides," Cat said neutrally, "but I'd rather have you tell me. That way there's no chance of a mistake."

Ashcroft hesitated, then shrugged. "There's no nice way to put it, babe. Your pictures are as cold and empty as you are."

Alone, Cat stood at the light table, her fine-boned face illuminated from below. Shadows haunted her eyes as she stared down at her rejected slides lined up in rows on the light table, their tiny squares of color gleaming like gems . . . blues and greens, ebony and cream, silky flesh tones and fiery sunsets.

She saw none of the colors, none of the grace, none of the beauty.

Your pictures are as cold and empty as you are.

She didn't need to wonder anymore why Travis had stepped into the wind, leaving her alone. Obviously she wasn't capable of returning the pleasure he gave her.

Cold and empty.

The sweet burning had gone no further than her own skin.

Cold.

Ecstasy's golden shadow of peace had shimmered only in her own mind, her own dreams.

Empty.

Cat's slender hands became fists as she fought not to cry out against her own inadequacy. She didn't even feel her fingernails cutting into her palms. She felt nothing but the bleak discovery of her own emptiness.

Gradually she became aware that she wasn't alone in the room. From behind her came the slow, measured breathing of another person.

Damn Ashcroft, she thought fiercely. *What more can he have to say to me?*

Despite Cat's anger, she forced her hands to relax and thought quickly. Before he left, he had agreed to let her try again. If he was back, he must have changed his mind. She couldn't let that happen. She needed the money too badly.

With a quiet breath she wiped all expression from her face. She turned only partway around before she saw him, dressed in clothes as black as her own, nearly invisible in the dimly lit room.

"Travis."

Cat hardly recognized her own voice, cool and remote, as untouchable as a winter halo around the moon. A voice for Ashcroft, not Travis, but she said nothing more because she couldn't. So much had gone wrong that she was afraid even to believe he was back.

And for how long? A night? An hour? A minute?

Not that it mattered. A lifetime was hardly enough, and Travis wasn't interested in sharing lifetimes.

"I knocked. No one answered," Travis said. "The door was open, so I came in." He shrugged, but the eyes examining her face were intent rather than casual. "What's wrong?" he asked bluntly.

Cat closed her eyes. Hearing his voice again, seeing him close enough to touch but so very far away . . .

Cold and empty.

Her hands clenched again, each nail returning to the red crescents that hadn't faded from her palms. Against her will her eyes opened again, hungry to see the angles and shadows of Travis's face.

"Cat?" he asked, his voice softening. Of all the things he had imagined when he came back to Laguna, this remote, brittle angel of exhaustion wasn't one of them. "You look transparent. Are you all right?"

"Long day, that's all," she said, trying for a light voice and failing badly, betrayed by her own body at a time when she most needed strength.

Travis was standing there as though nothing had happened, as though she hadn't lived in hell for five days.

"Just a long day," she said. "One in a long series. Getting longer every day."

Cat forced herself to look away from Travis's eyes, more black than blue or green in the low light, as sensual and mysterious as a midnight sea. Abruptly she unclenched her fingers and began to gather up the careful rows of slides she had built from Ashcroft's rejections.

Travis reached toward her without meaning to, then dropped his hand, angry and concerned at once. He had pleaded for her to come away with him and she had refused. He still wasn't sure why he had come back to her. He knew only that he hadn't had any real choice.

The discovery had made him uneasy and angry. Furious. But nothing had erased the need to see Cat again. So he had come back to her, something he had never done with any woman.

And now she was hardly falling all over herself to greet him. She acted as though it had been five minutes rather than five days since she had seen him.

Travis had wondered how much Cat would miss him. Now he knew. He didn't like the knowing any more than he liked the needing.

"How was your trip?" Cat asked.

Travis clenched his teeth. "Lonely."

The single savage word was like a slap. Her hands shook, spilling slides.

"Damn it!" she said violently. "You were the one who left!"

Travis crossed the room in three strides. His hands closed over her arms.

Strong hands. Warm hands. Familiar hands. Cat could no more hide the tremor that went through her than she could stop the beating of her own heart.

"Look at me," he demanded.

She shook her head, refusing, and stood rigidly beneath his hands.

Baffled, Travis gripped Cat's arms and stared at her bent head. He didn't know why she was angry when she had been the one who turned her back on his pleas as though they—and he—meant nothing to her. Yet despite that, despite his frustration and anger at being turned down flat, her scent was as warm and familiar to him as dawn; and like dawn, it stole over him, ravishing him.

He almost hated her at that moment. She made him defenseless, vulnerable, enraged.

And he barely touched her cool surface.

"I missed you," Travis said harshly. "Too much."

"It was your choice, both the leaving and the missing."

The words were like Cat herself, without heat, without emotion. As lifeless as ice.

"I wanted you to come with me," he said. "Remember?"

She forced herself to look at the blue-green gems that were his eyes. They were like his voice, savage.

"You didn't want me enough to wait for me." Cat stepped out of Travis's grip and turned back to the light table. "But thanks for the invitation," she said, blindly stacking slides. "It made me feel less like a piece of ass."

Cat heard Travis's sharply indrawn breath and almost regretted her words.

Almost.

But they were true.

"You're acting like you were the one who was dumped," he said bitterly.

"Wasn't I?"

"I had to go!"

"Fine. But did you have to be so cruel about the way you left?" Cat asked, gathering slides with jerky motions of her hands.

"Cruel? I didn't—"

"It was cruel to let me wake up alone in your bed," she interrupted, talking over Travis. "It was cruel to walk alone to my own house with the taste and scent and memory of you everywhere on my body, even inside me, and I knew every step of the way that you were gone, that you left me so easily when it cost me so much not to go with you."

"Cost you? *You?*"

Travis's uncertain hold on his temper snapped. He turned Cat to face him so quickly that the slides she was holding flew out of her hands and fluttered to the floor like brilliant butterflies. She cried out and reached to gather up the slides, only to find herself chained by his hands.

"My slides—" she began.

"Screw the slides," he snarled.

"They haven't been duplicated." Cat's voice was thin,

stretched to the point of breaking. "If they're ruined, I can't replace them."

Then she remembered Ashcroft's words. *Cold and empty.* Strength drained out of her, leaving her nearly limp in Travis's grasp.

"It doesn't matter," she whispered. "Ashcroft won't be using the slides. They're cold and empty. Like me." She looked at Travis with blank silver eyes. "That's why you left, isn't it? I wasn't worth staying for."

Travis was too shocked to speak.

As though unable to believe it was Cat talking, he ran his fingers over her face. Her skin was almost cold to his touch. The shadows below her eyes were deeper, the hollows beneath her cheekbones more pronounced, the bones in her face very close beneath her translucent skin, her eyes as colorless as winter. She looked both fragile and oddly powerful, a sorceress caught in a moment of human weakness.

Almost hesitantly, Travis brushed his lips over Cat's and gathered her into his arms, holding her as though she was more fragile than frost.

"We'll talk after the slides are safe," he said. "Neither of us is making much sense right now."

Before Cat could respond, Travis released her and began picking up slides. When she didn't move, he looked back at her. She was watching him. The expression on her face was puzzled and shaken and dazed, a cat that for once had failed to land on its feet. He smiled crookedly, relieved to know that he wasn't the only one who was off-balance.

"Where do you want the slides?" he asked.

Like his smile, his voice both soothed and disturbed Cat. She wanted to smile and cry at once.

"On the light table," she said faintly.

She bent down to pick up the rest of the slides. When she was finished, she started to put them on the light table.

That was when Cat realized he was studying the images

Ashcroft had rejected. Unlike the poet, Travis had figured out how to use the magnifying tool without instruction.

Cat had an almost overwhelming impulse to snatch away the slides and hide them. The feeling appalled her. She was used to criticism; it came with the territory called professional photography. She knew all about differences in taste as opposed to differences in artistic or technical quality.

Yet seeing Travis look at her slides made her want to crawl into a dark corner and pull the shadows in after her until she was invisible.

If Travis didn't like her work, she would be devastated on a level that had nothing to do with professional pride. Just as the *Wind Warrior* was part of his soul, these slides were part of hers. If he saw them as cold and empty . . .

Trying to drive away the chill that covered her skin more thoroughly than the black sweater, Cat dragged her palms over her arms.

Without looking up from the light table, Travis took her hand and rubbed it slowly against his beard, warming her skin. When he shifted the magnifying glass to another slide, he didn't let go of her. He worked one-handed, staring down at the slides with an intensity that was almost tangible.

His anger at her, at himself, at everything, had vanished. Nothing was real to him but the slides, intense visions that were as unflinching, intelligent, complex, and passionate as the woman standing next to him.

Finally Travis straightened and looked at Cat as though he had never seen her before. It was the way she had looked at him when she first realized that he was the designer of the ship that had sailed across the sun.

He kissed her palm and said simply, ''They're brilliant.''

Cat drew a ragged breath, realizing that it was the first one she had allowed herself for a long time.

''Ashcroft didn't think so,'' she said. ''He told me they were cold and empty. Like me.''

"Ashcroft has the aesthetics of diarrhea."

She laughed almost helplessly. "But he's the boss. I'm reshooting the lot. Postcards coming up. Boring, superficial, and pret-ty," she said, her voice mocking the last word.

"Pretty pictures for pretty boys, is that it?"

She nodded, then looked into Travis's eyes. "I'm very glad you don't feel that way."

His hand tightened on hers. He looked at the slides spread across the light table, colors glowing, exquisite visions enclosed in white squares.

"You see an extraordinary world," he said in a low voice. "Things stripped down to their essential curves. Colors that reveal rather than conceal meaning. Your images are as balanced, graceful, and powerful as a good racing hull."

Travis touched one slide, moving it into a place by itself. Cat recognized the slide. It was the one she had taken the day she met him, when the tide came in and he lifted her off the rocks.

"No wonder I had to drag you away," he said. "If I'd seen dragons and gold hiding in rocks and spray, I'd have forgotten the tide, too." He smoothed her palm against his beard, then kissed the pulse beating in her wrist swiftly, hungrily. "Thank you for sharing your world with me, Cat. It's so much like you, pure and brilliant, radiating life even in its darkest shadows."

Cat realized she was crying when she felt the hot tears spill over her cheekbones, tears salty on her mouth. She put her arms around Travis and held on until she ached. She had missed him more than she had admitted or even known until now. She had missed him since she was born.

Travis held her, rocking slowly, letting his warmth seep into her, kissing her temples and eyelids, her eyelashes, murmuring her name. The warmth he gave her returned redoubled, filling him and giving ease to an emptiness that had been part of him for so long that he hadn't even known it was there until she had filled it.

And then he had left her and measured the loss.

He had learned something from the five empty days. This time he wouldn't let his sexual hunger for her blind him to the need to put their relationship on a rational footing. He had money. She needed it.

They were made for each other.

All he had to do was get her to set the price. Once she did, there would be no more empty days, no more aching nights. Everything would be understandable, reliable, predictable. Safe.

Yet even as Travis thought about the necessity of finding out Cat's price, something bitter came to the back of his mouth. A part of him that he thought had died with his unborn child didn't want a price tag on Cat's company.

And that scared him more than anything else.

We'll sort it out soon, he vowed silently. *Tonight.*

FOURTEEN

TRAVIS TURNED off the light table and pulled Cat close.

"Pack an overnight bag," he said, kissing her lips slowly. "We're going on board the *Wind Warrior*. Tonight. No arguments, witch. I'm the boss now, just like Ashcroft."

Startled, she lifted her head and stared at him. "What do you mean?"

"Simple. You're doing the photos for my book. No arguments about that, either. So bring your cameras. Bring whatever you need." Travis bent until his lips were just touching Cat's. "Bring your warmth. Bring your fire. It's been so damned cold without you."

Cat couldn't say no. She didn't want to. She packed in a daze, fitting her few personal things into a bag no bigger than a purse. Her camera equipment was another matter. Not only did it take longer to pack up, it took a lot more room.

Travis shook his head in rueful amusement when he saw the five bulky cases that Cat carried over her shoulders on straps or in her hands like suitcases.

"An overnight bag that would fit in a bread box and enough camera gear to fill a truck," he said dryly. "Here. Give that lot to me. It's a wonder you can stand up under all that stuff."

"I could use a bearer," she admitted. "Are you looking for work?"

Instead of answering, he bent swiftly and lifted her in his arms.

"Not me," Cat said, laughing. "The cameras."

"You carry them. I'll carry you."

He started for the door.

"Wait," Cat said. "I forgot to put on the answering machine. Harrington will—"

"Yeah," Travis interrupted, putting her down. "I know. He's forever chewing on me for being out of reach. Serve him right if I just grabbed you and sailed to the ends of the earth, leaving no number at all."

She hesitated for a dreamy instant while his words kindled her imagination—freedom and Travis and the sea. Then she sighed and went to turn on the answering machine. Running away was a child's freedom. She wasn't a child anymore.

Travis picked up the camera gear and followed Cat out the front door, waiting while she locked it. Then he started across the patch of hardy plants that was her front yard and toward the steps that led to the street.

"Can we take my car?" she asked.

He turned and looked at her, surprised. "This will all fit in mine."

"I have more gear in my car trunk. It's stuff I don't always use but never know when I'll need it. Specialized equipment. Reflectors and tripods, extra flashes and a change of clothes, hiking boots and the like."

Cat laughed at the expression on Travis's face. "You guessed it. I keep my magic broom there, too."

"I was wondering where you hid it," he said mildly. He lifted the heavy, bulky garage door. "Back out. I'll lock up for you."

With the ease of much practice, she maneuvered the little Toyota out of the narrow garage and into the street. He lowered the door, snapped shut the padlock, and walked toward her with long strides, illuminated only by moonlight.

Cat watched Travis with open appreciation, planning how to take a picture that would capture both his animal grace and his intense intelligence. Sidelight, surely. Or perhaps illumination from below as she panned her camera with his movements, freezing him against a blurred background.

"Wake up," he said, opening the passenger door and piling stuff in the backseat. "Or do you want me to drive?"

"I'm awake," she said vaguely, balancing angles and lighting in her mind.

"Convince me."

"I was wondering whether to shoot you in sidelight or up from below, to freeze you against a blurred background or to do a close-up."

"What did you decide?" Travis asked as he slid into the passenger seat.

A slow smile curved Cat's lips. "To shoot you and then have you stuffed."

He snickered. "Sounds painful."

"Nope. I know a great taxidermist."

Travis waited until Cat drove the car onto the Pacific Coast Highway and turned right, heading toward Dana Point. Only then did he begin talking quietly.

"I didn't mean to be gone so long. *Wind Warrior*'s rigging is new, not only the lines but the sails as well. I'm doing some experiments with high-tech cloth, stealing some ideas from parachute designers."

Cat didn't know what to say, so she didn't say anything at all.

He glanced sideways. "Don't worry, I won't give you a pop quiz. I'll just say I'm trying out a few new sail designs, and a few new ways of controlling those sails. I had to get used to the rigging under various conditions of wind and sea. It took longer than I thought it would, and there are still some problems I need to work on.''

She nodded and concentrated on driving for the simple reason that she didn't like talking about those long days when she hadn't known if Travis would ever come back to Dana Point.

To her.

"If it helps," Travis added almost reluctantly, "I was surprised I'd only been gone five days. It felt more like five weeks. I missed you like hell."

Cat said nothing. Instead of looking at him, she concentrated on the highway winding between small shops and beach cottages.

"Still mad?" Travis asked neutrally.

She blew out a swift breath between her lips. She didn't want to talk about it, but she knew they had to or she would find herself waking up alone again and wondering what she had done wrong this time.

"Suppose I'd made love to you as though I could never get enough of you," Cat said, her voice as neutral as his had been. "Then I left you when you were asleep, and you woke up and found a note that said: 'Gone to take pictures somewhere on the ocean. Wish you had come with me.' ''

Travis's breath came in with a rough sound.

"And then I didn't show up for five days," Cat said, glancing quickly at him. "Or five weeks."

"Cat—"

"It just as easily could have been five weeks, couldn't it?" she asked.

His jaw tightened. "Yes."

"Yes," she repeated numbly. "You make your own rules, live in your own world. I can understand that. I live the same way. But how would you have felt if you'd been the one to wake up in my bed and I was gone and you had to walk home alone, wondering why?"

Cat braked smoothly for a stoplight and watched the red

circle with unblinking silver eyes. Travis's hand caught her chin, turning her face toward him.

"I'd have been mad as hell," he said, his voice deep and certain. "If I didn't have a ship to go after you, I'd buy one and chase you until I caught you."

She looked at his hard eyes, his unsmiling mouth, his tawny beard almost black in the dim artificial light.

"That's the difference between us, Travis. You're used to buying what you want. I'm used to going without. But we're alike in one way," Cat added coolly, turning away. "I was as mad as hell."

The light turned green. She accelerated smoothly, coaxing every bit of power from the Toyota's little engine.

Travis clamped down on his impatience. He didn't want to get stuck in a discussion of the immediate past when their immediate future needed to be settled. They would keep on misunderstanding each other, catching each other on the raw, unless they had a relationship that was rationally defined and understood by both of them, right down to a timetable if that's what she wanted. This tripping over each other's work had to stop.

What they needed was more honesty and less games.

But Travis didn't have to be a mind reader to know if he brought up the subject of time, work, money, and mistresses right now, he would find himself dumped by the side of the road. At the moment, Cat wasn't in a mood to be reasonable. She was still angry at having been left alone in his bed.

"I had to test the rigging modifications," Travis said finally. "I couldn't do it in the harbor."

"I'm not arguing that. I'm arguing the way you left."

"If you'd been awake, I couldn't have gone," he said flatly.

Startled, Cat turned to look at Travis. He was staring ahead, his eyes concealed in shadows, his profile hard beneath the erratic illumination of streetlights. She looked away, back to the road.

"I'm not sure I believe that," she said, her voice uncertain.

"Why?"

"I don't think I affect you the way you affect me."

"I know I don't. If I affected you the way you do me, you wouldn't have sent me out to sea alone."

"That isn't fair," Cat said instantly, angrily. "I have to work to survive. My choices aren't as easy as yours. And even if they were, I wouldn't have left you hanging for days, not knowing if we'd ever see each other again."

Travis's breath caught, but his voice remained calm. "Is that what you thought?"

"What else was I supposed to think, Mr. In-the-Wind Danvers? Or is it Mr. Hell-on-Women Danvers that I'm with tonight?"

"Damn Harrington," Travis snarled suddenly, finally understanding why Cat had been so reluctant to trust him in a negotiated relationship. "What did he tell you about me?"

"Nothing that I didn't already know."

"Which is?"

"I'm playing with fire." Cat smiled, but there was no humor in the curve of her lips, no warmth. "At first I thought I could just enjoy the flames."

Travis waited, but she said no more. "And now?" he demanded. "What are you trying to say? I'm not a mind reader, Cat."

"Now," she said in a tight voice, "the only question is how badly I'm going to be burned."

He drew in a long breath. Then, slowly, he relaxed and touched her cheek. He shouldn't feel better—nothing had been settled between them—but he did. He had needed to know, really *know*, that she missed him.

"Funny you should mention that," Travis said, but his

tone wasn't amused at all. "I feel the same way about fire. About you. I almost didn't come back."

Cat bit back a cry of protest and denial at the thought of never seeing Travis again.

After a mile of silence and darkness, she asked, "Why did you come back?"

"Why are you here with me now?" he countered softly.

"It's better than the alternative," she said, her voice rich with irony and something softer, yearning.

"Yes," Travis agreed simply. His voice was as gentle as his fingertips tracing the line of her hand, her arm, her cheek. "Much better."

He started to say more, to tell her that she didn't need to worry, they would get their relationship on a sensible footing as soon as she figured out how much she needed from him. But he couldn't bring himself to open up what would surely become another argument. He was enjoying the peace of her presence in a way that was too new and too fragile to destroy with business talk.

They finished the drive to the harbor in silence, touching each other from time to time. The touches were more reassuring than provocative. They were small, tangible statements of mutual pleasure at being within reach of one another.

It was a kind of undemanding intimacy that Cat hadn't known since she was a child, a warmth that sank all the way to her core. When Travis touched the corner of her smile, she turned and breathed a kiss across his fingertips.

"Cat," he whispered.

Just that. Her name.

It was enough.

With the shadow of a smile still softening her face, Cat drove into the nearly empty parking lot at Dana Point. In silence she switched off the engine and looked across the harbor to Travis's ship rising clean and dark and potent out of the moonlit sea. The *Wind Warrior* was both refined and wild, an elemental force drawn in black lines against a starry sky.

"I'd give my soul to capture just part of her strength, her elegance, her savage beauty," Cat said in a low voice.

"Yes." The word was short, almost harsh.

Travis was watching Cat rather than his ship, and he was thinking of the five long days when he had learned that the sea alone wasn't enough for him. He didn't like feeling the way he did then or now, almost helpless, certainly not in control.

We've got to settle this, he thought again. *Tonight.*

Cat turned toward Travis, wanting to say more about the impact of his creation on her, but her words caught in her throat. He was like his ship, fierce and powerful, and he was looking at her as though he wanted to melt through her into her soul.

His look held more than passion, more than lust. It was a shattering hunger that was as complex and compelling as Travis himself. She would have been frightened by his intensity if it hadn't been so like her own feelings when she looked at him.

Then Travis framed Cat's face in his hands and simply looked at her. The restraint he exercised at only looking, barely touching, was obvious in the muscles standing out tautly on his arms.

"I can't believe I didn't dream you," Travis said, his voice both harsh and wondering.

Before Cat could answer, he took her mouth in a swift, hard kiss, as though reassuring himself that she was real. Her lips softened, opened, invitation and demand. Then her hands went to his face, holding him as fiercely as he held her. They kissed each other without reservation, as though a single kiss could say everything, be everything, assure everything they wanted of each other and themselves.

A kiss wasn't enough. Their hunger went deeper than desire, but only their bodies could express what neither had the words to speak aloud. Only by blending together, sinking into one another, could they begin to describe or appease the levels of need they aroused in each other.

"Travis," Cat said raggedly.

"I know," he breathed against her lips. "Wrong time. Wrong place."

But still Travis couldn't bring himself to let go of her. Not yet. He caught her mouth, kissing her with a sweet hunger that made her moan. Then he swore very softly and released her while he still could.

Cat closed her eyes and fought the hunger that coiled through her in liquid waves.

Without looking at her, Travis got out, pulled camera gear from the backseat, and walked around to her side of the car. When he opened the door she climbed out and locked up the car with hands that wouldn't stop trembling. Not wanting to fumble with the buckle on her purse, she stuffed the car keys into her pants pocket.

Travis hung camera bags and straps around his neck, picked up several cases in one hand, and laced the fingers of his free hand through Cat's.

The frank sensual pleasure he took in even such a simple caress made her feel weak all over again.

"It would be easier if you didn't enjoy touching me so much," she said raggedly. "It makes me want to ... everything."

Travis rubbed her fingers against his beard and led her toward the dock where the Zodiac was tied up.

"You're the one who taught me how to enjoy touching," he said in a low voice.

"Me?" She laughed in disbelief. "You're the experienced one."

"Pleasure and experience aren't the same thing. That's what you taught me, Cat." Then, so softly that she almost didn't hear, Travis muttered, "And I hope to hell I won't regret learning it."

His hand tightened painfully in hers and he watched her with eyes as dark as the sea. She understood his fear. It was the same fear she had of him. If she was wrong about Travis, if he was less than he seemed . . .

The cost would be more than she could pay.

In silence the two of them loaded camera equipment and themselves into the Zodiac. When Travis started up the outboard engine, it sounded very loud in the quiet harbor. As though called by the sound of the engine, a lantern bloomed suddenly on the *Wind Warrior*'s stern. A shutter descended once, twice, blocking out light, then returning it in a long flash before the lantern was shuttered completely.

"Diego," Travis said beneath his breath. "He wants to talk to me."

Cat's fingers tightened in his hand, silently protesting the intrusion of another person into their world.

"I wonder what couldn't wait until morning," he said savagely. "It better be good."

Travis helped Cat up onto the ship's deck, handed over her camera equipment, and pointed her toward the steps leading below.

"I'll met you in my cabin," he said. "Whatever Diego wants, it won't take long, I promise you."

Before Cat went below, she watched him stride toward the dark figure of a man standing discreetly near the *Wind Warrior*'s helm. When Travis started talking to Diego in a low voice, she turned and went below.

"What couldn't wait?" Travis asked bluntly.

Diego winced. When he had seen Cat's silhouette climbing onto the ship, he had hoped his captain's temper would be improved. That didn't seem to be the case.

"Schoenfeld," Diego said. "Remember him?"

"The guy who thought he could sail anything, anywhere?"

"*Sí.*"

"What about him?"

"He ran aground."

"In my ship?"

Diego knew better than to comment on the captain's possessive feelings toward his hull designs, no matter who happened to own the hull in question at the moment.

"*Sí*, the hull is one of the Delta series."

"He ran aground in the hull I sold him," Travis said.

The first mate nodded.

"Fool," Travis said harshly.

Diego knew better than to ask who the fool was, Schoenfeld for going aground or Travis for selling one of his most recent hull designs to a man who wasn't much of a sailor.

"Was he drunk?" Travis asked.

"Undoubtedly, though nothing was said."

Travis grunted. "This could have waited until morning."

"Telling you about the hull, yes. But the rest, no."

"There's more?"

"The insurance company wants to know if the hull is a write-off or if it can be salvaged. The Australian expert took one look at the hull configuration below the water line and—"

"Australians? Where did Schoenfeld run aground?"

"Some nameless piece of the Great Barrier Reef. Nearly even with Brisbane, I believe."

"Hell."

"They will pay all expenses for you."

"I'm sure they will. And while they're at it, will they also hand me an extra week of time to make up for what I'll lose?" Travis asked ironically.

"I'll ask."

"Do that," he retorted, turning away. "But not yet. Call them tomorrow."

"Captain, they are eager for your answer. The hull, you understand, is not waiting in dry dock. It is still aground in a lagoon."

"If a storm gets there before I do, the insurance company

will have its answer. The hull will be a write-off."

With that Travis went downstairs to the captain's cabin. As irritated as he was with Schoenfeld, the idiot had provided a perfect opening for beginning a conversation with Cat about time, money, and relationships.

Yet as soon as Travis closed his cabin door behind him, all thought of a bottom-line negotiation evaporated. She was asleep in his bed with the sheet pulled up to her nose, as though she was enjoying the scent of where he had slept.

"Cat," he whispered, feeling helpless against the emotions twisting inside him, tying him in knots. "What am I going to do about you?"

Slowly, as though pulled against his will, Travis went to the bed. The subdued fire of Cat's hair had escaped from the clip that held it. Silky auburn curled over white sheets and cheeks that were almost as pale.

Tenderly he smoothed a lock of hair away from her eyes. When he saw how tightly drawn her skin was over her cheekbones, he frowned. She looked much too fragile to hold all the passion he knew was in her body.

"Why are you scowling at me?" Cat asked, her voice husky.

"You've lost weight. You're working too hard."

"It's only temporary," she said, yawning and rubbing against Travis's hand. "Just until January, when the major bills are paid."

His frown deepened. January, when her money crunch would be over. At least, that's what she had told him.

But he didn't know where he would be in January. Nor did he want to wait that long for some of Cat's time.

"You don't have to wait until January," Travis said. "All you have to do is tell me how much you need."

Cat woke up suddenly and cursed her sleepy tongue for touching on the subject of money. Every time the topic came up, she and Travis argued. She didn't want to argue tonight. She wanted to hold him and know again the joy and peace she could find in his arms.

She sure as hell didn't want to talk about money.

"What did Diego want?" Cat asked neutrally.

Travis hesitated. The stubborn lines of her face told him that she would have to be dragged screaming into a business talk. He told himself he couldn't let her get away with evasions much longer.

But he really didn't want to argue with her right now. He just wanted to climb into bed beside her.

"I sold one of my hulls to a fool," Travis said in a low voice. "He ran it aground somewhere off Australia's east coast. The insurance company wants my estimate of salvage value."

Cat made a sound that could have meant anything and watched him.

He peeled off the soft bedcover and slid in beside her. Pulling her over onto his chest, he covered both of them up again. She braced herself on one elbow, wanting to see his brilliant, changing eyes. Her fingers spread over his chest, savoring both the texture of the cashmere sweater he wore and the resilient muscle beneath.

"Nothing to say about Australia?" he asked.

"When are you going?" Cat asked, keeping all emotion from her voice.

Lean, masculine fingers moved up to her head and combed out the silver clasp that still held some of her hair in a twist. Locks of hair flowed over his hands like warm, silky sunset. His fingers clenched suddenly, chaining her.

"We," Travis corrected. "*We're* going."

Before Cat could argue or agree, his tongue invaded her mouth. He claimed the soft territory with long, slow strokes.

She didn't protest the bone-melting sensuality that robbed her of speech. She wanted him too much. They could argue later, when desire no longer clawed at both of them, making their tempers too short and their words too reckless.

Cat's hands slid beneath Travis's black sweater, along his ribs, over his chest. Her fingers tangled gently in his tawny, springy hair. Then she smoothed and caressed each ridge of tendon, each supple swell of muscle. When her nails brushed over his flat male nipples, he shuddered lightly. Instinctively she returned to the sensitive area, wanting to give as much pleasure to him as he gave to her.

The hunger of his kiss increased, making her ache, shortening her breath and speeding her heartbeat until it matched his. His legs parted until she sank between them. Then he locked his legs over her, holding her in a sensual vise. His eyes were an intense blue-green, narrowed, revealing his desire for her as surely as the slow, sinuous movements of his hips revealed his arousal.

"Come with me, my Cat, my woman," Travis said huskily, moving against her, coaxing with his body as much as with his words. "I know you don't have the time to sail to Australia. We'll fly."

"But—"

"It won't take long to see if the hull can be salvaged," he said quickly, ignoring her interruption. "When I'm done we can dive along the Great Barrier Reef, drift in diamond waters with fish more brilliant than any jewels. We can love each other and sleep in the sun, and then we can love again beneath a moon as big as the world. *Come with me.*"

As Travis's heat and need broke over Cat like a storm wave, he sensed her succumbing to his lure, felt the liquid heat of her passion matching his. The relief of knowing that she would come to Australia with him was almost dizzying.

And in the next heartbeat it was gone.

Cat's soft, giving smile changed into a determined line. He could feel her withdrawing even as he molded himself to the sultry heat between her thighs.

"I'm sorry," she said raggedly. She turned away from the hunger in her lover's eyes, hoping to conceal her own hunger from him. "I can't go with you."

"Why?" Travis's voice was as blunt and smooth as wave-polished stone. And as hard.

"My work."

"It's just money. I have plenty of it."

Cat's eyes flew open. "I don't want your money. Can't you understand that?"

"You work to get money."

"I love my work!"

"All of it? All the time?" he retorted. "Are you really looking forward to shooting fluff for Ashcroft?"

"No, but—"

"You need the money," Travis finished smoothly. "No problem. I've got money. How much do you need?"

Cat closed her eyes and shook her head. "You don't understand. *It's not money.*"

"Like fiery hell," he said under his breath. Then he bit back a curse and took a better grip on his temper. "Okay, we'll do it your way. If it's not the money, what's keeping you from going with me?"

She hesitated, then spoke in a rush. "Where is this going, Travis? Where are *we* going?"

There was a charged silence followed by a sound of disgust from him. "So that's it."

His hands opened, letting her hair spill away. His legs loosened, freeing her.

"So that's what?" Cat asked, not understanding.

"I told you the truth the first day we met," Travis said, trying to be reasonable despite the hot running of his blood and the furious chill of being wrong about Cat after all. "I'll never marry a woman less wealthy than I am. I'm sorry you didn't believe me when I told you. But that doesn't mean we can't—"

He stopped abruptly as she shoved away from him and

sat on the far end of the bunk. Her face was pale and very still. He could see her anger burning in red slashes across her cheekbones.

"Who said anything about marriage?" Cat demanded.

"You did." Travis saw the silver blaze of her eyes and realized that she was as furious as he was. "Wait, Cat. Listen. We're very special together. I've given up fighting it, whatever it is. I want to give you—want to share with you—a simple time of peace, companionship, pleasure, passion. And when the time is over, I won't be so vicious to you that you have to jump overboard and swim out to sea to escape me."

Cat closed her eyes and concentrated on the pain of her nails digging into her hands. *When the time is over.*

Not even *if*, just *when*.

She hadn't known how simple and devastating a single word could be.

And the worst part of it was that she still wanted to go with Travis, even if it was for only two weeks, two hours, a minute.

"No," she said tightly. "I can't. There's too much I have to do. Ashcroft's book. Some small jobs I've lined up. My show in L.A. Your book."

Travis could feel Cat slipping away. It enraged him. They wanted each other so much they were vibrating like a sail in a storm, and she was turning her back on it. On him.

"*Christ!*" Travis snarled. "Weren't you listening earlier? I know how important money is to you! I'll be glad to pay for the time you spend with me."

"What?"

"That's the first smart question you've asked," he retorted, deliberately misunderstanding her. "Five thousand dollars for a five-day trip to Australia. All expenses paid, of course, including clothes if you're worried about it."

Cat was too shocked to answer. Her body had gone cold,

all passion drained by Travis's relentlessly reasonable voice and cool, measuring eyes.

"No, that wouldn't be enough," Travis said as though Cat had refused an opening bid. "Not for a photographer like you. Ten thousand dollars. How about it? Ten thousand dollars for five days."

Holding herself very carefully, Cat climbed off the bunk. When she spoke, her voice was thin from the effort she made not to scream at him.

"If you stopped buying women, you might just find out that there are women who can't be bought."

"Twenty thousand."

Cat stepped backward and looked at Travis for a long moment. His face was closed. His eyes measured her with bleak assurance, certain that she would allow herself to be bought when the price went high enough.

"Forty." Travis's voice was like an ice pick chipping away at her composure. "Fif—"

"*No.*"

"Sixty. It would solve all your problems, Cat. The tuition, your mother, even a chunk of your house. Hell, I'll throw in some digital camera gear and a computer to go with it. Five days. Sixty thousand. Okay?"

She spun around and yanked open the cabin door.

"Running won't do any good," he said flatly. "I'm tired of all the games and uncertainty between us. I'm not letting you go until we agree on how much you need."

"Money?"

"What else?"

Rage shot through Cat. "Screw you!"

"That's the whole idea, darlin'," he drawled.

"Then screw yourself, T. H. Danvers—if you can agree on a price."

Cat slammed the door behind her, raced up topside, and ran the length of the deck. For an instant she hung poised against the shimmering moonlight. Then she flew from the

Wind Warrior's stern in a graceful dive that barely disturbed the dark surface of the harbor.

The water was chilly, but the shock waves of adrenaline that pumped through Cat's body kept her from feeling anything. With swift, angry strokes, she swam to the steps leading up the pier to the parking lot.

Dripping, shaking as much from emotion as from cold, she climbed the stairs and ran to her car, grateful that she had put her keys in her pants pocket instead of in the purse she had left behind on the *Wind Warrior*. As she unlocked the car she heard the snarl of the Zodiac's engine.

"Too late, you thickheaded bastard," she said through chattering teeth. "I'm gone. Go buy some other woman."

Cat was out of the parking lot and accelerating down the harbor road before the Zodiac reached the dock. She had one satisfying glimpse of an infuriated Travis silhouetted on the dock with his legs braced and his hands on his hips.

Then the road turned and he vanished.

Not until Cat drove into her garage did she remember what sheer rage had made her forget. She had left more than her purse behind.

Her cameras were on board the *Wind Warrior*.

FIFTEEN

CAT AWOKE from a daze that was more like a trance of exhaustion than true sleep. Dawn poured over her bed and filled the room with light. Automatically she looked through the open curtains toward the radiant sea.

A man's black figure cut across the shimmering waves, swimming powerfully, leaving a shadowed wake behind.

She watched while emotions warred in her and questions hammered her like hail.

Is Travis thinking of me?

Is he still angry?

Does he wonder if I'm watching him swim like a god through the heart of dawn?

Why did we have to meet now? Given enough time, I would have gotten past his cynicism to the man beneath, the man I could love.

The man who could love me in return.

Cat didn't like hearing her own fierce longing put in words, even in the silence of her own mind. She swept off the tangled covers and shot out of bed, buoyed by a surge of adrenaline.

The floor was cold beneath her feet. She shivered and rubbed her arms, remembering last night and the chill that even a steaming bath hadn't been able to ease. But she didn't want to think about last night. It had taken her three hours to get to sleep. Three hours of trying not to care, not to remember.

Yet even in her sleep there had been no peace. She had endured four hours of fragmented dreams, dreams that dragged her to the brink of consciousness only to let go of her at the last instant, sending her spinning back down into troubled darkness.

Dreams of cameras that didn't work, broken lenses, slides warped and torn . . . hell presided over by a shadow figure whose power was exceeded only by his grace, a voice as compelling as the heat that radiated from him; *he was smiling, touching her, and she was burning.*

Grimly Cat yanked on her clothes. She had had enough of her dreams last night. She refused to be captive to them in daylight. Anything was better than that.

Even trying to figure out how she was going to get her cameras off the *Wind Warrior*.

At least Travis had gotten home, even though she had driven off and left him without transportation. That meant she wouldn't have to confront him on the ship when she went to pick up her camera gear.

Cat tried to be grateful that she wouldn't be face-to-face with Travis again, but gratitude wasn't what she felt. She felt used up, spent, baffled, exhausted. The spurt of adrenaline that had goaded her out of bed was already gone. She was fresh out of anger to keep herself going.

With dragging feet she went to the kitchen, hoping that a cup of tea would put energy back into her. The first thing she saw was the blinking light on her answering machine. Even as the swift hope came that Travis had called to apologize to her, she slapped the thought aside.

He had been as angry as she was. Besides, he didn't see that he had done anything to apologize for. A simple business transaction, that's all.

Cat hit the play button and listened. Diego's clear, apologetic tenor lifted into the silence, saying her name. Her neck prickled. She doubted that she would like what she was going to hear next.

"Captain Danvers instructed me to tell you to pick up your camera equipment at nine o'clock this morning on board the *Wind Warrior*. If that is not convenient, please call the following number and make an appointment."

Staring out the window, trying to work up energy to replace emptiness and aching, Cat barely listened to the number Diego gave her. She kept telling herself it shouldn't hurt that Travis was as eager to avoid her as she was to avoid him. Being hurt didn't make sense. But she felt pain just the same, gnawing away at her, bleeding what little strength she had.

Cat couldn't see Travis anymore. He was a shadow lost among other shadows, and the colors of dawn flowed like wine over the ocean waves.

Breathing raggedly, she tried to shake off the pain and unhappiness that whipsawed through her. She should be out shooting now, when the light was best, taking pret-ty pictures for the pret-ty poet with the skim-milk mind.

But her cameras were out of reach. Like her heart. Locked up on an elegant black ship owned by a pirate who didn't know the value of love, only money.

Beneath the hot sun, Travis paced the length of the *Wind Warrior* wearing only swim trunks, a dark T-shirt, and deck shoes. The sun had taken forever to crawl above the ragged line of the land into Southern California's empty sky. Time was moving like it was chained to the deck. Yet even time in chains had to pass somehow. Eventually.

He looked at the shadows cast by the sun and knew that Cat would be coming soon, lured by the damned cameras that meant more to her than anything, most especially Travis Danvers. He was tempted to meet her out on deck, but didn't trust himself. Or her. He hadn't forgotten her swift, graceful dive from the ship's stern.

The memory of it still made him furious. He hadn't laid a finger on her, yet Cat had fled over the railing as though he was no better than the drunken wife beater she had married before she was old enough to know better.

Hell, the way she acted, you'd think I had taken a whip to her. All I did was offer her enough money that she wouldn't have to work herself into the ground. Enough money that she would have time to enjoy life a little. With me.

Granted, he hadn't made the offer with much finesse. But she hadn't exactly made it easy. Every time he tried to talk about how much money she needed in order to make room in her life for him, she acted as though she was deaf. Or she got angry.

Travis had been telling himself all night that Cat must have been holding out for marriage; that was why she had been so coy on the subject of money. But even as angry and frustrated as he was, he couldn't fully convince himself that marriage had been on her mind. Unless she was a staggeringly good actress, the look of shock on her face when he had accused her of trying for a gold ring had been as genuine as her outrage when she stormed out of the cabin.

Then screw yourself, T. H. Danvers—if you can agree on a price!

Warily his mind circled around the dangerous, alluring possibility that had made his night a hell of restlessness. What if Cat wasn't an actress? Did she really want to be with him for no other reason than the pleasure of his company?

Prickles of unease snaked coldly through Travis. If he had learned nothing else last night, he now knew how much he wanted to take Cat at her word. The depth of his hunger to believe in her shook him. He couldn't trust his judgment. Not where she was concerned. He wanted her too much.

Needed her even more.

She said she didn't want marriage. Hell, she insisted on

it. So why not just do it her way? Nothing said. Nothing nailed down. Nothing paid. Just enjoy each other and take the days as they come until there aren't any more days.

Then I'll step into the wind and sail to another place, another time, another . . .

But for the first time in his life, Travis couldn't imagine another woman in his bed. Anger and an uneasiness that was barely a breath away from outright fear warred within him. Before he could discover which was more powerful, the sound of the Zodiac's engine ripped across the water toward him.

Soon Cat would be here.

He was damned if she would find him hanging around like a lovesick teenager.

Other than a polite greeting, Diego didn't offer conversation to his passenger. Cat was grateful. It was all she could do to control her nerves. Small talk was beyond her. She was too worried about running into Travis on the ship. She didn't have the energy to face him now. She felt frayed, fragmented, no more strength than a handful of sand.

Travis won't be there, she assured herself quickly. *Even if he is, he won't bother me. He wants to buy a woman and I won't be bought.*

Yet Cat's hands trembled as she climbed aboard the ship. She felt as faded as the cutoff jeans and blue work shirt she wore.

"This way, if you please," Diego said. "Your equipment is in the captain's cabin."

Her throat closed and her stomach flipped, but nothing showed on her face as she followed Diego down to Travis's cabin. Her camera bags—all five of them—were lined up neatly on the bed. Next to them, on the pillow, lay a pen and sheets of paper covered in angular printing that fairly shouted of T. H. Danvers's male hand moving furiously across the lines.

"Please read these," Diego said, "and then sign where indicated."

"What?" Cat asked, startled.

Diego's eyelids flinched, but he said nothing more. He simply handed her the papers and stepped back.

She flipped through the sheets. They contained a summary of the contents of each camera bag, down to serial numbers where appropriate. She didn't understand why Travis had bothered until she read the last page. There, in slashing block print, was what she was supposed to sign.

I, CATHERINE COCHRAN, DO AGREE THAT THE AFORE-MENTIONED EQUIPMENT WAS RETURNED TO ME IN THE SAME CONDITION I LEFT IT ABOARD THE *WIND WARRIOR*. AT NO TIME IN THE FUTURE WILL I SUG-GEST OTHERWISE, OR ATTEMPT IN ANY WAY TO RE-CEIVE PAYMENT FROM T. H. DANVERS FOR ANY OF THE EQUIPMENT LISTED ABOVE.

There was more. It was like a slap in the face.

I, DIEGO MATEO RAFAEL DE LORENZO Y VELASQUEZ, WITNESS THAT MS. COCHRAN PERSONALLY CHECKED EACH PIECE OF HER EQUIPMENT TO VERIFY ITS CON-DITION.

Cat turned on Diego. Her gray eyes were narrowed and glittering at the unmistakable insult.

"Does he think I'm some little slut he picked up who can't wait to go through his pockets?" Cat said in a raw voice.

"I am sorry. I tried to talk him out of it, but . . ." Diego shrugged gracefully. "You do not know the captain when he is truly in a rage."

Then Diego looked again at Cat's pale face and swore

under his breath in Spanish. Obviously she had seen Travis in one of his famous tempers.

"I regret," Diego said quietly, "but I cannot release the equipment to you until you have checked each piece and signed that paper. The equipment is very valuable, I'm told. More valuable than anything else you have. It is your life, yes?"

She stared at Diego's firm, apologetic expression for a long moment, then at the pieces of paper that were headed "CATHERINE COCHRAN'S PHOTOGRAPHIC EQUIPMENT."

Savagely Cat turned to the first case and began examining the contents. Ignoring Diego, she worked quickly, efficiently, handling each lens and camera body with the familiarity that only came from long experience. When she finished the first case she closed it, set it aside near the door, and went to work on another, and then another.

Somewhere between the first and last camera case, her anger diminished, soothed away by the cool curves and familiar weight of cameras and lenses. They were old friends, loyal friends, her magic windows on the soul of the universe.

And Travis was correct. The equipment was very valuable. To replace it would cost at least fifty thousand dollars. Yet if she sold it, she would be lucky to get a quarter of that. It was the old story of secondhand not being as valuable as new, even though the pictures were the same regardless of the age of the camera.

Behind Cat, Travis silently walked into the cabin. He gestured, and Diego left.

"You know," Travis drawled, "if you need money so damn bad, you could always sell some equipment. You've got enough for three photographers."

Cat's heart stopped, then beat so frantically it made her dizzy. She might have been prepared for Travis's presence, but she wasn't prepared for the casual suggestion that she sell off her very life.

He didn't understand. He never would.

Rich men didn't know how to love anything but themselves.

Trying to control the waves of hot and cold coiling through her stomach, Cat put the last lens in its nest, closed the fifth case, and set it aside. She straightened but didn't turn around to confront Travis. She didn't trust herself. She had no idea what she was going to do next—scream or weep or claw him like a cornered animal.

Travis's legs brushed past Cat, stopping only inches from her as he leaned against the bunk. A tanned, strong hand shot out and scooped up the papers she hadn't signed.

Yet even now, even when she was gripped by anger and hurt, the sight of Travis made her want to run her palm over his arm, to feel his warmth, to savor his strength. Her weakness frightened her.

"I'd no more sell my cameras than I'd sell my children," Cat said harshly.

Then she heard the echo of her own words . . . *my children, my children.* A soft, anguished sound broke through her control. She looked up at Travis, her eyes blind, and when she spoke her voice shook.

"That's it, isn't it?" Cat asked. "I'm passionate, poor, and sterile. That makes me great mistress material but not worth more than a few nights in the sheets, not worth really caring about, certainly not worth loving."

Travis flinched at the pain he saw in her. He felt it as though it was his own, a razor of anguish slicing into him. Then he saw her look toward the door. Her desire to escape from him was as clear as the white lines of grief bracketing her mouth. She started toward the door.

"If you go overboard again," he said, "I'll throw your goddamn cameras in after you."

Cat stared at his face and knew that he meant precisely

what he said. Fury literally vibrated in him. She had never seen a man so angry, hadn't even known that such anger could exist without physical violence. Yet he made not one move toward her.

She looked at her cameras, then at the door that had never seemed farther away. Numbly she looked back at Travis. He was watching her as though he hated her.

No doubt he did. He would have to in order to look at her that way.

"The papers," Cat said, looking away because she couldn't bear to see Travis's contempt anymore. Her throat ached from the strain of not screaming. "I haven't signed them." She held out her hand, not looking at anything except the camera cases lined up by the door. "I'll sign, then I'll take my cameras and go."

Hard fingers closed on her chin, snapping her head around to face Travis.

"Last night you wouldn't stay on board for love or money," he said coldly, "but you'll meekly stay for a few piles of metal and glass. What the hell kind of woman are you?"

Cat flinched and went white before color returned in a desperate spurt of anger and adrenaline.

"Tired, beaten, and cornered," she said, her voice as ragged as her nerves, "that's what kind of woman I am. My cameras are all I have left since you tried to buy what I'd have given you for a few gentle words, a touch, your warmth in the cold center of night. . . ."

She stopped because she couldn't say more. She hated the tears burning in her eyes, choking in her throat, drowning her.

Travis stared at Cat for an aching moment before he closed his eyes, unable to take any more. She was tearing him apart, saying everything he had ever wanted to hear from a woman, love and need that had nothing to do with money . . . and she said it with grief and rage in her eyes instead of tenderness and invitation.

"Damn you," Cat managed finally. "Give me my cameras and let me go."

"Cat," Travis said starkly. "Don't."

She shuddered. His voice hurt even more than her unshed tears.

"Don't leave."

Swiftly Travis put his arms around Cat and held her as though afraid that she would run away from him again and never return. And he was.

"I'm sorry," he said, kissing Cat's eyes, her cheeks, her hair, rocking her. "I didn't understand. I couldn't believe that there was a woman alive who didn't want to be bought. I believe you now. God help me," he whispered, "I believe you. Don't leave me, my woman, my Cat. Stay with me . . . warmth in the cold center of night."

Hearing her own needs, her own words, spoken in Travis's shaking voice unraveled her anger, leaving her too spent to stand, much less to fight. With a ragged sigh she gave herself over to his irresistible strength, floating on him as though he was a wave rising up out of the sea, carrying her irresistibly to an unknown, beautiful shore.

Cat didn't object when Travis lifted her onto his bed and lay down beside her.

"Hold me," he said, sliding his arms around her again. "Just hold me for a minute. Then I'll let you go. If you want to go." He shuddered and whispered, "Don't go, Cat. Please, don't go. I need you."

She felt the shudder that went through Travis when her arms circled his body, heard his broken sigh against her hair, and knew that he was drinking her presence as hungrily as she was absorbing his. The realization went through her like fine cognac, heady and powerful and swift, fire spreading through her, freeing her from the cold, numbing emptiness of last night.

Cat moved her head slightly and found Travis waiting for her, hoping for her to make the first move. With a low sound she opened her lips against his mouth, tasting his heat and sweetness. She kissed him deeply, pouring herself into him until she realized that she was shaking with desire.

And so was he.

She made an incoherent sound, telling him of the fire burning inside her. Her hands moved beneath his dark T-shirt, tugging upward impatiently, hungry for the feel of his naked skin beneath her palms. He shrugged out of the shirt with a muscular twist that made her breath shorten.

"You're . . . beautiful," Cat said.

Travis laughed and touched her lips. "Not likely. But you are. You make me ache."

She just smiled and looked at him in the half-light of the cabin . . . smooth skin rippling over his male strength, tawny hair catching light, his face drawn by need and anticipation until his teeth were two hard white lines divided by the tip of his tongue.

He pulled her mouth down to his and filled himself with her taste. While she returned the deep kiss, his hands moved over her, pulling off her blouse and bra. At the first touch her nipples became hard, vibrant buds nuzzling his hands. He groaned and plucked at her passionate gift until she was writhing and twisting against him.

Liquid waves of pleasure slammed through Cat, a pleasure that built with each caress Travis gave her. Lost, she arched against him, her whole body drawn with a need only he had ever been able to create and satisfy in her.

He moved suddenly, turning over, taking her with him, pinning her beneath him. With a hoarse sound he tore his mouth from hers. Before she could protest the end of the kiss, she felt his tongue on one breast, his teeth closing around the hardened nipple. And then she was sucked into his hot, hungry, demanding mouth and caressed with a fierce thoroughness that made her want to cry out with surprise and intense pleasure.

Slowly Cat twisted against Travis, barely able to breathe for wanting him. Her hands raked down his chest to his swim trunks. She wanted to feel all of him, his strength and his passion and his arousal. That most of all. She loved measuring and pleasuring him with her hands, feeling the heat and tension of his rigid flesh.

When her fingers stroked him through the close-fitting trunks, his body tightened like a drawn bow. For a few seconds he thrust helplessly against her hands, his eyes closed, his lips thinned by the force of the desire raging in him.

Then Travis shifted without warning, peeling off the rest of Cat's clothes. His hands moved almost roughly over her soft skin. His mouth searched hungrily over her, touching every part of her, making her whimper with pleasure. Yet even that wasn't enough for him. He had to know that she wanted him as much as he wanted her.

He slid one hand between her thighs and turned it, opening her legs. The steamy heat of her licked over his fingertips and then over his hand. Waves of pleasure curled tangibly through her to him, a sultry feminine perfume that made him feel dizzy and incredibly powerful at the same time.

She wanted him as much as he wanted her.

"No more talk about leaving," Travis said thickly.

Slick fingers stroked and probed, claiming Cat with deep caresses that didn't stop even when rhythmic waves of pleasure curled and broke, shattering her, transfixing her soft flesh.

Smiling narrowly, wild and fully controlled at the same time, Travis lowered his mouth to taste his lover's climax.

"No more running from me," he said.

His teeth closed with ravenous delicacy on her, sending yet another wave of ecstasy ripping through her. He tasted it, tasted her, and then he fed on her climax, driving her higher, wilder, until she cried out and convulsed again.

Only then did Travis shift until his hips lay between her thighs, opening her completely. One of his hands tangled in the hair at the nape of her neck in a claiming as fierce as the passion burning behind his eyes. He held her motionless while his other hand caressed her shivering, sultry flesh, his fingers sliding deeply into her heat, retreating, returning, probing, until she moaned and arched bonelessly into his touch and he smiled, watching her.

"You're mine, sweet Cat, my woman. You're mine and I've only begun to touch you. . . ."

She saw the hunger and stark need in his eyes, and felt it in his touch, in his fiercely erect flesh like a burning rod against her belly. Fire ate at nerves still quivering with the shocking ecstasy he had given her. She wanted to do the same for him, to feel him succumb helplessly to a passionate storm of her making.

Calling his name, she cried out and reached for him, wanting only to give him a pleasure to equal what he had given her. Her hands kneaded down his body, savoring him with palms and fingertips and delicate raking nails.

It wasn't enough. She wanted to taste him, to know him as passionately as he had known her. She pulled at his swim trunks, but her hands trembled too much to peel the stretchy fabric away.

Laughing with sheer pleasure at Cat's hunger for him, Travis finished undressing himself with a few swift motions.

"Let me—" she began.

His mouth closed over hers and the world narrowed to the feel of his tongue moving over hers, his fingers between her legs echoing the slow rhythms of love.

Waves of pleasure went through her, pleasure she shared with him, melting over him while she made small, reckless sounds at the back of her throat. When he finally lifted his head, she was covered in a fine mist of heat, her eyes wide and almost wild. She whispered his name, her hands and eyes asking for something she didn't know how to put into words.

"Yes, my woman?" Travis said thickly against her throat, his hand still buried in her hair, holding her while her body arched and quivered. "What do you want? Tell me and I'll give it to you. Anything."

"I want—" A shudder moved over her, tightening muscles inside her body in a reflex as old as passion and as new as her next ragged breath.

Travis smiled, his teeth a vivid flash of white against his tawny beard.

"What is it that you want, little Cat?"

He lowered his head until he could lick the mist off her breasts with quick, light strokes of his tongue. She made a ragged sound and shuddered again. His mouth moved, enjoying her.

"Do you know how good you taste?" he asked.

"Travis," Cat began, only to have her voice unravel into a moan. "That's what I want, only—" Her nails dug into his shoulders as another wave of pleasure broke over her.

"Only what?" he said, his blue-green eyes burning as they watched her lifted by a wave of pleasure.

"I—" Cat took a deep breath as the wave passed, giving her back her body and her voice until the next wave would come, claiming her. She touched his erection lightly, longingly. "You once said I could touch you anywhere, any way I wanted to. Did you mean that?"

His lips curved in a smile that took her breath. "Yes."

Her fingers traced the length of his body, lingering over his heat and maleness.

"I've never been touched the way you touched me," Cat said, hesitantly. "I've never wanted to touch a man the way I want to touch you. Let me touch you. Please."

Travis's hand tightened almost savagely in her hair,

chaining her for an instant while his lips drank the pulse beating rapidly in her neck.

"Whatever you want," he said hoarsely.

He released her, letting her slide down his body, a wild, sweet fire licking over him.

She flexed her fingers like a cat, rubbing her palms down his chest and stomach and thighs, teasing him by just avoiding his aching, sensitive flesh. She let him feel the sharpness of her nails and the softness of her tongue, then looked up and found him watching her with eyes that burned too vividly to be real.

Cat smiled and Travis fought to breathe. She looked impossibly beautiful to him with her hair licking like flames around her naked breasts, her mouth flushed, her body sultry and shivering with the pleasure she wanted to share.

With a ragged sound Cat leaned forward until her hair fell over Travis in a silky, seething cloud. Hesitantly, then with increasing confidence, she explored his body, running her cheeks and mouth over the smooth muscles of his abdomen, enjoying the textures of warm skin, taut muscles, tawny hair that was hot and springy, the softer hair of his thighs and calves.

She savored him, fascinated by his male body, his strength and potency. When her tongue finally, tentatively, traced his arousal, the long muscles of his thighs contracted.

Travis made a hoarse sound. His hips moved sinuously, telling her without words that he reveled in the intimate caress.

Desire shook Cat as thoroughly as it shook him. To have the freedom of his body and to feel his uninhibited response was as exciting as any caress he had ever given her. With a small, reckless sound she bent to him, letting the rest of the world slide away. She forgot everything, even herself, in the violent pleasure of loving Travis as she had never loved any man.

"Cat—" Travis's voice was unrecognizable, torn between a groan and a fierce cry of pleasure.

She escaped the hands blindly trying to drag her back up his body. Caught as completely as he was in the wildness building between them, she wanted only to continue setting fire to him with the changing pressures of her mouth.

For a few moments more Cat held Travis captive with her tongue and teeth. Then the world tilted crazily and she found herself imprisoned in the grip of a man whose strength she had only begun to measure. He was looking at her with hot blue-green eyes and a dark smile.

"Witch," Travis muttered thickly. His hands shifted, fastened behind her knees, pulling her legs up, opening her completely. "I hope you want what you've been asking for, because I'm going to give you every bit of it."

Cat arched her hips hungrily, seeking him, giving her newly discovered wildness to him, certain that he would enjoy it as much as she did.

With a deep male sound Travis took what she offered, filling her with a single savage thrust that undid her. Even as she convulsed he drove into her harshly, repeatedly. Each slam of flesh into flesh sent her higher, her world tearing, shattering, soaring, exploding into a glittering black where colors pulsed. Only his mouth over hers kept her from screaming as fierce ecstasy transformed her.

With a hoarse, grating cry, Travis ground his hips against Cat and pumped himself into her, his body corded and shuddering, his eyes glazed and wild.

It was a long time before the aftershocks of passion stopped shivering through their spent bodies. When their breathing no longer caught and broke, Travis forced himself to lift some of his weight from Cat's body. She made an inarticulate sound of protest, not wanting to be separate from him. His finely scarred fingers framed her face.

"I've never lost control like that, even when I was a

kid,'' Travis said roughly, searching Cat's misty gray eyes. "Did I hurt you?''

"Hurt me?'' She licked her lips, tasted him, and tightened her body, savoring the feel of him locked deep within her slick heat.

"Damn,'' Travis said. He took her mouth almost hungrily, tasting her, tasting himself, tasting passion. When he finally lifted his head, his breathing was ragged. "The way you answer my questions could get you in trouble all over again.''

Cat laughed and rubbed her cheek against his beard. Her hands moved slowly over the muscles of his back to his buttocks, enjoying him with an intensity that was reflected in her warm gray eyes. He moved inside her, letting her know that she was playing with fire.

"Insatiable, aren't you?'' she teased.

"Not usually,'' he said, his hands stroking languidly over her body, "not like this. This is new, Cat.'' He buried his head in the fire of her hair. "Everything you bring to me is new. I want to make love until I can't tell who is you and who is me.'' His fingers rubbed through her hair in sensuous assault even as he moved inside her. "I want to fill you until you'll be empty if I'm not there. *I want you.*''

"Yes,'' Cat said, lifting herself against his strength. "Yes, I—''

Then her breath caught and she couldn't say anything more, only hold on to Travis as he loved her with mouth and hands and body.

A shimmering wave of passion claimed them, swirling them around, tumbling them over and over until they dissolved into each other, holding back nothing. They were enclosed in a primitive, radiant world where nothing existed but the ecstasy they gave and took and explored until they had strength left only to lie spent, breath and heartbeat tangled, a single body shared between them.

SIXTEEN

IN THE next three weeks, Travis didn't bring up the subject of Australia or any other exotic, distant location. Cat kept waiting for it, waiting for Travis to step into the wind and leave her behind. The thought of losing him gave her an odd sinking feeling, as though the ground was slowly dissolving beneath her feet until nothing was left but emptiness and she was sinking slowly, spinning.

"You sure you need more pictures of me at my computer?" Travis asked, watching Cat narrowly. "Why don't we laze around on the beach instead?"

Though they had spent most of the night asleep in his big bed with a humid, almost tropical breeze flowing over their skin, this morning Cat looked ghostly to Travis. Her rich auburn hair was startling against her pale skin. She was as unexpected as a flame burning in the center of cotton candy—in this case, his cousin's wallpaper in the room he had taken over as his office.

Even though Travis fed Cat every time he thought of it, he was certain she had lost weight. Not much. A few pounds. Just enough to remind him how close to the end of her physical resources she was.

It haunted him. He wanted to make life simpler for her, easier; yet everything he did just complicated it. It took time to eat. Time to sleep. Time to laugh. Time to love. And time to work. That most of all.

Cat needed more sleep than Travis did, yet when he got up for his dawn swim, he was alone. He would look out the window and see lights burning in the house across the ravine, lights throwing pale rectangles of yellow into the predawn darkness. When he finished his swim and was ready for breakfast, he would have to go next door and drag her away from her light table or her dunning letters or her files. He would make a big breakfast and watch her eat a quarter of what he ate, no matter how much he coaxed and teased and spoon-fed her.

Travis no longer counted the times he bit his tongue against offering Cat the money she so obviously needed. The best he had managed in the way of help was sneaking off to the supermarket and stocking up her refrigerator and cupboards while she was out shooting corporate lions and making babies smile for Mommy. Although she had said nothing about it, he was certain that the Big Check from Energistics hadn't come, which meant she had been forced to find other sources of cash.

Work and more work. Small jobs that were only stopgap measures, an effort to stay afloat until she had some other kind of luck than bad.

Though Travis waited, not once had Cat asked him for help paying bills. He knew she would make a nice bit of money when she finished his book, but she was taking too much time on it. Time she should have spent sleeping or sorting slides or simply doing nothing at all. He suspected that the extra hours and days she put into his book was her way to be with him, squeezing precious time out of her relentless schedule.

"Cat?" Travis brushed his palm over her cheek. "Where are you?"

She blinked, banished the empty, sinking feeling, and smiled up into beautiful tourmaline eyes. With a sigh, she kissed the broad palm that was caressing her. Travis was right here, within reach, touching her. There was no need to think about the future when he would be gone and there would be nothing but work and more work and solid ground dissolving beneath her feet, leaving her adrift, slowly spinning.

No reason to borrow unhappiness from tomorrow. It would come soon enough.

"Just planning my shots," Cat said, focusing on the here and now. "Do you have some drawings you wouldn't mind having made public? Stuff that's already patented?"

"I keep my old drawings on a hard disk," Travis said, gesturing toward a box of multigigabyte disks that sat on the floor next to his computer. "What do you need?"

"Real paper. It's hard to photograph bytes."

Travis smiled and tugged lightly on a lock of Cat's hair. "I have a printer."

"That does drawings?"

He nodded.

"Good," Cat said. "Find me a drawing that's simple, elegant, and mysterious without being alien to a layman."

"Swear to God, Cochran, you're hard to please."

"You've been talking to Harrington again."

"He's fussing around me like a mother hen," Travis admitted.

"Why?"

"He's wondering if I'm going to get in the wind before the book is done, but he's too canny to ask outright."

It was an effort, but Cat managed to keep her smile in place. "Harrington's nothing if not canny."

"Don't you want to know what I told him?" Travis asked softly.

Cat didn't want to know when she would lose the only man she had ever loved, but she kept her voice casual as she bent over and rummaged in one of her camera cases.

"Sure," she said. "What did you tell Harrington?"

"That I wasn't going anywhere until I could talk a cer-

tain redheaded witch into sailing off to the ends of the earth
with me."

Cat's heart turned over with a longing that made her
ache. *If only that was true. If only Travis would wait for
me until January.*

"Well, sailor," she said lightly, "in that case you're going to be in port for quite a while. It's about this book I'm
working on. . . ."

A book she would find a way to continue working on
until January, at least. But she wasn't going to say that
aloud. She would take one day at a time. And one night.

"Now you've got it," Travis drawled.

"I do?"

"Yeah. Pack up your gear. We'll set sail and you can
take pictures for the book until your camera melts or hell
freezes over, whichever comes first."

Temptation prickled over Cat, a yearning so great that
she shivered with it. "There's a small problem," she said
in a low voice.

"Just one? Go pack. The problem is solved."

"You don't even know what it is."

"Have faith in your pirate."

"Even pirates can't develop film at sea," Cat said, smiling sadly, silently begging Travis to understand that she
still wasn't free to put her hand in his and step into the
wind.

"So develop film when we get ashore," he said.

"Sorry. Doesn't work that way. Foreign film developers
are dicey, at best. You ruin more rolls than you keep."

"Okay. We'll send them back here."

"Snail mail," Cat said, keeping her voice cheerful. "Too
slow. I have to know which images fly and which die, and
I have to know in time to get more of what's needed."

Travis bit down on the anger and restlessness that surged
up out of nowhere. He wanted Cat more than anything on
earth. She wanted him more than any woman ever had.

But not enough.

"What about a digital camera?" he suggested neutrally. "You can see an exact preview of each shot. You can store the images in a computer, call up one of my programs, and play with the image any way you want. Don't like the contrast? Change it. Don't want the clouds? Delete them. Focus sucks? Fix it. Presto. Welcome to the miraculous world of photography in the twenty-first century."

"When I get there, I'll welcome it. Digital is moving up on my must-have list."

"What if I bought a digital camera?"

In the abrupt silence, each of them could hear the bold rhythm of a wave coming apart on the shore. Light dimmed and then redoubled as a cloud whipped across the path of the sun. The storms off of Mexico had been flirting with Southern California for weeks.

"I didn't know you were into photography," Cat said, smiling carefully. But her eyes were the cool gray of pewter.

"Just one of my many interests," Travis muttered. He raked a hand through his hair and turned away before he said something he would regret. "Come on."

"Where?"

"Lunch."

"We just had breakfast."

"So who appointed you to the Meal Police? Besides, that was hours ago. You need more food."

Cat started to protest, then decided not to. If she told him she was too tired to eat, he would find some way to get her in bed early and keep her in bed late. As much as she would have enjoyed that, she simply didn't have the time.

At least Travis had dropped the topic of a shockingly expensive digital camera. And they hadn't argued about money this time.

Progress. Definitely.

January, Cat thought with a combination of fear and

hope. *We can make it until January. Then I'll put my hand in his and step into the wind.*

But all she said aloud was, "What do you think of shrimp salad and fresh rolls?"

"As a nibble, fine. I had lunch in mind."

"Dare I ask?"

"Enchiladas, quesadillas, burritos, and tacos. In no particular order."

"The stomach churns."

"The stomach needs food," Travis shot back. "C'mon. Jason told me about this really fantastic Mexican place his dad took him to before he flew off back east."

"Jason is gone?" Cat asked, startled.

"No. His dad. That's the first sign, you know."

"Huh?"

"Malnutrition," Travis said, sliding an arm around Cat's narrow waist. "Your thought processes fry."

"You're not making any sense."

"Uh-oh. That's the next stage. Starvation. We'd better hurry."

Laughing, Cat put her arm around Travis's waist. She could always make up for time lost at lunch by slipping out of bed even earlier than usual tomorrow.

Or not sleeping at all.

The phone woke Travis up. As usual, he was alone in the big bed with its fussy lace sheets and pink satin pillows. Groaning, he looked at the clock.

Three A.M.

Three! When did Cat leave? he wondered with a combination of irritation and anger.

The phone kept ringing.

And who would call at this hour?

There was one way to find out. Travis snatched the pink receiver and snarled a word into it.

"Ah, there's the sweet boy I know and love," Harrington said dryly.

"What the hell do you want at this hour?"

"Are you alone?"

"Yes."

"That explains it. You're surly because Fire-and-Ice had enough of your piratical charm and left you to stew in your own rude juices."

Travis smiled and yawned. "Cat is next door, trying to cope with that damned gallery's demands. Can you believe it? Swift and Sons asks for sixteen images originally, she sends them, and then they up it to twenty-two. So she busts her ass and makes up the extra. Then they demand a total of forty-six and an exclusive contract for—"

"Yo, Danvers, this is me, remember?" Harrington interrupted. "The agent for the photographer in question."

"Some agent. You're killing her."

"A showing like this is a watershed in an artist's career," Harrington said simply. "They moved her from one of the side galleries on the second level to the main floor. Not just one room. Three. She's the whole thing, Travis. Not just a sideshow."

"Then they should send someone out to help her put it all together."

"Does that mean you finally have someone to help you put together your designs?"

"Of course not. Of all the lamebrained . . ." Travis's voice trailed off into a sigh. "Hell. I really walked into that. I must still be asleep."

"Where's Cochran?"

"Where do you think?"

"It's too dark for photography, so I assumed I would catch both of you, um, at home."

"You're half right. What's up—besides me?"

"Just wanted to see how things were going," Harrington said casually.

"Things are going fine."

"Everything on schedule?"

Instead of answering, Travis scratched his beard thoughtfully, then the hair on his chest. He might wake up slowly without the help of a good swim, but he did wake up.

Harrington wanted something.

Travis had an idea of what it was.

"Seems like it," Travis said. "Dawn is starting to take a big bite out of night. The tropical storm that has been churning around off Mexico is slowly dying. The warm El Niño ocean and big waves had made a lot of surfers happy this summer. Temperature is—"

"Much as I hate to interrupt your riveting little weather report, I do have important things to do. Combing my hair comes immediately to mind."

"Go for it. Should I tell Cat to call you?"

"Does that mean you're still speaking?"

"To you?" Travis asked innocently.

"Swear to God, Danvers, you'd piss off a saint! Are things fine between you and Cat?"

Travis smiled grimly. "I thought you'd get down to it."

"I did. Why don't you?"

"Things are just fine."

"What does that mean?"

"It's your question, not mine. What does fine mean?"

The next silence gave Travis plenty of time to enjoy dawn slowly consuming the night.

"If things are so bloody fine between the two of you," Harrington said coolly, "why is she working so hard?"

"Money."

"Then give her more," Harrington snarled. "God knows you can afford it."

"She won't take one penny."

"What? Then how has she survived? Energistics hasn't paid and that mealymouthed poet is taking forever choosing the pictures—excuse me, *soul images*—for his book. Tuition is coming due and Cat's dear mother just spent a fortune on her trousseau!''

Travis didn't say anything.

"Not a penny?" Harrington asked after a moment.

"Not one."

"What happened to your rule about women?"

"I broke it, just like Cat broke her rule about combining business and pleasure."

"Broke it. Swear to God. Amazing. What next?"

"That's the whole show," Travis said evenly. "We're two responsible adults and we're enjoying the hell out of each other."

"What about the future?"

Travis went still. He didn't like thinking about the future. He liked talking about it even less. "What about it?"

"Cat isn't like your other women," Harrington said.

"I know."

"What are you going to do about it?"

"Stop pushing me, Harrington."

"After you answer my question."

"I can't," Travis said simply.

The sun was halfway across the afternoon when Travis and Cat emerged from his cabin on *Wind Warrior*.

"I knew you had enough time for a nap," he said, tracing her cheek with his fingertips.

"Nap, huh? Is that what we were doing?"

"Eventually."

Casually Travis looked out over the water and smiled rather grimly. The Zodiac was tied at the pier, as he had ordered. Everyone was ashore. They had orders not to come back until evening. He didn't like having to scheme like a teenager just to be alone with his woman, but he was getting good at it.

And like a teenager, he was getting good at pretending tomorrow would never come.

In order to be with Cat, Travis had turned himself into her assistant. When she went to photographic assignments, he was there. He not only carried her heavy camera bags, he began to anticipate her needs, handing her a piece of equipment before she could ask for it.

The first time that had happened she simply stared at him and whispered, *What did I ever do without you?* His answer had been as swift as it was fierce. *The same thing I did without you—go through life not knowing what the hell I was missing.*

Travis didn't know how much longer he could go on juggling his professional demands, his hunger to be at sea, and his consuming need to be with Cat. He only knew he didn't want to find out. He didn't want that ultimate tomorrow to come.

"Where is everyone?" Cat asked, looking around the deserted ship.

"Shore leave," he said laconically.

"What about us?"

"If it's urgent, we'll just have to swim."

Cat yawned and stretched languidly, feeling boneless from Travis's loving and a long, wonderful nap. "Swim? Ha. I'd go down like a brick. Looks like you're stuck with me."

Travis tilted her face up and kissed her swiftly. "Remember that, witch. You're mine."

Her eyes widened into misty silver pools. She looked up at him through dense lashes that glinted red and gold.

He smiled.

"You really *are* a pirate, aren't you?" Cat muttered.

"Where you're concerned, yes."

The sensual rasp in Travis's voice sent echoes of ecstasy shimmering through her. His smile was rakish and utterly male, reminding her of what it was like to have him deep inside her.

It was all Cat could do not to simply stand and stare at

her lover. In the slanting afternoon light his eyes had a
jewel-like purity of color. His skin was taut, deeply
bronzed, and his beard was spun from dark gold. Beneath
his faded black T-shirt and casual shorts, his body radiated
ease and power.

"Don't move," Cat ordered, heading back to the cabin.

"Where are you going?"

"Don't move!"

She raced below deck, grabbed the two camera cases she
used most often, and ran back on deck. While Travis
watched her with a lazy, sexy gleam in his eyes, she pulled
out a camera and a small telephoto lens. When she retreated
a few feet back along the deck, he moved as though to
follow.

"No," she said. "Stay right where you are. You're perfect."

"Cat," he said, amusement curling in his voice, "what
are you doing?"

"Taking pictures of an off-duty buccaneer."

The motor drive surged quickly, pulling frame after
frame of film through the camera.

"You're supposed to be taking pictures of the *Wind Warrior*," Travis pointed out.

"I am. You're part of the ship. The most important part.
Creator, owner, soul."

She caught the sudden intensity of his expression, an
elemental recognition of her words. The motor drive
whirred in response to her command. After a few more
frames she lowered the camera and walked back to him.

"Get used to looking into a camera lens," Cat warned
Travis. "I've been itching to photograph you since the first
time I looked into those gorgeous, sea-colored eyes of
yours."

Laughing softly, he snaked one arm around her and
pulled her snugly against his side. Together they walked
the deck of the ship from bow to stern and back again,

talking about the book project. Energy and ideas bubbled through her.

It was the special enthusiasm that came only when Cat had been working on a project, and working on it, and suddenly it all came together. From one breath to the next, she began seeing both Travis and his ship with a new understanding. Now she knew what she would need for the book and how she would get it.

Cat worked tirelessly, absorbed in the subtle changes of light and texture and composition. She darted around Travis like a fire, taking photos of the captain and his ship from various angles.

Travis didn't interfere or require her conversation. He could sense the excitement of creation flooding through her as clearly as he felt it in himself when elusive details of hull design would condense in his mind.

Smiling, he watched his lover, enjoying her intense concentration on her work. She handled cameras and lenses with the same total familiarity he handled wind and sail. When her determination to catch the sunlight on the rigging made her forget he was alive, he sat cross-legged on the deck and began splicing rope, not at all upset at being ignored.

When Cat realized that Travis wasn't nearby anymore, she lowered her camera and looked around for him. She found him halfway back on the deck, sitting in a pool of sunlight. His head was bent over some task. Sun glinted over his tawny hair like a miser running fingers through gold.

Her heart hesitated, then beat with redoubled strength. She set aside her camera and went to Travis. Without a word she took the rope out of his hands and started pulling off his T-shirt.

"What are you doing?" he asked, surprised.

"Taking off your shirt."

He blinked, then relaxed beneath Cat's hands with a pirate's smile of anticipation. She smiled in return, the serene smile of a sorceress, and threw his T-shirt aside. Then she put rope back into the hands that were reaching for her and picked up her camera once more.

"Come back here and finish what you started," Travis said.

"I'm finished."

"What about my pants?"

"They make a nice contrast with the deck."

"Well, damn."

Disappointed, Travis made a face at the camera, then resumed splicing rope. Cat photographed him as he worked, seated like a god in the center of a golden cataract of light. He watched her with intense, blue-green eyes, measuring her progress around him while she climbed the rigging and the railing in search of the perfect angle.

At one point she miscalculated. He came to his feet in a single motion and snatched her off her perch before she could fall. She laughed and let herself slide down his body, her hands savoring his supple, sun-warmed skin.

Then he held her close, breathless, kissing her until she made soft sounds and melted over him like sunlight. When he was certain that work was the furthest thing from her mind, he took her below and sank into her, drinking her cries and muffling his own.

When Travis fell asleep, it was to the sound of storm surf thundering against the breakwater that protected the harbor.

Cat listened to the relentless waves and tried not to think about the time when she would be listening alone.

I'll ask him tomorrow, she told herself. *Then I'll know how long we have.*

Yet just the thought of putting her worst fear into words made her skin clammy.

She knew then that she would never ask Travis when he was going to leave. It was agonizing enough simply to know that someday he would board the *Wind Warrior* and sail over the curve of the world, never to come back to her again.

Cat didn't want to know the date of the last hour they would have together, the exact moment when everything solid would dissolve around her, leaving her adrift, sinking, alone as she had never been before.

SEVENTEEN

WHEN TRAVIS came into Cat's office carrying a cardboard carton, she was sitting at her light table sorting slides and trying to ignore her growling stomach. She looked up and smiled hopefully.

"Is that dinner?" she asked.

"Didn't you eat lunch?"

She shook her head. "These slides should have been in the mail weeks ago. Tomorrow I'll make time to go to the market."

Guiltily Travis realized that he hadn't been to the store for almost a week. He had been caught up in a new design for a hull, plus going on various assignments with Cat, and a round of negotiations for building a shipfitting and repair installation close to Laguna Beach.

And then there were the plans he had drawn up to refit one of the guest cabins on the *Wind Warrior* as a traveling photographic lab. Working with Harrington, and swearing him to secrecy, Travis had bought various pieces of equipment for Cat to use. He knew she wouldn't be able to leave her work behind.

And he knew he wouldn't be able to stay in Laguna all the time.

"I'll bet you haven't eaten since we had peanut butter and cocoa with Jason this morning," Travis said.

Cat didn't bother to deny it.

"You don't know the first thing about taking care of yourself," he said. "You work too hard. Damn it, if you'd just let me pay—"

Abruptly Travis shut up. The amount she worked was directly related to her need for money. Money was one subject he had vowed not to bring up until she did.

Cat hadn't even hinted at it.

Silently she looked at Travis, knowing what he was seeing in her face. Shadows of fatigue surrounded her eyes. Her cheekbones were too sharply drawn. Her skin was too pale. She was tired, driven, relentless in her demands on herself.

She knew she was pushing herself too hard. Her weekly visits to the doctor were a brutal reminder. Her hips were bruised from iron shots and her ears were burned from Dr. Stone's caustic remarks about endurance and exhaustion.

Yet Cat didn't know what else she could do except keep pushing until January. She needed the money that came from her work, but she couldn't deny herself time with Travis. She knew that someday he would leave her as suddenly as he had come to her.

Until that day came, Cat would beg, borrow, bribe, and steal every instant she could from the rest of her life, hoarding seconds and minutes and hours to give to him. And her only regret would be that there was never enough time.

Travis bent and kissed Cat in silent apology. "I'm sorry. I know I take up too much of your time."

"No. Never that. I'm just . . . greedy. World enough and time." She smiled ironically, rubbing her aching neck. "Not much to ask, is it? Just everything."

This time his kiss deepened until it was just short of bruising, but he said only, "I'll bring you something to eat."

He reappeared in a few minutes, balancing a plate of pasta in one hand and a bowl of salad in the other.

"Did you steal Sharon's dinner?" Cat asked, startled.

"Nope. The miracle of take-out pasta," Travis said, smiling triumphantly. "A new place opened up on the high-way."

She eyed the mound of pasta, appalled at its size. "My God, Travis, it'll take me a week to eat that."

He smiled sheepishly. "I remembered that I hadn't eaten, either."

"How's the hull design coming?" Cat asked, under-standing exactly why he had forgotten to eat.

"Slowly. But it's coming. It would be easier if a ship's hull was as supple as a dolphin."

"Swear to God," she said dryly. "You don't ask much."

"Speaking of Harrington, how is he?"

"Ready to get on the next plane and pick slides for me if I won't do it myself."

"Swift and Sons is getting restless?"

"Big time."

Travis sat at the small table Cat had set up in the corner of her office so that he would have a place to work on his hull designs while she pored over the endless boxes of slides.

"So let Harrington help you," Travis said, handing Cat a fork.

"There's a family crisis. A sister getting divorced. Very messy. It wouldn't be fair to ask him to hold my hand, too. Besides, the reasons I choose one slide over another can't be put into words, but it does make a difference in the continuity of the show."

"Eat," was all Travis said.

Both of them attacked the food. Cat filled up quickly. When she couldn't eat any more food no matter what Travis threatened, he calmly finished the pile of pasta, cleared away the dishes, and set a cardboard carton on the table.

"What's in the box?" Cat asked.

"Whittling."

She blinked. "Come again?"

"Carving. You know, sharp knives and pieces of wood." Travis reached into the box and pulled out several blocks of wood that were bigger than his hand. "Do you think Jason would like dark or light wood better?"

Cat looked at the intelligence and warmth in Travis's eyes and felt a familiar, sweet heat ripple through her. Her lips quivered slightly as she smiled.

"Dark, of course," she said huskily. "Like the *Wind Warrior*. Is that what you're going to do—make Jason a ship?"

Travis put away all but the piece of nearly black wood. Then he touched Cat's cheek with a gentleness that made her ache.

"How did you know what I was going to do?" he asked.

"I just did. Jason worships you."

"It's mutual," Travis said. He turned over the ebony block in his hand, looking for the *Wind Warrior* trapped within solid wood, and added absently, "I'd like a son like Jason."

Cat closed her eyes, afraid that Travis would see the pain slicing through her. She knew that he hadn't meant to wound her with his words. In any case, she was both proud and pragmatic enough to realize that even if she could have children, they wouldn't be his.

In the time she had spent with Travis, she had come to understand that there was nothing personal in his refusal to love her. Love required trust. Travis required a certain level of wealth before he could trust a woman. Cat didn't have that wealth.

It was a fact, like gravity. Nothing personal at all.

But that didn't make the hurt any less.

Lost in thought, Travis turned the dark block of wood over and over in his hands. Cat didn't interrupt his concentration. She gave him the same undemanding companionship that he gave her when she was absorbed in her own work.

Absently he fished a thin, razor-edged knife out of the carton. He turned on and adjusted the gooseneck lamp that arched shoulder high above the table. A shaft of white light poured over the rich wood. The same light that picked up hints of chestnut and mahogany in the densely grained block of wood turned the hair on his forearms into spun gold. The wood and his skin glowed against the deep tourmaline green color of his shirt.

Before Travis even touched blade to wood, Cat knew that she had to photograph him—his concentration, his exquisitely sensitive hands, his vivid eyes, the flow of light and shadow over his face.

Travis was so accustomed to Cat at work that he didn't even notice the whirring of the motor drive or the occasional flash she used when the existing light didn't please her. She worked with an intensity that equaled his, narrowing her world to the width of a camera lens, trying to capture the essence of the man she loved.

As minutes slowly built into hours, an image of the *Wind Warrior* emerged from the black wood. It was very difficult work, for ebony was almost too hard to be carved. Travis's concentration never wavered, even when the knife inevitably slipped and nicked the backs of his fingers, leaving behind a hairline of red that bled freely. He didn't stop carving until blood threatened to stain the wood.

"Damn," he muttered, licking the backs of his fingers. "One more scar." He stretched the tight muscles across his shoulders and flexed his cut hand ruefully. "I usually have a choppy sea to blame for my clumsiness."

"Blame it on the hour," Cat said, stretching as he had stretched.

Startled, he glanced at the clock.

Two in the morning.

He looked at her dark eyes and the litter of empty film

containers scattered on the floor around the table, mute evidence that she had been working as hard as he had.

"Ah, Cat," Travis said deeply, shaking his head and pulling her onto his lap, "I had other plans for tonight."

She smiled and rubbed her mouth lightly over his. "It's still tonight."

"It's late, and you're so damn tired."

"When I'm *that* tired, you can call 911. Besides," she added, yawning delicately, then closing her teeth on his ear, "I'm going to make you do all the work."

His hands hesitated, then moved knowingly over her body. "Are you sure, sweetheart? I can wait."

"I can't. I've been wanting you every second since you told me you were making a ship for Jason."

Cat tugged at Travis's shirt, needing to end this night as she had so many others, deep in his arms. There were times when she didn't know which was the greater pleasure, sharing his mind or sharing his body.

She did know that nothing would be the same without him, that he had become as much a part of her as her own skin, her own dreams. She loved him as she had never thought to love any man. It had been hard not to tell Travis about her feelings, but she hadn't. She wouldn't. To say *I love you* is to ask that your love be returned, to ask for a lifetime together. She wouldn't do that.

There was no point in asking.

She knew the answer.

Travis had told her in the first days of their affair that he would never be able to trust a woman who had less money than he had. Cat believed him. Not once in the nine weeks they had been together had he lied to her.

She hoped that in time he would change his mind about trusting her, but she sensed that time was running out.

Five short weeks until January. Just five. He won't leave before then.

She told herself that over and over, but she didn't believe

it. Lately Travis had been watching the sea with the hunger of a sailor who had been too long ashore.

"Jason will be over the moon," Cat said, touching the miniature *Wind Warrior* with reverent fingertips. She could hardly believe that Travis had finished the elegant sculpture in a night and a morning. "It's so beautiful. I hope he's careful with it."

Travis looked up from the crumbs of the omelet Cat had cooked for them. They were in her kitchen, not his. They hadn't made it to his house at all last night. They had simply fallen into her bed and spent the few remaining hours of darkness tangled first in passion and then in sleep.

The silky memories made him want to kiss her generous lips and stubborn chin, and then move on to the soft, pink-tipped breasts that hardened so quickly in his mouth.

"If Jason loses this in the surf," Travis said, touching the little sailing ship, "I'll make another one for him."

."The surf! Over my dead body! This little beauty is going inside a glass bottle just as soon as I can figure out how to squeeze it past the neck."

Laughing, Travis eased his fingers into Cat's soft, autumn-colored hair. The scent of lemon shampoo and the warmth in her eyes intoxicated him.

"It doesn't work that way," he said, caressing her scalp.

"You sure?"

"Uh-huh. Trust me."

Cat smiled slowly at Travis, remembering just how exquisite it was to trust her body to his keeping . . . and to take his in return.

"You keep looking at me like that," he said in a deep voice, "and Jason will find us naked on the kitchen table."

She gave a delicious little shiver of memory and anticipation. "Don't tempt me."

"How about if I tease you instead?"

Travis's hand slid from Cat's hair to her breasts. The

cotton shirt she wore was no barrier to sensation. Her breath caught, broke, and then became a ragged sigh when knowing fingertips circled one nipple.

A young voice called from the beach. "Cathy? Am I too early? Are you up?"

"I'm in the kitchen," Cat called.

Jason's footsteps drummed on the stairway outside. "Is Travis up, too?"

"Definitely," Travis muttered. "Damn." He caressed her hard nipple one more time and dropped his hand before the kitchen door flew open. None of his frustration showed when he turned to Jason. "We're just finishing breakfast. Have you eaten?"

"Nah. The babies were screaming and Dad was on one phone talking to Boston and Mom was on the other phone talking to her sister in Georgia."

Cat smiled, tucked the hand holding the toy boat behind her, and gave Jason a quick, one-armed hug. "You've come to the right place. I'll scramble some eggs for you."

"Make some for yourself, too," Travis muttered. "You only had about two bites of the omelet you made."

She ignored him, not wanting to argue over how much she did or didn't eat. Her appetite had gone on holiday. Even after five hours of sleep, the smell of food didn't appeal to her.

"I'll do the toast," Jason said eagerly.

"I'll get the orange juice," Travis said. "But first I get a good-morning hug."

Delighted, Jason launched himself at Travis, confident from past experience that he would be caught and hugged back.

Cat took advantage of Jason's distraction to hide the black boat in the refrigerator when she got out some more eggs. Before she had them cracked into a pan, the kitchen was full of Jason's whoops of laughter. Travis had the boy up on his shoulders for a "pirate" ride.

Like a tyrant on a throne, Jason supervised the making of breakfast from his high perch. He would have eaten from there, too, but Travis drew the line at having toast crumbs dribbled down the neck of his T-shirt.

"Okay, tiger," Travis said, lifting Jason off his shoulders and setting him on a chair to eat. "Time to come back to earth. When do you have to be ready for school?"

"It's Saturday," the boy said.

Cat and Travis exchanged a quick look. They both sensed the silent appeal that Jason was too polite to put into words; he wanted company, and everybody in his family was busy. She nodded slightly to Travis while she frantically rearranged her day in her mind.

Not enough time. Never enough time. But she would do it, somehow. January was only five weeks away. She could keep on juggling for five more weeks.

If Travis stayed that long.

She shoved the unhappy thought away. She couldn't live in tomorrow. She could only live in today.

"No school, huh?" Travis said. "Then I think it's time Jason saw a real-for-sure pirate boat up close."

"Real-for-sure? You mean it?"

"Yeah."

"Cool!"

"If it's all right with your parents," Travis amended quickly. "I'll call them."

"It will be forever before they're off the phone!" Jason wailed, disappointed.

Travis smiled. "You and Cat eat breakfast while I run over and talk in your mom's other ear."

Jason was too excited at the prospect of going on board a real ship to notice that he ate Cat's breakfast and his own, too. He just shoveled in food and talked about pirates and sailing ships and blood on the high seas.

By the time Travis came back, Jason was sitting in Cat's lap while she cleaned jam off his hands, cheeks, and chin with a paper towel. It was tricky work, because the boy was still talking.

"Ready?" Travis asked. "We'll take my cousin's car. It needs a run or its battery will go dead."

Jason shot out of Cat's lap and raced for the back door.

"Hold it, tiger," Travis said. "Use the front door and the sidewalk. The tide is coming in."

Jason looked out at the waves. "Nah. It's okay. The sidewalk is for babies."

"Then I guess I'm a baby," Travis said calmly.

The boy's lower lip came out, but he didn't say any more. He just headed for the front door. He had learned that Travis was like Cat—fun most of the time and adult the rest.

"Hide the boat in a camera bag and bring it along," Travis said softly.

"Okay." Cat stood on tiptoe, brushed her mouth over his, and smiled at the soft tickle of his beard around her lips. "You're a sneaky, wonderful man, T. H. Danvers."

"Comes with being a pirate."

He grabbed her and kissed her quickly, completely, before going off to catch up with Jason.

By the time they parked and locked the car at the harbor, Jason was bouncing with excitement. "I've never been on a boat before. Not a real-for-sure one. Boy, that's something babies can't do!"

Travis smiled and swung the boy up onto his shoulders for the walk across the weekend-crowded parking lot. After a brief tussle over whether Jason would wear a life preserver—the boy lost—the ride in the Zodiac was a giddy adventure for Jason, one that left him round-eyed and laughing with glee. Diego was so taken with him that he extended the ride by going around the *Wind Warrior* twice.

Cat kept taking pictures of Jason and Travis and the transparent affection that flowed between them. Once they were aboard, Jason asked a thousand questions about the ship while he trotted around beside Travis, still wearing the bright red vest that was the price of being allowed on board a pirate ship.

Patiently Travis answered each question with as much detail as the boy wanted to absorb. He talked about the long nights on the sea, nights filled with a dazzling river of stars and storms that shut out all light. He talked about sunrise in the tropics, a sunrise that was another kind of storm, one made entirely of light and heat and color. He talked about the deep night silences broken by the hiss of the ship's bow parting the sea, and about the sudden, gigantic breathing of a whale surfacing nearby in the darkness.

Cat heard all that Travis didn't put into words, the aching hunger in him to be on the ocean again, to be free of land and smog and people, to be a captain with a good ship under his feet and a strong wind blowing through his hair, to have the past behind him and the future radiant with the endless miracle of the sea.

Working tirelessly, Cat caught it all on film, the longing and the love of the sea; the intelligent, earnest, excited child and the equally intelligent, earnest, excited adult. She tried not to grieve that she would never know the joy of sharing their own child with Travis, but the sadness was there in the images she took, a poignant shadow defining the brightness of the day, the dark certainty of future loss.

Hearing the elemental yearning for the sea in Travis's voice, Cat knew that tomorrow was coming. Soon.

Too soon. January was too far away.

At least I have Jason to love, Cat told herself as she changed rolls of film. *Until his parents move, anyway. I wonder if that's what all the telephoning was about early this morning at his house.*

I hope not. I'll miss my bright little tornado.

Cat put away the thought of the future and the bitter losses that it would bring. She would grieve for both of them. She loved both of them. The love was very different, equally deep. Seeing the two men she loved so much enjoying each other made her want to laugh and weep at the same time, emotion overflowing her heart, breaking it and healing it in the same breath.

I love. That's more than I thought I would ever have in my life. Each of them returns my love in his own way. That's enough.

It has to be.

"Cat?"

She looked up from her camera and realized that Travis had called her name more than once.

"I think you have something, don't you?" Travis asked. "In your camera bag?"

"Close your eyes, Jason," Cat said, remembering. "And no peeking!"

Without a word the boy put his small, perfectly formed, and slightly grubby hands over his eyes.

Shielding the boat with her body just in case, Cat passed the carving to Travis.

"You made it for him," she whispered. "You give it to him."

"But I wanted you—"

"Go on," she interrupted, folding his long, finely scarred fingers around the boat. "Okay, Jason. Look what your pirate made for you."

The boy's hands moved away from his face. His eyes grew big and then bigger still. Almost hesitantly he reached for the darkly gleaming boat. "For me?"

Travis crouched down on his heels, bringing his eyes nearly level with Jason's. "Just for you."

Jason threw himself at Travis and gave him a big kiss. "You're the best pirate ever!"

Travis caught the boy and stood slowly, wrapping Jason in his arms, holding him tight. "And you're the best boy ever."

Then Travis saw the longing in Cat's eyes as she watched the boy, tears that shimmered on the edge of falling.

And he found himself wishing he could give her a child.

In that instant Travis understood that he could fall in love with her. The realization was shocking. It told him how reckless he was. Despite the scars and savage lessons of the past, he believed that Cat was exactly as she seemed to be—a woman who loved without thought of money.

She isn't like other women, scheming and lying in order to get a free ride for life. Cat is different.

She has to be.

Anything else was unthinkable.

At least this time, if I'm wrong, I'll be the only one who suffers.

It wasn't much consolation for the terrifying risk Travis was taking, but it was all he had.

Slowly he put Jason back on the deck of the ship. "Go show your new boat to Diego. He has a whole collection of carvings from all over the world."

As soon as Jason ran off to show his trophy to Diego, Travis turned to the woman who watched him with pain and joy in her beautiful eyes.

"Tomorrow, Cat. Tomorrow we'll go to sea together. Just for a few days. Please."

She closed her eyes against the naked plea in his. She knew Travis was being pulled apart by conflicting needs. She was being pulled apart in just the same way.

She couldn't go.

It was impossible.

There was too much to be done. January was coming down on her like an avalanche, fast and hard and furious.

Then she opened her eyes and looked at the face of the man she loved.

"Yes. Tomorrow I'll go to sea with you."

EIGHTEEN

As the *Wind Warrior* glided toward the exit to Dana Harbor, Cat leaned against the railing. Air that smelled of salt and cool water flowed over her face. Travis was a warm presence at her back, two strong arms bracketing her body, male laughter in her hair. She moved against him with a feline ease and sensuality, enjoying the heat and strength that radiated from him.

"Like this, do you?" Travis asked, catching her close against his body with one arm. "I thought you would. Other than man, cats are the only land animals that live well at sea."

She laughed softly and lifted her hand until she found the rough silk texture of his beard. Her fingertips moved along the line of his lips, his jaw, the smooth lobe of his ear.

On either side of the *Wind Warrior* the rocky barriers of jetties rose out of the sea, baffling the smooth-backed waves, creating a tranquil harbor for the myriad pleasure craft dozing at their white slips. The channel itself was a straight green ribbon leading to the ocean. There was no swell yet, simply a subtle rocking motion that hinted at the immensity of the Pacific waiting beyond the narrow thrust of jetties.

"You've made a beautiful world for yourself with the

Wind Warrior," Cat said, looking at the limitless sea that beckoned just ahead.

"This is nothing," Travis said, taking Cat's hand and kissing her palm. "Wait until she spreads her wings."

At the farthest reach of the jetties, seagulls soared and cried. Ocean swells creamed around the rocks, reaching for *Wind Warrior*'s black elegance. The ship's motion changed subtly, eagerly, responding to the approach of unconfined ocean.

At the edge of Travis's awareness, the crew moved in silent concert, preparing the ship. Normally he would have worked with the men, but he wanted to be close to Cat at the exact instant that his ship stepped into the wind.

The *Wind Warrior* rounded the outer jetty and slid into the sweeping embrace of the sea. Overhead, maroon sails unfurled in a sleek rush of canvas. The ship quivered, transfixed by wind.

And then she heeled over and flew like the great black bird she was.

Laughing softly, exultantly, Cat stretched out her hands to the horizon. She had been to sea before, but never like this, carried with such grace and elegance and silent power.

Travis drank her response as totally as his ship drank the wind. Then he turned Cat in his arms and kissed her until they became a single figure swaying to the rhythms of the untamed ocean. Finally he lifted his head and looked down into her radiant gray eyes.

"Thank you," he said.

"For what?" she asked, smiling up at him, loving him the only way she could, silently.

"For being here, for being alive, for being you."

Cat blinked back unexpected tears. She couldn't speak for fear she would say what must not be said. *I love you.* So she stood on tiptoe and kissed Travis as though for the first time or the last.

Silently, holding each other, they watched the blue-green

ocean divide around the ship's bow. Water seethed and foamed along the *Wind Warrior*'s elegant hull, wind filled her sails, eagerness vibrated through every sleek centimeter of her. The ship took the swells cleanly, rising to meet the looming liquid walls with an economy of motion that made her easy to ride despite her experimental rigging.

Yet after a time, Cat was forced to admit the growing uneasiness of her stomach. It didn't particularly worry her. For her, seasickness had always been something that rarely happened. And if it did, the queasiness vanished after a few hours.

She hoped that hadn't changed after her long absence from the sea. Motion sickness pills acted more like sleeping pills on her. They knocked her out.

"Hungry?" Travis asked.

"Um . . ." Cat swallowed.

"You should be. You were so busy packing camera gear that you ate about three bites of toast."

"That's probably why my stomach is jumpy. It's empty."

He looked at her closely. Beneath her skin she was vaguely green. "Let's go below and get you some food."

But Cat took no more than two steps down the stairs before her stomach clenched in warning.

"Nope," she said, retreating swiftly. "I'm staying above deck."

Travis didn't argue. In some people, being confined made seasickness worse.

"I'll bring you some food," he said. "How about a nice cheese sandwich?"

She was on the point of saying yes when her stomach rebelled in vivid warning of what would happen to any food she ate.

"No. Nothing," Cat said hurriedly.

"Dry toast? Fruit?"

She shook her head, swallowed hard, and thought of

something else besides food, anything—the cry of gulls and the blue-on-blue where sky met sea.

The ship swooped down the side of a particularly large wave. Cat closed her eyes.

It was a mistake.

Her eyes snapped open. She saw Travis's rueful, sympathetic smile.

"Getting to you?" he asked softly.

She nodded.

"Want something for it?" he asked.

"No. Everything I've ever taken was worse than the queasiness. It should pass. It always has before."

Cat breathed deeply through her nose, then let the breath hiss out from between clenched teeth. It was a trick she had learned when she had first gone to sea, a means of avoiding the nausea of mal de mer. Usually it worked. When it didn't, there was always the head or a nearby railing.

This time the nausea didn't pass quickly. Cat spent the next few hours leaning on the rail, breathing out through her teeth and letting the wind blow over her. When the grip of nausea finally eased, she tried to take up her cameras and shoot the *Wind Warrior* under sail as she had planned to do.

Another mistake. Changing her perspective from normal to through-the-lens, adjusting to the shifting focus, and switching her own position to get the angle she wanted nearly undid her. When Travis appeared in front of her with a pale yellow pill and a glass of water, she accepted without argument.

"I'll be better soon," she said. "It's been years. I just have to get my sea legs back."

"Uh-huh," Travis said, doubtful.

He had seen all kinds of seasickness. Cat looked green. He doubted that it would pass any time soon.

As soon as the pill took effect, Cat's eyelids turned to

lead. Travis took her to his cabin. She was asleep before he tucked her into his bed.

She slept for sixteen hours.

Cat didn't notice Travis as he came and went, checking on her. Or when he simply sat, watching her, holding her slack hand in his. Finally he lay next to her and slept, too, letting the fresh salt air from the open porthole wash over them.

When Cat awoke, nausea was a fist in her stomach. Thanks to Travis's help, she made it to the tiny head. Instead of leaving her on her own, he held her and wiped her face, taking care of her as though she was no older than Jason.

"Okay now?" Travis asked when she stopped retching.

"Yes. I think. Hope."

"You'll feel better up top."

Travis was right. Cat felt better up on the deck. Yet she was tired despite her long sleep. The slow rhythms of the sea unraveled her ambition. She was supposed to be climbing masts and scooting about in the Zodiac, dangling from the railing and performing all the rest of the contortions a photographer went through to get the best angle for a picture.

And each time she tried to look through a lens, her stomach flipped over.

She had no better luck with breakfast. As long as she didn't smell food or try to eat anything, her stomach behaved. When the crew ate breakfast, she was careful to find a spot at the bow, upwind of the galley. There she sat with her face tilted up into the fresh air while exhaustion consumed her, leaving barely enough strength to huddle on the bow and let the sea part before her.

When Travis sat down behind Cat, she looked over her shoulder with an apologetic smile.

"I'm sorry to be such a disappointment," she said. "I

don't know what's wrong. I've never been a bad sailor before.''

He smiled gently and pulled her between his legs, settling her weight against his chest.

"What could be disappointing about holding you?" he asked, burying his face in the gentle fire of Cat's hair. "Go ahead and curl up in my arms. You make me feel like a god bringing you the gift of sleep."

"But I'm supposed to be shooting the ship and the sea," she said, relaxing against him despite her words.

"The sea was here before civilization began. It will be here when civilization ends. Sleep, darling. There's all the time in the world."

Sighing, Cat burrowed into his warmth and let the world slide away, keeping only him.

Travis wanted to turn and head back the next morning, but Cat insisted she would get better. She was right, up to a point. She didn't spend any more time with her head in the toilet, but she stayed very drowsy even though she refused to take any more motion sickness pills.

Feeling lazy and thoroughly spoiled, Cat spent the remaining two days of the trip curled in Travis's arms. She let the gentle winter sun wash over her, counted waves, counted heartbeats, slept, and awoke to his smile.

Yet no matter how much she slept, her body cried out for more rest. Though nausea came back only once in a while, she didn't want to eat any of the time.

The lack of appetite didn't surprise Cat. Her desire for food had varied from slim to nothing during the past five weeks. The same thing had happened a few times before, when she got too wrapped up in her photography, worked too hard, and slept too little.

"Here," Travis said, appearing with a milkshake in his hand.

"Thanks, but I'm not—"

"Hungry," he finished for her. "That's okay. This isn't food. Drink up."

Cat did her best, but only managed to swallow half of the milkshake in the next half hour.

Watching her without seeming to, Travis worried about her lack of energy and appetite. He had known men who were hit by seasickness so hard that they only recovered back on shore. Yet from all that Cat had said, she hadn't been seasick on Harrington's boat.

The thought that something else might be wrong with her, something serious, was gnawing in Travis's gut.

"Don't look so worried," Cat said, giving him a chocolate-mustache smile. "I'll go back to eating normally as soon as I'm on land."

"I'll hold you to it," he promised.

And he did. As soon as the *Wind Warrior* anchored in Dana Point Harbor, Travis drove Cat to her house, dropped her off, and gave her a level look.

"I'll be back with a five-course meal," he said. "You're going to eat every bite of it."

"Oh. Goody," she said without enthusiasm.

He kissed her hard and headed down the beach stairs to his house.

Cat stood in the kitchen, watching Travis dodge between the big winter waves and sprint along the wet sand to his own stairway. Then she sat at her little table and wished food had never been invented.

She stayed there, just sitting, until sunset light sent scarlet shadows over her hands. Occasionally she wondered what Travis would bring back with him. Every food that occurred to her sounded either uninteresting or outright disgusting.

Even the thought of food made her stomach jerk.

She flattened her palms on the cool table, breathed sharply through her nose, then gritted her teeth and let the breath hiss out. It helped, but not enough.

"Damn," Cat groaned, her head in her hands. "I forgot that it takes me as long to get used to being on land as it took me to get used to the sea."

Even though she had been off the *Wind Warrior* for several hours, the room still swayed gently when she closed her eyes . . . and her stomach swayed a good deal less gently whether her eyes were open or closed.

The idea of dinner defeated her.

Tired.

God, I didn't know what the word meant until now. I'm too tired even to yawn, and I spent the last three days dozing in Travis's arms.

Cat shoved away from the table, went to her workroom, and slumped into the chair next to the answering machine. The message light was blinking.

How much energy can it take just to listen? she asked herself, yawning.

Sighing, Cat hit the play button. The chair wasn't as comfortable as leaning against Travis had been. A tingle of longing and memory went through her. She wished she was back in the arms of her pirate, listening to a deep east Texas drawl that caressed her more warmly than California's bright winter sunlight.

The first message roused Cat from her lazy, sensual memories.

"Cathy-baby, where the hell are you? Just wanted to say that the pictures are great, babe, really great! Just what I wanted, all soft and warm and creamy. I knew you could do it if someone just showed you how."

Cat let the words flow past her. It was like the arrogant Crown Prince of Treacle not even to identify himself. But then, no one else she knew was insensitive enough to call her Cathy-baby.

At least Ashcroft was happy with the slides. That meant money, pure and sweet and desperately needed. The last half of the advance for Ashcroft's book wouldn't cover her siblings' final tuition payment or her mother's monthly expenses, much less her own photographic expenses; but the money would help her hang on until the Big Check from Energistics came.

The Big Check simply had to come. Soon. She had already spent fifteen hundred dollars on lawyers to pry out the thousands Energistics owed her. Without that check she wouldn't make it to January. In the past few weeks she had maxed out her credit cards and borrowed heavily on signature loans, knowing she could pay them off the day the Energistics check arrived.

Cat closed her eyes. Her stomach quivered. She forced her eyes open. It would be better in a few hours. It had to be. It couldn't get much worse.

The second message clicked on.

"Stoddard Photographic. Your slides are in."

She sighed. More processing to pay for. More slides to sort and duplicate, mail and file. Which reminded her, she had to buy film soon. She had only enough for a few days of shooting.

Money and more money, dollars disguised as light-sensitive emulsion coated on a perforated ribbon of film. But there was no choice. No film, no slides. No slides, no income.

"Hi, this is Sue from Custom Framers. When are you going to come in and select mats and frames for the prints Swift and Sons needs? You did say your show was in December, didn't you?"

Cat took a very deep breath and hissed it out between her teeth. Yes, her show was in a few weeks. Yes, she had to select mats and frames to go with prints she hadn't even paid for yet. Thirty-five images left to do, ten prints of each.

Not all of the prints had to be framed, of course. Just a few of each, and a few more of the ones the gallery owner expected to sell most quickly. Three hundred fifty prints costing her between $60 and $200 each for the enlargement, depending on size and special instructions. Then the framing. Another $150 to $800 each, depending on how fancy the gallery wanted to get.

Cat groaned. Thousands of dollars. Money she didn't have. Money Energistics owed her.

"Damn damn damn!"

Frustration didn't help her nausea one bit. Only the thought that somewhere on the tape there might be a call from her green angel kept Cat from quitting and hanging her head in the toilet.

Sure enough, the next call was from Harrington.

"Hi, Cochran. Glad to see you have the damn machine on for a change. Energistics is now returning my calls, but they aren't saying anything very interesting. I'll keep you posted on that one. I know tuition and Mum's check are due pretty quick. Ashcroft called to tell me that he loves the postcards you took for him. Swear to God."

Cat grimaced and kept listening.

"Unfortunately the Crown Prince of Treacle has developed poet's block. Or is it simple constipation? The last section of poetry just isn't coming along. Naturally the publisher won't pay your part of the contract until Ashcroft fulfills his part."

Cat's stomach flipped. She swallowed hard. And then she had to swallow again before she could concentrate on the rest of Harrington's message.

". . . that guy who wanted the pret-ties? He decided to redo his image along other lines. Chartreuse hair, black fingernails, and safety pins in unlikely places. I'm sending the slides back to you. Sorry. Better news next time. Swear to God it can't get worse. Say hi to In-the-Wind for me."

Cat looked at the readout on the machine. One message left.

For a second of pure cowardice she almost turned off the answering machine. She had had all the bad news she could take for a while. On the other hand, maybe a fairy godmother had died and left her a pile of gold dust. . . .

Smiling thinly, Cat waited for the last message to begin.

"Cathy, this is Dr. Stone. I hope you're sitting down. This time the reason your period is late is that you're pregnant. If you hope to stay pregnant, come in and see me immediately."

Stunned, disbelieving, Cat simply sat in the chair and listened to the surf growling along the beach below.

I must have heard wrong. Wishful thinking. Sheer wish, soul-deep and wild as the ocean.

With a trembling hand she hit the replay button and advanced to the last call. She listened to it again. And then again.

And again.

Then Cat simply stared at the answering machine in dazed fascination, hearing over and over the impossible word.

Pregnant.

Laughing softly, Cat pulled herself to her feet. She went to her bedroom and stared at herself in the full-length mirror. Pregnant! A world of possibilities growing inside her, another heartbeat, another mind, another living being.

Travis's baby.

Her baby.

Their baby.

Cat was still laughing softly, hugging herself, when she heard Travis come in the front door.

"Cat?" he called out from the kitchen. "Where are you?"

"Travis!" she said, laughing and running to him.

He was putting grocery bags on the kitchen counter when he heard her behind him and turned around. The joy on her face made him grin.

"What is it?" he asked, lifting her in a big hug. "Did the Big Check finally come?"

Unable to speak for the happiness overflowing her, Cat simply returned Travis's warm hug.

"You look like you swallowed the sun," he said, kissing her lips, smiling at her because it was impossible to see her joy and not share the delight.

Cat smiled in return, her eyes huge and brilliant with emotion, looking at him as though she had never seen him before: Travis H. Danvers, the man she loved, father of her child.

"Do you believe in miracles?" she asked breathlessly, then kissed Travis before he could answer. "I do," she said, kissing him quickly after each word. "I do! I'm pregnant, my love. I'm pregnant!"

At first Travis thought he hadn't heard correctly.

And then he was afraid he had.

"What did you say?" he asked carefully.

She caught his face between her hands. "A baby! Travis, my man, my lover, my love. Our baby!"

Even as the world shattered around Travis, he fought to believe that it wasn't true. Cat hadn't lied to him that deeply, that finally.

She couldn't have.

He couldn't have been so wrong again. Trapped by a cold-blooded schemer.

Again.

A baby.

His whole body tightened until he was afraid he would break apart along with the warm world he had lived in for the past weeks. He couldn't breathe. Couldn't move. Couldn't think.

And then rage came, a freezing kind of rage that numbed the scalding pain of betrayal. Rage made it possible to breathe, to move, to think.

Laughing softly, Cat turned her head to catch Travis's lips again, but couldn't. She was sliding down his body, no longer held in a strong hug. Her feet hit the floor so hard she staggered and grabbed his arm to steady herself.

"Travis?"

When Cat saw his face she instinctively stepped backward, out of reach. Violence and rage burned blackly in the depths of his tourmaline eyes. His body rippled with the involuntary motion of a predator poised for the killing leap, adrenaline pumping, muscles tensed.

Then Travis closed his eyes, saying more clearly than words that he didn't trust himself to look at her.

Like his eyes, his expression was closed, his face as bleak and unyielding as the rocks lining the beach. When he spoke, chills coursed over Cat. His voice was soft, cold, vibrant with rage.

His eyes opened, watching her, measuring her.

"And your Big Check, Cat. Did it finally come?"

She shook her head, but it was as much in baffled reaction to the change in Travis as in answer to his question.

"No, but what does that have to do with me being pregnant?" Her voice was small, shaken, more poignant than tears.

"Very good," Travis said coolly.

"What?"

"The voice. It would make a stone weep. But I'm not a stone. I'm a fool."

"Travis . . . ?" Cat's voice died.

She had the eerie feeling that she was talking to a stranger who just happened to look like the man she loved. Blankly she watched as he reached into a pocket of his red windbreaker and whipped out a checkbook and pen.

"You're as good an actress as you were a lover," Travis said carelessly. "But then, you were acting all the time, weren't you?"

He made a savage gesture, cutting off whatever Cat might have said.

"Actress, mistress, whore, it doesn't matter," he said. "Not anymore. But listen up, bitch kitty, and listen good."

Cat took another step backward and wondered if she had just fallen off the edge of the world.

But it wasn't that easy. She was still here, Travis was still here, and he was talking, flaying her alive. He was writing in his checkbook as he spoke, slashing at the paper as though it was an enemy.

"You're going to have that baby and then it will be *mine*," he said. "No running off for an abortion. No holding the child for ransom. You'll have it, I'll raise it, and you'll never see either one of us again." He tore out the check and held it out to her. "My attorney will have the papers to you in a few days."

Cat stared at the check quivering in front of her nose.

One million dollars.

The price Travis had paid to be free of his wife.

A black, terrible kind of lightning went through Cat, burning her until she wanted to scream with pain. At a distance she understood that when there was nothing left for the fire to consume, she would be free, safe beneath an armor of ice.

But until then it still burned. She burned.

"Take it," Travis said harshly, his voice shaking with all that he wouldn't reveal, all that he had lost. "Take it or I'll tear it up and write a smaller one."

Cat's hand moved with the speed of a striking snake. She took the check so quickly that the edge of the paper sliced through Travis's skin. Blood welled.

He smiled with contempt. "So that was your price." He flexed his hands as though hungry to feel her neck between his fingers. "Christ. You'd think whores would be more original and men would be less gullible."

With quick, savage motions Cat shredded the check. "You're right, T. H. Danvers. People should be more original. But then, 'I love you' isn't the most original phrase in the universe."

"Whores don't love anything but money."

She opened her fingers. Tiny, pale blue pieces of paper fluttered to the floor.

Travis slapped his checkbook on the counter again. His pen stabbed across the paper. Moments later he held out a check to her. The amount was nine hundred thousand dollars.

"That little gesture cost you a hundred grand." Rage tightened his face, making his sensual mouth a hard line.

Cat's only answer was the sound of paper ripping and ripping and ripping again.

Cold blue-green eyes raked over her. Then Travis began writing again. "It will cost you a hundred thousand dollars every time you tear up a check."

"Write faster and smaller until you reach zero, you bastard," Cat snarled. "I can't wait to see your back going out that door."

He ignored her and kept writing.

Suddenly she snatched the checkbook out from under his pen. "My way is faster."

With one hand she snapped on a gas burner on the stove. With the other she held the checkbook deep in the fire. She felt nothing, not even heat as flames scorched her. She watched her hand in the flames with a total lack of interest. She was too cold to feel fire. She was buried in ice as old as the world and as thick as time.

"Cat! Jesus!" Travis yanked her hand back from the fire and shut off the gas.

She turned on him, her eyes empty. "It's my baby now. You can go out and knock up a string of women if you want kids. This one is mine. Even if I could get pregnant again, I wouldn't give up this child to be raised by a man who can't see love when it stands in front of him. Like me, now. I love you, Travis," she said, each word hard and cold. "But that's my mistake. I should have known better. My husband was such a fine teacher. Rich men just don't know how to love. And we both know how *rich* you are, don't we?''

"So that's it," Travis said. His lips curled in a travesty of a smile. "A million wasn't enough." He shrugged. "I'll make it two million. You were worth it, lady. Really great. But," he added casually, brutally, "if you're holding out for marriage, you can forget it. Marrying a whore is the kind of mistake I don't make twice."

Cat took the smoking checkbook and crushed it into his hand, burning him.

"Thank you for my child," she said, "even though it was an unwilling gift. I'll take the baby. And you, T. H. Danvers, you can take your money and go to hell."

She watched fury ripple through Travis. Distantly she wondered if he would lose control now, giving in to the violence that seethed visibly through him, shaking his restraint like winter storm waves pounding against a crumbling sea wall.

"You have my phone number," he said harshly. "When you want the money, call. The papers will be waiting for you to sign."

"Never."

"Why not? You earned it. Too bad you didn't believe the final payment wasn't marriage. Well, live and learn, kitty cat. I sure as hell have. This time."

The back door shut softly behind Travis. Too softly.

Then a sound came back through the wood, a sound that could have been the surf or the throttled cry of a man who had been betrayed.

And then he walked down her stairs, out of her life. The set of his body said that she didn't exist anymore, had never existed.

Cat flew at the door and hammered her fists against it as though it was alive and able to feel pain. As soon as the adrenaline storm passed, nausea hit. She barely made it to the bathroom in time.

As darkness came she kept listening for the phone or the sound of Travis coming up the stairs from the beach. She heard nothing but the wind and the sea and the taut silence between breakers.

She tried to sort slides. She found herself staring aimlessly at the white plastic frames, arranging and rearranging them in random patterns across the light table. Abruptly her hands shook, scattering slides. When she bent to pick them up her fingers were as clumsy as a child's.

Empty-handed, Cat straightened and leaned against the light table. After a long time she realized that she was staring at the clock on the wall across the room.

Midnight. Exactly.

The second hand swept on its downward curve, marking out the first instants of the new day.

Wearily Cat pushed away from the light table and went to bed. For a time queasiness kept her awake. Eventually she drifted into a haunted sleep. There wasn't anything truly menacing in the dream that came to her, neither monsters nor pursuits nor sleeting colors of terror. There was simply . . . *nothing*. A great black hole in the center of her universe, a place that was no place at all, a horrible expanding emptiness where the sun should have been.

Cat awoke in a rush. She was clammy, nauseated, her body rigid. For a few awful moments she didn't know where she was. She reached out automatically, searching for the comfort of living warmth next to her in bed.

"Travis?"

The raw whisper echoed as memories came like ice water.

She turned on her side and curled around herself. Motionless, she lay without sleeping, her eyes fastened to the black rectangle of the window, straining to see the first hint of dawn.

NINETEEN

By seven-thirty Cat was sitting in her car outside Dr. Stone's office. She knew the office didn't open until nine, but she didn't care. She had taken all the silence she could, silence and listening for sounds that didn't come, footsteps and laughter and Travis's voice calling her name.

He'll think about it and he'll believe me, Cat told herself again and again. *He'll see that it isn't his damned money I want. It's him.*

Just him.

All he needs is time to get past his surprise and anger. That's all. A little time. He'll miss me and he'll come back to me, hold me, tell me that he—

"Cathy?"

Cat started. It took her a moment to focus on Dr. Stone's dark, neatly tailored suit and her concerned face.

"Are you all right?" asked the doctor.

When she didn't get an answer immediately, she opened the car door and leaned in. Skilled fingers pressed against Cat's wrist over her pulse.

"I'm okay, Dr. Stone. Just a little—"

"—Exhausted," the doctor finished crisply, taking in Cat's rumpled shirt and jeans and her stark pallor. "I've buried patients who looked better than you do. Can you walk, or should I bring out a wheelchair?"

Cat started to laugh, then realized Dr. Stone wasn't joking. "Nausea isn't my most becoming color," she explained, trying to smile. "But I can walk just fine."

The other woman didn't smile back. "Have you eaten?"

"This morning?"

The doctor's eyes narrowed. "Let me rephrase that. When was the last time you ate?"

"Tea and crackers. Yesterday."

"And before that?"

Cat shrugged. "Travis—" Her voice broke over his name. She swallowed and tried again. "I went sailing for a few days. I was seasick, which hadn't ever happened to me before, not like that. I had a little juice, some tea, toast, half of a milkshake."

"How many days?"

"Sailing?"

"No. Since you've eaten a decent meal."

Frowning, Cat tried to remember.

"Never mind," the other woman said curtly. "You've told me all I need to know." She pulled keys out of a small leather purse. "Stand up."

Under the doctor's critical eyes, Cat climbed out of the small Toyota. Nausea coiled in her stomach. She let her breath hiss out through her teeth.

Dr. Stone's expression softened with rueful sympathy. "Come on. I'll make you some tea with lots of honey. And you'll drink every bit of it."

When Cat was seated with a steaming mug in her hands, Dr. Stone settled into her comfortable desk chair. Over folded hands she watched her patient sip tentatively at the sweet tea and nibble on the soda crackers she had been given.

The doctor pulled out a list of the day's patients and began reviewing folders. When she was finished, she went to the bank of files and pulled out the folder with Cat's name on the tab. She sat down and began reading, making notes on a pad on her desk.

After ten minutes Dr. Stone looked up at Cat. The crackers were gone. The tea mug was empty. Cat was either dozing or in a daze.

"How's it going?" Dr. Stone asked. "Everything staying down?"

Blinking, Cat turned and looked at the doctor. She was still queasy, but she thought she could hang on to the meager breakfast. "Yes. Thanks."

"How often are you nauseated?"

"Most of the time, lately."

"How often do you vomit?"

Cat grimaced. "I hate throwing up. But last night, this morning. Yes. Twice. Once while we were sailing."

"Are you still spotting?"

"Yes."

"How often?" Dr. Stone asked, her voice calm.

"All the time, I guess."

"How much?"

"Not much, usually. Not like a real period. This morning, though . . ." Cat's voice faded.

"Cramps?" the doctor said neutrally.

Cat nodded.

Dr. Stone's questions continued in a rapid fire that gave Cat no time to weigh her answers. Finally the doctor examined her short, unpolished fingernails, sighed, and looked at the notes she had made.

"Do you want this pregnancy?" she asked.

"*Yes.*"

The doctor's head snapped up. Cat looked as intense as she sounded.

"Then I hope you're stronger than I think you are," Dr. Stone said bluntly. "Obstetrically speaking, you're among the worst risks I've taken on in my career."

Cat's gray eyes widened in her white face. "What do you mean?"

"Right now, this instant, your body is doing everything

in its power to abort this pregnancy. And frankly, I think your body is wise. It's a simple survival reflex. You can barely sustain your own physical demands right now. Where on earth will you find the resources to support the additional demands of pregnancy?''

''But—but pregnancy is natural for a woman.''

''So is illness. So is death. So is spontaneous abortion. So is birth, health, laughter.'' The doctor's smile was calm and accepting. ''We just like some of those things better than others, so we call them natural.''

Cat closed her eyes and wished she could close her ears as well. ''I want this baby.''

''I'll do what I can,'' Dr. Stone said. ''All anyone can. The first trimester of pregnancy is always high risk. Much higher risk than we ever suspected before we could determine pregnancy after only a few weeks.''

Numbly Cat listened, but all she really heard was her own deep need to have this baby.

''No matter what you do,'' the doctor said, ''no matter what I do, you must understand that your chance of a successful pregnancy is very, very low.''

Cat made a stifled sound of pain.

''Would you rather I lied to you?'' Dr. Stone asked gently.

''I—no.''

Leaning forward, the doctor took Cat's tightly clenched hands between her own.

''Think very carefully about this, Cathy. You aren't sterile. I suspect your vaginal chemistry was simply too acid for your husband's sperm to survive. It's not an uncommon problem, and one that is easily solved.'' Dr. Stone smiled. ''Obviously you're quite chemically compatible with at least one man. If this pregnancy doesn't work out, there will be other chances for you.''

Cat stared through the doctor. Other chances meant nothing to her. She didn't want them. She didn't want just any man's baby. She wanted a child with tourmaline eyes and tawny hair and a smile to break her heart.

"I want *this* baby."

There was silence followed by a sigh. "All right. Let's get you in the stirrups and see what we have to work with."

When the examination was over, Dr. Stone took Cat back to the private office. The nurse had arrived, followed shortly by the first of the doctor's appointments.

"If your spotting was just a bit heavier," the doctor said, "our previous discussion would be academic and spontaneous abortion a fact."

Cat had to fight to force words past the fear closing her throat. "No! It can't happen. I want this baby."

"I believe you. I'll call the hospital and tell them to expect you."

"Hospital? Unless it comes with a money-back guarantee, I can't afford it. I'm not insured."

When Cat heard her own words, she swallowed and closed her eyes. The hole that had expanded in her dreams was still there.

Waiting for her.

Her eyes snapped open. "Never mind. If going to the hospital is the only way to keep this baby, I'll get the money somehow."

When you want the money, call. The papers will be waiting for you to sign.

Cat stopped breathing and wanted to scream, but she had no breath.

"Relax," Dr. Stone murmured. Gently she rubbed Cat's cold, clenched hands. "This kind of tension doesn't do you or the baby any good."

"Relax?" She laughed wildly, then stopped, afraid she would scream after all. "How long will I have to stay in the hospital?"

"As long as it takes. Weeks, surely. Months, possibly."

Cat turned white as salt.

The papers will be waiting for you to sign.

Signing away her baby to a man who didn't know how to love.

"But you won't be going into the hospital," the doctor said, watching Cat's distress. "The more I think about it, the more certain I am that lying in a hospital ward worrying over money would only make things worse. Not to mention exposure to staph infections in your run-down state."

Cat's breath trickled in and out, but not much. She was still reeling over the idea of weeks in a hospital, thousands and thousands of dollars, money that could only be paid by signing away her baby.

Too bad you didn't believe the final payment wasn't marriage. Well, live and learn, kitty cat. I sure as hell have. This time.

Frowning, Dr. Stone absently tapped her clean nails against a medical folder. "No hospital, but only if you can find someone to take care of you."

Deep inside the freezing of her soul, Cat glimpsed a picture of warmth and caring that burned: Travis smiling at her, kissing her, tucking tidbits of food past her lips.

A shudder went over her, leaving her dizzy. She couldn't allow herself to think about Travis. At all. She hadn't the strength.

"You need regular meals," Dr. Stone continued. "You must have bed rest until the spotting stops. If it stops."

"Can I get up long enough to go to the bathroom or fix a quick meal?" Cat asked.

The doctor's nails tapped thoughtfully on the file, weighing alternatives. "The bathroom, yes. The meals, possibly. But who would shop for you? Who would wash your dishes? Who would do your laundry? Who would take care of the house? Who would—"

"I'll find someone," Cat cut in, not wanting to hear more. "I'll hire someone."

Frowning, thinking quickly, Dr. Stone opened Cat's folder. "You live on the beach, don't you?"

"Yes."

"Stairs?"

"Yes."

"You can't climb them," the doctor said bluntly. "You can't lift anything heavier than a cup of tea. No photography for you, Catherine Cochran."

Cat wanted to protest, but didn't. She wouldn't risk the baby for a handful of photos, no matter how much she needed money that assignments would bring in.

"Someone from Home Volunteers will be calling you," Dr. Stone said, writing quickly. "They'll bring you one hot meal a day. Drive home and then don't drive again. Go straight to bed."

"All right."

The doctor set aside her pen and took Cat's cold hand between her own. "Think carefully about what you're doing. You can't work for a living and you don't have enough money not to work."

"I'll pay you, no matter—"

"Don't irritate me," the doctor interrupted. "I'm not talking about my fees. I'm talking about living expenses. If you go to bed and stay there for weeks or months, how will you cover your expenses?"

"I'll manage. I earn my keep."

Dr. Stone winced. "Then please understand this. No matter what you do or don't do, the odds are overwhelming that you'll miscarry before the second trimester begins."

"No."

"Yes," the doctor said simply, holding Cat's hand, trying to rub warmth into it. "This isn't your only chance for a baby. Next time you get pregnant, we'll talk about happier things, like cranky babies and diaper rash."

Cat knew that there wouldn't be a next time. She wouldn't trust herself with a man to that extent.

Fool me once, damn you. Fool me twice, damn *me*.

Somewhere, somehow, vulnerability had to stop and survival had to take over. For her that somewhere was here and now, however she could, whatever it took.

"I'm giving you antinausea pills for a few weeks," the doctor said, releasing Cat's hand and writing briskly on a prescription pad.

"Won't that hurt the baby?"

"No. What hurts the baby is not having a strong mother. You can't build up your strength unless you eat. The nurse will give you some shots before you leave. I'll visit you once a week unless you need me more often. Any questions?"

Numb, Cat shook her head.

Dr. Stone smiled. "There will be. Call me, Cathy. I'm here to help."

Cat drove home slowly, thinking only of what must be done. Grocery shopping, opening and closing the garage door, climbing down the stairs to her house, carrying bags of food, putting away the food. She wasn't supposed to do any of it, yet she had to eat and eat well.

When she felt like she was drowning in details and the impossibility of what must be done, she forced herself to think of only one thing at a time.

She would find a way to shore. She always had. She was a very good swimmer.

Cat turned in to her driveway, looked at the closed garage door, and mentally shrugged. The Toyota's paint job would just have to suffer exposure to salt air until she could raise and lower the garage door again.

She let herself out of the car and descended the steps slowly, taking excruciating care. Inside the house two more flights of stairs waited. She had weighed the effort carefully and decided that calling Sharon made more sense than taking on her neighbor's stairs, which were steeper than her own.

As soon as Cat reached the phone in her workroom, she called Jason's mother.

"Sharon? This is Cathy."

"Oh, God. Did Jason miss the school bus?"

"No." Cat hesitated. Asking for help was very hard for her, but she had no other choice. "I have a very big favor to ask of you."

"Name it," Sharon said cheerfully.

Cat spoke in a rush, trying to get it over with. "I have to take it easy for a while. Bed rest. I can't lift anything, not even a camera."

"Cathy! What happened? Did you have a fall?"

There was real concern in Sharon's voice. In his own charming fashion, Jason had stitched together the two most important women in his life.

"A fall?" Cat laughed oddly. "Not the way you mean. I'm pregnant. And I want to stay that way. So it's bed for me until I stop spotting."

"Cathy . . . oh, Cathy, I don't know whether to congratulate you or cry. Is Travis happy about it?"

"This is a solo flight." Her voice was flat, completely colorless. "But congratulate me anyway. I want this baby. I'm going to move heaven and earth to have it."

Silence. Then Sharon said, "I'll do whatever I can. I miscarried twice before I had the twins, and they were born five weeks too soon in spite of all I did."

Cat couldn't think of anything to say. Knowing that Sharon had miscarried both frightened her and made her feel less alone.

"I'm sorry," Cat whispered. "I didn't know."

"Women don't talk about miscarriages. It makes them feel inadequate. Stupid, but there it is. Don't get caught in that trap, Cathy. Losing a pregnancy is bad enough. Beating yourself up over it can destroy a marriage."

"No problem there."

Sharon made a funny sound, half laugh, half cry. "Hang up the phone and go to bed. I'll be over as soon as the baby-sitter arrives, unless there's something you need right now."

"No. I'm fine. Just fine. Thank you, Sharon."

"Don't thank me. If it weren't for you, Jason and I wouldn't even be speaking."

That evening Cat lay in her bed, watching sunset transform the western sky. Colors flamed up from the horizon, spilling molten beauty over the sinuous waves.

And then she saw the *Wind Warrior* skimming over the burning sea, ebony strength and beauty following the dying sun into the darkness beyond the horizon.

Going . . . gone . . .

Travis sailing into night on the wings of a great black bird, leaving Cat with nothing but the shadow of the sun burning behind her eyes.

She slept finally, badly, twisting and turning. She awoke in the heart of night, a stifled scream on her lips.

There was no bed, no house, no earth. Falling. She was falling.

And there was nothing to hold on to except the hope of dawn.

Sweating, cold, tangled in covers, Cat lay frozen in place for a long time, afraid to move and risk vertigo again. Beyond the window, darkness stretched from horizon to horizon, unbroken.

Jason and the dawn arrived at Cat's house together. She sat up quickly, pulled on the robe Sharon had left over a chair next to the bed, and waited for the boy's brilliant smile to chase away the last of the nightmare. When he appeared in her bedroom door, he was clutching several packets of instant cocoa and grinning with pride.

"Mom taught me how to make this," he said proudly. "You don't have to do it anymore."

He vanished before Cat could answer. She heard sounds from the kitchen, including a crash that had her holding her breath.

A few minutes later Jason rushed into the bedroom carrying empty mugs and a tray of toast. He put everything on the bedside table and ran back to the kitchen. This time he returned slowly, carrying a pot full of hot cocoa.

He poured with more determination than grace, but most of the chocolate ended up in the cups. With a flourish, he handed Cat a dripping piece of honey toast and a mug of cocoa.

She smiled at Jason, thankful that her antinausea pills were working. "Smells and looks delicious. Thank you. You can cook my breakfast anytime."

The boy grinned proudly. "I told Mom I could do it alone. Besides," he said, reaching for a gooey piece of peanut butter toast, "she would have to bring the twins, and only a mother would eat with two screaming babies."

There was no tactful way for Cat to disagree with her benefactor. Instead, she took a tentative bite of the toast, half expecting her stomach to rebel. She was relieved when her body accepted the toast without comment.

"You want something else before I go to school?" Jason asked, licking his fingers. The cocoa mustache he wore gave his face a rakish air that went well with his tumbled black curls.

"No, thanks," Cat said. "This is more than I've eaten for a week."

He frowned. "You're gonna get skinny."

"Slave driver."

She took another piece of toast and honey from the haphazard heap in the center of the tray. At first she nibbled hesitantly, then with more confidence. It actually tasted good. She reached for the pot of cocoa, only to have Jason grab it first.

"Mom said you're not s'posed to lift anything." Frowning intently, he poured more cocoa.

"Thank you," she murmured, discreetly licking up dribbles of chocolate before they ran off the cup onto the bed.

The phone rang.

Cat's heart turned over in the instant before she remembered that it couldn't be Travis. He was in the wind, gone as completely as yesterday's sunlight.

Automatically she started to get up and answer the phone. Then she remembered that she wasn't supposed to get out of bed, much less take on the flights of stairs to the workroom. She had left the phone there yesterday, because it was heavier than a cup of tea, which was her maximum weight-lifting range.

"I'll get it," Jason said, racing off.

He came back in a few minutes. "It was Mom. She's going to the store and wants to know if you need anything."

Cat reached for the tablet on her bedside table and tore off the sheet that held the grocery list. "Could you put my purse on the bed, please?"

Jason grabbed her purse and plunked it down on the bed next to her. His smile was as bright as the sun. The idea of being her legs hadn't lost its attraction yet. She hoped it wouldn't. After seeing the *Wind Warrior* sail into the night, she needed Jason's lighthearted company.

Cat fished out her checkbook, wincing when her scorched hand scraped against the zipper. The burns were more startling than painful. Travis had yanked her hand out of the flames before any blisters formed. All she had were streaks of red skin that would split and peel away in a few days, like a sunburn.

She wished that the rest of her would heal as quickly.

"Give this to your mom," Cat said, handing Jason the

check and the list, "and tell her thank you very much. When you get home from school you can teach me how to play Go Fish."

"Oh boy!" He turned and raced toward the back door.

"Wait!" Cat said. She looked out the bedroom window at the advancing ranks of waves. "The tide's up. Use the front door."

"That's okay. I just go between waves."

Jason was out the back door before she could object. Anxiously she watched him dart down the stairs to the beach. Because her bedroom jutted out beyond the kitchen deck and the bluff itself, she could see the bottom of her stairs as well as the bottom of Jason's stairs.

The boy waited on the last step of her stairs until a wave retreated. Then he scurried across the beach and up his own stairs before the next wave even got close to his feet.

Relieved, Cat lay back on the bed. After a few moments sleep finally came, washing over her in a black tide, carrying her out to sea.

TWENTY

THE PHONE rang, waking Cat. She was halfway out of bed before she remembered that she wasn't supposed to get up at all. She lay back and wondered if she had remembered to turn on the answering machine.

She hadn't. Between rings, other sounds came from the kitchen. A cupboard door closed. The refrigerator closed. Something thumped on a shelf.

"Sharon?" Cat called as the phone rang for the fourth time.

"Just putting away groceries," Sharon called from the kitchen as the phone rang again. "Do you have a phone with you?"

"No. And I forgot to turn on the answering machine."

"I'll get it after I answer this call."

A few minutes later Sharon appeared in Cat's bedroom. She was carrying the telephone in one hand and the answering machine in the other.

"That was the framer," Sharon said. "They've got some finished stuff for you to look at." She looked around the room. "Where's the phone outlet?"

"There." Cat pointed to the wall by her bed. "Thanks. I really appreciate you taking the time to help me."

"Hey, no problem. It's great to have another adult to talk to." Sharon plugged in the phone, connected the answering machine, and dusted her hands off on her jeans. "What else needs to be moved around?"

"Nothing urgent. When I'm more rested I'm going to sort and mail some slides." Cat grimaced. "Correction. I'll sort and you'll mail." She rubbed her eyes and looked at her friend and neighbor. "Sharon, are you sure you have enough time to run my errands?"

"All the time you need." She pushed a wisp of chestnut hair behind her ear and tucked in her blue-striped blouse. "If it hadn't been for you these last four months, Jason and I would have driven each other crazy. Tonight I'll send Steve over to move your bed right next to the window. Then you'll be able to watch the ocean and the beach and whoever wanders by."

"Thanks." Cat laughed oddly. "Seems like that's all I've been saying to you lately. Thanks and thanks and thanks."

"So enjoy," Sharon said, smiling. "Heaven knows you've done enough for me. It's about time you were on the receiving end."

The house seemed very empty when Sharon left. Normally Cat would have gone to her workroom and sorted slides, or she would have sat at her desk to handle the endless correspondence and bookkeeping chores.

But nothing was normal anymore. She was confined to her bed with only her own thoughts for company. She couldn't even turn to her cameras for consolation and distraction. All she could do was lie in bed and try not to think.

It didn't work.

Her thoughts kept jumping between Travis and checkbooks, the cramps that coiled in her abdomen, and the spotting that terrified her now that she understood its cause.

When thinking about those things became too painful, there was always money to worry about. Or lack of it. In four days she would have to write out checks for loans and credit card companies, the twins and her mother. The amount Cat had to pay would exceed her combined checking and savings accounts by $12,650, give or take a few dollars.

If Cat had been able to work, the deficit would have been a hill to climb rather than Mount Everest. She had lined up corporate jobs that were worth more than twelve thousand, but she would have to cancel them.

If the Big Check from Energistics didn't come, she didn't know what she would do.

Her stomach clenched.

Don't worry about money, Cat told herself quickly. *It's bad for the baby.*

Staring at the ceiling, she repeated the doctor's advice about not worrying. Then she wondered why it wasn't possible to think of nothing at all.

Memories twisted through her like black lightning, Travis and love and anger, memories burning her until she twisted as though trying to escape the relentless pain.

Crying would have helped, but tears were beyond her. Travis had left her nothing, not even hope. Without hope there could be no tears.

The phone rang, startling in the silence. Cat started to get up, remembered, and groped for the receiver without sitting up.

"Hello," she said hoarsely.

"Is that you, Cochran?"

Cat cleared her throat. "Hi, green angel. It's me."

"Didn't sound like it. Is Danvers around? I called his cousin's house, but no one answered."

Fighting her emotions, unable to speak, Cat hung on to the phone until her hand ached.

Slowly she rallied herself. She would have to get used to hearing Travis's name unexpectedly. She would have to get used to knowing that she would never again wake up next to his solid warmth, never again see his eyes brilliant with passion, never again see his lips smiling as he bent to kiss her, never again taste the salt-sweet flavor of him, never again. . . .

"Cochran? You there?"

"Yes." Cat forced herself to swallow past the vise of loss gripping her throat. "I guess I'm a little fuzzy. You finally caught me napping."

Harrington hesitated. "Are you all right?"

"Fine," she said, sounding anything but. "Just fine."

He made a sound that said he wasn't convinced.

Cat took a deep breath. She had to tell Harrington something. At the very least she must tell him that *The Danvers Touch* was a write-off unless the publisher would be satisfied with the photos she had already taken.

"Rodney?" she managed.

"I'm sitting down," Harrington said dryly. "Go ahead."

"Travis is in the wind. I'll send you the slides I've taken for the book. If they aren't enough, you'll have to get another photographer."

The words tumbled out as though by speaking quickly Cat could get it all said and over with before Harrington suspected how she felt.

"Hey," Harrington said gently, "not to worry. Danvers gets restless, he leaves, he comes back."

"Not this time." Cat's voice was very clear, very certain.

There was a long silence followed by a sigh. "You sure you're all right?"

"I'm working on it."

"That's the ticket. Work. I'll line up a few foreign gigs for you. In fact, just this morning I was talking to Miller in Paris and—"

"No," she interrupted.

"What? Why not? You have something against Frenchmen?"

Cat hung on to the phone and thought of the lies she could tell her green angel. But of all the people in the world, she owed Harrington the truth. He had helped her when she crawled out of the sea, a naked stranger badly needing kindness, refuge. He had given them to her without hesitation or question and never asked for one thing in return.

"My doctor told me to stay off my feet for a while," she said, her voice flat. "No work allowed."

There was a shocked silence.

"It's just temporary," Cat continued. "I'll call you when I can take assignments again."

"Cochran, what the hell is going on?"

There was no way to duck it. No way to finesse it. No way to ignore it.

"I'm pregnant," she said baldly. "And since I want to stay that way, I have to spend some time in bed."

"Pregnant! Sweet Jesus. What the hell were the two of you think—" Harrington bit his tongue and managed to swallow the rest of his comment.

Cat smiled despite her own pain. "Don't sound so horrified."

"Shocked, not horrified, and only because Travis is a damned fanatic on the subject of unwanted, uh, that is . . ."

"Hey," she said. "Don't worry. I thought I was sterile. This baby is a miracle."

"Some miracle. You're flat on your back when you most need to be working."

"Nobody said miracles were convenient."

Yet Cat was smiling. Just the thought of being pregnant made her emotions lift with delight at her own unexpected fertility, the miraculous gift growing inside her womb. With that she could survive anything.

Even a rich bastard with a velvet drawl.

"Does Danvers know?" Harrington asked bluntly.

"Yes."

"Then why in God's flaming hell did he leave you!"

"Ask him when you find him. If you find him."

"I will. And he'll tell me, if I have to hire someone to

hold him while I beat the truth out of him. No one treats you like that and gets away with it. No one. Not even my best friend.'' Harrington made a disgusted sound. ''Especially my best friend. To think I hoped he and you would . . . ah, *shit*. I'm sorry, Cochran. I wish I'd never thought of a book about a son of a bitch called Danvers.''

''You shouldn't have any regrets,'' Cat said. ''I don't. Everybody should ride a wild, breaking wave at least once.''

There was a long silence before Harrington asked, ''Do you need anything?''

''Just the check from Energistics.''

There was another silence.

''That's why I called,'' he said reluctantly. ''Energistics is tits-up in the bankruptcy court. They're paying their debts at six cents on the dollar. Our lawyer is filling out claim forms right now.''

Cat heard little beyond the word ''bankruptcy.''

''Cochran? You still there?''

''Yes . . .''

''What about the L.A. show? Are you ready?''

''There's a batch of prints ready at the framers,'' she said mechanically. ''A lot more still to go. I haven't had time to select mats and frames.''

''So let the gallery do it. They never like what the artist chooses anyway.'' Harrington hesitated, swore under his breath, and plunged on. ''I know you were counting on that Energistics check.''

''I'll manage. I always have.''

''You weren't pregnant. Surely Travis owes—''

''No.''

A single word. Nothing more. Nothing more was needed.

''Then I'll give you—'' Harrington began

''No,'' Cat interrupted again. ''Not Travis. Not you. Not anyone. *I earn my own keep.*''

She heard the echo of her own voice, as savage as

Travis's had been when he offered her the check for a million dollars.

Kept woman.

Whore.

The memory enraged Cat, but Harrington had done nothing to deserve her fury. She closed her eyes and worked very hard to keep her voice calm.

"But thank you anyway, green angel. I appreciate the offer. I appreciate even more that you care enough to make it."

"We'll talk about this later," Harrington said after a moment. "When you feel better."

Cat didn't answer. As far as she was concerned, the subject was closed.

"Cathy . . . ?" He sighed. "Take care. I'll call you soon."

"Sure," she said mechanically. "'Bye."

The phone clicked back into its cradle.

For a long time there was no sound but that of her own breathing and the muted voice of the sea. Cat lay on the bed and stared at the two beautifully framed prints that hung on the wall on the opposite side of the bedroom. She had been so eager to show them to Travis, but she had made herself wait until the prints were properly matted and framed.

Now they were ready.

And now he was gone.

The first print had been blown up to life size. It was a close-up of Travis that she had taken the night he carved Jason's boat. Light from the gooseneck lamp slanted across Travis, striking gold out of his hair, making the color of his eyes the jeweled blue-green of fine Brazilian tourmaline. His intensity, concentration, and intelligence were as vivid as his eyes. Light bathed his hands, revealing the fine scars, the strength, the tension of his lean fingers holding the unyielding block of ebony, the steely flash of the knife coaxing dark curves from wood.

The photo was so real Cat kept feeling that if she called his name, Travis would look up at her and smile.

The second print was as big as an open newspaper. It was one of the shots she had taken the first time she had seen the *Wind Warrior,* before she knew the ship's name or creator. In the print the sun blazed across half the darkening sky. The ship was a shape out of ancient legend, ebony grace and power, daring to sail across the incandescent eye of God.

It was an extraordinary image, one of the best Cat had ever taken. And there was no one to share it with.

She closed her eyes, yet still she saw the *Wind Warrior* flying through twilight into gathering night. Emotions raked through her, shaking her.

She wanted to hate Travis.

And she knew she couldn't.

Anger, rage, fury—yes, Cat could feel all of that and more for Travis, emotions she had no easy labels for. But hate?

No, not that.

He had created too much beauty. He had taught her what passion was.

I can give you a chance to run before the storm, to feel ecstasy in every motion, every touch, and when the storm sweeps down, I'll be there. Let me love you, Cat.

Travis had been a fire burning in the icy center of night. She had known his dangers, yet she had chosen to stand too close to his flames.

Her fault, not his.

And when all was said, when the last word was buried beneath silence and ice, there was the fact that Travis had given her a beauty few women ever knew. For a time she had been a part of his fierce and tender fire, as graceful and wild as flame itself, burning with him. Now the time of fire was gone, flames scattered in darkness and wind, nothing left but the memory of warmth . . . and a single ember hidden inside her, fighting to live.

That ember deserved its chance to burn.

Slowly Cat turned to the telephone, picked up the receiver, and pushed in seven numbers. There were three rings before a woman answered.

"Tidewater Auction House, may I help you?"

Cat wrote out the last check, sealed the last envelope, licked the last stamp. Then she lay back on the heaped-up pillows and stared at the stack of envelopes. The credit card companies would be held at bay for a month. The signature loans would have to wait. So would the rent, the processor, and the framer.

She would worry about them next month. She would worry about a lot of things next month, but not now.

Not now.

Today she would be grateful that tuition and trousseau were paid for and she had enough money left in the bank to live on for three weeks. Maybe even four, if she was very, very careful. If that wasn't enough . . . well, somehow she would find a way to keep her head above water.

I'm a good swimmer, she thought. *It will work out. I'll make it work.*

Cat eased herself onto her side, pressed an extra pillow against her abdomen, and tried to ignore the cramps that gripped her. She kept telling herself that the spotting had eased up in the long days she had spent in bed. She didn't know if she believed it.

Cramps coiled harshly, relaxed, then returned with redoubled force. Heat flushed Cat's body, followed by a prickling chill and clammy waves of nausea.

The sound of someone knocking at the front door drifted into her bedroom, followed by Dr. Stone's voice.

"Cathy?"

"The door is open," Cat called.

Dr. Stone came into the bedroom and looked around. "Very nice. Much better than a hospital room."

Cat managed a smile despite her cramps. "You say that every time. And I say, 'Cheaper, too.' "

The doctor smiled. "True, too. New shells?" she asked, looking at the drift of shells on her patient's bedside table.

"Jason brings more every day."

Idly Cat stirred a fingertip in the shells. They made light and shadow curve into shapes that were both fascinating and serene. Sunlight streamed in from the full-length window by the bed. Light filled the room, picking out all the white envelopes and crumpled papers left by Cat's bill-paying spree.

"Working?" Dr. Stone asked, looking at the envelopes.

"Just taking care of a few details. Sharon will mail them for me tomorrow."

"No need. I'll mail them on my way home."

Dr. Stone gathered the envelopes and put them in her leather attaché case. Then she gave her patient a quick, expert examination. When she was finished, she sat in the chair that had been drawn up to Cat's bed for visitors.

"It's not any worse, is it?" Cat asked anxiously.

"It's been ten days. Frankly, I'd hoped for some progress. Are you staying in bed?"

"Yes. I only get up to go to the bathroom."

"Are you eating well?"

Instead of answering, Cat handed over a list of her meals since the last visit. Doctor Stone read it in silence, nodding approvingly from time to time.

"What about sleep?" the doctor asked.

Cat looked down at her hands, willing them not to clench. She hadn't had a whole night's sleep since Travis had sailed the *Wind Warrior* over the curve of the world.

"I sleep," she said.

"How many hours a night?"

"A few."

"How many is a few? Two? Four? Six?"

"Three, most of the time. Sometimes . . . less."

Dr. Stone frowned. "Do cramps wake you up?"

"Dreams."

"Describe them."

"There's only one, really." Cat's fingers laced together. "At least, only one ending. I stumble into the hole at the center of the universe and fall and then I wake up cold and shaking. It takes me a while to figure out that it was just a dream."

"Sleep with a light on."

"I do. It's just that"—she took a deep breath—"the dream is very real."

Dr. Stone put her hand over her patient's clenched fingers. "You never talk about the baby's father. Does he know you're pregnant?"

Cat's face became smooth, utterly expressionless. "Yes."

"I see." The doctor chose her next words carefully. "You're not the type of woman to sleep with a man just because you can. Do you still love him?"

"I don't hate him," Cat said, unwilling to assess her own raw feelings any more than that.

"Even though he abandoned you?"

Cat's breath came in sharply as she remembered Travis's rage and . . . agony. His sense of betrayal had been as deep as hers.

Deeper.

She could see that now, where before she had seen only her own terrible hurt.

"I don't hate him," she said in a soft, certain voice.

"That's why you want this baby. Other men, other babies just don't interest you, is that it?"

"Yes."

"No wonder you can't sleep. The man is gone and you're losing the battle to keep the baby."

"*No.*"

Dr. Stone's hand squeezed gently over Cat's fingers.

"Listen to me," the doctor said. "You must begin the process of accepting what almost certainly will happen."

"No."

"Yes, Cathy. If you don't, there will be a time you won't wake up when you stumble into that hole. You'll just keep on falling."

Cat closed her eyes, not wanting to see the other woman's compassionate face.

"Don't blame yourself," Dr. Stone continued gently. "It's a miracle that you're still pregnant at all. You have an amazing will. But even you can't keep willing miracles day after day, week after week."

Slowly Cat opened her eyes. She saw the doctor's concern and her calm certainty that the pregnancy would be lost.

"Why?" Cat whispered.

Dr. Stone hesitated, then said, "I've seen thousands of pregnancies, delivered thousands of babies. I've learned not to question the wisdom of a woman's body, particularly in the first trimester of pregnancy. Learn to accept all the possibilities, Cathy. Then, when your mind is calm, let your body decide what is best. It knows more than either of us."

Cat drew in a long, tight breath. "I'll try. But I want this baby so much!"

The doctor's smile was both sad and comforting. "Nothing would give me greater pleasure than to deliver a healthy baby into your arms."

Cat looked quickly at Dr. Stone's dark, compassionate eyes. "I'll think about . . . what you said."

"Good." The doctor stood up. "I'll see you in three days. Call me immediately if the pattern of bleeding changes or the cramps become rhythmic or truly painful. Do you need anything else?''

"Nothing. Just . . .'' Cat's voice died.

Her hands opened and settled protectively over her womb, saying all that she couldn't say in words.

"Think about what I said, Cathy. Find what peace you can with yourself.''

Cat didn't answer.

The door closed behind Dr. Stone.

Slowly the light flowing over the bed shifted from yellow to gold to deep orange. Motionless, Cat lay watching the supple transformations of the sea, trying to understand the unthinkable, accept the unspeakable.

It's a miracle that you're still pregnant at all.

I've learned not to question the wisdom of a woman's body.

Let your body decide.

"No,'' Cat whispered. "I can't.''

If you don't, there will be a time you won't wake up when you stumble into that hole. You'll just keep falling.

Accept. Accept. Accept.

Yet Cat couldn't. She simply could not accept losing the tiny ember inside her.

So she thought of other things, her mind floating free, adrift in twilight, seeking the black shadow of a vanished ship.

TWENTY-ONE

NIGHT OR day, moonlight or sunlight or storm, the Pacific rolled in untamed waves from horizon to horizon. Usually the simple magnificence of the sea cleansed Travis of impatience and anger, but not this time. He had lost track of how many days he had been on the water.

He knew only that it hadn't been enough time.

Cat hadn't called his cousin's house. She hadn't called his lawyer.

She will, Travis told himself with bitter certainty. *She doesn't have enough money to support a baby. If she's too coy to talk to an answering machine, she'll get the number I left with Harrington or he'll patch her through to the ship on a radio link.*

Cat's a big girl. She'll figure it out. She was going for the lifetime ride, but she's shrewd enough to cut her losses and take the cash instead of the gold ring.

Sterile.

My God, how could I have been taken in so easily?

Like the waves rolling beneath the ship, Travis kept going over and over his relationship with Cat, from its rocky beginning to its brutal end. He needed to figure out where he had gone wrong, how he had been so completely fooled by her.

It wasn't as though he had ignored the possibility of getting Cat pregnant. He had asked her outright.

I'm not contagious, but I have to know if you're protected against pregnancy.

She had answered with a reluctance that set off warning bells.

I won't get pregnant.

He had pressed her hard, needing to know the truth.

Are you certain?

I'm very certain. But it doesn't matter.

Like hell it doesn't. I was caught in the baby trap once. Once was more than enough.

Not to worry, Mr. T. H. Danvers. I'm fresh out of baby traps.

What does that mean?

I'm sterile!

Cat's rage had been so real, her pride so vulnerable, that Travis hadn't pushed beyond her words to real proof of sterility.

She had lied to him, beginning to end. He had believed her.

Beginning to end.

Spray lifted past the bow, brushed across Travis's hands like cool, salty kisses from a passionate yesterday. He tightened his grip on the railing and kept replaying scenes as he had done day and night since Cat betrayed him. He tore each memory apart again and again, seeking . . . something.

Some truth. Some answers.

Something to make him feel more alive, less a fool.

She had been so convincing, so proud, so strong and yet so vulnerable.

When Billy found out I was the reason we weren't having kids, he was furious. He wanted to know how I would earn my keep since I couldn't have babies. I wasn't educated, my mother was broke, and I was sterile. What damn good was I to a man?

Even in memory, Cat's words squeezed Travis's heart.

The knowledge that she still could reach inside him made him want to scream in raw fury. Because underneath it all, the pain and the memory and humiliation, he was hungry for her. He couldn't sleep for remembering how it felt to push into her tight, wet body and listen to her rippling cries of pleasure.

Travis didn't want to remember Cat's surprise and passion when she climaxed that first time. And he had believed it was her first.

What an actress. Shit, why didn't she go onstage? Money would have been the least of her problems.

Hot memories sleeted through him, sex better than he had ever had before, so damn good he never questioned the truth of Cat's response. He knew women could fake climax—and he also knew there were some things that couldn't be faked. Wet sheets were one of them.

All right. So she enjoyed it. So what? She lied about the rest and I went for it all, hip-deep and buried to the hilt.

Furious with Cat and with himself, Travis spent his waking moments balanced on the razor edge of self-control. It had never been this bad. Not even with Tina.

He couldn't go back to shore yet. He was still too vulnerable. He was still haunted by the sight of Cat's hand in the flames and the ice in her eyes when she told him to take his money and go to hell.

But most of all he was consumed by something he called himself a fool for even thinking.

What if she wasn't lying? What if she really thought she was sterile?

The possibility teased him, taunted him with all that he wanted to believe, all that he hungered to believe, with an intensity that left him shaken.

He needed her.

She only needed his money.

He had to remember that. Women and money was a lesson that had cost too much to learn. He couldn't allow himself to forget that.

Travis's hands squeezed the cold railing hard enough to leave marks on his palms.

"Captain?"

He spun toward Diego. "I told you I didn't want—"

"There is a call for you," the first mate interrupted quickly. "Very urgent."

A savage combination of triumph and despair twisted through Travis. The triumph he understood.

Cat got my number from Harrington and called.

Travis ignored the despair. He didn't want to examine why being right about what Cat really wanted from him should make his gut twist.

Nobody was standing around the radio phone when Travis got there. Every crew member had vanished. No one wanted to be within range of their captain's hair-trigger temper.

"Yes?" Travis said into the transmitter.

"Well, if it isn't Hell-on-Women Danvers. Finally. Do you know how long I've been trying to get this call through?"

"Harrington," Travis said. Disappointment made his voice rough.

"That's me, boy-o. Mind telling me why you aren't picking up your phone messages?"

"I am."

"Delightful," Harrington said sarcastically. "Then why in hell haven't you returned just one of my ten calls?"

"Eleven."

"But who's counting, right? Talk to me, Travis. Tell me why I shouldn't hire a boatload of thugs and beat you into a thin paste."

"Nice to know who my friends are."

"You're lucky to have any."

"Am I to assume Cat told you the heart-wrenching—or

is it gut-wrenching?—tale of her sterility followed by her miraculous fertility?'' Travis asked.

"I talked to Cochran."

"Then you know what kind of a fool I've been."

"I know what kind of a fool you're *being*. Cathy isn't a lying, scheming piece of ass like Tina."

"The proof is in the pudding. Or isn't Cat pregnant?"

"That's up for grabs right now."

Travis felt as though the ship was sliding down the side of a wave as tall as the sky. "Are you telling me that she's going to have an abortion?" he asked savagely.

"An abortion? Are you on drugs? Get it through the rock that passes for your brain: *This isn't Tina.* Right now Cathy is flat on her back in bed, doing everything she can to hang on to your baby."

"Yeah yeah yeah," Travis said, not believing a word of it. "You're breaking my heart."

"I'd rather break your head," Harrington snarled.

"Just because I don't think old Fire-and-Ice is an innocent little angel? Hell, Harrington. You're the one who's always telling me that a man can't really know a woman until he sleeps with her. I've slept with Cat. Have you?"

"Of course I haven't. She's my friend."

Travis told himself he wasn't going to ask. It was none of his business.

But it would explain why Cat hadn't called him or his lawyer.

"Did her Big Check from Energistics come through?" Travis asked.

"No," Harrington said curtly. "And it won't. Energistics is tits-up. Hardly enough left for the lawyers to snarl over."

Then why hasn't Cat called? Travis demanded silently. *She's dead broke and the twins' tuition is due.*

"So how much did you give her?" Travis asked.

"What are you talking about?"

"Cash and Cat."

"I tried to help her. She refused."

"Playing for keeps, isn't she?"

"Listen, you muleheaded son of a bitch," Harrington said, spacing each word so there could be no misunderstanding. "Cat isn't playing at all. She's honest to a fault. She has more integrity than any ten people and more stubbornness even than you!"

"So says the man who hasn't slept with her. Watch it, pal. Next thing you know she'll have you in front of a minister."

Silence stretched. Then Harrington spoke, his voice all but purring. "What a wonderful idea. Thank you. Should I send you an invitation? It will be a small ceremony, of course. Do RSVP at your convenience."

Before Travis could get his voice back, Harrington broke the connection.

Travis stood there, staring at the radio phone, for a long time. He knew his friend wouldn't be getting married. Not to Cat. If she had wanted to marry Harrington, she would have by now. But she hadn't even been his lover.

The thought transfixed Travis. He had been assuming that Cat wanted him for his money, but Harrington was richer than Travis.

What if Harrington is right about Cat's integrity?

Then, like ice water, came the second question: *What if he isn't?*

Travis didn't know the answer to either question. He did know that nothing was being solved at sea.

"Diego!" he yelled up the stairway.

"Yes, Captain."

"Set course for Dana Point."

Travis listened to the creak and snap of sails as the ship came about. Automatically he shifted his weight, adjusting to the different feel of the sea. Something close to calm stole over him. Cat needed his money. No matter how stubborn she was, she couldn't get past that fact.

She would see his ship returning, know that he was back, and call him.

Lying in bed, watching a restless dawn, Cat saw the *Wind Warrior* sail back out of the night, heading down the coast to Dana Point. Her heart beat so fast that it frightened her as much as the cramps gripping her body. She would have given anything but her baby to get up and look through a telescope, to see Travis again, if only at a distance, if only for an instant.

He came back, she thought, dizzy with relief. *He thought about it and now he knows it wasn't the money I wanted. Just him.*

Soon he'll call me, hold me, trust me, love me as much as I love him.

Tears burned behind Cat's eyes. In an agony of hope, she waited for the phone to ring.

She waited all day.

She endured another dream-haunted night.

Sometime during the second day, Cat finally understood that Travis wasn't going to call her. He wasn't going to see her. She was no more to him than spindrift torn from a storm wave.

Sometime during the second night, Cat realized that even good swimmers could drown.

Finally she slept, only to wake up shaking, breathing brokenly, sweating, bolt upright in bed. *Just a dream,* she assured herself frantically. *Wake up. It's just that damned dream.*

But being awake didn't end the nightmare. It was there in the blackness beyond her window, in her shallow breaths, in the fear that made her body rigid. Silently she endured it all, the sweating and the cramps, the darkness and the nightmare, the blank emptiness that awaited her with such terrifying patience.

I'll be better in the morning.

The bleeding will stop. The baby will be fine. This will all be worth it, every bit of it, when I hold our baby in my arms.

Motionless, Cat watched color seep into the starless arch of sky beyond her window. She lay on her side, trying to ease the cramps that held her lower body in a vise. She could feel the dampness between her legs.

After three weeks of bed rest, the bleeding wasn't better. If anything, it was worse.

Like the pain of not hearing from Travis.

Below Cat's bedroom window, surf exploded over black rocks beneath a slate-colored sky. The ranks of storm waves were enormous, rhythmic, almost reliable. Almost. The ocean was like a person, never truly predictable. Sometimes a larger set of waves would sweep in without warning, booming and tumbling onto the shore, making the house tremble with the power of the unleashed sea.

Cat held her breath, waiting for the beautiful violence of the biggest waves, waiting for the clash of fluid force and stone. Eagerly her eyes searched for the telltale dark lines of the larger waves looming out of the brightening day. And when the huge breakers came in their fives or sevens, bringing their own vicious thunder, she smiled triumphantly, glorying in the violent sea.

It was like having someone scream for her when she was too proud to scream for herself.

She made a low, pleased sound when she finally spotted another dark line looming on the horizon, the first of another series of smooth-backed monsters leaping up out of the sea.

Then, from the corner of her eye, she caught a slight motion partway down the cliff. Cold horror drenched her when she saw Jason darting down his stairway to the beach, coming to visit her as he had on so many dawns. He was too young to understand the danger of the big waves hump-ing up on the horizon, rolling toward shore with lethal power.

Cat screamed even though she knew Jason couldn't hear. "No! Jason, go back!"

Still screaming, she raced for the back door. She yanked it open and sprinted across the deck to the stairway that went down to the beach.

"Jason, go back! *Jason!*"

But even Cat's screams couldn't cut through the relentless roaring of surf and wind. Cataracts of water smashed over rocks, burying the lower quarter of her stairway in a deceptively creamy froth.

Jason paused on the beach, but not to go back. He was waiting for the pause between waves. When the pause came, it would be shorter than he expected and the following wave would be larger, the first of the big ones Cat had seen leaping darkly on the horizon.

Bruising her bare feet without feeling it, she bolted down the stairs. Her whole being was focused on the distance between her and the boy who was even now dashing over the foamy beach.

Somewhere in her mind she counted off the seconds since the wave had retreated, counted the steps Jason had made along the beach, counted the stairs he had to climb before he would be beyond the reach of the combers that were rising up out of the sea to explode in blue-green violence on her stairway.

Too much distance.

Not enough time.

Cat didn't scream again, even when she saw the next wave come apart, burying the beach in a powerful, deadly wall of surf. She simply ran faster than she ever had in her life, racing down the steps with reckless speed.

Not enough time.

Heart bursting, breath sawing, Cat reached Jason at the same instant the wave did. She wrapped her arms around him and the twisted iron railing and hung on with all her strength.

A wall of water slammed into her, over her. She held her breath and Jason and the rail until the wave reversed, trying to suck everything back down to the sea. Coughing, strangling, blind, she managed to stagger up three stairs with the boy when the force of the water pulling at her weakened.

Cat neither heard nor saw the next wave. It burst over her, burying her in a violent explosion of green and white. Before she could recover, the third big wave hammered her to her knees. With a burst of strength that came from desperation, she hung on to Jason and the railing.

The retreat of the third wave combined with the incoming power of the fourth. It was a cold ocean slamming over Cat, bruising her, crushing her, and not retreating at all. The fifth wave hit before the fourth was gone. There was no time for breath, no air to breathe. Her head was spinning from lack of oxygen, yet it was the thought of Jason that frightened her. He was a slack weight in her arms, threatening to slip away.

Half-conscious, Cat forced herself to her feet. Desperately she tried to lift Jason's limp body above the reach of the devouring sea.

It was like trying to lift the world.

The clock in her mind ticked off the seconds between waves, telling her that it was already too late.

The sixth breaker consumed Cat, dragging her down, clawing at the boy who was too heavy for her to carry. Barely conscious, she sensed the brief second of calm while the wave was balanced between advance and retreat.

She knew that when the balance shifted, when the wall of water rushed back to the sea, it would take her with it.

I'm sorry, Jason.

But she couldn't even say the words, nor could Jason have heard her if she spoke.

The wave hesitated, then began its powerful retreat.

Cat felt the rough railing slip away beneath her clutching hands. Before she could renew her grip, the world jumped crazily, throwing her off her feet. Dimly she thought another wave had come in, a wave so strong that it was washing her up the stairs on its crest.

Then she realized that someone was carrying her, carrying Jason, taking them both beyond the reach of the violent sea. When she saw her own deck, she struggled free and reached for Jason.

"He needs—"

It was all Cat could manage for the water choking her, strangling her. Fighting for breath, retching water, she went to her knees on the deck next to Jason. She tried to give him artificial respiration, but she was coughing too violently to breathe for herself, much less for him.

Hands crisscrossed by fine scars reached past Cat and wrapped around Jason, hands strong enough to defeat the wild sea and gentle enough to coax breath back into a small child.

Travis.

Cat closed her eyes, braced herself against the wracking coughs, and kept counting seconds in the back of her mind.

It seemed like a lifetime before Jason coughed, yet she had counted off less than eighty seconds before the child was breathing on his own.

She coughed wrenchingly again and again, clearing water from her lungs. Then she felt something break inside, felt a single searing pain. Warmth rushed out of her, taking her remaining strength. With a small cry she sank to the deck.

Travis heard, and turned to her. His face was grim, his eyes haunted, his voice ragged.

"You're bleeding, Cat. You must have cut your leg."

She looked down, saw the blood mixed with sea water on her legs, blood pooling on the deck.

Blood flowing out of her womb.

The scream that clawed from her throat was a savage denial that she could lose everything she had wanted out of life, that in the space of a few weeks she could be peeled like a living shell until nothing was left but a transparent, bleeding core.

And then nothing at all.

The scream was still raw in Cat's throat when another kind of wave surged up and broke over her. She gave herself to its blackness with a passion she had once saved for life.

Travis waited for Dr. Stone to emerge from the hospital room that Cat shared with three other people.

"How is she?" Travis asked.

"Sleeping. I gave her something."

"That's not what I asked." He met and matched the doctor's cool, assessing look.

"Are you related to Cathy?"

Travis's eyes narrowed. "Not legally. But we're . . . close."

"I see. Have you had those cuts and bruises looked at?"

"There's nothing worth looking at."

"Does Cathy have anyone who should be notified?"

"You're looking at him."

The doctor's eyebrows rose. "Come with me."

She led Travis to what looked like an interns' lounge. Scarred plastic chairs, ratty tables, battered food and drink machines. The magazines were old enough to vote but too worn to make the effort.

"Sit down," Dr. Stone said.

"I'd rather stand."

"Did I ask?"

Travis measured the doctor's calm determination. Then he lowered himself into a nearby chair.

"Well, you don't limp and your legs are still flexible," she said crisply. "How is your back?"

"It will be stiff tomorrow. Nothing that a swim or a hot tub can't take care of. How is Cat?"

"Cat? Oh, Cathy. She lost the pregnancy."

Travis hoped the knife turning in his guts didn't show. He sensed that the good doctor would probably enjoy his pain.

"Nothing to say?" Dr. Stone goaded.

"Just tell me how she is."

"I have. She's not pregnant."

"Are you saying she'll never have children because of this?" he asked tightly.

"No. Cathy had a relatively simple miscarriage. No complications, physically speaking."

Travis closed his eyes and let out his breath. The relief made him weak. "Thank God. She'll be all right, then?"

"I don't know."

His eyes snapped open as relief vanished. "What?"

"My dear young man," Dr. Stone said, yet her eyes said Travis was anything but dear to her, "Cathy has spent the last three weeks flat on her back in bed, alone, terrified of miscarriage. She described her feelings to me very well— a hole at the center of everything. She stumbles in and then she falls and keeps on falling."

Grimly Travis fought to keep his emotions from showing. "If Cat knew she was at risk of miscarrying, why wasn't she in the hospital?"

"No insurance. No money."

Travis flinched as though the doctor had struck him. "Are you saying that she would still be pregnant if she had been in the hospital?"

"Odd. She asked me the same thing."

"What did you tell her?"

"The truth."

"Damn it!" Travis exploded. "Do I have to drag it out of you word by word?"

Abruptly Dr. Stone sighed. "However satisfying it would be to torment you for your callus treatment of your lover, I find I haven't the stomach for it. I can see, despite your attempt at a poker face, that you're already doing an excellent job of tormenting yourself."

"Don't stop now. Twist the knife again. *Tell me about Cat.*"

The doctor smiled slightly, liking the fierce-looking stranger in spite of herself.

"Mr. Danvers, no matter what care Cathy received, she was simply too physically depleted to sustain a pregnancy. Everything we did was too little, too late. Her body started trying to shed the pregnancy as soon as conception occurred. She wanted that baby. She fought for it. She is a very strong-willed woman. But in the end . . ." The doctor spread her hands, palm up, empty.

Travis forced himself to breathe past the pain he wouldn't reveal. "Cat's money worries are over. Move her to a private room. Get her whatever she needs that money can buy. Do it now."

"Too little, too late."

"Shit," he said, closing his eyes for an instant. "You're really enjoying this, aren't you?"

"No. I'm telling you that money is too small a bandage to put on a wound like Cathy's."

Ice settled in Travis's stomach. "You said she was all right."

"She is, physically. That's less than half the battle after a miscarriage. Depression is common. The male doctors call it hormones and shrug it off. But hormones are only part of it. The rest is something fundamentally female. I doubt if a man could understand the loss."

"Try me."

This time when Dr. Stone measured Travis, he made no

attempt to conceal his own grief. There was no need. He could see the doctor's pain; she was talking about her own loss as well as her patient's.

For a time she was connected in the most intimate possible way with another life. Now that is gone.

For everyone.

TWENTY-TWO

WHEN CAT woke up she thought she was still caught in the last violent wave, green and white pouring over her, surrounding her. Her heart squeezed and then beat frantically before she realized that the green was pale, calm, and the white was clean, smooth, and dry.

Sheets. Walls. A bed.

Quiet.

Her body ached everywhere. When she moved to ease her muscles, she realized that a man's hand was wrapped around her wrist.

Cat blinked, focused, then blinked again in disbelief. Travis was asleep in a chair next to her bed. His hand was around her wrist, fingertips resting on her pulse as though even asleep he needed to be reassured that her heart still beat.

With a small shudder she closed her eyes. At a great distance she heard the waves breaking, cataracts pouring over her, drowning her and the boy she couldn't have loved more if he had been her own.

But Jason was safe now, thanks to Travis.

Jason is safe and I drowned.

That means I'm safe, too. Nothing can hurt you when you're already drowned.

The thought soothed Cat, surrounding her with numbness. In being close to Travis she had lost far too much,

more than she thought she could lose . . . more than was
hers to lose and still survive.

Deliberately she eased her wrist from his grip.

The motion woke Travis. His eyes opened, blue-green,
vivid, seeing through Cat to her core. Something inside her
moved beneath his look, something very like pain. She
couldn't bear that, couldn't bear him seeing her empty core.

When he took her hand again she removed her fingers
with cool finality.

"Jason," she said.

A single word. It was all she could say, for her throat
was raw from salt water and screams.

"He's fine," Travis said quickly. "The ER doctor
checked him over, read him the riot act about storm waves
and common sense, and then turned him over to his mother
for scolding and hugging."

Even as Travis spoke, the last stubborn bit of Cat's emotions that had struggled against numbness quietly gave up.

Jason was fine.

That was all she needed to know, the best she could have
hoped for since she saw blood pooling around her on the
deck.

"Thank you for saving him," Cat said, closing her eyes,
her voice colorless. "I wasn't strong enough."

Silence came to the room, an emptiness haunted by the
sounds of surf breaking against black rocks. But the waves
lived only in Cat's mind. She hoped if she slept, they would
go away, leaving her in a silence to equal her numbness.

Warm fingers touched her hand, then closed around her
wrist in hard demand.

"Aren't you going to ask about yourself?" Travis said.

Cat opened her eyes. She saw nothing but the emptiness
inside her where an ember of life had once burned. She
didn't need to say anything, ask any questions. There was
nothing to say, no reason to ask after the dead.

The utter lack of animation in Cat made her a stranger

to Travis. He had seen her in so many ways—exhausted, furious, passionate, laughing, focused in work—but never like this. Indifferent. Completely.

Fear slid cool claws over Travis's skin, stirring the hair at his nape. He had prepared arguments for her, pleas for her, reasons for her . . . *but she wasn't there.*

Slowly his fingers loosened on her wrist. Tenderly he stroked it, feeling for her pulse. Finding it reassured him at a primitive level.

"Dr. Stone told me you would be depressed," he said quietly, "even though you knew how great the odds were against a successful pregnancy."

Cat didn't even blink.

"She said that your depression will pass," Travis continued. "Physically, you're fine. Exhausted, a little bruised, but nothing that rest won't cure."

She said nothing.

He turned her face so that she had to look at him. When he saw the emptiness in her eyes, he whispered her name and gathered her against his chest to comfort her, rocking her.

Cat neither responded nor retreated. She was as still as a photograph in his arms.

Fear condensed in Travis's stomach. He smoothed the cool fire of Cat's hair away from her face. Her eyes didn't change as he touched her, didn't focus on him, didn't even see him. She was looking through him to the hallway beyond.

It was as though he wasn't there.

"Listen to me," Travis said urgently. "We'll be able to have another baby. Cat? Do you hear me?"

She heard him, but his voice was far away, muffled by layers of blessed numbness, layer on layer of icy water enfolding her, a whole silent ocean to drown in.

His arms tightened as though he knew she was slipping away finally, irretrievably, drowning in silence. He held her close again, rocking her slowly, trying to warm both of them.

"I know you hate me," Travis said in a ragged voice. "I came back to you too late. If you don't want my baby, then another man's. Anything, Cat, anything, but don't look like that. Scream and call me names. I deserve all of them. At least cry. Tears will heal you faster than anything else."

There was no answer, no movement, nothing.

Travis looked down at the woman who lay motionless in his arms. If he hadn't felt Cat's weight, he wouldn't have believed that he held her. *She was not there.*

No matter how he searched, he didn't see the woman whose photographs hummed with passion and intelligence, the woman whose mind and body had become a part of him, the woman whose incandescent fury had burned through all his hours since she had taught him how little money could buy.

Too little. Too late.

She had retreated beyond his reach, beyond the reach of anyone or anything.

With aching tenderness Travis kissed the tumbled mass of auburn hair.

"This isn't you," he whispered, plea and command at the same time. "In a few days you'll feel better. You'll take your cameras and catch the waves coming up over the edge of the world, waves that came thousands of miles just to touch your feet. Smart waves." His lips brushed her cheek. "Lucky waves. I learned from them, but I learned too late."

Cat spoke then, her voice as lifeless as her eyes. "I sold all my cameras."

Travis didn't want to believe that he had heard her correctly. Yet he knew he had.

"Cat."

The word was hoarse, an involuntary cry of pain and regret. He didn't have to ask why she had sold her cameras, her heart, her life's blood. He knew. He could hear his own voice coldly suggesting it: *If you need money so damn bad, you could always sell some equipment. You've got enough for three photographers.*

She had done more than sell extra equipment. She had sold her future to buy enough time to have his baby. The baby of a man who had more money than trust. The baby of a man who would have given anything for that child.

Too little.

Too late.

Cat rolled away from Travis, turning her back on him and the world, staring at the far wall without seeing it, seeing nothing at all.

With a hand that shook, he stroked tangled coils of hair away from her still face, remembering her cheeks flushed with excitement, her gray eyes misty and luminous as she watched him, touched him, laughed with him. Memories like razors sliced through his fear of repeating the past until truth finally bled out, unmistakable, unavoidable.

She had loved him.

Do you believe in miracles? I'm pregnant, my love. I'm pregnant! A baby! Travis, my man, my lover, my love. Our baby!

Head bowed, Travis measured the depth of his loss, her loss, their loss. He sat for a long time, motionless but for his hand smoothing her hair with endless patience, his eyes as dark as hers were pale.

He didn't call Cat's name again.

When Cat opened her eyes the next day, Travis was there. He had been there every time she awakened, night or day, since he had carried her and Jason beyond the reach of the storm waves. After she told Travis that she sold her cameras, he had said nothing, demanded nothing of her, not even an acknowledgment that she wasn't alone.

Travis was simply there.

Cat ignored him. She didn't know what he wanted of her. She didn't want to know. His presence threatened the emotional numbness that was all that protected her from being overwhelmed. She could cope with the rest of the world, after a fashion. But not Travis, not in any fashion.

"Sharon and Jason are here," Travis said. "He thinks it's his fault that you were hurt. Sharon thought if Jason saw you, saw that you were all right, he would feel better."

Travis waited, unwilling to ask any more of Cat than he already had, knowing he had no right to ask anything of her at all.

For the space of several slow breaths, Cat thought of Jason, young and laughing and so very vulnerable.

"He doesn't know about—about—" She stopped, unable to talk about her miscarriage.

"Don't worry," Travis said quickly. "All Jason remembers is seeing you reach for him just as the first wave hit."

The part of Cat that hadn't drowned realized that Travis understood that she didn't want Jason to know about the miscarriage. Deep inside her numbness a faint echo of anger and grief trembled, then faded. Travis had always understood everything about her except the one thing that mattered.

She had loved him.

"All right," she said tonelessly. "Send Jason in."

Not until Travis let go of her hand did Cat even realize that he was holding it, had been holding it the whole time, night or day, asleep or awake. It would have disturbed her, if she had been able to feel anything.

"I'll be right back," he said.

She didn't answer.

After a few minutes Travis returned with Sharon and Jason. Cat saw Jason's strained, too old expression and troubled blue eyes. Emotion rippled beneath her numbness. She was deeply grateful that this small boy was alive.

"Jason," she said softly, and held out her hand.

A smile lit the boy's face. He ran to her and buried his face against her neck in a fierce hug. Then he pulled back and looked at her with eyes made huge by tears.

"I th-thought you wouldn't want to s-see me," he said.

Unable to speak, Cat simply shook her head. Her fingers trembled as she pushed thick black curls back from Jason's forehead and hugged him again.

"I'm very glad to see you," she finally said in a voice that was husky from lack of use. "You're my very favorite little boy."

Jason snuggled against Cat and then pulled back, energy overflowing in an electric smile.

"This is for you," he said, holding out his hand. "I found it this morning."

On the boy's narrow palm lay a shell that had been rubbed smooth by countless waves and then flung carelessly up on the beach by the storm. The rough outer layer of shell had been completely worn away, leaving bare the pearly layer beneath. What remained was an object stripped to its essential form, revealing the gleaming beauty that had been hidden until time and storm waves peeled the shell to its iridescent core.

At one time Cat would have itched to photograph the shell. Now it was all she could do to accept it.

"It's beautiful," she managed, looking at the silent plea in Jason's eyes. "Thank you."

Sharon glanced at Jason and then at Travis, who was standing in the doorway. He crossed the room and lifted the boy onto his shoulders.

"I saw this big ol' candy machine in the lobby," Travis drawled. "Bet they have your favorite kind of tooth poison. Watch your head, now. We're kinda tall, stacked like this."

Travis ducked, Jason squealed, and the two of them got through the doorway to the hall. The sound of the boy's giggles floated back.

Cat closed her eyes.

"It isn't fair," Sharon said in a low voice. "It just isn't fair that you should lose your baby to save my son."

Cat forced herself to look at the other woman's clear blue eyes, eyes as troubled as Jason's had been. Cat tried to smile, to reassure Sharon.

"Jason is alive," Cat said. "That's all the 'fair' anyone can expect."

"But you—"

"I'd do it again in an instant," Cat interrupted. "I love Jason."

Tears gathered and slid down Sharon's cheeks. Cat felt a dim envy for the other woman's ability to cry.

"Thank you," Sharon said shakily. "You saved his life."

"Thank the man who carried Jason up the stairs. He saved Jason. I wasn't strong enough."

"If you hadn't held on until Travis got to you . . ." Sharon took a sobbing breath and squeezed Cat's hand. "You won't have to worry about Jason getting into trouble while you get back on your feet. We're going to my sister's house in Georgia for a while. I haven't been able to sleep, knowing the ocean was out there, day and night, waiting. . . ." Her voice broke. "Jason is so small. So terribly small." She bent and kissed Cat's pale cheek. "I was told not to stay long, not to tire you out. But thank you, Cathy. Thank you for Jason's life."

After Sharon left, Cat lay and looked at the ceiling. She heard footsteps and knew that Travis was back. She neither moved nor spoke, ignoring him even when he took her hand. Only when Dr. Stone walked into the room did Cat stir.

"I want to leave," she said.

"You would be better off with a few more days of rest," the doctor said, looking at Cat's chart.

"I can rest at home better than I can rest here. Tell the cashier's office to make up my bill."

Surprised, Dr. Stone looked from Cat to Travis.

Cat's emotions might have been frozen, but her intelligence wasn't. She knew instantly that Travis was paying for her hospital room. Something like anger flickered in her pale eyes as she turned on Travis.

"Rich man," she said in a smooth, empty voice, "I'll sell myself on street corners before I take one dime of your money."

Cat turned away from Travis and looked back to Dr. Stone. "I'm leaving whether you agree or not."

There was no emotion in Cat's voice, just certainty. She would not stay here one moment longer than she had to. Once she was home, she wouldn't have to tolerate Travis by her bed, his blue-green eyes following her every movement, counting each breath she took, each heartbeat, searching for a way beneath the ice that was her only refuge.

Dr. Stone hesitated, then gave in to the inevitable. "If you feel you must leave, I can't stop you."

"You told me she should stay here for several more days," Travis protested.

"She should. But I'm not going to tie her to the bed."

He hissed a word under his breath. He knew Cat's true reason for wanting to get out of the hospital. She didn't want to be near him.

"If you will excuse us, Mr. Danvers," Dr. Stone said, "I would like to examine my patient."

Without a word he stood and walked out of the room. As soon as he found a public phone, he punched in a long string of numbers and started counting the initials scratched on the battered steel face of the phone.

Harrington picked up his very private number on the second ring. "Well?" he demanded.

"What would you do if it wasn't me?" Travis asked.

"Hang up."

Travis almost smiled despite his unholy turmoil of anger,

pain, and desperation. "Cat's physical condition is better than we had any right to expect."

"Good. What about the rest?"

"She saw Jason this morning, and even managed a smile for him."

Harrington let out an explosive breath. "Then she's coming out of it."

"You couldn't prove it by me. She's checking herself out of the hospital so she won't have to put up with me anymore."

"Shit."

"Amen. I'll play it your way for a few more days, just like I promised. Then I'll change the game. And you'll help me, just like you promised."

"Travis . . . ah, *hell*. What do you want me to do?"

"Get her aboard my ship."

"And then?"

"We're in the wind. Together."

"What good will that do?"

"She's hiding from what happened, from me, from herself. I can't reach her. But I know what can. Her cameras. She loves them more than anything else on earth."

Especially Travis Danvers.

"You said she sold them," Harrington objected.

"I tracked them down. They're aboard the *Wind Warrior,* along with the lab I designed and a computer setup that will let Cat do anything she wants with the images she takes. Thanks to your contact at Nikon, she'll have a chance to test state-of-the-art digital cameras and software, as well as the old-fashioned kind."

"Old-fashioned? Swear to God, Fred would kill you if he heard that. His autofocus zoom lenses are to cameras what your hulls are to racing—innovative and unbeatable."

"Good. I have a full set of his latest, from micro to macro to stuff that could count rocks on the moon."

For a time Harrington didn't say anything. Travis could fairly hear his friend's brain humming.

"Cathy will have a fit when she finds out you bought her all the gear," Harrington said finally.

"A fit would be welcome. It would tell us that we're both alive."

Harrington made an involuntary sound of sympathy at the pain tightening Travis's voice.

"No point in digging any deeper a hole than you already have," Harrington said. "I'll just tell her Nikon is so impressed with her photography that they want her to test lenses for them. Swear to God, the way her show is going in L.A., camera types are going to be beating down her door with equipment to use."

"The show is going well?"

"They can't hang the stuff fast enough. Swift and Sons are walking around rubbing their hands and mumbling about Catherine Cochran, the twenty-first-century Stieglitz."

"Have you told her?" Travis asked.

"Not yet. I'm waiting until it's sold down to the bare walls, then I'm going to drop the good news on her."

"Don't wait too long. Time is running out."

"Time or your patience?" Harrington retorted.

"Same difference. Three more days, Rod. Then we do it my way."

"On two conditions."

Travis bit off a curse. His temper was raw and he knew it. And he knew why. "What?"

"Dr. Stone has to approve of Cathy being on her feet and at sea."

"She does."

"How do you know?"

"The usual way. I asked. If you don't believe me, call the doctor yourself."

"I will, if only to shut my conscience up."

"You didn't do anything to Cat."

"That, boy-o, is a matter of opinion. My second condition is that if you lure Cathy out of her shell, and she still doesn't want you, you'll put in to the first port and let her go. Alone."

For a time Travis couldn't force any words past the fist squeezing his throat shut. He closed his eyes and remembered the horrifying sight of Cat hurtling down her stairway, Jason blithely climbing up, and a cold wall of water rising, rising, rising, then exploding over them.

He had come so close to losing her, so damned close. He didn't know if he could lose her again, feel again the cold black wings of loss wrapping around him, freezing him all the way to his soul.

"Travis? I mean it. If I had known what doing that damned book would cost Cathy, I never would have thrown the two of you together. If she wants to walk, *let her*. Let her find a man she can love. She deserves to be loved, and loved well."

When Travis finally could speak, his voice sounded like a stranger's.

Like Cat's.

"If that's what she wants."

For three days Cat didn't allow anything to disturb her solitude. The answering machine picked up all incoming calls. She returned none of them, listened to none of the messages. She simply lay on her bed and let the sun and darkness wash over her.

Though Travis didn't come to the house, she knew he was next door, just a few steps away. Each dawn she saw him swimming. When she watched him, she wondered if his nights were like hers.

When he falls asleep, does he stumble into the hole at the center of the universe? Does he wake up sweating, cold, disoriented?

When Cat heard her own thoughts, she would have laughed bitterly if she had the energy.

Rich men don't have nightmares. They don't care enough about anything to let it disturb their sleep.

The phone rang. Dully Cat focused on it. She knew who it would be. Only one person would call her at dawn.

Harrington. Swear to God. I don't have the energy to talk to him. But I should. It's the least I owe him.

Guilt forced Cat to struggle to the surface of her lethargy long enough to answer the phone. She knew she should have called Harrington the day she got out of the hospital, or any of the days since.

"Hello," she said, and wondered if her voice sounded as strange to the rest of the world as it did to her.

"Cathy?"

It was Harrington's voice. His concern was as clear as the rosy light of dawn filling her room.

"Must be a wrong number," Cat said. "This is Cochran."

Static crackled softly on the line, filling the silence.

"I talked to Dr. Stone," Harrington said bluntly.

Dimly Cat wondered how he had gotten the doctor's name. Travis, probably.

"Are you still there?" Harrington asked.

She felt a wild impulse to laugh or scream. *Of course I'm not here. I drowned. Didn't Travis tell you?*

"Cathy—damn it!—say something!"

"Hello, green angel," she said without inflection. "How are you. I'm fine, thank you. Just fine."

There was a startled pause before Harrington collected himself. "Good. Then there's no reason why you can't finish the Danvers assignment, is there?"

Cat stared at the phone, speechless. Something finally stirred beneath her indifference.

"You're crazy," she said. "I sold my cameras."

"Not to worry. It's all taken care of. You're a famous

photographer now. Nikon is dying to lend you equipment.''

"What are you talking about?''

"Didn't someone from Swift and Sons call you?''

"No. I don't know. My messages are . . . piled up some-where.''

"Your show sold out,'' Harrington said cheerfully. "You're back-ordered for more. You're a sixty-thousand-dollar hit, Cochran. And Ashcroft's publisher came through. If you don't like the gear that was sent out to the *Wind Warrior,* buy a different camera. Hell, buy twenty. Money doesn't matter anymore. You're over the hump.''

Cat knew she should feel something, if only relief. She could pay off the hospital, the signature loans, the credit cards, her mother's expenses, education loans for the twins, everything.

But Cat felt nothing, nothing at all, except a certainty that she couldn't set foot on the *Wind Warrior* again, couldn't look at Travis again, couldn't see her own emp-tiness reflected in his eyes.

"No.''

"Cathy,'' Harrington said softly, "I've never asked you to do something for me, have I?''

"No . . .'' she said, swallowing, afraid of what he would say next.

"I called in a lot of debts to get the Danvers book going. I didn't say anything before because there wasn't any way you could do the work. But Dr. Stone said you were well enough to spend a month shooting the *Wind Warrior* under sail, as long as you took it easy the first week.''

"Angel—'' Cat's voice broke.

She swallowed and tried again, desperately wanting to refuse Harrington but knowing she owed him so much more than a few photos. Her mind raced frantically, trying to find a way out of the trap.

"On one condition,'' she said finally. "That Tra—'' Her voice broke again. She couldn't say his name aloud. It was bad enough to hear it in the numbing silence of her mind. "Only the crew," she managed. "No one on board but me and the crew. *No one.*"

"Done," Harrington said quickly. "Be at the harbor in an hour."

"That isn't enough time to—"

"How long does it take you to drive to Dana Point?" he interrupted. "Everything you need is aboard, and I mean everything. Even clothes. Swear to God. I knew you wouldn't let me down. Remember, one hour. 'Bye, Cochran. I'm counting on you."

Harrington hung up before she could protest.

In a daze Cat dressed and stuffed a few things in an overnight bag. She drove to the harbor where the *Wind Warrior* rode quietly at anchor, its superb maroon wings furled. Diego met her, took her aboard, and showed her to a cabin.

Cat was relieved that it wasn't the one she had shared with Travis. She didn't think she could have stayed in his bed without remembering everything that she must forget. And if she couldn't forget, it must remain buried beneath ice and silence.

As she opened cupboards looking for a place to put her few things, she found the camera equipment Harrington had said was on board. In silence she examined item after item—the very latest models of autofocus zoom lens, state-of-the-art Nikon camera bodies and motor drives, film carriers, and more variety of lenses than she knew existed.

It was everything she might possibly need, more equipment than she had ever dreamed of owning. There were even four camera bodies and a lens system that duplicated the equipment she had sold, as though Harrington had been afraid that she wouldn't be comfortable with different camera models and lenses.

Numbly Cat looked at all the equipment, trying to add up its cost in her mind. The wide-angle lens she held in her hand was the latest model put out by Nikon. It cost well over five thousand dollars. The big new autofocus zoom cost at least fifteen thousand. She knew its price because she had promised herself one as soon as she had the money to buy it.

She doubted Harrington's explanation that Nikon had lent her the equipment she saw spread out in the tiny cabin. He had bought it himself.

Or Travis had.

Unable to stop herself, Cat opened every cupboard in the cabin. Then she stood silently, staring at what had been concealed by polished wood—a very sophisticated computer system that mated with a digital camera. A flat scanner. A slide scanner. A printer whose product was indistinguishable from a quality photographic print.

And if Cat wanted to go back to the twentieth century for inspiration, the cabin had been fitted out as a seagoing photo lab tailored to her precise needs. There was a refrigerator packed with film. A slide processor had been cleverly suspended to counteract the inevitable surge of waves. The slide duplicator was new, far better than the one she had at home. There was a nondigital system for enlarging and printing images.

The cabin was a photographer's dream. Everything that money could buy. Cat looked at the room and wanted to feel something, pleasure or anger or outrage or . . . anything.

The camera equipment might have been bought recently, but the cabin itself couldn't have been designed and executed in a few days, no matter how much money was spent. It had to have been done when Travis was trying to get her to run before the storm with him.

Come away with me. Avalon. Ensenada. Or farther. Hawaii. Papeete. The Seychelles or Tasmania or the China Sea. Anywhere in the world the wind blows, and it blows everywhere, Cat. Come with me.

Then she had told him that she was pregnant, the storm broke over her, and she was alone.

Slowly Cat turned in a circle, seeing Travis in every polished length of wood, in the cleverly designed lab, in the computer equipment, in the gleaming symmetry of cupboard and sink. Ordinary things had been reshaped by his mind into a beauty that sang beguilingly of skilled, sensual hands.

Emotion rippled through Cat, a feeling like warmth breathing over the ice surrounding her, threatening it. Threatening her. She shuddered once, violently.

Slowly, carefully, she packed away the camera equipment, closed the cupboards, and went up on deck. She felt the timeless rhythm of the open sea as the ship spread its wings and stepped into the wind. Standing at the railing, she watched the coast of California slide away behind her.

Wind blew around Cat, and sunlight. The sea air tasted of the tears she couldn't cry.

Not until it was dark did she go below. When she opened her overnight bag, she remembered that she hadn't brought anything to sleep in.

Everything you need is aboard, and I mean everything. Even clothes. Swear to God.

"Everything better be," she said wearily. "Swear to God."

Cat went through the cedar drawers beneath her bunk. There were clothes in all styles and only one size. Hers.

Harrington was right. Everything she needed was aboard, including an emerald silk nightgown and one of indigo. She ignored both of them.

In a different drawer, stuffed way back into a corner as though overlooked and forgotten, she found a black T-shirt. It was soft from many washings and smelled of cedar. She stripped and pulled the shirt over her head.

It was far too big for her. Only one person could have worn it.

Cat shoved the thought from her mind. She would rather wear one of Travis's forgotten T-shirts than the sensuous silk gowns. She lay down on the bunk and felt waves rocking her, heard the wind and the hiss of water dividing on either side of the bow. A vague sparkle of stars came through the lozenge-shaped porthole above her bunk. Finally she slept.

Three hours later she awoke in a cold sweat. Nausea somersaulted in her stomach. She knew immediately that it wasn't seasickness. She had simply stumbled into the hole again, falling and turning endlessly.

The feeling of disorientation faded when she found the lighter shade of black that was the porthole. She fastened onto it like a lifeline.

Cat didn't go back to sleep that night. She didn't want to. It wasn't worth it, just to wake up sweating and shaking, holding on to herself so she wouldn't scream. She knew it would pass, eventually. It had before, darkness dragging slowly toward dawn.

But in the icy center of night, time itself froze, sweating seconds as slowly as a glacier sweated water. Quietly, desperately, she stared out the porthole and counted stars.

Maybe tomorrow night it will be better, she told herself. *Maybe, at least, it won't be worse.*

Cat was up on deck before the last stars faded into dawn. She spent that day and the following five days sitting at the bow of the *Wind Warrior*, staring into the horizon, seeing nothing, saying nothing, dreading the coming night when she would wake and stare out the porthole, looking for a dawn that never came.

At sunrise of the seventh day, Travis was waiting on deck for her.

TWENTY-THREE

THERE WAS nothing but ocean in all directions. No ships, no shore, nothing to swim toward even if Cat had the strength to flee.

After the initial overwhelming realization of Travis's presence, her first thought was that Harrington had lied to her. Though she said nothing, though she refused to speak to Travis at all, the accusation was written across the taut lines of her face.

Travis saw it, as he had always seen so much of her. So much, and still not enough. He had understood too late that he had been so busy looking over his shoulder at the mistakes of the past that he had missed the most important truth of all. Cat, his future.

"Rod didn't lie to you," Travis said. "The captain is part of the crew."

Cat closed her eyes. *Of course. And Travis is captain of this ship. I should have phrased my demand more carefully.*

But she said not one word aloud. Speaking would make it all too real. Make Travis too real.

When she made no move to speak, he did. "I knew I couldn't lure you out of your . . . silence. But I thought your cameras would. I thought you would succumb to the beauty of photographing the *Wind Warrior* as she sailed a long reach at dawn."

Cat looked past Travis. Through him.

Though he wasn't surprised at her reaction, he was surprised at how much it still hurt. Like having his guts pulled through the eye of a needle. Like watching her slide further and further away with each dawn.

"But you didn't respond to the cameras," Travis said, his voice hard. "In six days you haven't so much as unwrapped a roll of film. You're not sleeping and you're not eating. Since neither your cameras nor I can seduce you back to life, it's time for the direct approach." He shoved a wet suit into Cat's hands. "Put this on."

Her eyes flew open. She looked in disbelief at the wet suit, and then at Travis. She saw nothing in his face but the hard planes and angles of his determination. And the shadow of another emotion that she flinched from seeing at all.

"If you don't put it on," he said flatly, "I'll do it for you."

Once she would have flung his suit and his pity in his face. Now it simply didn't matter. Nothing did.

As soon as Cat went below, Diego appeared at Travis's elbow. "Now, at least, we won't have to hide you with the cook."

"Is everything ready?"

"As you ordered, Captain."

Travis grunted and stalked to the stern of the *Wind Warrior*.

When Cat emerged on the deck again, she was wearing the wet suit. It, like the other clothes Travis had bought her, fit perfectly.

The ship was hove to, resting quietly on the roller-coaster back of the sea. At the stern, Travis was waiting for her, a tall black figure looming against the dawn.

"I'll go first," he said. "The ladder can be slippery."

Cat waited with absolute indifference until Travis called to her from the diving platform below. She climbed down and went into the water without looking at him. He dove cleanly, surfaced beside her, and swam alongside her, watching her.

Diego watched too, ready to launch the Zodiac if it was needed.

At first Cat swam erratically, more of a flight from the *Wind Warrior* than a coordinated effort to stay afloat. Gradually the ingrained rhythms of swimming settled her body. Then she swam mindlessly, arms and legs churning, ignoring everything.

She didn't know how long she swam. She knew only that when it came time to climb back onto the diving platform, she hadn't the strength.

With a smooth motion Travis levered himself onto the platform. He pulled Cat out of the sea, stood her on her feet, and pushed her up the ladder.

"Captain," Diego asked anxiously, "is she sick?"

"She's fine. Just tired from the exercise. I'll bring breakfast to her."

Travis picked Cat up and carried her back to her assigned cabin. He peeled off her wet suit, toweled her dry as impersonally as a nurse, dressed her in warm clothes, and left her staring at the door in a combination of shock and disbelief.

He returned in a few minutes, carrying breakfast.

The first thing she saw was the medicine Dr. Stone had prescribed to help get her menstrual cycle back to normal.

"Take it with this," Travis said, holding out a glass of juice.

Cat didn't move.

"You aren't strong enough to fight me," he said bluntly. "If I have to, I'll shove this pill down your throat and pour juice in after it."

She took the pill.

When she made no move toward the food, Travis picked up the fork and loaded it with scrambled eggs.

"Open up."

His words and actions reminded Cat of the night at the restaurant, when they had fed each other dessert and Travis licked up his mistakes. A single look at his smoldering blue-green eyes told her that he was remembering too.

Pain moved beneath Cat's indifference. She took the fork away from Travis.

She would eat, but not from his hand.

"I'm not leaving until the tray is clean," he said. "Take as long as you like."

Cat ignored him completely, but the plate was empty when Travis took it away. Moments later he was back in her doorway. She hadn't moved. Her eyes were as empty as her hands.

"Up," Travis said curtly. "Get your cameras."

Slowly she focused on him. She said nothing, simply looked at him, her pale eyes dazed with exhaustion and disbelief.

He can't do this to me.

Travis leaned over Cat. She could see nothing but him, a tawny-haired giant filling her world until there wasn't room for anything else, even breath.

"No mercy," he said softly. "I'm going to push you until you fight me. Somewhere under all that ice a fire still burns. I'm going to find it. *Get up.*"

Cat stood up, knowing that if she refused, Travis would simply carry her up to the deck. She didn't want that. When he touched her, she remembered things better left buried under layers of ice and silence.

For the rest of that day and all the days that followed, Cat didn't look directly at Travis, didn't argue with his orders, didn't speak to him at all. He gave up trying to break through her silence and settled for being her nurse and her nemesis, driving her physically in the hope that she would be tired enough to sleep through the night.

But she wasn't.

No matter how far she swam, no matter how many meals

she ate, no matter how many exercises she did or how many pictures she took under his critical eye, the hole in the universe was still there beneath her feet.

And each time she slept, she fell through, awakening to terror.

When night came and the sea anchor was put out and the crew went below, Cat dreaded going back to her cabin to face the freezing core of darkness. Yet she did just that. Every night. Night after night after night.

Halfway through the third week at sea, she woke as she had every night, sick, cold, fighting not to scream. When she looked out the porthole to begin the ritual of counting stars, something gave way deep inside her.

I can't take this anymore.

With a choked sound she stumbled out of her bed and fled silently up to the deck. She found a place out of the wind and huddled there, staring blindly into the night.

Though she had made no noise, Travis appeared. When he picked her up and began carrying her toward the stairs, she went rigid in his arms.

"No," Cat said, her voice soft, shattered. "I won't go back to that cabin. Do you hear me? I won't."

It was the first time she had spoken to Travis in all the long days since he had appeared on the *Wind Warrior*.

His arms tightened around Cat as he looked at her drawn face. In the moonlight she looked otherworldly, as fragile and beautiful as frost.

"It's all right," he said very gently. "I won't take you to your cabin. I promise."

Slowly Cat's body relaxed. Travis carried her to the cabin at the bow of the boat.

His cabin.

She didn't protest. She would do anything, endure anything, rather than count the stars beyond her porthole again.

"Easy now, sweetheart," Travis said softly. "We're almost there. You're safe."

Gently he put Cat on his bed and covered her with a blanket. When he lifted a hand to smooth her hair back from her face, she flinched as though he meant to strike her. His mouth flattened into a bleak line. He sat near the bed, close to Cat but not touching her.

And not touching her was like feeling his skin peeled from his living body.

Eventually Cat slept, only to awaken shaking and cold and nauseated. Her low sounds of distress woke Travis.

"Cat," he whispered. "You're safe. It's all right, darling."

She shuddered.

"Easy, sweetheart," Travis said in a low voice. "I won't hurt you. I just want you to know that you aren't alone."

He lay down next to Cat and gently, very gently, gathered her into his arms.

Cat wanted to fight his touch, but couldn't. At that instant she could no more have turned from his warmth than the sea could have turned from the pull of the moon.

For a long time Travis held her, rubbing out the knots of tension in her neck and shoulders, soothing her, stroking her without sensual demand. Yet still she shuddered on some breaths, her body and mind wound too tightly to go on much longer without breaking. Travis wasn't even certain she knew that she was being held.

"Cat . . . Cat, don't fight against showing your feelings. Scream or cry or smash things, do whatever you have to. Let go, Cat. Let go. You can't go on living like this."

Her only answer was a shudder that wracked her body.

Travis held her, warming her cold flesh until finally she slept again.

This time Cat didn't wake up until long after sunrise. It was the most sleep she had had since telling Travis she was pregnant. She was still trying to understand why she was able to sleep next to him but not alone when he appeared in her cabin. He was wearing a wet suit and carrying hers.

The daily routine began. Neither one of them said anything about how the night had been spent. When Travis did speak, he didn't require an answer from Cat. He had learned that she wouldn't give one. Except for that one stark demand not to be taken back to her cabin, she hadn't spoken to Travis at all.

It was as though he no longer existed for her.

At some point during the day, Cat began to do more than go through the motions with her cameras. The beauty of *Wind Warrior*'s magnificent maroon sails swelling against the cloud-layered sky finally had seeped through her numbness. She said nothing to Travis about it. It wasn't something she wanted to put into words, to face. It was easier just to let reflexes take over.

When the time came to sleep again, Cat went to her own cabin. She woke up shaking and cold, making muffled sounds, trying not to scream. When she was able, she dragged herself off the bunk and started for the deck.

Travis was waiting outside her door. Wordlessly he carried her back to his cabin. He tucked her between the sheets, climbed in beside her, and pulled her against his body. Saying nothing, she accepted his embrace and his warmth.

In time the shuddering finally stilled. Travis settled Cat more closely against him. She didn't resist. Nor did she move closer on her own. He closed his eyes and fought to conceal the rage and despair and anguish that were tearing him apart.

"Cat," he said softly, raggedly, "don't be too strong. Let me help you. Bend before you break. Before we both break."

She didn't answer.

His lips brushed her forehead again and again, the caresses like tiny breaths whispering over her. He tried not to think about what might have been, love and time and the future, all the things that money can't buy. Instead, he watched moonlight and shadows move over her face, staring at her as though if he looked closely enough, he would be able to see through darkness to the end of her pain.

It was the same on the nights that followed. They slept until Cat awakened, and then Travis held her until she slept again. But he didn't sleep again. He couldn't.

Her nightmare had become his.

Each night after Travis soothed Cat back to sleep, he slipped out of the bed and went out on the deck alone. There he stood with the moonlight and sea, the ship steady beneath his feet and the night haunted by voices, voices turning and crying around him like black gulls, voices telling him how little he could do, how much he had lost.

Cat's voice, alive with wonder. *I'm dreaming. First you, then that ship. Don't wake me up, Travis, not yet.*

Cat's voice caught in pain. *Why? Why couldn't I have met you in January, when we might have had a chance to love?*

Ask me to go away with you again in January. By then I'll have paid all my debts that matter.

I don't want your money. Can't you understand that?

If you stopped buying women, you might just find out that there are women who can't be bought.

But Travis had been afraid to believe.

And then he had believed, only to be betrayed.

Do you believe in miracles? I'm pregnant, my love. I'm pregnant! A baby! Travis, my man, my lover, my love. Our baby!

The joy in Cat's voice could wound him even in memory. Especially in memory. He should have shared that joy, should have gone down on his knees and thanked God for a miracle. Instead, he had been locked within his own fear of making the same mistake all over again, costing another baby its chance to live.

You're going to have that baby and then it will be mine. My attorney will have the papers to you in a few days.

He had let the past and Tina's lies blind him to the present and Cat's truth.

Travis looked at midnight without seeing it. His hands were locked around the railing, his whole body taut with pain and the voices cutting him until he bled silently, invisibly, hearing his own words with a kind of numb horror.

If you're holding out for marriage, you can forget it. Marrying a whore is the kind of mistake I don't make twice.

Yet it was Cat's voice that stripped Travis to his soul.

I wouldn't give up this child to be raised by a man who can't see love when it stands in front of him. Like me, now. I love you, Travis. But that's my mistake. I should have known better. Rich men just don't know how to love.

Thank you for my child, even though it was an unwilling gift. I'll take the baby. And you, T. H. Danvers, you can take your money and go to hell.

Dr. Stone's voice, each word another drop of agony eating at Travis's naked soul as she outlined the many ways he had failed Cat.

She was simply too physically depleted to sustain a pregnancy. Everything we did was too little, too late.

For a time she was connected in the most intimate possible way with another life. Now that is gone.

She described her feelings to me very well—a hole at the center of everything. She stumbles in and then she falls and keeps on falling.

Money is too small a bandage to put on a wound like Cathy's.

And money was all Travis had.

The despair that lay beneath anger and pain lapped at his will. He had been so certain that Cat would respond to her cameras, to the sea . . . to him.

She wouldn't speak to him.

She wouldn't even look at him.

He didn't blame her. If he could have, he would have shed himself like an ugly skin and walked away, but that wasn't possible. He wanted to cry her name and his love to the night, but his throat was blocked by grief. Like Cat, he could only endure each moment in a silence haunted by all the mistakes of the past.

Head bowed, Travis endured because it was the only thing he could do for Cat, the only way he could be close to her, joined by grief as he had refused to be joined by love.

I know you hate me. I came back to you too late. If you don't want my baby, then another man's.

Anything, Cat, anything. Scream and call me names. I deserve all of them. At least cry. Tears will heal you faster than anything else.

It seemed to Cat that no sooner had she been soothed out of nightmare and back into sleep by Travis than she awakened again. She didn't know what had disturbed her. There was no nightmare clawing her out of sleep. Nor was she cold.

Slowly Cat realized that she had awakened because she was alone in the bed. She was used to being within reach of Travis in the terrible darkness, within touch, breath and warmth mingling.

Making no noise, Cat went up onto the deck. Though she wore only the soft T-shirt she had found forgotten in a drawer, she wasn't chilly. The night was like velvet. *Wind Warrior* had taken them south to summer.

All around the ship, a school of dolphins leaped in silver calligraphy against the seamless midnight sea. Balanced on the horizon, a full moon poured radiance over the night.

It was a moment before Cat saw Travis at the bow, outlined against moonlight. His arms were braced against the rail, his head was bent, his body rigid. Despite being half turned toward her, he didn't see her. He seemed to be looking at the ebony sea and the dolphins' quicksilver grace.

Cat stood without moving, without breathing. The crystal

beauty of the moment sliced through her. She heard a harsh sound and thought that she had cried out. Then she realized the sound had come from Travis. He buried his face in his hands, but not before she saw the silver sheen on his cheeks.

He can't be. Crying. Rich men don't care enough about anything to cry.

Confused, shaken, Cat stumbled back to Travis's cabin, his bed. She lay awake, sorting through certainties that had been shattered by moonlight and a man's tears. No matter how many times her thoughts scattered, they re-formed around one impossible truth.

Travis had cried for her when she was unable to cry for herself.

Guilt might make him replace her cameras. Pity might make him bully her into health. But neither guilt nor pity could force tears out of his strength.

Trembling, almost afraid, Cat wondered how many nights Travis had comforted her and then gone out on deck alone with no one to comfort him.

As quietly as moonlight, tears came to her, burning her, searing through ice to the agony beneath.

Cat didn't know how long it was before she heard Travis walk softly into the cabin and ease himself onto the bed. Silently she turned toward him, fitting herself against him, holding him as he had held her so many times. She tried to speak, but her breath came out in a ragged sob that was his name.

It was all she could say, over and over. She wept even harder when his arms closed around her, crying because he had cared enough to cry for her when she couldn't cry for herself.

Travis buried his face in Cat's unexpected warmth, holding her as tightly as she held him, sharing the terrible wrench of emotions returning to her.

When there were no more tears, they still held one another, warmth in the cold center of night.

Cat awoke with the taste of Travis on her lips, bittersweet residue of tears. He was watching her as though he was afraid she would turn away.

And he was. When she moved closer to him, his arms tightened to hold her. He breathed raggedly, no longer fighting against the pain that ate at his soul.

"I should have been with you," Travis said. "I should have cooked your meals, bathed you, carried you into the sun, held you." His voice tightened into silence as he fought for control. "I didn't believe you loved me. I kept telling myself that you would call, you would come to me, that all you wanted was to marry my money. Then you told me you sold your cameras."

Travis was holding Cat so hard that she couldn't breathe, but she didn't notice. She knew nothing but his face, his eyes, his words, his warmth.

"You sold your cameras to keep my baby and never called me, never spoke to me, never asked one thing of me."

When Travis closed his eyes, Cat almost made a sound of protest. His face was so bleak without their unique light, so despairing.

"I thought," he said slowly, "that nothing could be worse than seeing that wave break over you and Jason, seeing your blood pooling on the deck, hearing you scream."

Cat tried to speak, to protest, but the pain she saw in Travis was too great for words to ease.

"I was wrong," Travis said. "The last few weeks have been like watching you die by inches, knowing I'd killed you but not cleanly, not quickly. Nothing I did helped you. The nights, Cat. My God, the *nights*."

She tried to speak, but couldn't for all the emotions twisting through her, telling her she was alive.

His eyes opened, but there was no comfort in them, no beauty, no life. His face was turned away from her.

"And the nightmare will go on forever because I can't change the past," Travis said in a raw whisper. "I can't take back the moment when you saw blood on the deck and fell into nightmare, screaming."

"Travis," Cat said, her voice husky from lack of use.

"I can still hear you screaming beneath your silence. I can't stop it. I can't help you. I can't change the past. I can only relive it one savage memory at a time. And hate myself."

"You didn't do any—"

"The hell I didn't," Travis interrupted. "I've seen you locked in nightmare because of the miscarriage. I can't change the nightmare. I can't help you live with it. There is no end to it."

"The nightmare," Cat said painfully. "The nightmare began before I miscarried, not after."

At first Travis wasn't sure he had heard correctly. Slowly he turned his head, facing her, revealing himself.

What Cat saw shocked her, turning her world and her heart inside out. She touched his cheek tenderly, wanting to take the certainty of despair from his eyes. She saw his breath hesitate at her caress, then still completely, as though he was afraid to believe. To hope. To trust.

She took a shaky breath. "I knew from the beginning that I would almost certainly miscarry. And I knew that it wasn't my last chance, that I could have other babies. But I didn't want another man's child. I wanted yours. I wanted you, but I'd lost you. That's when the nightmares started. When I lost you."

A shudder ripped through Travis. He started to speak, but she covered his lips with her fingers.

"Please," Cat said. "Let me finish. Let me be like you, strong enough to bend."

His lips moved against her fingers, and he said nothing.

"For seven years I prided myself on standing alone, and then I fell alone," she said. "I'm still falling. Don't leave me, Travis. Not yet. I know I'm not rich enough for you to trust, to love. I don't care about that anymore. All I care about is here, now, you. Let me run before this storm with you. And when it's over you won't have to say anything, do anything. I'll know, and I'll leave."

Travis's breath came out in a rush as his lips moved from her fingers to her palm to the pulse beating in her wrist.

"You're richer than I ever was or ever will be," he said. "You're fire and life and love. If I thought I could buy you, I'd sell even the *Wind Warrior,* my soul. But you can't be bought, can't be begged, and borrowing isn't good enough."

Without warning, his arms moved swiftly, fitting her body against his.

"But you can be stolen, sweet Cat. And that's what I've done. The *Wind Warrior* owns three quarters of the world. No one can find you and take you away from me."

He held her so tightly that she couldn't move or speak. It didn't matter. She didn't know what to say and she didn't want to go anywhere except even closer to him.

"But I promised Harrington I wouldn't keep you against your will," Travis said.

"What?"

"You didn't really believe that your green angel would force you back to work just to meet a deadline, did you?"

She just blinked and looked at Travis like a puzzled cat.

"The publisher told me your photos were so good that he'd cheerfully wait until hell froze over to get the rest of them," he said. "The rest was just a lie to get you on board."

"Some angel," Cat whispered, but the line of her mouth was soft.

"He's no angel at all. He wouldn't help me until I promised to let you go when you were well, to let you find a man you could love. And he's right. You deserve that love, Cat. I'll let you go, I promise it."

Yet even as Travis spoke the words, he sensed the hole at the center of the universe opening beneath his feet. Waiting for him. Waiting to swallow the man who learned to love too late.

"But don't leave me yet," he whispered raggedly. "Don't make me let you go right away. I . . . can't."

Cat traced his mouth with fingers that trembled. "I've already found the only man I could love. Nothing has changed that. Nothing ever could. I love you."

"Then marry me," he said urgently, his beard caressing her cheek, her neck, his lips warm and firm on her skin. "Please marry me, Cat. I need you so much that I can't—don't know how to say—don't know what to say."

She pulled away and stared at Travis.

"I know it isn't fair to ask you now," he said in a low voice. "You should have time to recover, but I'm afraid that once you're well you won't need anyone, and I need you . . . I *need* you. Marry me."

"Don't," Cat whispered. She closed her eyes, afraid that if she looked at him, she would accept without asking whether guilt or passion made Travis offer marriage. "The miscarriage wasn't anyone's fault. Not yours. Not mine. Not Jason's. Don't marry me out of pity. I can take anything but that."

Travis made a harsh sound. "Pity? I'd as soon pity a storm. You're so strong."

"Strong?" Cat's voice was frayed. Her eyes opened, luminous with tears. "Yeah. Right. That's why I wake up in a cold sweat every night."

"You spent a month going through the nights alone. I've

spent only a week and it's tearing me apart."

"You helped me just by being here, holding me. It's much better now. Don't feel guilty. Don't feel you have to marry me."

"I love you, Cat."

Travis felt the tremor that went through her, saw shadows of pain and doubt in her haunted gray eyes. His lips brushed hers as his tongue licked at the corners of her mouth.

With a small sound she opened her lips, let him fill her mouth with his breath, his taste, his tongue meeting hers until she forgot to breathe. She felt the sweet heat of his skin beneath her hands, felt his body change, felt his need break over her.

His lean, scarred hands moved beneath the T-shirt she wore, his shirt, a shirt he had envied for too many nights. He stroked her hungrily while she trembled and sighed, telling him how much she liked his touch. His hands moved from her hips to her shoulders, and then over her head, leaving her naked.

Cat lay in the dawn pouring through the porthole, watching Travis, asking nothing of him but his presence here, now. He bent until his lips could brush her face, his warmth touching her temples, her eyes, her mouth. His tongue lingered over hers for a time, moving slowly, deeply, sending desire quivering through her.

When he ended the kiss she made a sound of protest. He called her name and buried his hands in the silky fire of her hair. She arched against him, asking him to touch all of her.

His fingers curled around her breasts, caressing her as his tongue rasped softly over her skin. With slow, unhurried movements he cherished her, moving over her like the sun, warming every shadowed hollow.

She changed beneath his touch, his tongue setting fire to her until she moaned. Her hands clenched rhythmically in his hair as she cried out in the wordless language of ecstasy.

With a deep male sound of pleasure he held her straining hips until the storm passed. Then slowly, reluctantly, his mouth released her sultry flesh. He tasted his way back up her body, savoring the salt-sweetness that misted her skin.

"I didn't steal you out of pity or guilt," Travis said against Cat's mouth, catching her lower lip in his teeth, moving his hips hungrily against her and drinking her ragged moan of pleasure. "I stole you because I had to. I want to sink into your soul the way you sank into mine. You taught me how to love. And then I drove you away before I could discover how much I loved you. Now I know. I'll give you whatever you want, even a life without me. If that's what you want. Is that what you want?"

She looked at the tourmaline depths of his eyes, felt his arms hard and strong around her, the heat of his aroused body burning against her. He had given her everything, asked nothing, not her love, not even the easing of his own need.

"You," Cat whispered, pushing Travis over onto his back, her hands sliding down his body. "I want you."

"Are you sure? The money hasn't changed." His lips twisted in a sad, ironic smile. "I'm rich and getting richer every minute."

"Fuck your money."

Travis looked startled. Then he laughed until Cat's hands slid knowingly between his legs. He made a hoarse sound and rolled her onto her back.

"I have a better idea," he said. "Marry me. Then the money will be yours and you can do what you like with it. Even that."

Before Cat could answer, his hips moved against her sensually, opening her. But he stopped just short of the union she wanted.

"Travis . . ."

The word was both name and plea.

"Do you want me?" he asked, moving just a bit, touching her, teasing her.

"Not fair," she said. Lightning raced through her again, seething currents that promised to consume and renew her in the same burning ecstasy. "Not fair."

"Whoever told you pirates fought fair?" he drawled.

His eyes were blue-green fire, fierce and loving. He laughed and moved again, touching her, but not enough, not nearly enough.

Cat melted in liquid waves of pleasure. "I want you."

"How do you want me?" he asked, his voice husky, deep. "Husband or lover? Friend or partner? Companion or father of your children?"

"Yes," she said, closing her legs around him, trying to draw him into her liquid warmth.

"Yes, what?" Travis asked, fighting the desire that shook his strength, showing what it cost him to wait for her answer.

"*Yes.* Everything you can be. Everything we can be."

Travis whispered Cat's name and his love as he took her and gave himself. For a time he simply held her, murmuring his love over and over, hearing the words return redoubled from her lips. Only then did he begin to move with the timeless, potent rhythms of the sea and love, melting her, melting into her, stealing her away.

Above them the *Wind Warrior* spread its wings and soared through the incandescent dawn, a radiant pirate ship sailing to the ends of the earth and beyond.

If you enjoyed *To the Ends of the Earth,*
then sample the following brief selection from

JADE ISLAND,

Elizabeth Lowell's captivating romance,
available now from Avon Books.

"LET ME get this straight," Kyle Donovan said, staring in disbelief at his older brother. "You want me to seduce the illegitimate American daughter of a probably corrupt Hong Kong trading family in order to discover whether said family is involved in the sale of cultural treasures stolen from a Han emperor's grave?"

Archer tilted his head as though thinking it over and studied the cold salt water beyond Kyle's Pacific Northwest cabin, and finally nodded. "Yeah, that's about it. Except for the seduction part. That's optional."

"I don't believe it."

"Fine. So seduce her."

"This is a joke."

"I wish."

Kyle waited but his brother wasn't feeling talkative. Kyle was afraid he knew why. Archer hated involving family in any of the gray areas of his past. Uncle Sam was definitely one of those areas. But the U.S. government, like the past, never really went away.

"What's going on?" Kyle asked finally, shifting in his chair. "And don't give me any fairy dust about hands across the water and international cooperation."

Archer looked at his brother. Sunlight glinted in Kyle's tarnished blonde hair and made his hazel eyes look more gold than green, but even sunlight couldn't brighten the dark rims around the irises. Nor could light take away the lines and shadows of experience—experience Archer would rather have spared his younger brother.

"Would you believe business?" Archer asked neutrally.

"Monkey business, yeah."

Archer's smile was fast but real, like the anger narrowing his gray-green eyes.

Kyle simply waited. This time he wasn't going to be the one to break the silence.

Archer got out of his chair. He was tall, rangy, quick, a darker echo of his younger brother. Silently Archer prowled the cabin's homey main room, touching things at random: a computer that bristled with Kyle's personal additions, books on everything from international banking to five thousand years of Chinese jade, a small vase with a branch of rosemary in it, a letter opener that could slice to the bone, and a fishing lure that looked like a tiny hula skirt. Beneath the slithery, glittery skirt was a hook so sharp it could stick to rock. It certainly wanted to stick to flesh.

"You've changed," Archer said, smiling as he carefully set aside the lure. "Before that amber fiasco last year, you couldn't out-wait me if your life depended on it."

"Does it?"

Archer's smile vanished. "Not as far as I know."

"Which brings up an interesting question," Kyle said. "What *do* you know?"

"Enough to worry. Not enough to do anything useful about it."

"Welcome to the human race."

For a moment longer Archer studied the windswept fir forest outside the cabin and the water beyond, where currents more powerful than rivers coiled beneath the peaceful surface of Rosario Strait.

"I don't know any more facts than I already told you," Archer said.

"Can you get more?"

"Soon? I doubt it. My contact was unofficial."

"Unofficial. Uh-huh. Do you really believe that?"

"Most of the real work is done that way. Off the record."

Subtly, Kyle flexed his left shoulder, trying to work out the ache. The wound had long since healed, but the shock wave from an off-the-record bullet had done unhappy things to nearby cartilage. When it came to predicting rain, he had a much better average than the expensive weather guessers on TV.

"So this guy calls you," Kyle said, "and says that there are rumors of the kind of cultural theft that will make diplomats reach for tranquilizers while governments beat the drum of nationalism and everyone with any sense heads for cover."

"Yes."

"Why did he come to you?"

"He didn't say, beyond the obvious."

"Which is?"

"Donovan International is in the right position and I know how the game is played."

"With real bullets," Kyle muttered.

"No. With real permits, passports, and paper. If we tell Uncle to bugger off, life becomes a lot trickier for Donovan International. It's hard to run an import/export business without the cooperation of the U.S. bureaucracy."

"And we owe them one, don't we?" Kyle asked quietly. "For cleaning up my mess on Jade Island."

Archer shrugged, but the tight line of his mouth said a lot.

"Mother," Kyle said, disgusted. He had been afraid of that. "I tried to keep the family out of it."

"So did I."

Kyle flexed both hands, trying to work off the tension that came to him every time he realized how close he had come to dying—and taking his sister Honor with him.

"Let's go over it again, just to make sure I don't fuck this one up, too."

Turning, Archer looked straight at the big blonde man who had once been his little brother and would always be his younger brother. "What happened on Jade Island wasn't your fault."

"Yeah, right," Kyle said, disgusted. "I'm surprised you trust me with this."

"That's bullshit. The only one lacking trust around here is you, in yourself."

"Did your contact ask for me by name?" Kyle asked, changing the subject.

"No. But you're the one Lianne Blakely has been watching for the past two weeks."

Kyle's odd gold-green eyes widened. "What are you talking about?"

"The illegitimate daughter of—"

"Not that," Kyle interrupted. "The rest of it."

"Simple. She was looking at you and you were so busy looking at cold jade that you never noticed a warm woman trying to catch your eye."

"Jade isn't cold and I've never met a woman of any temperature who wouldn't crawl over my bleeding body to get to you."

Archer bit off the kind of comment that would devolve into a family argument. He had never understood why everyone considered him a lady killer. As far as he was concerned, Kyle was the best-looking of the Donovans, with Justin and Lawe very close behind.

"Not this lady," Archer said. "Lianne was looking at you. That's one of the reasons I agreed to ask for your help in penetrating the Tang Consortium."

"Penetrating, huh? First the woman, then the whole damn clan. You've got an overblown idea of my libido, not to mention my stamina."

Archer made a choked sound that was a combination of exasperation and humor.

"In any case," Kyle said, "if the lady was looking at me rather than you, we can be sure of one thing."

"What?"

"It's a setup."

Archer blinked. "I'm having trouble following you."

"Take it one word at a time. In the last two weeks you and I have gone to three jade previews together."

"Five."

"Two were so lousy they don't count. If Lianne saw past you to me, then it's because the Tang Consortium figures that I'm an easier nut to crack than you."

"You don't think it's possible that Lianne prefers blondes?"

Kyle shrugged. "Anything is possible, but the last time a woman passed up a tall, dark, and handsome type for me, I nearly got killed before I figured out exactly what kind of screwing was on her mind. That kind of lesson sticks with a man."

For a moment Archer didn't know what to say. Kyle was certain that the only thing women wanted was to use him and lose him. It hadn't been like that before last year.

At times Archer missed the old Kyle, the one who laughed easily, the golden boy touched by the sun. But Archer never would have asked that golden boy to do anything more serious than match wines with meals.

"Maybe it's a setup," Archer agreed. "And maybe there's a different game. That's up to you to find out. If you want to."

"And if I don't?"

Archer shrugged. "I'll put off my trip to Japan and take a run at the Tangs myself."

"What about Justin? He's blonde. Kind of."

"Justin and Lawe are ass deep in their own alligators,

trying to get a line on a new emerald strike in Brazil. Besides, they're too young.''

"They're older than I am," Kyle pointed out.

"Not since Marju."

Kyle smiled. It wasn't an open, sunny kind of smile. It was like Archer's, more teeth than comfort.

"I'm in," Kyle said. "When and where does the game begin?"

"Tonight. Seattle. Wear a tux."

"I don't have one."

"You will."

Lianne Blakely sat in her mother's elegant Kirkland condominium and watched Lake Washington's gray surface being teased by cat's-paws of wind. Never quite still, never predictable in its changes, the lake licked slyly at the neat lawns and sidewalks that crowded its urban shores. In balcony planters and along streets, tree branches were just beginning to shimmer with the kind of green that was more hope than actual announcement of spring's return. The bravest of the daffodils were already in bloom, lifting their cheerful faces to the cloud-buried sun.

"Do you want green, jasmine, or oolong?" Anna Blakely called from the open kitchen.

"Oolong, please, Mom. It's going to be a marathon tonight. I'll need all the help I can get."

And all the courage, Lianne acknowledged silently, wryly. She had promised herself that if Kyle Donovan was at the ball tonight, she would pick him up. Or try to.

Putting off the encounter hadn't made it any easier, so she had decided to just get it over with. If she failed, she failed, and her father would just have to chalk up one more disappointment from his bastard daughter. In truth, she knew she didn't have the kind of recklessness or innate female confidence to approach a good-looking stranger with the idea of getting acquainted for business purposes, much less for sexual ones.

But Lianne was definitely the kind to repay a favor or keep a promise. Engineering a meeting with Kyle Donovan was both.

Her stomach hitched at the thought. She tried to calm herself by saying that Kyle wouldn't be at the ball tonight. He had no patience for that kind of arts-and-culture crush and no need to siphon money from society's cream.

Lucky him.

"Nervous?" her mother asked from the kitchen.

Lianne barely prevented herself from jumping up and pacing the room. "Of course I'm nervous. I chose every single piece of the Jade Trader's display myself. Wen Zhi Tang never gave me that much responsibility before."

"Wen's eyes are going. Besides, the crafty old bastard wanted goods that would appeal to the Americans as well as to overseas Chinese."

"And his bastard granddaughter is as close as he can come to American taste, is that it?" Lianne retorted.

The sound of a teaspoon hitting the granite countertop made her wince, but she didn't apologize for her bluntness. She had spent thirty years pretending that she was the legitimate daughter of a widow, while knowing full well that Johnny Tang was her father and Wen was her grandfather.

Lianne was tired of the charade, just as she was tired of watching her mother treated like an unwelcome stranger by the Tang family. As far as Lianne was concerned, bastards were made, not born.

And the Tang family had made more than its share of them.

Anna Blakely walked into the room carrying a lacquered tea tray that held a pale bone china teapot and two elegant, handleless cups. She wore a scarlet brocaded silk jacket, slim black silk pants, and low sandals. Pearls gleamed at her neck and wrists, along with a Rolex. On her right hand she wore a diamond and ruby ring that was worth more than half a million dollars. Except for her height and glorious blonde hair, she was the picture of a prosperous Hong Kong wife.

But Lianne's mother was neither prosperous nor Chinese nor a wife. She had built her life around being mistress to a married man for whom family, *legitimate* family, was the most important thing in life; a man whose Chinese family referred to Anna only as Johnny's round-eye concubine, a woman who didn't even know who her parents were, much less her ancestors. Yet no matter how often Anna came in at the bottom of her lover's list of family obligations, she didn't complain.

Watching her mother's quiet elegance as she poured tea, Lianne loved her but didn't understand the choices the older woman had made. And still made.

Bitterness stirred, a bitterness that was as old as Lianne's realization that she would never be forgiven for not being one hundred percent Chinese. She was too much an American to understand why any circumstance of birth, blood, or sex should make her inferior.

It had taken Lianne years to accept that she would never be accepted, much less loved, by her father's family. But she had vowed she would be respected by them. Someday Wen Zhi would look past her wide whiskey eyes and thin nose and see a granddaughter rather than the unfortunate result of his son's lust for an Anglo concubine.

"Is Johnny coming by later tonight?" Lianne asked.

She never called her mother's lover by anything other than his given name. Certainly not Father or Dad or Daddy or Pop. Not even Uncle.

"Probably not," Anna said, sitting down. "Apparently there's a family get-together after the charity ball."

Lianne went still. *A family get-together.*

And she, who had spent three months of her free time

preparing the Tang Consortium's display, wasn't even invited.

It shouldn't have hurt. She should be used to it by now.

Yet it did hurt and she would never be used to it. She longed to be part of a family: brothers and sisters, aunts and uncles, cousins and grandparents, family memories and celebrations stretching back through the years. Except for her mother, the Tangs were Lianne's family, her only family.

But she wasn't theirs.

Without realizing what she was doing, Lianne ran her fingers over the jade bangle she wore on her left wrist. Emerald green, translucent, of the finest Burmese jade, the bracelet was worth three hundred thousand dollars. The long, single strand necklace of fine Burmese beads she wore was worth twice that.

She owned neither piece of jewelry. Tonight she was merely an animated display case for the Tang family's Jade Trader goods. As a sales tactic it was effective. Resting against the white silk of her simple dress and the pale gold of her skin, the jewelry glowed with a mysterious inner light that would act like a beacon to jade lovers, connoisseurs, and collectors.

Lianne's own jewelry was less costly, though no less fine to someone knowledgeable about jade. She chose her personal pieces with an eye toward her own desires rather than worth at auction. The trio of hairpicks that kept her dark hair in a swirl on top of her head were modern shafts of Burmese jade carved in a style four thousand years old. When she wore them, she felt connected to the Chinese half of her heritage, the half she had spent her whole life trying to be part of.

Distantly, Lianne wondered if she would have been invited to the party if Kyle Donovan was her date. Johnny, Number Three Son in the Tang dynasty, was hell-bent on getting entree into Donovan International. He had pressured

Lianne to get acquainted with Kyle: *Come on. Don't go all modest and fake Chinese on me. You're as American as your mother. Just do what the other girls do. Go up and introduce yourself. That's how I met Anna.*

The memory of her father's words went down Lianne's spine like cold water. She couldn't help wondering if Johnny figured that what was good for the mother was good enough for the daughter: a life of guaranteed second-best in a man's affections.

A mistress.

As Lianne drank tea from ancient, unimaginably fine china, she told herself that Johnny only wanted her to meet Kyle, not to bed him for the sake of Tang family business.

"Lianne?"

She swallowed the bracing tea and realized that her mother had asked a question. Quickly, Lianne replayed the last few minutes in her mind.

"No," Lianne said. "I won't be staying for the ball. Why would I?"

"You might meet some nice young man and—"

"I have work piled up," Lianne interrupted. "I've spent too much time on Tang business already."

"Johnny appreciates it. He's so proud of you."

Lianne drank tea and said nothing at all. Disturbing her mother's comfortable fantasy would only lead to the kind of argument that everybody lost.

"Thanks for the tea, Mom. I'd better get going. Parking will be a bitch."

"Didn't Johnny give you one of the Jade Trader passes?"

"No."

"He must have forgotten," Anna said, frowning. "He has been worried about something a lot lately, but he won't tell me what."

Lianne made a sound that could have been sympathy. Careful not to jerk the handle, she closed the door of her mother's condo behind her and headed out into the gusty night.

The benefit ball for Pacific Rim Asian Charities was one of the big social events of the season in Seattle. Invitations were reserved for the rich, the powerful, the famous, and the fabulously beautiful. Normally, Kyle and Archer wouldn't have bothered attending this kind of show-and-tell in the name of charity and social climbing.

"At least the tux fits," Kyle muttered.

"I told you we were the same size, runt."

Kyle didn't say anything. He was still surprised that he fit into Archer's long-legged, wide-shouldered clothes. No matter how old Kyle got, part of him was still the youngest of the four Donovan brothers, the butt of too many brotherly jokes, the runt of the litter always fighting to prove that he was as good as his bigger brothers in everything from fishing to karate to exploring the face of the earth for gems.

"You see her?" Kyle asked, looking past the herd of limousines to the glittery crowd filing toward Seattle's newest hotel.

"Not yet."

"Not ever. I didn't know this many people owned tuxes. Not to mention stones." He whistled softly as a matron walked past wearing a diamond necklace whose central feature was a pendant the size and color of a canary. "Did you see that rock? It should be in a museum."

Archer flicked a glance at the woman and then looked away. "You want to talk museum pieces, try the companions of the Taiwanese industrialists who just walked in. Especially the woman in red."

Kyle glanced past his brother. The red silk sheath—and the body beneath it—was an eye-popper, yet it was the woman's headdress that sent murmurs of appreciation and greed through the crowd: a lacework cap of pearls encased her gleaming black hair. Teardrop pearls as big as a man's thumb shimmered and swayed around her face. A triple strand of matched teardrop pearls the size of grapes fell from the back of the cap down to the cleft in the woman's rhythmically swinging ass.

"Companion, huh? As in mistress for the moment?" Kyle said.

"It's common enough. Most of the Asian men leave their wives at home with the in-laws when they come to the States."

"Afraid their little women will bolt to greener pastures if they get the chance?"

"Wouldn't you?"

"I wouldn't be fenced like that in the first place. Let's try the atrium. That's where the Jade Trader has its display. SunCo's stuff will be there, too. Ever since China took over Hong Kong, the Sun clan has been whittling away at the Tangs."

Archer smiled slightly. "Been doing some research?"

"If I had to research in order to name the competition, I wouldn't be much good to Donovan International, would I?"

"You're really serious about dragging Donovan Inc. into the jade trade, aren't you?"

"I've been serious about it ever since I held my first five-thousand-year-old jade *pi*," Kyle said simply. "I'll never know why the piece was carved, but someone back then was like me. He loved the smooth weight of jade. Otherwise he never would have tackled a stone that hard with little more than rawhide, sticks, and grit."

When Kyle turned and started toward the atrium, Archer put a hand on his arm, stopping him.

"There's only a limited market for Neolithic jade artifacts," Archer said neutrally.

"The market is expanding every day. Even New York

has caught on. Besides, there's a lot more to jade than Neolithic artifacts.''

"Do you feel expert enough to advise us on the full spectrum of jade, to go one-on-one with the Pacific Rim's best?''

"Not yet. But Lianne Blakely is. Or didn't your contact mention that?''

"He didn't make a point of it. He just said she was a kind of back door into the closed world of the Tang Consortium.''

"So let's go see if I can learn more from sweet Lianne than she can learn from me before she's finished using me for whatever old man Wen Zhi Tang has in mind.''

Archer blinked. "That's scary.''

"What?''

"I understood you.''

Kyle forged a way through the crowd with Archer at his side. Once inside the atrium, the crush of people broke into clots centered around various exhibits of corporations that were donating pieces to the midnight auction.

"Forget it,'' Kyle said, pulling Archer away from a Mikimoto pearl exhibit. "Lianne Blakely is into jade, remember?''

"Any harm in looking at something else?''

"You're as bad as Faith when it comes to pearls.''

"As bad as you and jade?''

"Worse,'' Kyle said, looking around.

Against the towering greenery-and-glass backdrop of the atrium, people from three continents and several island nations revolved around the central fountain, creating a kaleidoscope of languages and fashion. The fountain itself was striking: a clear, cantilevered glass sculpture of rectangles and rhomboids where light and water danced with a grace that people could only envy. The sweet music of the water blended with the languages of Hong Kong, Japan, and several regions of China, as well as English accented by countries as distant as Australia and Britain and as close as Canada.

"The jade must be on the other side of the atrium," Kyle said.

"Why?"

"Most of the Anglos are right here, crowded around the rubies and sapphires from Burma or the Colombian emeralds or African diamonds. Jade is a more subtle, civilized taste."

"Crap," Archer said mildly. "Civilization has nothing to do with it. Jade was available in ancient China. Diamonds weren't. Same goes for Europeans. Clear gemstones were more available than jade. Tradition is created from the materials at hand."

Kyle and Archer continued arguing about culture, civilization, and gems while they circled around the fountain. On the way they passed museum-quality pre-Columbian jade artifacts from Mexico, Central, and South America that were displayed on slabs of hand-hewn stone. Fright masks of gold and turquoise grinned or snarled, scaring off demons whose names were known only by people thousands of years dead. Mixed in among the artifacts were modern examples of gold and jade art.

Everything—ancient and modern—had a card in front of it naming the corporation that owned the object. Corporate displays of support for the arts were as much the purpose of the evening as the charity auction that would precede the ball.

By the time the two brothers came to the section reserved for offshore Chinese exhibits, Kyle was wishing he was aboard the *Tomorrow*, sharpening hooks and tying leaders for a dawn fishing raid. He snagged a glass of wine from a passing waiter, sipped, and grimaced. At a function like this he had expected higher quality.

"Bingo," Archer said softly.

Kyle forgot the mediocre wine. "Where?"

"To the left of SunCo's jade dragon screens, near the Sikh in the jeweled turban."

Though they were less than ten feet away, Kyle at first didn't see any woman. Then the Indian Sikh stepped aside.

Kyle stared. "You're sure?"

"Positive."

"Damn."

Kyle didn't know what he had been expecting, but he knew Lianne Blakely wasn't it. With a combination of skepticism, disgust, and grudging male interest, he watched the sleek, petite young woman who supposedly was so smitten with him that she had been watching him from afar for two weeks.

Yeah. Right. He was standing close enough to see that she had on real silk stockings and her patrician little nose was buried in an exhibit of Warring States jade ornaments as though he didn't exist.

Then Lianne turned and for an instant looked right at Kyle. Her wide tilted eyes were the color of cognac. She hesitated as though recognizing him. But if she had, she wasn't going to do anything about it. She went back to studying jade as though no one else in the room existed, certainly not a man she was interested in meeting.

"You're sure that's her?" Kyle asked quietly, praying it wasn't.

"I just said so, didn't I?"

"She doesn't look like an international art thief."

"Really?" Archer asked softly. "How many have you known?"

"Not as many as you. So tell me, is she?"

"A thief?"

"Yeah."

"They don't wear labels."

Kyle didn't say anything more. He simply watched Lianne Blakely.

Archer looked from his brother to Lianne, wondering

why Kyle had come to a point like a bird dog scenting warm pheasant. Lianne was attractive, even beautiful in an exotic way, but she wasn't in the fabulously beautiful companion category. The simple white dress she wore fit well enough, but wasn't slit from hem to crotch or throat to pubic bone in order to draw and hold a man's eye. The jade bracelets she wore were doubtless Burmese and of the highest quality, as was her necklace, yet Kyle didn't seem to have noticed them. He was looking at the woman and ignoring the jade.

Not good.

"Maybe we should forget the whole thing," Archer said abruptly. "I'll put off the trip to Japan."

"My shoulder is good as new," Kyle said without looking away from Lianne.

"Nothing is good as new after a bullet."

Kyle shrugged, then winced. Though he wouldn't admit it aloud, his shoulder still ached when the weather was setting up for rain. In the Pacific Northwest, that was pretty often.

"I know much more about jade than you do," Kyle said.

"Considering how little I know, that's not much of an argument for your participation in this little waltz."

Kyle smiled crookedly. The non sequitur hadn't even made Archer pause before he answered. That was the good thing about family: you knew them well enough to follow their thoughts.

It was also the bad thing about family. That kind of knowing could be claustrophobic when there were six kids. But Kyle had learned the hard way that running off to the other side of the world didn't prove anything except what he already knew.

He was four years and one century younger than his brother Archer.

"What's really bothering you?" Kyle asked, looking at

his brother. "Afraid another woman will grab me by my dumb handle and lead me into trouble?"

"If you get hurt because of me, Susa will have my ass for a wall hanging."

"Our own mother? Ha! You're her favorite son."

Archer gave him a look that would have backed off anyone else.

Kyle wasn't feeling like backing anywhere. He felt like he had just taken a sucker punch to his gut.

Lianne Blakely was everything that appealed to him in a woman, and he hadn't even known until he saw her. He had thought he liked big women; she was small. He had thought he liked blondes; she was dark. He had thought he liked outgoing, laughing women; she was quiet, poised around an inner stillness.

One thing Kyle did know for certain was that he never wanted to be at the mercy of his cock again. Yet he wanted Lianne in a way that had nothing to do with old knowledge, old learning, old promises.

Kyle's sudden, primitive arousal made him furious. He must be a slow learner on the subject of being used by a woman.

Maybe he could be a fast learner on how to use one.

"Don't wait up for me," Kyle told his brother, starting forward. "I've got some monkey business to conduct."